Edward Hayes

The ballads of Ireland

Edward Hayes

The ballads of Ireland

ISBN/EAN: 9783742829122

Manufactured in Europe, USA, Canada, Australia, Japa

Cover: Foto ©Andreas Hilbeck / pixelio.de

Manufactured and distributed by brebook publishing software
(www.brebook.com)

Edward Hayes

The ballads of Ireland

Delia T. S. Parnell

THE
BALLADS OF IRELAND.

COLLECTED AND EDITED,

WITH NOTES

HISTORICAL AND BIOGRAPHICAL,

BY EDWARD HAYES, ESQ.

FIFTH EDITION.

VOL. I.

The Emigrants.—P. 308.

DUBLIN:
JAMES DUFFY, 15, WELLINGTON-QUAY;
LONDON: 22, PATERNOSTER-ROW.

Dedication.

―――――

TO GAVAN DUFFY, Esq., M.P.

My Dear Sir,

PERMIT me to dedicate to you this collection of the Ballads of our native Country,—enriched as it is by some of your own admirable compositions. As no man living has more thoroughly identified himself with the native Literature of Ireland, and particularly with its Ballad Literature than yourself, I feel I am discharging a public duty as well as indulging a private feeling of the most heartfelt regard, in dedicating to you a volume, the materials of which, either directly or indirectly (to a very considerable extent at least) would probably never have existed but for you.

Believe me, my dear Sir, yours most sincerely,

EDWARD HAYES.

3 Blenheim Square, Leeds.

CONTENTS OF VOL. I.

Descriptibe Ballads.

Historical Ballads.

CONTENTS.

Political Ballads.

Emigrant Ballads.

Pathetic Ballads.

CONTENTS.

INTRODUCTION.

―――――――――

" If you would find the ancient gentry of Ireland," said
Swift, "you must seek them on the coal-quay, or in the
Liberties." The ancient minstrelsy of Ireland has shared
the fate of her gentry; you must seek for it in the peasant's
cabin or in the dusty corners of the libraries of Europe.
This parallel is by no means surprising. The common fate
of our ancient gentry and our ancient minstrelsy is perfectly
natural. While they lived, they were the body and soul of
Irish nationality; and like body and soul they departed
together. When adverse circumstances made the gentry
fugitives to foreign lands, the bards became fugitives at
home. Their praises were heard no more in the old baronial
halls—the voice of their song had ceased. From the days
of Amergin to those of Swift, our minstrelsy is a blank in
the literature of Europe. The poems of Ossian may form an
exception; for notwithstanding the ingenious imposture of
MacPherson, those most capable of judging and expressing
an opinion upon the subject, even amongst his own countrymen, have almost uniformly credited Ireland with their pa-
ternity.* This absence of an extensive native literature is
one of the saddest features of Irish history. But when it is
known that the use of the ancient tongue was prohibited,
and the cultivation of the new declared a felony by law,—
if that privilege were not purchased by the renunciation of
the ancient faith; and that this struggle between the tongues

―――――――――

* Among these may be named Dr. Shaw, Wm. Buchanan, David
Hume, Edward Davies, Dr. Johnson, O'Conor, O'Halloran, &c.

and creeds had been cruelly maintained for hundreds of years,
—and has ceased only in our own time,—it cannot be a
matter of surprise that Ireland is looked upon as an illiterate
nation,—and that the accumulated product of her intellect
bears no adequate proportion to her genius.

Periods of great excitement are unfavourable to the development of letters, or the progress of civilization. History
teems with illustrations of this truth. After the impetus given
to English literature by Chaucer, its progress was completely
checked by the civil contentions which succeeded. The
Wars of the Roses threw English poetry back for two hundred
years. We almost lose sight of it from the fourteenth to the
sixteenth century, when Surrey and Wyatt make their appearance upon the silent stage. The troubled reigns of Henry,
Edward the Sixth, and Mary, were also singularly barren of
poetry. The vigorous policy of Elizabeth having quelled the
storms of those troublous times, national victory inspired the
popular voice. Jeffrey, speaking of literature in the reign of
James the First, says, it would probably have advanced still
further, in the succeeding reign, had not the great national
dissensions which then arose, turned the energy and talent
of the people into other channels;—first to the assertion of
their civil rights, and afterwards to the discussion of their
religious interests. The graces of literature, he adds, suffered
of course in these contentions, and a shade of deeper austerity
was thrown over the intellectual chronicler of the nation.
If the absence of civil rights or religious freedom, or the
struggle for their assertion, be a barrier to intellectual progress, Ireland may well be poor in literature to-day. Indeed
the wonder is, how she has even a literature at all, when we
consider the proscription of her intellect. Her history is one
long series of warfare and disaster; and from the Battle of
the Boyne to this hour, her energies have been absorbed
either in struggles for religious liberty or in contests for
political power.

Even the dramatic literature of England has never recovered from the hostility of the Puritans. In 1642, it was
enacted, that all stage-plays should be discountenanced.
Theatricals were constituted a public offence, punishable by

fine or imprisonment. Germany also affords a remarkable instance of the injurious influence of warfare on intellectual, and more particularly, on poetic, development. From the fourteenth to the sixteenth century, the days of the Meister-singers, she was rich in song; but the religious dissensions of the seventeenth century created a blank in German Minstrel-sy. In the eighteenth century, when the devastating influence of the sword was passing away, the Black Forest of German literature, as it has been happily designated, soon passed away also. And we are now, fortunately, issuing from the Black Forest which has darkened Irish genius, ever since the days "when Ireland was the school of the West, the quiet habitation of sanctity and literature." * The excitement before or after a nation's struggle is the hot-bed of poetry. When peace is restored, then triumph is chanted, or defeat mourned, in national song; and the daily increasing means of education will quicken Ireland's acknowledged poetical ge-nius, hitherto prostrated by adversity, and shed a glory around the land and the language which it celebrates and adorns.

When the chivalry of the Middle Ages developed the ro-mantic poetry of Provence, Ireland had only then succeeded in driving the Danish invader into the sea, after a warfare of two hundred years. When the Italian schools of poetry started into existence under the inspiration of Dante and Petrarch, a fiercer foe than the Dane had nestled in her bosom. She was harassed from without by English invasion and from within by native faction. When Saxon barbarism was softening down under the influence of Norman chivalry and refinement, Ireland was denied the protection of Eng-lish laws, and, according to the Statutes of Kilkenny, was scourged if she adopted her own! Such was her unhappy condition, when the Saxon tongue was first softening its rudeness through the favoured lips of Chaucer. And in the commencement of the fifteenth century, when Spanish min-strels were singing the story of Charlemagne and the Twelve peers of France, of Bernard del Carpio and the Cid, Ireland was engaged in a fierce struggle against English power, and

* Dr. Johnson.

succeeded to such an extent, as to elicit from the Speaker of
the House of Commons, the admission, that the Irish had
"conquered the greater part of the Lordship of Ireland."
When Ariosto reigned in Italy by the grace of genius and
the favour of Cardinal d'Este, and rendered his country still
more celebrated by the immortal productions of his muse;
when Cardinal Ximenes, by his statesmanship and munificent patronage of literature, lifted Spain to a glory that
made her worthy of Columbus; when the illustrious family
of the Medici were more than royal in their encouragement of
intellectual culture, literature, and art; when, in fact, the
sovereigns of all the petty states of Italy vied with each other
in their princely endowments of genius, and, in a single century, within the small principality of the House of Este, were
produced,—besides the important works of Guarini and
Tassoni,—the three great epics of Italy, the "Orlando In-
namorato," the "Furioso," and the "Gerusalemme Liberata"
—at that very time, English law in Ireland, by way of ame-
liorating the condition of the country, legalized the murder of
the natives! When Tasso was summoned to Rome, at the instance of Clement the Eighth, for his coronation in the Capitol
as the successor to the laurel of Petrarch—when Spenser borrowed the wild legends of Munster, and stamped them with the
gorgeous colouring and chivalrous character of his "Faery
Queen," the horrors depicted in his "View of the state of
Ireland," and the prostrate condition of the country at that
time, are illustrated in his own experience; for he was then
in possession of the confiscated estates and castle of the Earl
of Desmond; and from the banks of the "gentle Mulla" we
may perceive how his Poem is pictured with that fair, Munster scenery. In that right royal age of British literature,
when the English language was assuming consistency and
beauty, the language and literature of Ireland were withering
under the deadly shade of persecution. When the poets of
the Elizabethan era stamped upon their glorious productions
the romantic beauties of that age of chivalry, Ireland was
prostrated by famine, pestilence, and war. When the stern
enthusiasm of the Puritans moulded the English tongue into
forms of sublimity, Ireland was still bleeding under the ter-

rible scourge of merciless conquest. Had England been thus treated, no Shakspeare would ever have immortalized her literature and her language. When Philip the Fourth nursed the genius of Spain, and invited the poets to the festivities of the palace as his friends; when the monarch himself contributed some of the best dramas of the day to the rich storehouse of Spanish poetry, and instituted those poetical tournaments, at which poets improvised and noble ladies judged, and which operated so powerfully in the development of dramatic literature—then had Ireland passed under the confiscating hammer of that royal auctioneer, James the First, who effected his plunder of the land from the native chiefs by "cruelty, subornation, and perjury." When Louis the Fourteenth pensioned his poets like princes, and in his appreciation of the genius of Moliere, when this author was calumniated, stood sponsor for his innocence by becoming the godfather of his child; when Milton's majestic muse produced the "Paradise Lost," Ireland was then, also, in an unfavourable condition for the cultivation of literature, exposed as she was to the tender mercies of Cromwell. But that total ignorance which the sword could never produce was achieved by the infamous penal laws, which disgrace the name and the Statute-book of England. This barbarous code, in the language of Edmund Burke, "had a vicious perfection—it was a complete system—full of coherence and consistency: well digested and well disposed in all its parts. It was a machine of wise and elaborate contrivance, and as well fitted for the oppression, impoverishment, and degradation of a people, and the debasement in them of human nature itself, as ever proceeded from the perverted ingenuity of man."

Ireland has been happily called the "Cinderella of Nations." She had sisters who enjoyed all the luxuries of education, while she was jealously excluded from any participation in such favours. She was abused and scourged alternately; and if her beautiful voice burst forth in song, in imitation of her sisters, she was forthwith gagged. Ireland has been compared to Spain under the dominion of the Moors, but there is no point of resemblance between them, except that of foreign conquest. She had the long crusades of Spain but she had not the conquest of Granada to thrill her like an inspiration. Victory sways the poet more than the soldier. When Henry the Fifth forbade his subjects to sing the Battle of Agincourt, they had already either begun to chant the strains of triumph, or defied the prohibition. Ireland had the feuds of her Zegris and Abencerrages; and while the policy of the invader fomented these feuds, his proscriptions did not permit her to sing them. She had an adventurous foe struggling bravely against her nationality, but she had not the chivalrous foe of Moorish Spain. She fell beneath the sword of the invader, but the bloody blade did not flash with the light of Saracen civilization. She was conquered; but instead of being consoled in her desolation by the elegance and philosophy of the East, she was crowned with the thorns of ignorance and persecution. Instead of the Moorish colleges and libraries of Cordova, Granada, and Seville, her halls of learning were demolished, or turned into barracks for a merciless soldiery. Instead of being taught the philosophy of Aristotle, which was expounded at Cordova by Averroes and other Moorish doctors, her conquerors taught her the higher philosophy of dying well! Ben Zaid cheered fallen Spain with the light of a glorious history, but the invader in Ireland wrote history with the torch and the sword. Moorish genius presented Spain with an Encyclopædia of Science; while the Genius of Misrule presented Ireland with an Encyclopædia of Horrors! Mahometan teachers invited christian students to their schools and became their masters and their friends, while the christian invaders of Ireland prohibited education under penalty of death.

These facts must be borne in mind in connexion with Irish literature and its history; they account for the blank of a thousand years. We disclaim any intention of exciting animosity or old jealousies, by these remarks. We regret the occasion of them as much as any of our readers; but this is not the time to blink the truth. In our own day the world is becoming wiser or more magnanimous; it is beginning to look boldly at the faults of the past. All parties have much to learn from such sad experience as the history of Ireland affords. The characteristic of modern history is the contrast drawn between the barbarism of our forefathers and the civilization of to-day. If Irish history be wisely studied to this end, there will be little danger in the knowledge or expression of the truth. But we can no more overlook the influence of persecution, in relation to this subject, than we can ignore the conquest of the country when treating of its history and the social condition of its people.

And yet, an Irish minstrelsy was never wanting in Ireland. The external world knew it not, because it was ignorant of her sweet tongue. But from the days of the Druids it existed—patronized by her chiefs, and sung by her people. Without wandering so far back as the misty ages of Milesius, we may safely say, that Ireland was not behind any nation of Europe in her ancient minstrelsy. Greece and Rome are, of course, excepted. The rhapsodies of Homer were recited before the Poems of Ossian; but both are alike immortal. Rome conquered the Greek Empire; but Greece enslaved the intellect of Rome, when the latter borrowed her literature. Yet Rome has no ancient ballads; and if she ever had any, they have not escaped the wreck of years. Macaulay *supposes* such ballads, and makes this idea the foundation of his " Roman Lays." But Homer and Ossian are the inspired giants of the shadowy past, whose productions will ever triumph over time.

The Irish bards were divided into three classes—the Filens, who celebrated the strains of war and religion; the Brehons, who devoted themselves to the study of the law, which they versified and recited to the people, after the manner of the Ionian bards; and the Seanachies, who filled the offices of antiquarian and historian. Almost every homestead of importance had its own Seanachie, whose duty it was to sing the exploits, and trace the genealogy, of the family up to Milesius. The ancient Irish felt proud of their oriental descent from this monarch; and the Irish of to-day are as strongly attached to this idea as were their ancestors. Even Dr. Petrie's elaborate Christianity of the Round Towers, will not divest thousands of the belief, that these grand structures are the relics of an oriental civilization, with whose history we are unacquainted.

No country is richer than Ireland, in those poetic records which form the early history of all nations. The productions of her bardic historians are most ample; but they are as dumb oracles to our generation. It is no wonder that she is rich in such records, for in that early age her Kings were the munificent patrons of literature. They founded colleges for the education of the bards, whose term of study was, at least seven years. Out in the green woods, beneath the shade of the sacred oak, these poetic institutions flourished. And when this term of study was completed, the degree of Ollamh, or doctor, was conferred upon the students. Then they went forth and sang the war-songs of the clans, and the dogmas of religion; versified the proclamations of the law, the axioms of philosophy, and the annals of history; and traced the genealogies of their respective patrons up to Milesius. Such were the offices of this venerated and privileged class.

The Irish bards were remarkable for the epigrammatic style of their productions, which frequently consisted of quaint wit, healthy morality, and sound advice. Their teachings are the popular maxims, even at the present day, in the vernacular—maxims which, for shrewd sense and wisdom, can scarcely be surpassed. The genius of the Celtic language assisted in the formation of this terse style. Its subtile grace and vigour, as idiomatic as its soul-touching tenderness, rendered it an appropriate vehicle for the exquisite touches of the poet, or the pregnant wisdom of the philosopher. The influence of the bards over the multitude, and the superstitious veneration attached to their office, soon elevated their dignity next to that of the king. The different orders of the state were distinguished by the number of colours which adorned their dress; and while the peasant's garment consisted of only one colour, the bards were allowed four, one less than the number worn by the monarch himself. Moore remarks, that this law argues the high station accorded to learning among the ancient Irish, as well as a remarkable coincidence with that Hebrew custom, which made a garment of many colours the distinguishing dress of royalty and rank.

Christianity superseded druidism; and though the bards were still in favour, the character of their song was changed.

The productions of the heathen muse were given to the
flames, in a moment of extravagant zeal, and the breathings
of the new lyre were crowned with the sweetness of christian
morality. No more do we see the herald-bards, clad in their
white flowing robes, marching with their chiefs at the head
of the armies, and singing their war-songs to the music of
the harp. The hymn of peace superseded the strain of battle;
and if Christianity destroyed those early records of a nation's
infancy, her truth and beauty imparted to the muse a higher
and a holier inspiration. The Lives of the Saints inspired
that lyre which once bowed down before the idol of paganism. The Church took Song under her protection, and used
it in her warfare against the world. The most remarkable
of Irish ecclesiastics were poets of a high order, among whom
we may mention St. Columbanus, one of the restorers of early
European christianity. But they wrote in the favoured language of the church; and though, according to Bede, the
Celtic, the Welch, the Teutonic, and the Latin languages
were spoken in Ireland in the seventh century, the strains of
their muse never lived in the hearts of the people. Politian
is remembered in Italy to-day, not by his accomplished Latin
productions, but by the few Italian verses he has left behind
him. The Arabians are said to have introduced rhyme into
Europe in the eighth century; but it is well known that
rhyme was employed in Ireland in the time of St. Patrick,
four centuries previously. Music, poetry, and literature,
were the characteristics of the country in those ancient days
when the students of Europe crowded to her schools.

The bardic productions of Ireland have an importance unknown to similar records of other lands. The strict super-
vision exercised over the historical records surpasses even the
scrutiny of the present day. A council was specially appointed to investigate their truth; and Moore says, that
" whatever materials for national history the provincial annals
supplied, were here sifted and epitomized, and the result
entered in the great national register, the Psalter of Tara."
Strange to say that while the beauties of the Persian tongue
are studied in Ferdusi by our learned antiquaries; while they
unravel the tangled web of Sanscrit, explore the ruins of

Nineveh, and decipher the hieroglyphics of Egypt, the ancient records of Ireland have never been deemed worthy of notice. The ruins of a great civilization at our own door have been all but completely overlooked. A paltry grant of two hundred pounds has been lately procured from Government for the translation of the Brehon Laws, which are said to be an epitome of ancient wisdom. It is thus that Irish history has been neglected. Every country of Europe has her biography except Ireland. While other nations are rich in chronicle and memoir, she has few besides those which speak of her as a barbarous enemy. These are not the national records over which a people might well exult. The truest history of Ireland will be found in the stray ballads of her persecuted bards, and the memoranda of her banished monks.

Ireland had once a glorious history, when she was the mart of learning, and the resort of the students of all nations. When Europe was a corpse beneath the hoof of the Vandal, then was Ireland famous—then was she "the school of the West, the quiet habitation of sanctity and literature." She had a glorious history before the crowning of Charlemagne— before the Crescent waved over the fair fields of Andalusia. And when war raged like an angry demon in the heart of Europe, she held up the torch of knowledge as a beacon, and received with open arms all those who sought shelter and science within her peaceful bosom.

Her history has been neglected, but the day will yet come when it will be lovingly written. France is rich in chronicle and memoir. French biography has been scrupulously active since the thirteenth century. Every Frenchman that has risen above the crowd, has his niche in the temple of contemporary history. Such memoirs are the most important portions of a nation's biography—the lives of the great movers in the national drama. Every city in Italy had its own historian from the same period; but they do not show the inner life of a nation like the biographies of France. The chronicles of Spain are ample from the days of Alphonso the Wise down to the time when it almost ceased to have a history, but the social habits and peculiar characteristics of the people have been illustrated by no other history than the beautiful ballads which attest the ancient chivalry of that degenerate land. Ireland is not without such records and chronicles : but, as yet, the majority of them are little better than waste paper in the illustration of her national existence. The biographies of her children would be an epitome of European history, for she has given soldiers and statesmen to every country from Spain to Russia. The breaking-up and migration of the nations which succeeded the fall of the Roman Empire, and which scattered to the winds all the civilization of the past, have been the characteristics of Ireland for a thousand years.

At the end of the eighth century, a tribe of that robber race which had previously overrun the fair lands of the South, invaded and desolated the happy homes of Ireland. The Danish Goth, true to the instincts of his barbarian nature, aimed the first blow at the literature of the land—that glorious treasure which had been so generously dispensed to the pilgrims of every clime. Monasteries were razed—Religious were persecuted—and the Bards, who had hitherto been regarded as sacred in the eyes of monarch and people, were exterminated with savage ferocity. For nearly three centuries, these pirates desecrated the soil of Ireland ; and, on their expulsion in the eleventh century, literature revived without resuming its former sway. Another invasion in the twelfth century brings us in a stride down to the present time. The bards were still held in high estimation by chiefs and people. But the reign of Elizabeth inaugurated the renewal of another Danish persecution. The obnoxious bards were victims once more at the altar of tyranny ; and thenceforth their character declined. Penal laws ruled the land, and laid the foundation of that ignorance for which Ireland is so unjustly blamed to-day. The Catholic who imparted or received education, was guilty of treason against the crown. The Catholic schoolmaster and the priest were both outlawed ; and as if these laws were not considered sufficient to keep the country ignorant, they were rendered still more stringent in succeeding reigns. We know that there are thousands in England at the present time, who would battle to the death against such injustice ; and we make these remarks to excite their charity for the ignorance and their sympathy for the sufferings of a country, which has been so systematically misgoverned.

Under the rigorous enactments of Elizabeth the bards gradually declined. But the fidelity which was so characteristic of the order still distinguished them amid all their misfortunes. The gold of the treasury was laid at their feet to sing her "Majestie's most worthie praises," but they spurned the base bribe, and fled to the mountains. The gold of England could not make them swerve from the path of duty. From time immemorial they were the personification of Ireland's chivalry, and to this hour that chivalry has had no truer exponents than the Children of the Lyre. Some of the finest characters in English history, are, also, some of her sweetest poets. It has been well remarked of Sir Philip Sydney that you may survey him as you would survey an antique statue ; you must walk round him to perceive all his beautiful proportions. And it is a remarkable item in poetical biography that Sir Philip, as well as many others of the English poets, such as Spenser, Raleigh, and Harington, were connected with Ireland as the first stage on which they appeared—the starting point of their illustrious career. Spenser, while he praises the productions of the bards who lived in his time, is severe in his strictures upon their character. In the reign of Charles II., an act was passed to prevent the wandering minstrels from exacting meat or drink from the people, "for fear of some scandalous song or rhyme to be made upon them." The act further states, that all "such persons may be bound to loyalty and allegiance, and committed till bond be given with good sureties." We see here the position to which the order was reduced by the oppressions of former reigns. The warfare of centuries had struck down the native chiefs, who had ever regarded them with a species of paternal affection. Around the oak of power the ivy of song had lovingly twined itself, and when the former was violently torn from the land, the latter was flung upon the world to float like a weed upon every wind.

It was this persecution of the bards by Elizabeth and Cromwell, which led to the dreamy allegory in which the national hopes were shrouded. Ireland was the poet's love, but a jealous stepmother stood between him and his mistress, And so consistent were his political rhapsodies, on some occasions, with the wailings of the tender passion, that it is almost impossible to discriminate whether they were intended for his country or his mistress. Of this class is Mangan's "Dark Rosaleen," which some consider political, but which we have placed among the Ballads of the Affections. The very extravagance of allegory employed on these occasions, is an unmistakable index to the intensity of the persecution by which the bards were harassed, and ultimately destroyed.

Ossian's Poems and Mangan's translations from the Irish, may be regarded as fair specimens of the old and later poets of Ireland. And as far as the latter are concerned, it may be well said of Mangan, what was once remarked of a celebrated French translator, that it is doubtful whether the dead or living are most obliged to him. Ossian is stamped with the freshness of national infancy—the later translations with the allegory of national prostration and trembling hope. And both are pregnant with the history of their respective periods. In the latter, voice and pen are stifled; and the muffled wail of a trampled nation sounds like a death-bell upon the ear. We see the Penal Laws in full operation, and the native population stricken to the earth, but still living in the hope of a better day. We see the national religion banned, and a price set upon the head of its priesthood. We become acquainted with the intrigues and struggles to get these priests educated in distant lands by the Garonne and Guadalquiver, and we see them concealed on their return in the fastnesses of the mountains, and the caverns of the rugged shore. Yet amid all these adverse circumstances, Ireland did not manifest an indifference to the spirit of song in this day of her dolour, nor a want of taste for its cultivation. Still was she, as in the olden time, the mother of patriot bards; and though a price was set upon the minstrel's head as well as upon the priest's, every valley resounded with the praises of ancient heroes—elegies for the martyred brave—dark curses for the native traitor and the ruthless stranger—proud invocations of the Genius of Liberty—and passionate aspirations for the glory and independence of Erin.

And thus we perceive the existence of a native minstrelsy in Ireland, from the landing of the Milesians almost to our own time, in one unbroken wreath of song. We have sketches of more than two hundred Irish writers, principally poets, from the days of Amergin, the chief bard of the Milesian colony, down to the beginning of the present century. Their poems are, in many instances, still extant, from the hymns of St. Columb to the Lamentation of M'Liag, the biographer and family bard of Brian Boru; and still downwards to the dreamy allegory of the proscribed poets of the Penal Days. The stores of native minstrelsy which Ireland possesses, both in the memory of her people and the cabinet of the antiquarian, are astonishing, when we consider the characteristics of her history, and the condition of her people, for the last seven centuries. Rome had lost her ballads long before she reached the zenith of her power. Mr. Macaulay remarks that, in spite of the invention of printing, the old ballads of England and Spain narrowly escaped the withering blight of years, and that Scott was but just in time to save the precious relics of the Minstrelsy of the Border. In truth, he adds, the only people who, through their whole passage from simplicity to the highest civilization, never for a moment ceased to love and admire their old ballads, were the Greeks. But we think Ireland equal to Greece in this respect, as far as the comparison can be instituted. Since these pagan days when Bride was the Queen of Song, her bards have ever been scrupulously venerated, and their productions cherished with a traditional love which Greece never surpassed; and her people have been as true to this ballad-worship in the days of her distress as in those of her glory. We can easily understand how deep was the reverence, and how unchanging the affection, with which Ireland clung to her minstrelsy, from the ample relics of it which still live in the hearts and memories of her people, and from those, also, which unfortunately lie dead in the ancient tongue. The influence of the old bards on popular tastes and habits is still observable. Not many years ago the rustic schoolmaster was elected by a species of poetic tournament. A prize poem was generally the test of merit; and the successful candidate was chosen more for his skill in the muses than for his acquaintance with the doctrines of Political Economy.

The rage for street-ballads is another trace of their influence. And so strict is the resemblance, in one respect, between the present and the past, that a collection of these ballads will be a versified record of the principal events of modern Irish history. But this is the only point of resemblance between them. The contemptible street-ballad of to-day will not bear comparison with the racy, vigorous minstrelsy of old. There are few people more susceptible to song than the Irish. They are swayed by its influence as the tides by the moon. We may assign this, in some degree, to Ireland's unconquerable attachment to her ancient minstrelsy, and, also, to the fact that, till a late period, the street-ballad has been the only popular literature which she possessed. Nothing but this deathless love of song could have saved the precious relics of our bardic muse from the hand of time, the torch of war, and the still more destructive influence of foreign conquest. Seldom has the successful invader spared either the life or literature of the fallen land. The Caliph Omar burnt to ashes the magnificent library of Alexandria when he captured that city. The Persians burnt the books of the Egyptians, and the Romans of the Jews, the philosophers, and the Christians. The Jews in turn destroyed the books of the Christians and the pagans. And the Christians again, the books of the pagans and the Jews. The Turks destroyed the grand libraries of Constantinople; the Spaniards, the painted histories of Mexico; and such, also, was the fate of the national records and literature of Ireland which fell into the hands of the English conquerors. Its ruin was inevitable, but the relics are numerous and beautiful, reminding us of the porticos and stately columns which shine through the ashes of Pompeii.

Since the reign of Elizabeth, Ireland produced twenty-six poets in the Gaelic language. Some of these were of a high order, and of distinguished attainments. In connection with this portion of our subject we are tempted to sketch them

individually; but their biography would prove uninterest-
ing to the general reader. The lives of the bards would
form no inconsiderable portion of Irish history, from the
influence which they exercised in the direction of its events,
and in stimulating the spirit of resistance. The strains of
O'Gnive, the bard of Shane O'Neil, often flung the stirrup-
less lancer of Ulster like a falling rock upon the armies of
Elizabeth, and gathered round the national standard the
hesitating chieftains of the North. Angus O'Daly's war-song
of the Wicklow clans prompted the O'Byrnes to many a fierce
raid, from their mountain fastnesses, against the clan London
of the Pale, carrying destruction across the English Border,
under the chieftainship of the famous Feagh Mac Hugh.
The martial muse of O'Mulconry, the bard of Breifny and
laureate of Ireland, summoned Clan Connaught to the battle-
field against the invader, and helped to inspire that determined and protracted struggle which ended only with the
death of Bryan O'Rourke. He was Prince of Breifny, and
was betrayed by James VI. of Scotland into the hands of
Elizabeth, who beheaded him in 1592. But there is one
serious drawback observable in the strains of these ancient
bards, and a glance at the titles of their productions will
render it apparent. Their sympathies were more factious
than Irish, more clannish than national. Not that they loved
Ireland less, but that they loved their Sept more. We have
appeals to the O'Neils and the O'Donnels of the North, to
the O'Briens and M'Carthys of the South, to the O'Moores
and O'Byrnes of the East, to the O'Connors and O'Rourkes
of the West; but, unfortunately, seldom an appeal to the
spirit and energies of universal Ireland, except when some
great victory inspired the national voice, and lifted it up to
higher hopes and grander aspirations. But this is scarcely
to be wondered at, when we consider the rivalries of the
clans, and their constant struggles for ascendency and personal aggrandizement—the natural result of the feudal system
upon the warm and impulsive character of the Irish people.

Nor are the poets of the last century entirely free from
blame in this respect, though their fault lies in a different
direction.—The proscription of the ancient faith attracted

them to it more powerfully, and called forth their sympathiz-
ing strains for its suffering sons and bleeding martyrs. They
almost lost sight of nationality, and the political privileges
of which they had been deprived, in their anxiety for the
blessing of religious liberty. This was the want they felt
the keenest, and expressed the heartiest. It made their
religion bitter and sectarian, though in good truth their
charity had such little scope that it could scarcely be otherwise. They looked forward more to a religious, than to a
political deliverer; and, hence, their effusions were more
dynastic than national—more Jacobite than Irish. When
they sang of Ireland, it was in connection with the fallen
dynasty. They longed for the union of Una and Donald, or
in other words, Ireland and the Stuart. They addressed
their country as a beloved female to disguise the object of
their affections. Sometimes it was Sabia from Brian Boru's
daughter of that name; sometimes it was Sheela Ni Guira,
or Cecilia O'Gara, Moreen Ni Cullenan, Kathleen Ni Houl-
ahan, Roseen Dhuv, and more frequently Granu Weal, or
Grace O'Malley, from a princess of Connaught who rendered
herself famous by her exploits and adventures. The poet
beheld his beloved in a vision, and wandering in remote
places bewailed the suffering of his country. He rests himself beneath the shade of forest trees, and seeks refuge from
his thoughts in calm repose. Then appears to his rapt fancy
one of those beautiful creations we have named. Language
is not sufficiently copious to describe all her charms. He ad-
dresses her, and asks her if she be one of the fair divinities
of old or an angel from heaven to brighten his pathway
through life, and restore peace to his afflicted country. She
replies that she is Erin of the Sorrows, once a Queen, but now
a slave; and after enumerating all the wrongs and indignities
which she is enduring, she prophesies the dawn of a brighter
day, when her exiled lord shall be restored to his rightful
inheritance. This was the style adopted by most of the
Jacobite poets of the last century to express the sufferings
of their country, and their hopes of deliverance from oppression.

We question if imagination could originate a style of song

c

more pathetic in its allusions, or more powerful in its results. Allegory, in this instance, had lost its inherent weakness, and acquired an influence which no directness of expression could have produced. Woman has ever been honoured in Ireland with especial reverence. Since those ancient days which Moore has celebrated in one of his exquisite lyrics, when the fairest lady might travel the land from shore to shore without harm or danger, the Irishwoman's virtue and beauty have commanded universal respect, and made her a national deity almost to be worshipped. This national chivalry imparted to the poet's allegory an insinuating and enduring power over the heart which no appeal to the passions could possess. Ireland was no longer an abstraction, but a familiar being; and still more an afflicted woman, a forlorn mother, a fallen Queen, mourning over her sorrows, and calling upon her sons to avenge her wrongs and restore her to the dignity from which she had fallen. As illustrative of these feelings, the following extract from Mons. Thiery will, we hope, not be out of place:—"Ancient Ireland," he says, "is still the only country which the true Irish acknowledge; on its account, they have adhered to its religion and its language; and in their insurrections they still invoke it by the name of Erin, the name by which their ancestors called it. To maintain this series of manners and traditions against the efforts of the conquerors, the Irish made for themselves monuments which neither steel nor fire could destroy; they had recourse to the art of singing, in which they gloried in excelling, and which, in the times of independence, had been their pride and their pleasure. The bards and minstrels became the keepers of the records of the nation. Wandering from village to village, they carried to every heart memories of ancient Ireland; they studied to render them agreeable to all tastes and ages; they had warlike songs for the men, love-ditties for the women, and marvellous tales for the children. Every house preserved two harps always ready for travellers, and he who could best celebrate the liberty of former times, the glory of patriots, and the grandeur of their cause, was rewarded by a more lavish hospitality. The Kings of England endeavoured more than once to strike a blow at Ireland in this last refuge of its regrets and hopes; the wandering poets were persecuted, banished, delivered up to tortures and death; but violence served only to irritate indomitable wills; the art of poetry and of singing had its martyrs like religion; and the remembrances, the destruction of which was desired, were increased by the feeling of how much they cost them to preserve. . . . . The Irish love to make their country into a loving and beloved real being, they love to speak to it without pronouncing its name, and to mingle the love they bear it, an austere and perilous love, with what is sweetest and happiest among the affections of the heart. It seems as if, under the veil of these agreeable illusions, they wished to disguise to their minds the reality of the dangers to which the patriot exposes himself and to divert themselves with graceful ideas while awaiting the hour of battle, like those Spartans who crowned themselves with flowers, when on the point of perishing at Thermopylæ."

The calumnies uttered against the character of the bards may be easily traced to the political influence which they exercised over the people. This was the head and front of their offending. They sang the hopes of the nation in strains of misty song which the circumstances and national shrewdness of the people rendered transparent. When the sword of O'Neil was broken, the minstrelsy which had made it start from its scabbard still lived and moved the pulse of the nation's heart. When the battle-axe of Tyrconnell had rusted, the strains which once nerved the arm of the fierce gallowglass still hung on the people's lips, and kept alive the spirit of national resistance. The warrior's strength dies with him; but the poet's power ever stirs like an immortal prophecy. The bards of Ireland were persecuted, because they excited hopes of national independence, as the ancient minstrels of Spain sang her struggles against the Moor, or the minstrels of Scotland the Border-battles of the Percy and the Douglas. And though these strains were not fortunate enough to crown the struggles of Ireland with success, they did not wholly fail, for they have embalmed her nationality to live throughout all ages. It is as distinct at this hour from that of England in all things, save language, as it was in the

days of The O'Neil. And Irish poetry is the power which
has achieved this result, linked as it has been to the life and
struggles of the national faith.   It has been well said that
poetry has an influence not to be measured by arithmetic, nor
expressed by syllogism.   And we know no instance in which
this is so true as with reference to Irish minstrelsy.   Great
poets are the legislators of the empire of the heart.   The
poetry of Spain flung back the Moor from the Asturian mountains to sigh for his fallen power by the banks of the Guadalquiver, and the fountains of the Alhambra.   The religious
feeling inspired by the struggle against the Saracen gave the
Spanish character a lofty enthusiasm which no disaster could
wholly destroy.   Centuries of suffering, instead of crushing
the national spirit, but kindled it into higher resolves, and
prompted it to deeds of nobler daring.   Religion is ever a
powerful element in a national struggle, and no unfailing
source of poetic inspiration.   When Tasso lived, Europe
throbbed from end to end with religious excitement.   The
sword of the Ottoman was at her throat, and her own members
were arrayed against each other, while she trembled for her
safety on the brink of ruin.   It was then that the victory of
Lepanto burst like an inspiration over the religious genius of
Tasso; and the moral grandeur of his muse, in which he
almost stands alone in his glory, shows how much religion
may effect for poetry.   Ireland had all the benefit of this inspiration in her warfare and in her muse; and though it has
failed to secure for her what it did for Spain, the enthusiasm
it evoked has preserved the same faith unsullied—the same
feeling unsubdued.

No nation can afford to despise its ballads.   They are an
important portion of its history—the first efforts of its civilization.   And in the record of a nation's ballads, we find the
history of its progress and its triumphs—or its decay and
death.   The shepherd grazing his flock in the peaceful valley,
the warrior heading his men to battle, the disasters of defeat
or the rapture of triumph, the throbbing of broken hearts, or
the happiness of successful love—all these will be the inspiration of a nation's infant poetry.   Fancy or imagination will
have little to do with it; all will be as simple and natural as

the unsophisticated heart of the people. Nature offers her
inspirations in gloomy woods and lofty mountains reposing
in her lap of beauty, while the feelings of primitive life ani-
mate them with the breathings of emotion. As society
advances, the language of passion will be better defined and
more cultivated. Thought will grow more vigorous, and
will require a corresponding degree of elevation and ner-
vousness of expression. The pathetic ballad will follow
quickly upon the gray dawn of the legendary and pastoral
literature of a nation's infancy. The adversities of life soon
develop their strain of sorrow. But when the inspirations of
nature are rejected for flights of fancy and imagination, poetry
loses its strongest impulse, and its most attractive influence.
Nature is thrown aside for art—the flush of health for the
artist's colouring—and the breathing beauty of life for the
graces of Dædalus. The warmth of emotion is supplanted
by the cold glitter of fancy; and that poetry which once
swayed the hearts and kindled the enthusiasm of the multitude,
now becomes a fashionable toy for people of quality. The
soul of poetry departs with its simplicity and feeling.

The ballad is a species of narrative poetry, short and pithy,
simple in its structure and language, accurate in its incidents,
consistent in its dates, costume, and colouring, graceful in its
ease and beauty, and perfect in all its parts. It was the
first record of the events and the laws of all nations. Its
measured music assisted the memory, and popularized whatever knowledge it clothed. Though at first rude in structure
and unpolished in expression, it soon rose with advancing
civilization, and became an important element of power. It
scorned its lowly origin, assumed all the importance of history,
all the fascination of romance, and all the grace and dignity
of poetry. It was the first vehicle of instruction, the earliest
perpetuation of thought, the first parent of literature. The
rhapsodies of the wandering minstrels of Iona were ballads
borrowed from the epic of Homer. The epic, which was a
development of the ballad, was again broken up into its
original elements for the accompaniment of the harp. And to
the same necessity are we indebted for the ballad literature
of modern times. The Norman romances were broken up

into fragments by the jongleurs of the twelfth century for the same purpose; and to that age may be traced the form of our modern ballads.

Lyrical poetry requires the highest degree of inspiration and intellectual development. What narrative is to the ballad, sentiment is to lyrical poetry. It is frequently an epitome of the ballad, and in such cases, it is not easy to draw the line. Ballads so compressed may be denominated suggestive songs. The literary perfection of ancient Greece developed some of the best specimens of the lyric muse. Italy excelled in this high department of minstrelsy since the days of Petrarch, who tested the melody of his verses by the breathings of his lute. Moore is the Petrarch of modern times. In every line of his muse, the fancy revels in an atmosphere of melody, till his artistic elaboration seems but the perfection of nature. Burns is the highest of simplicity and feeling; his inspired song sways all hearts.

Although Plato excluded the poets from his republic, the influence of poetry has been felt in all ages. Patriotism and virtue are still nourished by the strains of a national minstrelsy. It holds up to posterity the mirror of a proud past to guide it to a triumphant future. The province of poetry is to soothe and cheer the heart in the struggles of life, and to dignify human nature by prompting it to aspire to that virtuous heroism which the world too often repudiates. It borrows from the past all that is beautiful, to throw around fallen man a paradise of its own creation. And if sometimes it pictures the dark side of nature, its corrective power is still true to its mission—by teaching us that error is frequently the best warning. Poetry is the aspiration of humanity for that happiness and perfection which the world lost in the Fall, and which it strives to attain by substituting the shadow for the substance. History pictures the world as it is—poetry as it ought to be. It lifts the standard of heroism, and invites to follow by climbing the rugged path of duty.

The poet is the oracle of dumb nature's divinity; and poetry the harmonious embodiment of his inspired revelations. The greatest poet is he who expresses this divinity the truest and the sweetest. He who fails in poetry, fails for want of

truth to nature, or of eloquence and harmony to make that
truth attractive. Nature's oracle must first study nature's
mysteries. From the farthest fixed star to the humblest
daisy must his study range. He must be familiar with all
the miracles of creation between the poles of space; and he
must hear every sound within these limits, from the waves of
celestial music rolling against the flying planets, to the hoarse
gurgle of the ocean, and the sighing of the summer wind.
What is vacant he must fill up; what is uninhabited he must
people; what he does not know he must imagine. But his
imaginings must be always consistent with truth and nature.
Those who possess thought and feeling, a harmonious ear and
an eloquent expression, are poets, if they but add the fervour
of sincerity to their natural qualifications. Any one who
sees more in nature than the ordinary run of mortals, has the
germ of poetry within him. If he express in harmonious
language, this mystery which he perceives, he is uttering
poetry. He tells some what they think, but cannot say; and
he tells others what they should think if they had thought at
all. Homer and Shakspeare stand unrivalled in this respect;
and, hence, they are the world's poets.

If poetry creates a paradise of its own, and tends to make
mankind happier, Ireland has indeed need of song. Scarcely
had her history emerged from the " twilight of fable" when
her annals became blackened with disaster. The days of her
mourning are not yet ended. The dirge of a thousand years
still swells over the land of numberless sorrows. The voice
of her song is still plaintive over the razed homesteads of her
valleys—over the sweltering plague-ship and shattered bark
of the Western Main. For long, long years she has had
nothing but her faith and her poetry to call her own, and by
the sincerity with which she has clung to these she has preserved her distinct nationality through storms of conquest,
tears, and blood. Ireland needs poetry; and it is deep in
her people's heart.

One may now refer historically to the wrongs of Ireland
without incurring the risk of being pounced upon as an
agitator. In writing of Irish Minstrelsy, we cannot avoid re-
ferring to Irish history with which this subject is so intimately

interwoven. Our object is not to excite angry recollections,
but to vindicate the poetic fame of Ireland, and to claim as
high a rank for her in ballad literature as that of any other
nation. We have shown the difficulties which fettered her in
the path of literature, and their distinctive influence on that of
other lands. Nationality imparts a peculiar charm to song.
It has embalmed Spanish poetry, and endowed it with a life
that will endure for ever. The proud Castilian and chivalrous
Granadine stand out almost in relief in the early ballads of
Moorish Spain. The sun, the soil, the sky, as well as the
struggles and characteristics of the people, are reflected in
this glorious national minstrelsy. Scotland may also thank
her nationality for the beautiful ballad-literature which she
possesses. Her clan-feuds, her wars against England, her
Jacobite struggles, her chivalrous loyalty to the Stuarts, her
wild mountains and picturesque lakes—all these tended to
develop that ancient national minstrelsy which has been the
inspiration of the immortal peasant-poets of that land of song.
In its earlier ballads we see the distractions and barbarism of
the feudal system, which rendered the names of the Barons
more prominent than even that of the reigning sovereign.
We see in them also the gloomy ferocity of those times when
men held life and land at the point of the sword. Nationality in all its phases is mirrored in Scottish song. English
character and the durability of the British Empire owe more
to Shakspeare than to the British Constitution; and "Ye
Mariners of England" has done more for the British Navy
than Copenhagen and Trafalgar. The peculiar beauty of Irish
music, is its eloquent interpretation of the national character,
in all its moods of joy and sorrow; and though our present
Minstrelsy is written in the English tongue, it is still as true
to our nationality as our music. When Scott's "Marmion"
made its first appearance, Jeffrey abused it heartily for its
want of Scottish feeling. "There is scarcely one trait," said
the Reviewer, "of true Scottish nationality or patriotism introduced into the whole poem ; and Walter Scott's only expression of admiration for the beautiful country to which he
belongs, is put, if we remember, into the mouth of one of
his Southern favourites." How this happened to be said

of Scott, whose nationality was his inspiration, we know not ; but we trust that no critic will be able to pronounce a similar censure upon the ballads which we introduce to our readers in the present volumes.

When an eminent Scotch professor delivered a series of lectures on poetry, some time ago, to the fashion and beauty of London, his intense nationality called forth the strictures of the press. An able reviewer remarks that the Lecturer scarcely ever referred even by name, to "Paradise Lost," introduced Chaucer with an apology, Pope with condemnation, Ben Jonson with pity, and Moore with a rebuke for his Eastern stories; that Scott was placed upon a pedestal just lower than that of Shakspeare, but higher far than those of Chaucer, Milton, and Spenser. Campbell is faultless, and they who wrote the ancient ballads immortal. Such is the epitome given of these lectures. "He is more Scottish than British," adds the reviewer, "more national in his tastes than universal in his sympathies. In politics and poetry the Professor is national to a fault; but the fault is amiable, and criticism involuntarily applauds even while it deliberately condemns." This nationality so amiable in a Scotchman is frequently wicked in an Irishman. Nationality is amiable everywhere but in Ireland. The aroma of these volumes is the patriotism which pervades and characterizes them; and while it imparts vigorous life to this Irish minstrelsy, it seeks not to depreciate the literature of any other country and so far at least disarms the resentment of the critic. We hereby put forth our claim for the "amiability" of Irish nationality, more particularly in its association with song. We trust the Press will look with favour upon this Irish minstrelsy which adds new graces to the English tongue, as Irish blood grows new laurels to the brow of England and swells the tide of British glory.

Our modern minstrelsy loses much by its recent origin. It suffers from want of the shadowy background of antiquity. But with the greater part of our ballads this was simply unavoidable, except those translated from the Irish. The sonorous melody of the Celtic tongue would be preferable, though the wish to return to it now might be considered

impracticable.   It has been well said that we can be
thoroughly Irish in thought and feeling although we are
English in expression.   The fathers of the early church struck
down paganism with weapons borrowed from its own armoury.
Augustine and Chrysostom dipped their wings in the fountain of Cicero's genius, and made their highest flights in
christian preaching through the heathen atmosphere of
Demosthenes.   And so, also, has Ireland conquered in her
captivity, by her successful cultivation of the English tongue.
Like the enslaved Israelites of old, she has carried off from the
Egyptian taskmasters the treasures of their learning, to develop
a literature that shall shine like a star in the firmament of
intellect.   It has been remarked that poetry and eloquence
rarely flourish on the same soil; they are set down as the
results of different states of life—the one of contemplation
and solitude; the other of intercourse with the world.   But
Ireland disproves this opinion.   The fountain of her song
is as deep as the sea; and her eloquence has never been
surpassed.   Though speaking a foreign tongue, she has wielded it with ease and strength, moulding it into gorgeous rhe-
toric and sweetest song.   Jeffrey, in his essay on the English
language, after tracing its progress from Chaucer to Swift
and Pope, and still downwards to Goldsmith, Johnson, and
Junius, attributes its present perfection principally to "the
genius of Edmund Burke, and some others of his countrymen."
If we have been compelled to adopt the English language,
we certainly have used it well.   It has not degenerated in
our hands.   The manners, customs, and superstitions—the
thoughts, feelings, and idioms—the struggles, the defeats, and
the aspirations of a people, constitute the essentials of its
nationality, not the language in which they are uttered.

Well might Jeffrey attribute the perfection of the English
tongue to Irish genius, and well may Ireland feel proud of
the men who achieved such a result.   There is hope for the
land which in the depth of its degradation could produce
such a galaxy of genius as that which illuminated the period
from Swift to Grattan.   There is a brilliant future before
that country which, in the darkest century of its history,
could produce Swift, Sterne, and Steele in literature; Boyle

and Berkley in philosophy; Parnell and Goldsmith in poetry; Francis (Junius), Burke, Flood, Grattan, Sheridan, Curran, and Plunkett in oratory;—and in our own day, the illustrious genius of O'Connell, and Moore, and the Historian of the peninsular war.

In the present volumes will be found names deserving a wider poetic reputation than they have hitherto attained. Mangan, M'Carthy, M'Gee, Ferguson, Simmons, Mrs. Wilde, and Richard Dalton Williams, are a few among the number. With few exceptions the present ballads are of recent growth, and the fruit of a comparatively few years. The great majority of them will be new to the English public; and as they become better known, it is hoped they will become still more esteemed. They are the throbbings of Ireland's heart, when it bounded with the life of a grand passion, which the magical genius of O'Connell called into existence. Till then Irish poetry was sadly neglected. The struggle for Catholic emancipation had produced little besides the immortal melodies of Thomas Moore, upon whom we principally depended to uphold the honour of our race and the poetic genius of our country. Even the old literature of the land had never been used as it might have been, for the development of a ballad minstrelsy. The treasures of our dead language were buried in oblivion, and none but a great poet could call them back to life, and clothe their new form with the vigour and raciness of the original. Such a poet arose in James Clarence Mangan; and his translations from the Irish show how much yet remains to be done for the development of the golden mine of our ancient minstrelsy.

The people after all are the great judges of poetry, and the most profound in their appreciation of its beauties. It sprung from them and belongs to them. They feel its influence, while others analyse its philosophy; and the muse is elevated or otherwise, according to the power with which it sways the people's heart, tunes the popular voice, and captivates the popular ear. It owns no other sway than the magic of the heart, and receives but its allegiance. The heart is the grand source of poetry; and from this throbbing throne of feeling, the muse looks down upon all nature as its dominions.

Dryden strove partially to exhibit Chaucer in the costume of modern phraseology, but the simple, vigorous verse of the original is preferred to the classic grace of the elaborate imitation. We have no great sympathy with philosophic poetry. Poetry, like history, has lost its primitive simplicity, and adopted the speculative and philosophic tendency.

Addison says—"an ordinary song or ballad, that is the delight of the common people, cannot fail to please all such readers as are not unqualified for the entertainment by their affectation or their ignorance; because the same paintings of nature, which recommend it to the most ordinary mind, will appear beautiful to the most refined." How thoroughly the people of Greece must have appreciated Homer, when the Iliad was not transcribed for centuries after the poet's era! And yet, the thunder of his wars is reverberating through the depths of the world's heart as loud as ever. Take philosophy and science to the cloister and the study, but poetry will always make itself felt in the home of the peasant, whose loving appreciation of the muse has snatched from the grave of time all the ancient minstrelsies of Europe. Where would be now the ballads of the Border, and the relics of our ancient Irish minstrelsy, were it not for the loving memories of the people? And need we ask, where is the sublime simplicity of Burns more truly admired than by the Cottager's fireside? Cellini states, that he exposed his celebrated statue of Perseus in the public square of Florence, by order of his patron, Duke Cosmo the First, who declared himself perfectly satisfied with it on learning the commendations of the people.

The poet who has sung for the people has rarely yet been neglected; and he who has been neglected by the people need sing no more. He may amuse a small class of readers who prefer the delicate touches of the artist's hand to the bounding passion of the poet's heart—the artificial flower to the simple daisy. With such persons, poetry is merely to tickle the fancy. It has no higher mission. Poetry should sway the passions and educate the affections; and the passions and the affections, which are the groundwork of poetry, are the common heritage of all humanity. They belong to the peasant as well as to the peer; and the poet who strikes these

chords will find as true and as hearty a response in the bosom
of the one as in that of the other. The poetry of fancy will
never stir the heart, nor awaken new feelings in the reader's
soul.

If the appreciation of poetry depended upon a reasoning
process, then would the test of popular approbation soon fall
to the ground. But it requires neither the abstraction of
analysis, nor the careful induction of logical investigation,
to unravel the mysteries of the muse. Poetry is judged by
the heart only, and its beauties are understood intuitively.
And those whose feelings are the most natural are the in-
fallible critics of its genuine and immortal inspirations.

Fletcher of Saltoun spoke truly when he said—"Give me
the making of a nation's ballads, and I care not who makes
its laws." We see in it the breathings of a people's inner life,
which history cannot possibly record. It is the reflection of
their wants and aspirations, and the truest history of their
feelings. Even the statesman may study it with advantage,
for it is the daguerreotype of the national mind. Heeren
observes that the poems of Homer were the principal bond
which united the Grecian states. And we have a eady
spoken of the influence of song in the struggles of Scotland,
and of Ireland. In the reign of Edward the First, the Welsh
bards exercised such sway over the people, stirring up in their
souls the memories of independence, that continual insurrection was the result, till an edict was issued against them
ordering their execution without mercy. Ritson, in his essay
on national song, says that the poetic squibs of the cavaliers,
during the Commonwealth, tended in no slight degree to
keep alive the trampled spirit of loyalty, and ultimately contributed to the Restoration. Lord Wharton used to boast,
that he rhymed King James out of his dominions by the
chorus of "Lillebullero," the only thing in the shape of a
song which the Revolution produced. It is stated of one of
the troubadours, who was seized by robbers, that he begged
of them, before taking his life, to hear one of his songs; and
so disarmed were the brigands by the touching pathos of the
poet, that they instantly restored him to liberty, and instead
of robbing him, loaded him with presents.

And if a national minstrelsy consecrate courage and nourish patriotism, its influence in the development of poetic taste is not less remarkable. The lyrical genius of Burns was half inspired by the fine old Scottish ballads which had made the land musical from the Orkneys to the Border. Scott, speaking of the books which he had read in childhood, says—"The tree is still in my recollection beneath which I lay, and first entered upon the charming perusal of Percy's Reliques." His infancy was surrounded by the traditions and legends of Sandy Knowe; and the old ballads of Scotland were as familiar to his infant tongue as the endearing expressions of his paternal grandfather, at whose house he resided. And to these old ballads may his future fame be traced as truly as his Border minstrelsy to the inspiration of Percy's Reliques, whose charming perusal made such a lasting impression upon his youthful mind. And the immortal "Melodies" of Thomas Moore have contributed, in no slight degree, to inspire the minstrelsy of the present volumes, invigorated as they are by the fire and feeling of popular passion, and flavoured with the simplicity of popular expression.

How much happiness life would lose, were it deprived of the soothing influence of poetry. In childhood we are charmed by its sweet sounds; in manhood we are thrilled by its inspirations or spiritualized by its pathos; and in old age, it calls back to the memory the simplest and most beautiful pleasures of the past. We must ever regard the poets who have adorned and elevated humanity by their genius as men of superior order, as philanthropists who have added a new pleasure to life—a pleasure which purifies the heart while it gratifies the sense, and which no mere utilitarian triumphs could ever supply. If there is any book of which we never grow tired, it is a book of ballads.

What better picture of the religious and domestic life of Ireland in the seventh century, when she was "the school of the West, the quiet habitation of sanctity and literature," than the "Itinerary of Prince Aldfrid," a translation of which will be found in its proper place among the Historical Ballads of this collection? Is not our entire history, our sorrows, our struggles, and our hopes, comprised in the melodious lyrics of Thomas Moore, from the "Landing of the Milesians" to the chivalry of "Brian the Brave," and still downwards to the "slave so lowly" of our own day?

There is a false poetry which has fastened itself upon the world, because the world has a quick ear for evil. But vice was never intended to be the theme of poetic strains. The beautiful in all things should be the poet's only theme. The Athenians prohibited the honoured names of Harmodius and Aristogiton from being ever given to slaves; those who freed their own country from the tyranny of Hippias and Hipparchus should never have their names profanely associated with slavery. Why desecrate the sacred name of poetry by conferring it upon the daring indecencies of the profligate? Or disgrace the Muses by associating them with vice?

Moore's melodies are said to have assisted powerfully in achieving Catholic Emancipation, by creating a sympathy for the wrongs of Ireland wherever they penetrated. Let us hope that our labours may have an effect in a similar direction—that they may create a more charitable feeling towards Ireland by inducing the English public to study the history of a country which they have hitherto strangely and unaccountably neglected. If we have added a new charm to Ireland's beautiful scenery—if we have excited curiosity regarding her legends and her traditions—if we have excited sympathy for her sufferings, or charity for her shortcomings—if we have paved the way to kindlier feeling between the people of both countries, or dispelled from the English mind a single prejudice against Ireland—if we have effected any of these objects, our labours have not been all in vain.

Descriptive Ballads.

THE FAIR HILLS OF IRELAND. *

(FROM THE IRISH.)

BY SAMUEL FERGUSON, M.R.I.A.

A PLENTEOUS place is Ireland for hospitable cheer,
Where the wholesome fruit is bursting from the yellow barley ear;
There is honey in the trees where her misty vales expand,
And her forest paths, in summer, are by falling waters fanned,
There is dew at high noontide there, and springs i' the yellow sand
    On the fair hills of holy Ireland.

Curled he is and ringletted, and plaited to the knee,
Each captain who comes sailing across the Irish sea;
And I will make my journey, if life and health but stand,
Unto that pleasant country, that fresh and fragrant strand,
And leave your boasted braveries, your wealth and high command,
    For the fair hills of holy Ireland.

Large and profitable are the stacks upon the ground;
The butter and the cream do wondrously abound;
The cresses on the water and the sorrels are at hand,
And the cuckoo's calling daily his note of music bland,
And the bold thrush sings so bravely his song i' the forests grand,
    On the fair hills of holy Ireland.

    1834.

* After the first and second lines of each verse in this ballad an Irish refrain
occurs of *Uileacan dubh, O!* which literally means, *a black-haired head of a
round shape or form.* It was used as a term of endearment by the early Irish
poets.

A

THE GREEN ISLE.

BY THOMAS MOORE.

FAIREST! put on awhile
  These pinions of light I bring thee,
And o'er thy own green isle
  In fancy let me wing thee.
Never did Ariel's plume,
  At golden sunset hover
O'er scenes so full of bloom,
  As I shall waft thee over.

Fields, where the Spring delays,
  And fearlessly meets the ardour
Of the warm Summer's gaze,
  With only her tears to guard her.
Rocks, through myrtle boughs
  In grace majestic frowning,
Like some bold warrior's brows
  That Love hath just been crowning.

Islets, so freshly fair,
  That never hath bird come nigh them,
But from his course thro' air
  He hath been won down by them.*
Types, sweet maid, of thee,
  Whose look, whose blush inviting,
Never did Love yet see
  From Heav'n, without alighting.

Lakes, where the pearl lies hid,†
  And caves where the gem is sleeping,
Bright as the tears thy lid
  Lets fall in lonely weeping.

---

* In describing the Skeligs (islands of the Barony of Forth), Dr. Keating
says, " There is a certain attractive virtue in the soil which draws down all the
birds that attempt to fly over it, and obliges them to light upon the rock."
  † " Nennius, a British writer of the ninth century, mentions the abundance
of pearls in Ireland. Their princes, he says, hung them behind their ears: and
this we find confirmed by a present made, A. C. 1094, by Gilbert, Bishop of
Limerick, to Anselm, Archbishop of Canterbury, of a considerable quantity of
Irish pearls."—*O'Halloran.*

Glens,* where Ocean comes,
   To 'scape the wild wind's rancour,
And Harbours, worthiest homes,
   Where Freedom's fleet can anchor.

Then, if, while scenes so grand,
   So beautiful, shine before thee,
Pride for thy own dear land
   Should haply be stealing o'er thee;
Oh, let grief come first,
   O'er pride itself victorious—
Thinking how man hath curst
   What Heaven had made so glorious!

———

TIPPERARY.

WERE you ever in sweet Tipperary, where the fields are so sunny
   and green,
And the heath-brown Slieve-bloom and the Galtees look down
   with so proud a mien?
'Tis there you would see more beauty than is on all Irish ground—
God bless you, my sweet Tipperary, for where could your match
   be found?

They say that your hand is fearful, that darkness is in your eye
But I'll not let them dare to talk so black and bitter a lie.
Oh! no, *macushla storin!* bright, bright, and warm are you,
With hearts as bold as the men of old, to yourselves and your
   country true.

And when there is gloom upon you, bid them think who has
   brought it there—
Sure a frown or a word of hatred was not made for your face so
   fair;
You've a hand for the grasp of friendship—another to make them
   quake,
And they're welcome to whichsoever it pleases them most to take.

* Glengariff.

Shall our homes, like the huts of Connaught, be crumbled before
    our eyes?
Shall we fly, like a flock of wild geese, from all that we love and
    prize?
No! by those who were here before us, no churl shall our tyrant be;
Our land it is theirs by plunder, but, by Brigid, ourselves are free.

No! we do not forget the greatness did once to sweet Erië belong;
No treason or craven spirit was ever our race among;
And no frown or no word of hatred we give—but to pay them
    back;
In evil we only follow our enemies' darksome track.

Oh! come for a while among us, and give us the friendly hand;
And you'll see that old Tipperary is a loving and gladsome land;
From Upper to Lower Ormond, bright welcomes and smiles will
    spring,—
On the plains of Tipperary the stranger is like a king.

FIONULA.

THE PILLAR TOWERS OF IRELAND.

BY D. F. M'CARTHY,

(Author of "Ballads, Poems, and Lyrics," and Professor of Poetry in the
Catholic University of Ireland.)

THE pillar towers of Ireland, how wondrously they stand
By the lakes and rushing rivers through the valleys of our land;
In mystic file, through the isle, they lift their heads sublime,
These grey old pillar temples—these conquerors of time!

Beside these grey old pillars, how perishing and weak
The Roman's arch of triumph, and the temple of the Greek,
And the gold domes of Byzantium, and the pointed Gothic spires,
All are gone, one by one, but the temples of our sires!

The column, with its capital, is level with the dust,
And the proud halls of the mighty and the calm homes of the just;
For the proudest works of man, as certainly, but slower
Pass like the grass at the sharp scythe of the mower!

The Pillar Towers of Ireland.—Vol. i., p. 4.

But the grass grows again when in majesty and mirth,
On the wing of the Spring comes the Goddess of the Earth;
But for man in this world no spring-tide e'er returns
To the labours of his hands or the ashes of his urns!

Two favourites hath Time—the pyramids of Nile,
And the old mystic temples of our own dear isle;
As the breeze o'er the seas, where the halcyon has its nest,
Thus Time o'er Egypt's tombs and the temples of the West!

The names of their founders have vanished in the gloom,
Like the dry branch in the fire or the body in the tomb;
But to-day, in the ray, their shadows still they cast—
These temples of forgotten Gods—these relics of the past!

Around these walls have wandered the Briton and the Dane—
The captives of Armorica, the cavaliers of Spain—
Phœnician and Milesian, and the plundering Norman Peers—
And the swordsmen of brave Brian, and the chiefs of later years!

How many different rites have these grey old temples known?
To the mind what dreams are written in these chronicles of stone!
What terror and what error, what gleams of love and truth,
Have flashed from these walls since the world was in its youth?

Here blazed the sacred fire, and, when the sun was gone,
As a star from afar to the traveller it shone;
And the warm blood of the victim have these grey old temples
    drunk,
And the death-song of the Druid and the matin of the Monk.

Here was placed the holy chalice that held the sacred wine,
And the gold cross from the altar, and the relics from the shrine,
And the mitre shining brighter with its diamonds than the East,
And the crozier of the Pontiff, and the vestments of the Priest!

Where blazed the sacred fire, rung out the vesper bell,—
Where the fugitive found shelter, became the hermit's cell;
And hope hung out its symbol to the innocent and good,
For the Cross o'er the moss of the pointed summit stood!

There may it stand for ever, while this symbol doth impart
To the mind one glorious vision, or one proud throb to the heart;
While the breast needeth rest may these grey old temples last,
Bright prophets of the future, as preachers of the past!

———

THE OLD CASTLE.

THERE is an old Castle hangs over the sea—
'Tis living through ages, all wrecked though it be;
There's a soul in the ruin that never shall die,
And the ivy clings round it as fondly as I.
Oh! proud as the waves of that river pass on,
Their tribute they bear to that Castle so lone,
And the sun lights its grey head with beams from the sky,
For he loves the dear ruin as fondly as I.

Right grand is the freedom which dwells on the spot,
For the hand of the stranger can fetter it not;
The strength of that Castle its day-spring has told,
But the soul of the ruin looks out as of old;
And the river—the river no tyrant could tame,
Sweeps boldly along, without terror or shame;
Yet she bends by that Castle so stately and high,
And sings her own love-song as gladly as I.

How weird on those waters the shadows must seem,
When the moonlight falls o'er them as still as a dream,
And the star-beams awake, at the close of the day,
To gaze on a river eternal as they!
How the ghosts of dead ages must glide through the gloom,
And the forms of the mighty arise from the tomb,
And the dream of the past through the wailing winds moan,
For they twine round the ruin as if 'twere their own.

There is an old Castle hangs over the sea,
And ages of glory yet, yet shall it see,
And 'twill smile to the river, and smile to the sky,
And smile to the free land when long years go by;
And children will listen with rapturous face,
To the names and the legends that hallow the place,
When some minstrel of Erin, in wandering nigh,
Shall sing that dear Castle more grandly than I.　　MARY.

THE HOLY WELLS.

BY JOHN FRASER.

[John Fraser, more generally known by his *nom de plume*, "J. De Jean," was born near Birr, in the King's County, on the banks of the river Brosna, and died in Dublin in 1849, about 40 years of age. He was an artisan—a cabinet-maker; a steady and unassuming workman,—enjoying the respect of his fellow-workmen, and the friendship of those to whom he was known by his literary and poetic talents. He possessed much mental power,—and had his means permitted him to cultivate and refine his poetic mind he would have occupied a higher position as a poet than is now allotted to him. As it is, he has clothed noble thoughts in terse and harmonious language; in his descriptive ballads he depicts in vivid colours, the scenery of his native district,—with all the natural fondness of one describing scenes hallowed by memories of childhood and maturer years.]

The holy wells—the living wells—the cool, the fresh, the pure—
A thousand ages rolled away, and still those founts endure,
As full and sparkling as they flowed, ere slave or tyrant trod
The emerald garden, set apart for Irishmen by God!
And while their stainless chastity and lasting life have birth,
Amid the oozy cells and caves of gross, material earth;
The scripture of creation holds no fairer type than they—
That an immortal spirit can be linked with human clay!

How sweet, of old, the bubbling gush—no less to antlered race,
Than to the hunter, and the hound, that smote them in the chase!
In forest depths the water-fount beguiled the Druid's love,
From that celestial fount of fire which warmed from worlds above;
Inspired apostles took it for a centre to the ring,
When sprinkling round baptismal life—salvation—from the spring;
And in the sylvan solitude, or lonely mountain cave,
Beside it passed the hermit's life, as stainless as its wave.

The cottage hearth, the convent wall, the battlemented tower,
Grew up around the crystal springs, as well as flag and flower;
The brookline and the water-cress were evidence of health,
Abiding in those basins, free to poverty and wealth:
The city sent pale sufferers there the faded brow to dip,
And woo the water to depose some bloom upon the lip;
The wounded warrior dragged him towards the unforgotten tide,
And deemed the draught a heavenlier gift than triumph to his side.

The stag, the hunter, and the hound, the Druid and the saint,
And anchorite are gone, and even the lineaments grown faint,
Of those old ruins, into which, for monuments, had sunk
The glorious homes that held, like shrines, the monarch and the
　　　monk;
So far into the heights of God the mind of man has ranged,
It learned a lore to change the earth—its very self it changed
To some more bright intelligence; yet still the springs endure,
The same fresh fountains, but become more precious to the poor!

For knowledge has abused its powers, an empire to erect
For tyrants, on the rights the poor had given them to protect;
Till now the simple elements of nature are their *all*,
That from the cabin is not filched, and lavished in the hall—
And while night, noon, or morning meal no other plenty brings,
No beverage than the water-draught from old, spontaneous springs;
They, sure, may deem them holy wells, that yield from day to day,
One blessing which no tyrant hand can taint, or take away.

GOUGAUNE BARRA.

BY J. J. CALLANAN.

[Jeremiah Joseph Callanan was born in Cork in 1795. He was educated for
the priesthood, but the delicate state of his health, and the restless spirit,
which afterwards became the bane of his existence, and which frequently led
him to abandon real good for some vain and shadowy prospect, impelled him,
after a residence of two years, to quit Maynooth, and to relinquish all his future
prospects in the clerical profession. In 1820 he entered Trinity College as an
out-pensioner, with the intention of studying for the bar; but, like his previous
choice, he renounced this also after a two years' trial. In 1823 he became an
assistant in the school of Dr. Maginn, in Cork, where he remained only a few
months,—but through Maginn's introduction he became a contributor to
" Blackwood's Magazine."

During these six years, and up to 1829, he spent his time in rambling
through the county, collecting the old Irish ballads and legends, and in giving
them a new dress in a new tongue. Early in 1829 he became a tutor in the
family of an Irish gentleman in Lisbon, and on the 19th of September of the
same year, he died there in the 34th year of his age.

His " *Recluse of Inchidony*," in the Spenserian metre, is his longest poem,—
but his verses on " *Gougane Barra* " have attained the widest popularity in
the south of Ireland.

The Lake of Gougaune Barra, *i. e.* the hollow, or recess of Saint Finn Barr,
in the rugged territory of Ibh-Laoghaire, (the O'Learys' country,) in the west
end of the county of Cork, is the parent of the river Lee. Its waters embrace

a small but verdant island, of about half-an-acre in extent, which approaches
its eastern shore. The lake, as its name implies, is situate in a deep hollow,
surrounded on every side, (save the east, where its superabundant waters are
discharged,) by vast and almost perpendicular mountains, whose dark inverted
shadows are gloomily reflected in its still waters beneath. The names of those
mountains are *Dereen*, (the little oak wood,) where not a tree now remains;
Maolagh, which signifies a country—a region—a map, perhaps so called from
the wide prospect which it affords; *Nad an' willur*, the eagle's nest, and
Faoilte na Gougane, i. e. the cliffs of Gougaune, with its steep and frowning
precipices the home of a hundred echoes.]

THERE is a green island in lone Gougaune Barra,
Where Allua of songs rushes forth as an arrow;
In deep-vallied Desmond—a thousand wild fountains
Come down to that lake, from their home in the mountains.
There grows the wild ash, and a time-stricken willow
Looks chidingly down on the mirth of the billow;
As, like some gay child that sad monitor scorning,
It lightly laughs back to the laugh of the morning.

And its zone of dark hills—oh! to see them all bright'ning,
When the tempest flings out its red banner of lightning,
And the waters rush down, 'mid the thunder's deep rattle,
Like clans from the hills at the voice of the battle;
And brightly the fire-crested billows are gleaming,
And wildly from Mullagh the eagles are screaming,
Oh! where is the dwelling in valley, or highland,
So meet for a bard as this lone little island?

How oft when the summer sun rested on Clara,
And lit the dark heath on the hills of Ivera,
Have I sought thee, sweet spot, from my home by the ocean,
And trod all thy wilds with a Minstrel's devotion,
And thought of thy bards, when assembling together,
In the cleft of thy rocks, or the depth of thy heather;
They fled from the Saxon's dark bondage and slaughter,
And waked their last song by the rush of thy water.

High sons of the lyre, oh! how proud was the feeling,
To think while alone through that solitude stealing,
Though loftier Minstrels green Erin can number,
I only awoke your wild harp from its slumber,
And mingled once more with the voice of those fountains
The songs even echo forgot on her mountains;
And glean'd each grey legend, that darkly was sleeping
Where the mist and the rain o'er their beauty were creeping.

Least bard of the hills! were it mine to inherit
The fire of thy harp, and the wing of thy spirit,
With the wrongs which like thee to our country has bound me,
Did your mantle of song fling its radiance around me,
Still, still in those wilds might young liberty rally,
And send her strong shout over mountain and valley,
The star of the west might yet rise in its glory,
And the land that was darkest be brightest in story.

I too shall be gone;—but my name shall be spoken
When Erin awakes, and her fetters are broken;
Some Minstrel will come, in the summer eve's gleaming,
When freedom's young light on his spirit is beaming,
And bend o'er my grave with a tear of emotion,
Where calm Avon-Buee seeks the kisses of ocean,
Or plant a wild wreath, from the banks of that river,
O'er the heart, and the harp, that are sleeping for ever.

MY OWN SWEET LEE.

MY own dear native river, how fondly dost thou flow,
By many a fair and sunny scene where I can never go,
Thy waves are free to wander, and quickly on they wind,
Till thou hast left the crowded streets and city far behind;
Beyond I may not follow; thy haunts are not for me;
Yet I love to think on the pleasant track of "my own sweet
    river" Lee!

The spring-tide now is breathing—when thy waters glance
    along,
Full many a bird salutes thee with bright and cheering song;
Full many a sunbeam falleth upon thy bosom fair,
And every nook thou seekest hath welcome smiling there.
Glide on, thou blessed river! nor pause to think of me,
Who only in my longing heart can tread that track with thee!

Yet, when thy waters wander, where, haughty in decay,
Some grand old Irish castle looks frowning on thy way;
Oh! speak aloud, bold river! how I have wept with pride
To read of those past ages, ere all our glory died,
And wish for one short moment I had been there to see
Such relic of the by-gone day upon thy banks, fair Lee!

And if, in roving onward, thy gladsome waters bound
Where cottage homes are smiling, and children's voices sound ;
Oh ! think how sweet and tranquil, beneath the loving sky,
Rejoicing in some country home, my life had glided by,
And grieve one little minute that I can never be
A happy, happy cottager upon thy banks, fair Lee !

Now, fare thee well, glad river ! peace smile upon thy way,
And still may sunbeams brighten, where thy wild rimples play !
Oft in that weary city these blue waves leave behind
I'll think upon the pleasant paths where thy smooth waters wind ;
Oh, but for one long summer day, to wander on with thee,
And rove where'er thou rovest, my own sweet river Lee !

MARY.

THE BELLS OF SHANDON.

BY REV. FRANCIS MAHONY,

Author of the " Prout Papers."

[The author was born in Cork about the year 1800. He was one of the
ablest contributors to Frazer's Magazine in its best days, about 20 years ago,
when it was edited by his townsman, the late Dr. Maginn. Some of the articles which he then contributed have been since collected and published under
the title of " Father Prout's Reliques," in two volumes. Mr. Mahony is a priest
of the Catholic Church, but has for many years ceased to perform any clerical
functions. He has been a long time connected with the London press, and is
at present, we believe, editor of the *Globe*.
"There is nothing, after all, like the associations which early infancy at-
taches to the well-known and long-remembered chimes of our own parish
steeple ; and no magic can equal the effect on our ear when returning, after
long absence in foreign, and perhaps happier, countries."—*Prout's Reliques.*]

WITH deep affection and recollection
　　I often think of those Shandon bells,
Whose sound so wild would, in days of childhood,
　　Fling round my cradle their magic spells.
On this I ponder, where'er I wander,
　　And thus grow fonder, sweet Cork, of thee ;
　　　With thy bells of Shandon,
　　　That sound so grand on
The pleasant waters of the river Lee.

I've heard bells chiming full many a clime in,
   Tolling sublime in cathedral shrine;
While at a glibe rate brass tongues would vibrate,
   But all their music spoke nought like thine:
For memory dwelling on each proud swelling
   Of thy belfry knelling its bold notes free,
      Made the bells of Shandon,
      Sound far more grand on
The pleasant waters of the river Lee.

I've heard bells tolling "old Adrian's Mole" in,
   Their thunder rolling from the Vatican,
And cymbals glorious, swinging uproarious
   In the gorgeous turrets of Nôtre Dame :
But thy sounds were sweeter, than the dome of Peter
   Flings o'er the Tiber, pealing solemnly.
      O ! the bells of Shandon,
      Sound far more grand on
The pleasant waters of the river Lee.

There's a bell in Moscow, while on tower and kiosko
   In St. Sophia the Turkman gets,
And loud in air, calls men to prayer
   From the tapering summit of tall minarets.
Such empty phantom, I freely grant them ;
   But there's an anthem more dear to me,
      'Tis the bells of Shandon, *
      That sound so grand on
The pleasant waters of the river Lee.

* The church and spire of Shandon, built on the ruins of Old Shandon Castle, are prominent objects from whatever side the traveller approaches the city
of Cork.   There exists a pathetic ballad, composed by some exile when "eastward darkly going," in which he begins his adieu to the sweet spot thus :
" Farewell to thee, Cork, and thy sugar-loaf steeple," &c., &c.   But as nothing
is done in Ireland in the ordinary routine of sublunary things, this belfry is
built on a novel and rather droll principle of architecture, viz., one side is all of
grey stone and the other all red,—like the Prussian soldier's uniform trousers,
one leg blue, the other green.

GLASHEN-GLORA. *

'Tis sweet in midnight solitude,
When the voice of man lies hush'd, subdued,
To hear thy mountain voice so rude,
      Break silence, Glashen-glora!

I love to see thy foaming stream
Dash'd sparkling in the bright moonbeam;
For then of happier days I dream,
      Spent near thee—Glashen-glora!

I see the holly and the yew
Still shading thee, as then they grew;
But there's a form meets not my view,
      As once, near Glashen-glora.

Thou gaily, brightly, sparklest on,
Wreathing thy dimples round each stone;
But the bright eye that on thee shone
      Lies quench'd, wild Glashen-glora!

Still rush thee on, thou brawling brook;
Though on broad rivers I may look
In other lands, thy lonesome nook—
      I'll think on Glashen-glora!

When I am low, laid in the grave,
Thou still wilt sparkle, dash and rave
'Seaward, till thou becom'st a wave
      Of ocean, Glashen-glora!

Thy course and mine alike have been
Both restless, rocky, seldom green—
There rolls for me, beyond this scene,
      An ocean, Glashen-glora!

* A mountain-torrent, which finds its way into the Atlantic Ocean through Glengariff, in the west of the county Cork. The name, literally translated, signifies " the noisy green water."

And when my span of life's gone by,
Oh! if past spirits back can fly,
I'll often ride the night-wind's sigh,
    That's breathed o'er Glashen-glora!

1824.   W.

GLANDORE.

BY THE REV. DR. MURRAY,

Author of the Irish Annual Miscellany.

THOUGH I have forsaken long
Fairy land of tuneful song,
Though my lips forget to tell
Thoughts they once could utter well,
How can I, with heart and tongue,
See unloved, or love unsung,
Scenes like those that rise before
The enchanted eye in sweet Glandore?

Though a high and holy call
Claims my soul and senses all,
Saints might sing a type like this
Of their own bright realms of bliss;
Man may tell in strains of love,
Oh! how fair the world above,
When such beauty beameth o'er
The heaven below of sweet Glandore!

Cloudless sky and sparkling sea,
Cliff and shore and forest tree,
Glen and stream and mountain blue
Burst at once upon the view;
The gay, the beautiful, the grand
Blending over wave and land,
Till the eye can ask no more
Than it hath in sweet Glandore.

But the sunshine on the sea,
And the emerald of the lea,
And the ever smiling skies
Charm not heart, or soul, or eyes,

Like the grasp of friendship's hand,
Like the welcome warm and bland,
As the sunlight gleaming o'er
The happy homes of sweet Glandore.

For the loveliest scenes that e'er
Smiled of heaven the image fair,
Like the beautiful in death,
Have nor soul, nor voice, nor breath;
Oh! 'tis but the kindly heart
Can to them true life impart.
Tree and flower, and sea and shore,
Thus live and breathe in sweet Glandore.

Time may chill and bow and bind
Glowing heart and chainless mind;
They droop—the flowers of fancy, youth,
Round the ripening fruits of truth;
Yet I feel, while here I stray,
Dawn again youth's sunny day;
Fancy, with her radiant store,
Comes again in sweet Glandore.

Lovely region of Glandore!
Friends beloved for evermore!
Mid the tranquil bliss I feel
One sad thought begins to steal—
Soon must come the parting day,
And my steps no more will stray,
And my voice be heard no more
Among the scenes of sweet Glandore!

1843.

THE BOATMEN OF KERRY.

Above the dark waters the sea-gulls* are screaming;
Their wings in the sunlight are glancing and gleaming;

---

* The fishermen of Tralee bay regard the appearance of sea-gulls in unusual numbers hovering over the water as a certain token of the approach of herring shoals—hence, at the commencement of the season, a frequent question among the boatmen is, "Did you see any signs to-day?"

With keen eyes they're watching the herrings in motion,
As onward they come from the wild restless ocean.
Now, praise be to God for the hope that shines o'er us,
This season at least will cast plenty before us.
When safely returning, with our hookers well laden,
How gaily will sound the clear laugh of each maiden.
Oh! light as young fawns will they run down to meet us
With accents of love on the sea-shore to greet us;
While merrily over the waters we're gliding,
Each wave as it rolls with our boat-stems dividing;
Till high on the beach ev'ry black boat is stranded—
Her stout crew in health and in safety all landed,
Near cabins, though humble, from whence they can borrow
Content for the day and new hope for the morrow.
   The loved of our maidens are Boatmen of Kerry!
   For stalwart and true are the Boatmen of Kerry!
   To guide the black hooker, or scull the light wherry,
   My life on the skill of the Boatmen of Kerry!

The rich man from feasting may seek his soft pillow—
The plank is our bed, and our home is the billow;
Our sails may be rent, and our rigging be riven,
Yet know we no fear, for our trust is in Heaven.
To waves at the base of dark Brandon's steep highlands,
To sand-bank and rock, near the green Samphire islands,
The nets that we cast in the night are no strangers—
The nets that we tend in all trials and dangers.
From north, east, or west, though the wild winds be blowing,
Though waves be all madly or placidly flowing—
Those nets get us food when our children are crying,
Those nets give us joy when all sadly we're sighing;
When signs in the bay lie around us and near us,
With thoughts about home to inspire us and cheer us—
When falls over earth the grey shade of the even,
When gleams the first * star in the wide vault of Heaven,
Through gloom and through danger each bold boatman urges,
With sail or with oar, his frail boat through the surges.
   Oh, loved of our maidens are Boatmen of Kerry!
   For stalwart and true are the Boatmen of Kerry!
   To guide the black hooker, or scull the light wherry,
   My life on the skill of the Boatmen of Kerry!

---

   * Until the first star appears, fishermen in Kerry never set their herring-
nets.

Though wealth is not ours, though our fortunes are lowly,
Our hearts are at rest, for our thoughts are all holy :
Oh ! who would deny it that saw, in fair weather,
Our black boats assembled at anchor together—
Their crews all on board them, prepared, with devotion,
To list to the Mass * we get read on the ocean ?
Oh ! there is the faith that of heaven is surest—
Oh ! there is religion the highest and purest—
Oh ! could you but view them, with eyes upward roving
To God ever living—to God ever loving ;
The deep wave beneath them, the blue Heaven o'er them,
The tall cliffs around them, the altar before them,
You'd say " 'tis a sight to remember with pleasure—
A sight that a poet would gloat o'er and treasure.
Oh ! ne'er shall my soul lose the lesson they've taught her—
Those fishermen poor, with their Mass on the water."
    Oh, loved of our maidens are Boatmen of Kerry !
    Religious and pure are the Boatmen of Kerry !
    To guide the black hooker, or scull the light wherry,
    My life on the skill of the Boatmen of Kerry !

                                                    HEREMON

LAMENT FOR TIMOLEAGUE. †

(FROM THE IRISH.)

BY SAMUEL FERGUSON, M.R.I.A.

LONE and weary as I wander'd by the bleak shore of the sea,
Meditating and reflecting on the world's hard destiny,
Forth the moon and stars 'gan glimmer, in the quiet tide beneath,
For on slumbering spring and blossom breath'd not out of heaven
        a breath.

On I went in sad dejection, careless where my footsteps bore,
Till a ruined church before me opened wide its ancient door,—

---

* The fishermen get a mass said once a-year on the bay, not with the idea
(as it is sometimes said) " of *bringing fish into the bay*," but with a spirit of
religion that dreads to commence any undertaking until the blessing of God
has been invoked upon it.
    † Teach Molaga—" The House of St. Molago"—now called Timoleague, in
Munster.   B

Till I stood before the portals, where of old were wont to be,
For the blind, the halt, and leper, alms and hospitality.

Still the ancient seat was standing, built against the buttress gray,
Where the clergy used to welcome weary trav'llers on their way;
There I sat me down in sadness, 'neath my cheek I placed my hand,
Till the tears fell hot and briny down upon the grassy land.

There, I said in woful sorrow, weeping bitterly the while,
Was a time when joy and gladness reigned within this ruined
      pile;—
Was a time when bells were tinkling, clergy preaching peace
      abroad,
Psalms a singing, music ringing praises to the mighty God.

Empty aisle, deserted chancel, tower tottering to your fall,
Many a storm since then has beaten on the gray head of your wall!
Many a bitter storm and tempest has your roof-tree turned
      away,
Since you first were formed a temple to the Lord of night and day.

Holy house of ivied gables, that were once the country's boast,
Houseless now in weary wandering are you scattered, saintly host;
Lone you are to-day, and dismal,—joyful psalms no more are
      heard,
Where, within your choir, her vesper screeches the cat-headed bird.

Ivy from your eaves is growing, nettles round your green hearth-
      stone,
Foxes howl where, in your corners, dropping waters make their
      moan;
Where the lark to early matins used your clergy forth to call,
There, alas! no tongue is stirring, save the daws upon the wall.

Refectory cold and empty, dormitory bleak and bare,
Where are now your pious uses, simple bed and frugal fare?
Gone your abbot, rule and order, broken down your altar stones;
Nought I see beneath your shelter, save a heap of clayey bones.

Oh! the hardship—oh! the hatred, tyranny, and cruel war,
Persecution and oppression that have left you as you are!
I myself once also prospered;—mine is, too, an altered plight;
Trouble, care, and age have left me good for nought but grief
      to-night.

Gone, my motion and my vigour,—gone, the use of eye and ear;
At my feet lie friends and children, powerless and corrupting here;
Wo is written on my visage, in a nut my heart would lie—
Death's deliverance were welcome—Father, let the old man die.

———

DUHALLOW.

(FROM THE IRISH.)

BY J. C. MANGAN.

Far away from my friends,
  On the chill hills of Galway,
My heart droops and bends,
  And my spirit pines alway—
'Tis as not when I roved
  With the wild rakes of Mallow—
All is here unbeloved,
  And I sigh for Duhallow.

My sweetheart was cold,
  Or in sooth I'd have wept her—
Ah! that love should grow old
  And decline from his sceptre!
While the heart's feelings yet
  Seem so tender and callow!
But I deeplier regret
  My lost home in Duhallow!

My steed is no more,
  And my hounds roam unyelling;
Grass waves at the door
  Of my dark-windowed dwelling.
Through sunshine and storm
  Corrach's acres lie fallow;
Would Heaven I were warm
  Once again in Duhallow!

In the blackness of night,
  In the depth of disaster,
My heart were more light
  Could I call myself master

Of Corracn once more
    Than if here I might wallow
In gold thick as gore
    Far away from Duhallow!

I lov'd Italy's show
    In the years of my greenness,
Till I saw the deep woe,
    The debasement, the meanness,
That rot that bright land!
    I have since grown less shallow
And would now rather stand
    In a bog in Duhallow!

This place I'm in here,
    On the gray hills of Galway,
I like for its cheer
    Well enough in a small way;
But the men are all short,
    And the women all sallow;
Give M'Quillan his quart
    Of brown ale in Duhallow

My sporting days o'er,
    And my love-days gone after,
Not earth could restore
    Me my old life and laughter.
Burns now my breast's flame
    Like a dim wick of tallow,
Yet I love thee the same
    As at twenty, Duhallow!

But my hopes, like my rhymes,
    Are consumed and expended;
What's the use of old times
    When *our* time is now ended?
Drop the talk! Death will come
    For the debt that we all owe,
And the grave is a home,
    Quite as old as Duhallow!

1848.

LOCH INA,

A BEAUTIFUL SALT-WATER LAKE IN THE COUNTY OF CORK,
NEAR BALTIMORE.

I KNOW a lake where the cool waves break,
    And softly fall on the silver sand—
And no steps intrude on that solitude,
    And no voice, save mine, disturbs the strand.

And a mountain bold, like a giant of old
    Turned to stone by some magic spell,
Uprears in might his misty height,
    And his craggy sides are wooded well.

In the midst doth smile a little Isle,
    And its verdure shames the emerald's green—
On its grassy side, in ruined pride,
    A castle of old is darkling seen.

On its lofty crest the wild cranes nest,
    In its halls the sheep good shelter find ;
And the ivy shades where a hundred blades
    Were hung, when the owners in sleep reclined.

That chieftain of old could he now behold
    His lordly tower a shepherd's pen,
His corpse, long dead, from its narrow bed
    Would rise, with anger and shame again.

'Tis sweet to gaze when the sun's bright rays
    Are cooling themselves in the trembling wave—
But 'tis sweeter far when the evening star
    Shines like a smile at Friendship's grave.

There the hollow shells through their wreathed cells,
    Make music on the silent shore,
As the summer breeze, through the distant trees,
    Murmurs in fragrant breathings o'er.

And the sea weed shines, like the hidden mines,
    Or the fairy cities beneath the sea ;

And the wave-washed stones are bright as the thrones
  Of the ancient Kings of Araby.

If it were my lot in that fairy spot
  To live for ever, and dream 'twere mine,
Courts might woo, and kings pursue,
  Ere I would leave thee—Loved Loch-Ine.

FUNCHEON WOODS.

BY B. SIMMONS.

[Mr. Simmons was born in Kilworth, in county Cork, the scenery of which he has described with such pleasing fidelity. He obtained a situation in the Excise Office in London, which he held till his death. He died on 21st July 1850, in Acton Street, Gray's Inn Road, and was buried in Highgate cemetery on the Sunday following. For many years he was a frequent contributor of lyrical poems to the Magazines and Annuals. *Blackwood*, whose pages he enriched by some of his finest productions, thus speaks of him:—" Simmons, on the theme of Napoleon, excels all our great poets. Byron's lines on that subject are bad; Scott's, poor; Wordsworth's, weak; Lockhart and Simmons may be bracketed as equal; theirs are good, rich, strong." His early death closed the career of one of Ireland's most promising young poets.

The river Funcheon rises among the remote fastnesses of the Galties, a range of lofty mountains, which run along the confines of the counties of Cork, Limerick and Tipperary. Its source is in a bog in Tipperary, about a mile to the south of these elevated hills; it soon enters the county Cork, through which it takes a winding course of about twenty-five miles, through an interesting country, full of monastic and feudal remains,—and flows into the Blackwater, about two miles east of Fermoy. In its course it passes Kilworth, the birthplace of the poet, enters the demesne of the Earl of Mountcashel, and flows past a natural grotto called by the peasants *Thiug-na-Filea*, or Teague the Bard, from a wandering minstrel of that name having traditionally made the cave his dwelling, in those days "when godless persecution reigned."]

DARK woods of Funcheon! treading far
  The rugged paths of duty—
Though lost to me the vesper star
  Now trembling o'er your beauty,
Still vividly I see your glades,
  The deep and emerald-hearted,
As when from their luxuriant shades
  My lingering steps departed.

That wild autumnal morning!—well
  Can haunted Thought remember
How came in gusts o'er Corrin-fell
  The roar of dark September,
When I through that same woodland path
  To endless exile hasted,
Where many an hour my lavish youth
  The gold of evening wasted.

Oh, for *one* day of *that* glad time!
  —Say, reckless heart, how is it
There's still so many a cliff to climb,
  And well-known nook to visit?—
The Filea's spring is gurgling near;
  And may I not, delaying,
One moment watch the glittering sand
  Beneath its crystal playing?

No!—" Onward!" cried the mighty breeze,
  " From all thy heart rejoices!"
And loud my childhood's ancient trees
  Then lifted up their voices,
As though they felt and mourned the loss
  (With heads bowed down and hoary)
Of him who, seated at their feet,
  First sang their summer glory.

Too like the fair beloved group
  From whose embrace I wended,
In vain the pine trees' shapely troop
  Their graceful arms extended;
And vainly fast as sisters' tears
  The pallid Birch was weeping—
While woke, like cousins' sad blue eyes,
  The winkle's flower from sleeping.

Farewell—I thought—ye only friends
  The heart can trust in leaving,
Untroubled by the primal curse,
  The dread of your deceiving.
I shall not see at least *your* fall,
  And so—when wronged and wounded—
Still feel secure of peace at last,
  By you, old friends! surrounded.

And since in nature's scenes, the grand
  Or beautiful or tender,
He who invests them with a light
  That sanctifies their splendour,
Finding no one abiding-place;
  Be his the deep reliance
That he for holier worlds received
  The bard's immortal science.

Green Funcheon-side! your sounding woods
  Heaved wide as tossing ocean
When my last glance that autumn morn
  Turned from their billowy motion—
Turned where the willow's tresses streamed
  Above the river stooping,
Dark as your own bright LADY's hair
  Magnificently drooping.

Ah, in that wild tumultuous hour
  When heaven with earth seemed warring,
And swept the tempest's demon-power,
  The landscape's lustre marring,
One gentle spirit, (haply then
  Of Funcheon's beauty thinking)
A fading GIRL—like a tired child
  On Death's calm breast was sinking.

They've made her grave far, far from all
  The haunts she prized so dearly,
O, place no marble o'er its turf,
  For there shall flourish yearly,
Such flowers as in her Bible's leaves
  She loved to fold and cherish—
Pansies and early primroses
  That, as they blossom, perish.

Rave on, loud Winds, from tranquil rest
  Ye never more shall stir her;
And ye, fair Woods, now vanishing
  From memory's darkened mirror,
Farewell; what meeter time for thought
  The lost and loved recalling,
Than in this solemn evening hour
  When autumn-leaves are falling.
October, 1841.

THE MOUNTAIN FERN.

BY THE AUTHOR OF " THE MONKS OF KILCREA."

Oh, the Fern! the Fern!—the Irish hill Fern!—
That girds our blue lakes from Lough Ine * to Lough Erne,
That waves on our crags, like the plume of a king,
And bends, like a nun, over clear well and spring!
The fairy's tall palm tree! the heath bird's fresh nest,
And the couch the red deer deems the sweetest and best,
With the free winds to fan it, and dew drops to gem,—
Oh, what can ye match with its beautiful stem?
From the shrine of Saint Finbar, by lone Avonbuie,
To the halls of Dunluce, with its towers by the sea,
From the hill of Knockthu to the rath of Moyvore,
Like a chaplet it circles our green island o'er,—
In the bawn of the chief, by the anchorite's cell,
On the hill top, or greenwood, by streamlet or well,
With a spell on each leaf, which no mortal can learn †—
Oh, there never was plant like the Irish hill Fern!

Oh, the Fern! the Fern!—the Irish hill Fern!—
That shelters the weary, or wild roe, or kern.‡
Through the glens of Kilcoe rose a shout on the gale,
As the Saxons rushed forth, in their wrath, from the Pale,§
With bandog and bloodhound, all savage to see,
To hunt thro' Clunealla the wild Rapparee!‖
Hark! a cry from yon dell on the startled ear rings,
And forth from the wood the young fugitive springs,
Thro' the copse, o'er the bog, and, oh, saints be his guide!
His fleet step now falters—there's blood on his side—
Yet onward he strains, climbs the cliff, fords the stream,
And sinks on the hill top, mid brachen leaves green,

* Lough Ine, a singularly romantic lake in the western mountains of Cork; of Lough Erne, I hope it is unnecessary to speak.
† The fortunate discoverer of the fern seed is supposed to obtain the power of rendering himself invisible at pleasure.
‡ Kern, an Irish footman, or foot soldier
§ Pale, that portion of Ireland first colonised by the English,—embracing five counties in the provinces of Ulster and Leinster. Beyond the precincts of the Pale, English law was not recognized till the reign of James I.
‖ Rapparees, men who were gradually driven by the English army and English law to the mountains and fastnesses, and who lived principally upon the spoil taken from the people in the English interest. Rapery was a kind of half-pike which was carried by these men, and hence Rapparee.

And thick o'er his brow are their fresh clusters piled,
And they cover his form, as a mother her child;
And the Saxon is baffled!—they never discern
Where it shelters and saves him—the Irish hill Fern!

Oh, the Fern! the Fern!—the Irish hill Fern!—
That pours a wild keen o'er the hero's gray cairn;
Go, hear it at midnight, when stars are all out,
And the wind o'er the hill side is moaning about,
With a rustle and stir, and a low wailing tone
That thrills thro' the heart with its whispering lone,
And ponder its meaning, when haply you stray
Where the halls of the stranger in ruin decay.
With night owls for warders, the goshawk for guest,
And their dais * of honour by cattle-hoofs prest—
With its fosse choked with rushes, and spider-webs flung,
Over walls where the marchmen their red weapons hung,
With a curse on their name, and a sigh for the hour
That tarries so long—look! what waves on the tower?
With an omen and sign, and an augury stern,
'Tis the *Green Flag* of Time!—'tis the Irish hill Fern!

THE VALE OF SHANGA'NAH.

BY D. F. M'CARTHY.

[By the "Vale of Shangánah," I understand the entire of that beautiful
panorama which stretches out from the foot of Killiney Hill to Bray Head, and
from the White Strand to the Sugar Loaf Mountains. These picturesque hills
were called in Irish "The Golden Spears." *Ben Heder* is the original name of
the Hill of Howth.

WHEN I have knelt in the Temple of Duty,
Worshipping honour and valour and beauty—
When, like a brave man, in fearless resistance,
I have fought the good fight on the field of existence;
When a home I have won in the conflict of labour,
With truth for my armour and thought for my sabre,
Be that home a calm home where my old age may rally,
A home full of peace in this sweet pleasant valley.

---

* The dais was an elevated portion of the great hall or dining-room, set
apart in feudal times for those of gentle blood, and was, in consequence, regarded with peculiar feelings of veneration and respect.

Sweetest of vales is the Vale of Shanganah !
Greenest of vales is the Vale of Shanganah !
May the accents of love, like the droppings of manna,
Fall sweet on my heart in the Vale of Shanganah !

Fair is this isle—this dear child of the ocean—
Nurtured with more than a mother's devotion ;
For see ! in what rich robes has Nature arrayed her,
From the waves of the west to the cliffs of Ben Heder,
By Glengariff's lone islets—Loch Lene's* fairy water,
So lovely was each, that then matchless I thought her ;
But I feel, as I stray through each sweet-scented alley,
Less wild but more fair is this soft verdant valley !
    Sweetest of vales is the Vale of Shanganah !
    Greenest of vales is the Vale of Shanganah !
    No wide-spreading prairie—no Indian savannah,
    So dear to the eye as the Vale of Shanganah !

How pleased, how delighted, the rapt eye reposes
On the picture of beauty this valley discloses,
From that margin of silver, whereon the blue water
Doth glance like the eyes of the ocean foam's daughter !
To where, with the red clouds of morning combining,
The tall " Golden Spears " o'er the mountains are shining,
With the hue of their heather, as sunlight advances,
Like purple flags furled round the staffs of the lances !
    Sweetest of vales is the Vale of Shanganah !
    Greenest of vales is the Vale of Shanganah !
    No lands far away by the calm Susquehannah,
    So tranquil and fair as the Vale of Shanganah !

But here, even here, the lone heart were benighted,
No beauty could reach it, if love did not light it ;
'Tis this makes the Earth, oh ! what mortal can doubt it ?
A garden with *it*—but a desert without it !
With the lov'd one, whose feelings instinctively teach her,
That goodness of heart makes the beauty of feature,
How glad, through this vale, would I float down life's river,
Enjoying God's bounty, and blessing the Giver !
    Sweetest of vales is the Vale of Shanganah !
    Greenest of vales is the Vale of Shanganah !
    May the accents of love, like the droppings of manna,
    Fall sweet on my heart in the Vale of Shanganah !

      * Loch Lene—The Lakes of Killarney

THE RETURNED EXILE.

BY B. SIMMONS.

BLUE Corrin!* how softly the evening light goes,
Fading far o'er thy summit from ruby to rose,
As if loath to deprive the deep woodlands below
Of the love and the glory they drink in its glow:
Oh, home-looking Hill! how beloved dost thou rise
Once more to my sight through the shadowy skies,
Watching still, in thy sheltering grandeur unfurled,
The landscape to me that so long was the world.
Fair evening—blest evening! one moment delay
Till the tears of the Pilgrim are dried in thy ray—
Till he feels that through years of long absence, not one
Of his friends—the lone rock and gray ruin—is gone.

Not one:—as I wind the sheer fastnesses through,
The valley of boyhood is bright in my view!
Once again my glad spirit its fetterless flight
May wing through a sphere of unclouded delight,
O'er one maze of broad orchard, green meadow, and slope—
From whose tints I once pictured the pinions of hope;
Still the hamlet gleams white—still the church yews are weeping,
Where the sleep of the peaceful my fathers are sleeping;
The vane tells, as erewhile, its fib from the mill,
But the wheel tumbles loudly and merrily still,
And the tower of the Roches stands lonely as ever,
With its grim shadow rusting the gold of the river

My own pleasant River, bloom-skirted, behold,
Now sleeping in shade, now refulgently roll'd,
Where long through the landscape it tranquilly flows,
Scarcely breaking, Glen-coorah, thy glorious repose!
By the Park's lovely pathways it lingers and shines,
Where the cushat's low call, and the murmur of pines,
And the lips of the lily seem wooing its stay
'Mid their odorous dells;—but 'tis off and away,

* The picturesque mountain of Corrin, (properly Cairn-thierna, i. e. the
Thane or Lord's cairn,) is the termination of a long range of hills which en-
closes the valley of the Blackwater and Funcheon (the Avonduff and Fanshin
of Spencer,) in the county of Cork, and forms a striking feature of scenery, remarkable for pastoral beauty and romance.

Rushing out through the clustering oaks, in whose shade,
Like a bird in the branches, an arbour I made,
Where the blue eyes of Eve often closed o'er the book,
While I read of stout Sindbad, or voyaged with Cook.

Wild haunt of the Harper!* I stand by thy spring,
Whose waters of silver still sparkle and fling
Their wealth at my feet,—and I catch the deep glow,
As in long-vanish'd hours, of the lilacs that blow
By the low cottage-porch—and the same crescent moon
That then plough'd, like a pinnace, the purple of June,
Is white on Glen-duff, and all blooms as unchanged
As if years had not pass'd since thy greenwood I ranged—
As if ONE were not fled, who imparted a soul
Of divinest enchantment and grace to the whole,
Whose being was bright as that fair moon above,
And all deep and all pure as thy waters her love.

Thou long-vanish'd Angel! whose faithfulness threw
O'er my gloomy existence one glorified hue!
Dost thou still, as of yore, when the evening grows dim,
And the blackbird by Downing is hushing its hymn,
Remember the bower by the Funcheon's blue side
Where the whispers were soft as the kiss of the tide?
Dost thou still think, with pity and peace on thy brow,
Of him who, toil-harass'd and time-shaken now,
While the last light of day, like his hopes, has departed,
On the turf thou hast hallowed, sinks down weary-hearted,
And calls on thy name, and the night-breeze that sighs
Through the boughs that once blest thee is all that replies?

But thy summit, fair Corrin, is fading in gray,
And the moonlight grows mellow on lonely Cloughlea;
And the laugh of the young, as they loiter about
Through the elm-shaded alleys, rings joyously out:
Happy souls! they have yet the dark chalice to taste,
And like others to wander life's desolate waste—
To hold wassail with sin, or keep vigil with woe;
But the same fount of yearning, wherever they go,
Welling up in their heart-depths, to turn at the last
(As the stag when the barb in his bosom is fast)
To their lair in the hills, on their childhood that rose,
And find the sole blessing I seek for—REPOSE!

* The cavern of *Thiag-na-filea*, or Trin the Bard.

THE SHANNON.

My youthful song I dedicate to thee,
  Oh mightiest of the floods
That swelled the pride of Dathy's heroic soul
  When Erin was the land of sombre woods
    And brave, true-hearted kings,
  Whose bosoms bounded wilder than thy sea--
When round the warm enrapturing wine-bright bowl
    Were quenched their idle quarrellings.

Methinks the banners of a hundred knights
  Were oft and oft beheld
By thee, thou stateliest river of the plains!
  And thou hast seen the Norman host repelled
    Before the dreadful spears
Which Cathal wielded in the blaze of fight—
  Cathal, whose thunders shook the ethereal far es—
    Whose fame o'erfloats the flow of myriad years

The days are gone when to thy flowery banks
  Soft minstrels might retire,
And, high extolling some celestial maid,
  Pour forth the mellow music of the lyre,
    Or tune the harmonious chord
To notes of deadlier sound—of kilted men—
  Of flying plumes and combatants arrayed
    With halbert, helm, and sword.

Thee have I loved, because with thee are twined
  A thousand golden thoughts
That waft my young life to the Munster vale
  Where, it is said, a stranger's bugle notes
    Shall sing a tyrant's doom.
Oh for one blast of that sweet evening's wind,
  To whistle o'er my plumage—Yea, or steal
    Along my peaceful tomb.

                              CONACIENSIS.

THE FAIR HILLS OF EIRE, O!

(FROM THE IRISH.)

BY J. C. MANGAN.

[James Clarence Mangan was born in Dublin in 1803, and died there in 1849. For a period of more than twenty years he had been a contributor to almost every magazine or periodical published in Ireland during that time. When scarcely fifteen years of age he obtained a situation in a scrivener's office, where he remained for seven years, and then became a solicitor's clerk for three years. Describing this period of his life, he says: "I was obliged to work seven years of the ten from five in the morning, winter and summer, to eleven at night; and, during the three remaining years, nothing but a special providence could have saved me from suicide. The misery of my own mind,—my natural tendency to loneliness, poetry, and self-analysis, the disgusting obscenities and horrible blasphemies of those associated with me—the persecutions. I was obliged to endure, and which I never avenged but by acts of kindness,— the close air of the room, and the perpetual smoke of the chimney—all these destroyed my constitution. No! I am wrong; it was not even all these that destroyed me. In seeking to escape from this misery, I had laid the foundation of that evil habit which has proved to be my ruin." Alas! It is too true that like many another child of song he drank long and deeply; and in his desire to forget himself,—to fly from the actual into the ideal, he became an opium-eater. He became connected with the library of Trinity College, where he acquired that knowledge of languages which he afterwards turned to such good account. In person Mangan was below the middle size. His face was ashy pale, but when kindled up by the light and brilliancy of his full, blue eye, under the influence of his favourite drug, he was perfectly beautiful. He usually wore a carmelite brown kind of frock coat, tightly buttoned, and occasionally over it a small blue cloak, in the shape of which the bias cut was carefully excluded. His hat, which was high-crowned and battered,—and the old umbrella under his arm, even the warmest day in summer, gave the finishing stroke to his quaint and spectre-like appearance. And yet there was something deeply but painfully interesting about him. On a friend of his presenting a looking-glass to his face that he might see the ravages which his wild habits were making, he said, "Yes, I see a skinless skull there,—an empty socket where intelligence once beamed; but when I look *within* myself I behold a sadder vision—the vision of a wasted life." His existence became like that of Savage and Poe, vagrant and dissipated, till he was taken from a garret in a mean street in Dublin to one of the public hospitals, where he died after a week's illness. His remains repose in Glasnevin cemetery, without a stone to mark the spot.

Amongst the poets whom Ireland has produced within the last ten or fifteen years, Clarence Mangan deservedly occupies a high place. As a translator he was inimitable; and he translated from the Irish, the French, the German, the Spanish, the Italian, the Danish, and the Eastern languages, with such a versatile facility as not only to transfuse into his own tongue the substance and sense of his original, but the appropriate graces of style and ornament, and idiomatic expression which are peculiar to the poetry of every country. He

frequently surpassed his originals in the freedom and fluency of his language;
and many of the poems which he has called translations, are entirely his own.
It has been well observed that he was a Dervish among the Turks, a Bursch
among the Germans, a Scald among the Danes, an Improvisatore in Italy, and
a Senachie in Ireland. His original poems exhibit the vigour of his style and
the vividness of his fancy; and embody every form of grace and dignity in the
wondrous flow and charming melody of his versification. The only poems of
his which are in a collected form are his translations from the German, which
were published in 1845, under the title of "Anthologia Germanica."]

TAKE a blessing from my heart to the land of my birth,
      And the fair hills of Eire, O!
And to all that yet survive of Eibhear's tribe on earth,
      On the fair Hills of Eire, O!
In that land so delightful the wild thrush's lay
Seems to pour a lament forth for Eire's decay—
Alas! alas! why pine I a thousand miles away
      From the fair Hills of Eire, O!

The soil is rich and soft—the air is mild and bland,
      Of the fair Hills of Eire, O!
Her barest rock is greener to me than this rude land—
      O! the fair Hills of Eire, O!
Her woods are tall and straight, grove rising over grove;
Trees flourish in her glens below, and on her heights above,
O, in heart and in soul, I shall ever, ever love
      The fair Hills of Eire, O!

A noble tribe, moreover, are the now hapless Gael,
      On the fair Hills of Eire, O!
A tribe in Battle's hour unused to shrink or fail
      On the fair Hills of Eire, O!
For this is my lament in bitterness outpoured,
To see them slain or scattered by the Saxon sword.
Oh, woe of woes, to see a foreign spoiler horde
      On the fair Hills of Eire, O!

Broad and tall rise the *Cruachs** in the golden morning's glow,
      On the fair Hills of Eire, O!
O'er her smooth grass for ever sweet cream and honey flow
      On the fair Hills of Eire, O!

* Cruachs,—Hills. The one referred to is that in the county Waterford,
near Dungarvan.

O, I long, I am pining again to behold
The land that belongs to the brave Gael of old;
Far dearer to my heart than a gift of gems or gold
    Are the fair Hills of Eire, O!

The dew-drops lie bright 'mid the grass and yellow corn
    On the fair Hills of Eire, O!
The sweet-scented apples blush redly in the morn
    On the fair Hills of Eire, O!
The water-cress and sorrel fill the vales below;
The streamlets are hush'd, till the evening breezes blow,
While the waves of the Suir,* noble river! ever flow
    Near the fair Hills of Eire, O!

A fruitful clime is Eire's, through valley, meadow, plain,
    And the fair land of Eire, O!
The very "Bread of Life" is in the yellow grain
    On the fair Hills of Eire, O!
Far dearer unto me than the tones music yields,
Is the lowing of the kine and the calves in her fields,
And the sunlight that shone long ago on the shields
    Of the Gaels, on the fair Hills of Eire, O!

* This river has its source in Slieve Ailduin (the Devil's Bit Mountain), in the county Tipperary, and after a circuitous route by Thurles, Holycross, Cahir, Clonmel, Carrick-on-Suir, and Waterford, joins the Nore and Barrow, six miles below the latter town, and then falls into the British Channel.

INNISHOWEN.

BY CHARLES GAVAN DUFFY, M.P.

[Innishowen (pronounced Innishone) is a wild and picturesque district in the county Donegal, inhabited chiefly by the descendants of the Irish clans, permitted to remain in Ulster after the plantation of James I. The native language, and the songs and legends of the country, are as universal as the people. One of the most familiar of these legends is, that a troop of Hugh O'Neill's horse lies in magic sleep in a cave under the hill of Aileach, where the princes of the country were formerly installed. These bold troopers only wait to have the spell removed to rush to the aid of their country; and a man (says the legend) who wandered accidentally into the cave, found them lying beside their horses, fully armed, and holding the bridles in their hands. One of them lifted his head, and asked, "Is the time come?" and when he received no answer—for the intruder was too much frightened to reply—dropped back into his lethargy. Some of the old folk consider the story an allegory, and interpret it as they desire.]

C

God bless the grey mountains of dark Donegal,
God bless Royal Aileach, the pride of them all ;
For she sits evermore like a Queen on her throne,
And smiles on the valleys of Green Innishowen.
    And fair are the valleys of Green Innishowen,
    And hardy the fishers that call them their own—
    A race that nor traitor nor coward have known
    Enjoy the fair valleys of Green Innishowen.

Oh ! simple and bold are the bosoms they bear,
Like the hills that with silence and nature they share ;
For our God, who hath planted their home near His own,
Breath'd His spirit abroad upon fair Innishowen.
    Then praise to our Father for wild Innishowen,
    Where fiercely for ever the surges are thrown—
    Nor weather nor fortune a tempest hath blown
    Could shake the strong bosoms of brave Innishowen.

See the bountiful Couldah * careering along—
A type of their manhood so stately and strong—
On the weary for ever its tide is bestown,
So they share with the stranger in fair Innishowen.
    God guard the kind homesteads of fair Innishowen,
    Which manhood and virtue have chos'n for their own ;
    Not long shall that nation in slavery groan,
    That rears the tall peasants of fair Innishowen.

Like that oak of St. Bride which nor Devil nor Dane,
Nor Saxon nor Dutchman could rend from her fane,
They have clung by the creed and the cause of their own
Through the midnight of danger in true Innishowen.
    Then shout for the glories of old Innishowen,
    The stronghold that foemen have never o'erthrown—
    The soul and the spirit, the blood and the bone,
    That guard the green valleys of true Innishowen.

Nor purer of old was the tongue of the Gael,
When the charging *aboo* made the foreigner quail ;
Than it gladdens the stranger in welcome's soft tone,
In the home-loving cabins of kind Innishowen.
    Oh ! flourish ye homesteads of kind Innishowen,
    Where seeds of a people's redemption are sown ;
    Right soon shall the fruit of that sowing have grown,
    To bless the kind homesteads of green Innishowen.

* The Couldah, or Culdaff, is the chief river in the Innishowen mountains.

When they tell us the tale of a spell-stricken band
All entranced, with their bridles and broadswords in hand,
Who await but the word to give Erin her own,
They can read you that riddle in proud Innishowen.
    Hurra for the Spæmen* of proud Innishowen!—
    Long live the wild Seers of stout Innishowen!—
    May Mary, our mother, be deaf to their moan
    Who love not the promise of proud Innishowen!

THE RIVER BOYNE.

BY THOMAS D'ARCY M'GEE.

CHILD of Loch Ramor, gently seaward stealing,
In thy placid depths hast thou no feeling
    Of the stormy gusts of other days?
Does thy heart, oh, gentle, nun-faced river,
Passing Schomberg's obelisk, not quiver,
    While the shadow on thy bosom weighs?

Thou hast heard the sounds of martial clangour,
Seen fraternal forces clash in anger,
    In thy Sabbath valley, River Boyne!
Here have ancient Ulster's hardy forces
Dressed their ranks and fed their travelled horses,
    Tara's hosting as they rode to join.

Forgettest thou that silent Summer morning,
When William's bugles sounded sudden warning
    And James's answered, chivalrously clear!
When rank to rank gave the death-signal duly,
And volley answered volley quick and truly,
    And shouted mandates met the eager ear?

The thrush and linnet fled beyond the mountains,
The fish in Inver Colpa sought their fountains,
    The unchased deer scampered through Tredagh's† gates;

---

* An Ulster and Scotch term signifying a person gifted with "second
sight"—a prophet.
† Tredagh, now Drogheda.

St. Mary's bells in their high places trembled,
And made a mournful music which resembled
   A hopeless prayer to the unpitying Fates.

Ah! well for Ireland had the battle ended
When James forsook what William well defended,
   Crown, friends, and kingly cause;
Well, if the peace thy bosom did recover
Had breathed its benediction broadly over
   Our race, and rites, and laws.

Not in thy depths, not in thy fount, Loch Ramor!
Were brewed the bitter strife and cruel clamour
   Our wisest long have mourned;
Foul Faction falsely made thy gentle current
To Christian ears a stream and name abhorrent.
   And all thy waters into poison turn'd.

But, as of old God's Prophet sweetened Mara,
Even so, blue bound of Ulster and of Tara,
   Thy waters to our Exodus give life;
Thrice holy hands thy lineal foes have wedded,
And healing olives in thy breast embedded,
   And banished far the littleness of strife.

Before thee we have made a solemn Fœdus,
And for Chief Witness called on Him who made us,
   Quenching before His eyes the brands of hate;
Our pact is made, for brotherhood and union,
For equal laws to class and to communion—
   Our wounds to staunch—our land to liberate.

Our trust is not in musket or in sabre—
Our faith is in the fruitfulness of labour,
   The soul-stirred, willing soil;
In Homes and granaries by justice guarded,
In fields from blighting winds and agents warded,
   In franchised skill and manumitted toil.

Grant us, O God, the soil, and sun, and seasons!
Avert Despair, the worst of moral treasons,
   Make vaunting words be vile.
Grant us, we pray, but wisdom, peace, and patience,
And we will yet re-lift among the nations
   Our fair and fallen, but unforsaken Isle!

THE ROCK OF CASHEL.

BY THE REV. DR. MURRAY.

[Cormac M'Cuillenan, King of Munster and Archbishop of Cashel, erected his royal Castle and Metropolitan Cathedral on this lofty and rugged Rock, about the year 900. This huge pile of building, covering, as it does, the native rock, and seeming as if it had been formed out of its summit, consists not only of Cathedral and Castle, but also of a Round Tower nearly one hundred and fifty feet high, in excellent preservation. The church was altered and rebuilt in the twelfth century by Donald O'Brien, and was again repaired and improved by Archbishop O'Hedian about the year 1430. Archbishop Price unroofed it in 1680, and now the mouldings, capitals, and arches, which were once richly sculptured with emblematical designs, are either defaced or in ruins. A profound silence has supplanted those hymns of praise and adoration which once resounded through its aisles, and the stillness is only broken by the discordant voices of birds and beasts which shun the light of day. The beautiful stone-roofed church, called Cormac's Chapel, is the oldest portion of the edifice, and is one of the most curious and perfect churches, in the Norman style, in the British Empire. Standing on the square tower there is within range of vision a splendid and picturesque country of one hundred and twenty miles in extent, embracing seven counties; the scenery is beautifully diversified by mountain, valley, wood, and stream.]

FAIR was that eve, as if from earth away
    All trace of sin and sorrow
Passed, in the light of the eternal day,
    That knows nor night nor morrow.

The pale and shadowy mountains, in the dim
    And glowing distance piled!
A sea of light along the horizon's rim,
    Unbroken, undefiled!

Blue sky, and cloud, and grove, and hill, and glen,
    The form and face of man
Beamed with unwonted beauty, as if then
    New earth and heaven began.

Yet heavy grief was on me, and I gazed
    On thee through gushing tears,
Thou relic of a glory that once blazed
    So bright in bygone years!

Wreck of a ruin! lovelier, holier far,
    Thy ghastly hues of death,
Than the cold forms of newer temples are—
    Shrines of a priestless faith.

In lust and rapine, treachery and blood,
    Its iron domes were built;
Darkly they frown, where God's own altars stood,
    In hatred and in guilt.

But to make thee, of loving hearts the love
    Was coined to living stone;
Truth, peace, and piety together strove
    To form thee for their own.

And thou wast theirs, and they within thee met,
    And did thy presence fill;
And their sweet light, even while thine own is set,
    Hovers around thee still.

'Tis not the work of mind, or hand, or eye,
    Builder's or sculptor's skill,
Thy site, thy beauty, or thy majesty—
    Not these my bosom thrill.

'Tis that a glorious monument thou art,
    Of the true faith of old,
When faith was one in all the nation's heart,
    Purer than purest gold.

A light, when darkness on the nations dwelt,
    In Erin found a home—
The mind of Greece, the warm heart of the Celt,
    The bravery of Rome.

But O! the pearl, the gem, the glory of her youth,
    That shone upon her brow;
She clung for ever to the Chair of Truth—
    Clings to it now!

Love of my love, and temple of my God!
    How would I now clasp thee
Close to my heart, and, even as thou wast trod,
    So with thee trodden be!

O, for one hour a thousand years ago,
    Within thy precincts dim,
To hear the chant, in deep and measured flow,
    Of psalmody and hymn!

To see of priests the long and white array,
    Around thy silver shrines—
The people kneeling prostrate far away,
    In thick and chequer'd lines.

To see the Prince of Cashel o'er the rest,
    Their prelate and their king,
The sacred bread and chalice by him blest,
    Earth's holiest offering.

To hear, in piety's own Celtic tongue,
    The most heart-touching prayer
That fervent suppliants e'er was heard among, —
    O, to be then and there!

There was a time all this within thy walls
    Was felt, and heard, and seen;
Faint image only now thy sight recals
    Of all that once hath been.

The creedless, heartless, murderous robber came,
    And never since that time
Round thy torn altars burned the sacred flame,
    Or rose the chant sublime.

Thy glory in a crimson tide went down,
    Beneath the cloven hoof—
Altar and priest, mitre, and cope, and crown,
    And choir, and arch, and roof.

O, but to see thee, when thou wilt rise again—
    For thou again wilt rise,
And with the splendours of thy second reign
    Dazzle a nation's eyes!

Children of those who made thee what thou wast,
    Shall lift thee from the tomb,
And clothe thee, for the spoiling of the past,
    In more celestial bloom.

And psalm, and hymn, and gold, and precious stones,
    And gems beyond all price,
And priest, and altar, o'er the martyr's bones,
    And daily sacrifice,

And endless prayer, and crucifix, and shrine,
    And all religion's dower,
And thronging worshippers shall yet be thine—
    O, but to see that hour!

And who shall smite thee then?—and who shall see
    Thy second glory o'er?
When they who make thee free themselves are free,
    To fall no more.

HOLYCROSS ABBEY.

BY B. SIMMONS.

[The Cistertian Abbey of Holycross, county Tipperary, was founded in the year 1181 by Donald O'Brien,[*] King of Limerick and North Munster. It was regarded through Western Europe with peculiar veneration, and for three hundred years was favoured by the pilgrimages of noble and illustrious persons of both sexes. At the confiscation of the Religious Houses and Lands, Queen Elizabeth granted the abbey and its dependencies to Gerald, Earl of Ormond. Its present ruins attest its former magnificence. Here are the noble remains of the gorgeous church, with its mullioned windows, canopied niches, perforated piscinas, and elaborate sepulchres, dispersed throughout the nave, transepts and side aisles. Here also may be traced the rich sacristy, the strong muniment-house,—the frugal kitchen,—the solemn chapter-house,—the studious cloisters, and the sequestered Abbot's quarters. But all is now a dreary ruin and a wide waste; where deeper silence reigns than that prescribed by the conventual discipline of the twelfth century.]

" FROM the high sunny headlands of Bere in the west,
To the bowers that by Shannon's blue waters are blest,
I am master unquestion'd and absolute "—said
The lord of broad Munster—King Donald the Red—
" And now that my sceptre's no longer the sword,
In the wealthiest vale my dominions afford,
I will build me a temple of praise to that Power
Who buckler'd my breast in the battle's dread hour."

* Lanigan's Ecclesiastical History of Ireland, vol. iv. p. 252.

He spoke—it was done—and with pomp such as glows
Round a sunrise in summer that Abbey arose.
There sculpture, her miracles lavish'd around,
Until stone spoke a worship diviner than sound.

There from matins to midnight the censers were swaying,
And from matins to midnight the people were praying;
As a thousand Cistertians incessantly raised
Hosannas round shrines that with jewell'ry blazed;
While the palmer from Syria—the pilgrim from Spain,
Brought their offerings alike to the far-honour'd fane;
And, in time, when the wearied O'Brien laid down
At the feet of Death's Angel his cares and his crown,
Beside the high altar a canopied tomb
Shed above his remains its magnificent gloom,
And in Holycross Abbey high masses were said,
Through the lapse of long ages, for Donald the Red.

In the days of my musings, I wander'd alone,
To this Fane that had flourish'd ere Norman was known;
And its drear desolation was saddening to see,
For its towers, were an emblem, O Erin, of thee!
All was glory in ruins—below and above—
From the traceried turret that shelter'd the dove,
To the cloisters dim stretching in distance away,
Where the fox skulks at twilight in quest of his prey.
Here, soar'd the vast chancel superbly alone,
  While pillar and pinnacle moulder'd around—
There, the choir's richest fretwork in dust overthrown,
  With corbel and chapiter "cumber'd the ground."

O'er the porphyry shrine of the Founder all riven,
No lamps glimmer'd now but the cressets of heaven—
From the tombs of crusader, and abbot, and saint,
Emblazonry, scroll, and escutcheon were rent;
While usurping their banners' high places, o'er all
The Ivy—dark mourner—suspended her pall.
With a deeper emotion the spirit would thrill,
  In beholding wherever the winter and rain
Swept the dust from the relics it cover'd—that still
  Some hand had religiously glean'd them again.
Then I turn'd from the scene, as I mournfully said—
" God's rest to the soul of King Donald the Red."

THE POET'S HOME.

BY JOHN FRAZER.

Wild forest of old Woodfield!*—God's blessing on the hand,
That spares thee, even as thou art spared—a relic on the land,
Of those Ily Falgian fortresses, that stood long years to foil
The conquest of the stranger o'er the children of the soil—
Albeit that, from their heritage, those children have been driven—
Albeit that, for thine ancient name, an alien name be given—
Thou art a record of the power bestowed on scenes sublime,
Or beautiful—to turn away a conqueror's arm from crime;
And, though the Saxon hold thee now, a trophy of the brand,
For every root and stem he spares, God's blessing on his hand!

I loved thee through a boyhood, nigh spent beneath thy shade—
I love thee now, in life's decline, though later love's decayed;
For, every day and season, thou wert redolent of joy,
That bathed my heart with freshening thoughts, no future could
        destroy;
Thy solitudes were peopled with dissolving visions then,
Of what I would encounter from my passions, and from men;
And if, at times, I sorrow that some visions were o'er-true,
Remembrance of thy sylvan world will come to cheer me too;
Some passage of the season and the scenery I trod,
Consoles me to endurance, like a whisper'd boon from God.

Oh! that amid thy mazy depths my heart could cease to burn
With manhood's hot ambition, and that boyhood's could return—
That, in voluptuous dreamings. I thy hills and dells could range,
Surrounded by new luxuries, with every daily change,
From spring's first bud till summer's sun, like rain, would pierce
        thy bowers,
Or spot the shadowy sward with lights, like multitudes of flowers—
From summer, till the withering leaves took up their harvest hymns,
And winter's stern anatomy exposed the quivering limbs
Of all thy forest progeny—except the ivy green,
And holly—bright, like truths at last, that long remained unseen.

* Woodfield is the remains of one of the ancient forests of the country, covering a considerable extent of finely undulating ground within about a mile of
the town of Birr. It is the property of the Earl of Rosse, and, I believe, has
belonged to the family since their settlement in Ireland.

To search thy lone recesses—in a pathless nook to twine,
For cottage shelf, or window pane, bluebell and columbine—
To climb the oak—the forest king of old and high renown,
And peep into the magpie's nest—that jewel of his crown—
To pick the vinous raspberry in some sequestered dell—
Or shake the hazel, till its hoard of auburn filberts fell—
To start the woodcock from his couch—the grey hare from her form,
My soul sublimed, or sooth'd, the while, by stillness or by storm;
Could these be mine, and thousands such too subtle for the pen,—
It were a sweet exchange to roam thy sylvan world again.

But it was still a deeper joy—to set before my soul
The names that burn the brightest on my land's historic scroll—
To feel whate'er in life, or death, was beautiful or grand,
Ordained me to the ministry of struggling for that land!
Of chivalry—truth—trusted friends—burst fetters—but above
All earthly things, save liberty, to dream of woman's love;
Till an embodied witchery was to my spirit shown
Without a fault, save faults that seemed, like virtues overgrown!
And these most hallowing dreams, alas! alone, or girt with men,
In city, or green solitude, I ne'er can dream again.

The spell is broke—life's low-hung clouds from hour to hour
     move by,
And veil the loftier golden ones, that fixed my gaze on high;
The struggle with the world is o'er that on my nature cast
A sadness, like the drip on leaves, when thunder-showers have
     passed;
And, were ambition all extinct, my energies of mind
Would be a heap, inert and cold, of cinders left behind!
No trusted friends! no woman's love! no spurned and broken
     chains!
Of all thy phantom prophecies, wild forest, what remains?
I might have been a meaner slave—a wretch more base and banned—
Had the kind Saxon spared thee not!—God's blessing on his hand!

THE HOLY WELL.

'Twas a very lonely spot, with beech trees o'er it drooping;
     The water gleam'd beneath.
Those fair green branches lowly stooping,
     A benediction seem'd to breathe.

And a deep and rich green light within the boughs came peeping,
    Where little insects dream'd.
A luscious calm on all was sleeping—
    The sunlight drowsy seem'd.

In that little silv'ry well, how many tears fell heavy,
    What homage there was pour'd,
To Mary sweet, how many an Ave
    Sought for her saving word.

I strayed one evening calm to this low gentle water,
    The Virgin there might be—
So holy look'd it, you'd have thought her
    Guarding it tenderly.

When from the silence soft, some one I heard a praying,
    A poor dark girl was she,
Upon her bare knees she was swaying,
    Telling her rosary.

Oh ! that little maiden blind, fair-hair'd she was and slender;
    Her sad smile lit the place;
Her blue cloak-hood had fall'n, and tender
    'Neath it gleam'd her face.

" *She the vah !* "* she murmuring said, " Queen of pow'r and
       meekness,
    Oh ! let me see the light;
My mother droops with grief and sickness—
    For her sake give me sight.

Oh ! my weeny sister's gone, and we're left lone and pining;
    But two in this world wide.
If I could greet the fair sun shining,
    And be *her* stay and guide ! "

You'd think Blind Bridgh saw the face of the Redeemer,
    So kindly was her air.
I thought that every moment brightly
    She'd see the Heavens fair.

           * Hail to thee.

Just like a saint, she seem'd God's pleasure waiting only ;
  I could not help but weep ;
And join her in that shrine so lonely,
  Breathing petitions deep.   SULMALLA.

CLONDALLAGH.

BY J. FRAZER.

ARE the orchards of Scurragh
  With apples still bending ?
Are the wheat-ridge and furrow
  On Cappaghneale blending ?
Let them bend—let them blend !
  Be they fruitful or fallow,
A far dearer old friend
  Is the bog of Clondallagh !

Fair Birr of the fountains,
  Thy forest and river,
And miniature mountains,
  Seemed round me for ever ;
But they cast from the past
  No home mem'ries, to hallow
My heart to the last—
  Like the bog of Clondallagh !

How sweet was my dreaming
  By Brosna's bright water,
While it dashed away, seeming
  A mountain's young daughter !
Yet to roam with its foam,
  By the deep reach, or shallow—
Made but brighter at home
  The turf fires from Clondallagh !

If whole days of a childhood
  More mournful than merry,
I sought thro' the wild wood
  Young bird or ripe berry ;
Some odd sprite, or quaint knight,
  Some Sinbad, or Abdallah,

Was my chase by the light
  Of bog fir from Clondallagh!

There the wild duck and plover
  Have felt me a prowler
On their thin, rushy cover,
  More fatal than fowler:
And regret sways me yet,
  For the crash on the callow;
When the matched hurlers met,
  On the plains of Clondallagh!

Yea, simply to measure
  The moss with a soundless
Quick step, was a pleasure
  Strange, stirring, and boundless;
For its spring seemed to fling
  Up my foot, and to hallow
My spirit with wing,
  O'er the sward of Clondallagh!

But alas! in the season
  Of blossoming gladness,
May be strewed over reason
  Rank seeds of vain sadness!
While a wild, wayward child,
  With my young heart all callow,
It was warmed and beguiled
  By dear Jane of Clondallagh!

On the form with her seated,
  No urchin dare press on
My place, while she cheated
  Me into my lesson!
But soon came a fond claim
  From a lover to hallow
His hearth with a dame—
  In my Jane of Clondallagh!

When the altar had risen,
  From Jane to divide me,
I seemed in a prison,
  Tho' she still was beside me;

And I knew more the true,
　From the love, false or shallow,
The farther I flew
　From that bride, and Clondallagh!

From the toils of the city,
　My fancy long bore me,
To sue her to pity
　The fate she brought o'er me!
And the dream, wood and stream,
　The green fields, and the fallow,
Still return, like a beam,
　From dear Jane of Clondallagh!

BEN-HEDER—(THE HILL OF HOWTH.)

BY R. D. WILLIAMS.

[Richard Dalton Williams was born about thirty-three years ago at the foot of the Devil's Bit mountain in the county Tipperary. He was educated in the Catholic college of Carlow, where he gave early promise of his genius and power as a poet. He writes with equal ability upon all subjects, whether they be grave or gay—pathetic or humorous; his sympathies are large enough to enable him to portray every human passion and affection. There is a giant strength in him, and yet a sweet native gracefulness. "He is tender,—he is vehement, yet without constraint, or too visible effort. There is in him the gentleness, the trembling pity of a woman, with the deep earnestness, the force and passionate ardour of a hero. Tears lie in him and consuming fire, as lightning lurks in the drops of the summer cloud." After he left college he went to Dublin and became a medical student. His beautiful ballad on the " Dying Girl " was composed after one of his visits to the hospitals. In 1850 he emigrated to America, and is at present professor of *Belles Lettres* in the Catholic college of Mobile, Alabama.]

I RAMBLED away, on a festival day,
　From vanity, glare, and noise,
To calm my soul, where the wavelets roll,
　In solitude's holy joys.
By the lonely cliffs, whence the white gull starts,
　Where the clustering sea-pinks blow,
And the Irish rose, on the purple quartz
　Bends over the waves below.

Where the ramaline clings, and the samphire swings,
   And the long laminaria trails,
And the sea-bird springs on his snowy wings
   To blend with the distant sails.

I leaned on a rock, and the cool waves there
   Plash'd on the shingles round :
And the breath of Nature lifted my hair—
   Dear God! how the face of Thy child is fair !—
And a gush of memory, tears, and pray'r
   My spirit a moment drown'd.
I bowed me down to the rippling wave—
   For a swift sail glided near—
And the spray, as it fell upon pebble and shell,
   Received, it may be, a tear.

For well I remember the festal days
   On this shore, that Hy-Brassil seemed—
The friends I trusted, the dreams I dream'd
   Hopes high as the clouds above—
Perchance of Fame, or a land redeem'd,
   Perchance 'twas a dream of love.
When first I trod on this breezy sod
   To me it was holy ground,
For genius and beauty—rays of God—
   Like a swarm of stars shone round.
Well! well! I have learned rude lessons since then
   In life's disenchanted hall,
I have scanned the motives and ways of men,
   And the skeleton grins thro' all.

Of the great heart-treasure of hope and trust
   I exulted to feel mine own
Remains, in that down-trod temple's dust,
   But faith in God alone.
I have seen too oft the domino torn
   And the mask from the face of men,
To have aught save a smile of tranquil scorn
   For all I believed in then.
The day is dark as the night with woes,
   And my dreams are of battles lost,
Of eclipse, phantoms, wrecks, and foes,
   And of exiles tempest-tost.

No more, no more! on the dreary shore
   I hear a caoina-song;*
With the early dead is my lonely bed—
   You shall not call me long;
I fade away to the home of clay,
   With not one dream fulfilled:
My wreathless brow in the dust I bow,
   My heart and harp are stilled.
Oh, would I might rest when my soul departs
   Where the clustering sea-pinks blow,
And the Irish rose, on the purple quartz,
   Droops over the waves below—
Where the crystals gleam in the caves about,
   Like virtue in humble souls,
And the Victor Sea, with a thunder-shout,
   'Thro' the breach in the rock-wall rolls!

BROSNA'S BANKS.

BY J. FRAZER.

YES, yes, I idled many an hour—
   (Oh! would that I could idle now,
In wooing back the wither'd flower
   Of health into my wasted brow!)
But from my life's o'ershadowing close,
   My unimpassioned spirit ranks
Among its happiest moments those
   I idled on the Brosna's Banks.

For there upon my boyhood broke
   The dreamy voice of nature first;
And every word the vision spoke,
   How deeply has my spirit nursed!
A woman's love, a lyre, or pen,
   A rescued land, a nation's thanks,
A friendship with the world, and then
   A grave upon the Brosna's Banks.

* *Caoina*—Dirge. Irish cry or lamentation for the dead.

D

For these I sued, and sought, and strove,
　But now my youthful days are gone,
In vain, in vain—for woman's love
　Is still a blessing to be won;
And still my country's cheek is wet,
　The still-unbroken fetter clanks,
And I may not forsake her yet
　To die upon the Brosna's Banks.

Yet idle as those visions seem,
　They were a strange and faithful guide,
When Heaven itself had scarce a gleam
　To light my darken'd life beside;
And if from grosser guilt escaped
　I feel no dying dread, the thanks
Are due unto the Power that shaped
　My visions on the Brosna's Banks.

And love, I feel, will come at last,
　Albeit too late to comfort me;
And fetters from the land be cast,
　Though I may not survive to see.
If then the gifted, good, and brave,
　Admit me to their glorious ranks,
My memory may, tho' not my grave,
　Be green upon the Brosna's Banks.

———

LOCH NEAGH.

BY THE REV. GEORGE HILL.

LOCH Neagh, I stood at close of day upon thy silent strand,
And saw the sun set o'er the hills of old Tir-Owen's land;
The fading light, how like the flight of Freedom from thy shore,*—
The old, proud place of Niall's† race shall know his name no more!

---

　* *In the course of time,* the English invasion of this country introduced a
better state of things; but when it first happened, and for a long series of years
afterwards, it was, in most instances, the triumph of might over right.
　† *Niall Naighiallach,* "of the Nine Hostages," and, in the history of Ireland, known also as *Niall the Great.* The following account of this once
powerful family is extracted from the admirable work, by Mr. Reeves, on the
" Ecclesiastical Antiquities of Down and Connor and Dromore." " In the year

How many a tale of human grief, sweet lake, thy waters know,
Since from their deep, mysterious spring they first began to flow,—
Since far along yon level plain arose the swelling flood,
And o'er Eachaïd's* fair domain in gathered strength it stood!

Loch Laogh! whilst thy broad expanse reflects th' impending sky,
And dimpling on thy glassy tide, the banks, in shadow, lie—
The tale of Mora's faithful love shall consecrate thy wave,
And thou shalt still remembered be as royal Bresal's grave!†

"Why comes he not?" sweet Mora cried, "the days are long
        and drear,
As by Loch Laogh's verdant side he hunts the flying deer;
Why comes he not?" "He will not come."‡ She heard the
        mournful tale,
And soon from all her sorrows free, she slept in Ollar's§ vale.

And many a nameless grave since then thy caverns have supplied
To those who, in old Uladh's‖ feuds, have on thy waters died;
When Yellow Hugh—and Phelim Dhu—and Shane, the fierce
        and strong,
Swept, in their curraghs, like the blast, thy wooded shores along!

1230, died Aodh Macaomh Toinleasc O'Neill, the chief of his princely race,
leaving two sons, Niall Roe, and Aodh Meith, in whose respective descendants
the common stock struck off into two distinct branches. To the *senior* line
the representation of the race and lordship of *Tyrone* was, with a few early exceptions, confined." "Anne, daughter of Bryan Curragh O'Neill, was the
second wife of Shane O'Neill, of Shane's castle, from whose *third son, Phelim
Dhu,* the present Viscount O'Neill is the *fifth* in lineal descent." Who shall
represent this ancient house when the present Lord O'Neill has passed away?

* Eachaïdh, from whom Lough Neagh derives its name, was drowned in its
eruption, with all his children. The earliest form of the word is *Loch-n-Eachach.*

† The Irish annals relate that, in the year of the world 3506, " *Loch Laogh*
broke forth." Tigernach, at the year 161 of the Christian era, thus records
the reign of a king of Ulster:—" Bresal son of Brian, reigns in Emania nineteen years, who was drowned in Lough Laigh; his spouse, Mora, died of grief
for his death; from her Rath-mòr, in Moylinny, is named."—See *Reeves'
Eccles. Antiq.,* pp. 272—280.

‡ These words refer to the following part of a legend in the Dinn Seanchus:
—" Mora said, ' I think Bresal's absence too long.' And a certain woman said
to her,—' It will be long to thee, indeed, for Bresal will never come back to his
friends until the dead come back to theirs.' Mora then died suddenly, and her
name remained on the Rath."

§ The ancient name of the Six-Mile-Water.

‖ "The ancient *Uladh,* in its superficial extent, was nearly the same as the
modern *Ulster,* inasmuch as it contained Louth, which is now in Leinster, instead
of Cavan, which then belonged to Connaught."—See *Reeves' Eccl. Ant.,* p. 352.

Alas! though feudal terror cease, thy children suffer still,
And keener weapons than the sword are raised to waste and kill;
In vain the care-worn peasant's fate appeals to lordly pride;
The humble hopes that toil inspired are ruthlessly denied!

"Loch Neagh," with drooping hearts, they say, "we loved thy
      pleasant shore,
And every year, through hope and fear, we loved thee more and
      more;
Yet must we seek a distant home beyond the western main,
Where hopes, that are extinguished here, shall light our steps
      again."

ADARE.

BY GERALD GRIFFIN.

[Gerald Griffin was born in Limerick on 10th December 1803. As a poet he is not so well known as he deserves; but as a novelist he takes his place by universal consent in the first rank, beside Banim and Carleton. His father's want of success as a brewer in Limerick compelled the family to remove to Fairy Lawn near Glin in the county, a distance of thirty miles from the city. Here the family lived for some time, but the parents were persuaded by an elder brother of Gerald's, an officer in the British army, who served in America, to emigrate to that country. Gerald, who was intended for the medical profession, remained with his brother, Dr. Griffin, who then resided at Adare, about eight miles from the city. With his two sisters who remained in Ireland, Gerald spent much of his time in rambling through the romantic demesne of Lord Dunraven,—fishing in the Mague, or watching its waters glide whisperingly along by the time-worn walls of the old castles and monastic ruins of that locality. Poetry was his first and greatest inspiration, and if his natural bent had been properly encouraged, he would probably have been the greatest of the Irish poets. He has, however, proved himself equal to any task which he deliberately undertook to perform. At the age of nineteen he wrote his drama of " Aguire," of which his brother thought so highly, that he consented to Gerald's going to London to seek his fortune as a dramatic writer,—without a single friend there to whom he could look for counsel or support. Imbued with the true poetic spirit, and anxious to devote his whole energies to create a name, as a poet, he brought misery and ruin upon himself by the pursuit of his darling passion. At the age of twenty he wrote " Gisippus," which has been pronounced to be " the greatest drama of our times." At twenty-five, he wrote " The Collegians,"—and thence forward till he withdrew from the world, he never ceased to pour forth the rich creations of his fertile and vigorous imagination, in verse and prose. But the success which he attained was too dearly paid for. His health was undermined by long vigils, by mental toil and blasted hopes. He became sad and heartbroken. His delicate sensibility of feeling forbade all intercourse with even those who were willing and able to help him,—and foremost amongst these were John Banim and Dr. Maginn. Although his distress was most severe,—being sometimes without food for three days, he acted firmly upon his resolute determination of trusting solely to his own efforts for success. As he approached the goal of his ambition, his keen enthusiasm became blunted and subdued by the anxieties and disappointments which met him on every hand. To his sister he says: "I look now upon success as a matter of mere business. As to Fame, if I could accomplish it in any other way, I should scarcely try for its sake alone." He wore away all relish for it in his too eager pursuit. The publishers for whom he wrote "cheated him abominably," he says. They forgot the first rudiments of arithmetic; they never counted his pages correctly! All of them, except Jerdan of the *Literary Gazette*. At this time he translated a volume and a half of Prevot's works for two guineas. To cheat a man of such hard earned money was to commit the sin of "defrauding the labourer of his wages." At last he says to his brother:—" I am tired of this stupid, lonely, wasting, dispiriting, caterpillar kind of existence, which I endure, however, in hope of a speedy metamorphosis. It would amaze you to know all I have done, and to no purpose.' His mind was deeply tinged with a strong religious sentiment, and in order to live, as it seemed to him, a more perfect life, he joined the Society of Christian Brothers in September 1838; a society of good and religious men, who, withdrawing from the world and its fleeting pleasures, devote their whole lives to the education of the poor alone. No one could describe in more felicitous language than Gerald, the new world of beauty and delight which education could open out to minds pent up in darkness; and no one could feel more anxious to transplant light and intelligence to where gloom and ignorance previously ruled supreme. It is this ignorance and not their poverty or toil that degrades men. On the 12th June 1840, he died in the North Monastery of the Christian Brothers in Cork, after having laboured for nearly two years in his new vocation. There is a graceful ease and elegance of versification in all his poems; and though they breathe the ardour and warmth of feelings peculiar to youth, they are ever remarkable for their chasteness and purity of thought and expression. His great historical novel of "The Invasion,"—his "Collegians," "Tales of the Munster Festivals," and other works, are sufficiently well known, we hope, not to require further notice.]

Oh, sweet Adare, oh, lovely vale,
    Oh, soft retreat of sylvan splendour!
Nor Summer sun nor morning gale
    E'er hailed a scene more softly tender.
How shall I tell the thousand charms,
    Within thy verdant bosom dwelling,
When lulled in Nature's fost'ring arms,
    Soft peace abides and joy excelling!

Ye morning airs, how sweet at dawn
    The slumbering boughs your song awaken,
Or linger o'er the silent lawn
    With odour of the harebell taken.

Thou rising sun, how richly gleams,
  Thy smile from far Knockfierna's mountain,
O'er waving woods and bounding streams,
  And many a grove and glancing fountain.

Ye clouds of noon, how freshly there,
  When summer heats the open meadows,
O'er parched hill and valley fair,
  All coolly lie your veiling shadows.
Ye rolling shades and vapours gray,
  Slow creeping o'er the golden heaven,
How soft ye seal the eye of day,
  And wreathe the dusky brow of even.

In sweet Adare the jocund Spring
  His notes of odorous joy is breathing,
The wild birds in the woodland sing,
  The wild flowers in the vale are breathing.
There winds the Mague, as silver clear,
  Among the elms so sweetly flowing,
There fragrant in the early year
  Wild roses on the banks are blowing.

The wild duck seeks the sedgy bank
  Or dives beneath the glistening billow,
Where graceful droop and clustering dank
  The osier bright and rustling willow;
The hawthorn scents the leafy dale,
  In thicket lone the stag is belling,
And sweet along the echoing vale
  The sound of vernal joy is swelling.

SWEET INNISFALLEN.

BY THOMAS MOORE.

Sweet Innisfallen, fare thee well,
  May calm and sunshine long be thine!
How fair thou art let others tell,—
  To *feel* how fair shall long be mine.

Sweet Innisfallen, long shall dwell
  In memory's dream that sunny smile,
Which o'er thee on that evening fell,
  When first I saw thy fairy isle.

'Twas light, indeed, too blest for one,
  Who had to turn to paths of care—
Through crowded haunts again to run,
  And leave thee bright and silent there ;

No more unto thy shores to come,
  But on the world's rude ocean tost,
Dream of thee sometimes, as a home
  Of sunshine he had seen and lost.

Far better in thy weeping hours
  To part from thee, as I do now,
When mist is o'er thy blooming bowers,
  Like sorrow's veil on beauty's brow.

For, though unrivall'd still thy grace,
  Thou dost not look, as then, *too* blest,
But thus in shadow, seem'st a place
  Where erring man might hope to rest—

Might hope to rest, and find in thee
  A gloom like Eden's, on the day
He left its shade, when every tree,
  Like thine, hung weeping o'er his way.

Weeping or smiling, lovely isle !
  And all the lovelier for thy tears—
For though but rare thy sunny smile,
  'Tis heav'n's own glance when it appears

Like feeling hearts, whose joys are few,
  But, when *indeed* they come, divine—
The brightest light the sun e'er threw
  Is lifeless to one gleam of thine !

Historical Ballads.

THE CELTS.

BY THOMAS D'ARCY M'GEE.

[T. D. M'Gee is a native of Monaghan, and is now little more than thirty years of age. Whilst he was a mere boy he emigrated to America, and there edited when scarcely eighteen a weekly journal. About 1844 he returned to Ireland, and after some time he was enrolled amongst the staff of writers for the "Nation." Subsequently he became sub-editor, and remained so till the suppression of that journal by the government in 1848. He was then proclaimed a rebel, and £300 offered for his arrest. He was hunted through the country by the minions of the law, and after having suffered severely escaped to America, and is now proprietor of the "American-Celt" in New York. During the disturbances of 1848, offices of trust and danger were delegated to him, the duties of which he discharged with the energy and fidelity of a brave and true man. M'Gee is thoroughly and devotedly national; he loves everything Irish, except the misery of his country, and the short-coming of the people. His ardent spirit imparts life and dignity to every subject he touches; and his poetry is instinct with the impulsive passion and glowing enthusiasm of the Celt. These characteristics combined with his earnestness and sincerity will preserve his name as a familiar household word to many generations yet unborn; whilst many writers of greater acquirements, and perhaps of higher genius who are less national, will be utterly forgotten.—Some poets and essayists who have lately passed away from us are scarcely cold in their foreign graves when they have ceased to be remembered by those for whom they wrote. But they wrote for English readers without a particle of nationality in their verse or prose to commend their memories to the safe keeping of their own people. They laboured for strangers, and having had their reward, they deserve to be forgotten.—M'Gee, on the contrary, imbues with his own loving spirit every theme which he illustrates; entirely forgetful of himself, his lofty aim is to reflect glory upon his country and to lift up her people to his own patriotic idea of her former valour and greatness. As a mere matter of profit, however, the writer who is national, and "racy of the soil," gains on all hands,—for he can secure fame and remuneration to a much greater extent than he who writes solely for English readers. A national literature has a strong and indestructible vitality in it. It inspires men with a passion for noble deeds and virtuous emulation; and as it is the record of their traditions, their poetry, and their history, it receives a ready welcome from the hearts of all men. The works of Banim, Griffin, and Carleton are better known and more read in England to-day than those of Prout and Maginn. A man who knows M'Gee well and intimately says of him ;—" To forty political prisoners in Newgate, when the world seemed shut out from me for ever, I estimated him as I do to-day. I said, if we were about to begin our work anew, I would rather have his help than any man's of all our confederates. I said he could do more things like a master than the best amongst us since Thomas Davis; that for two or three years I had seen him daily, and found his mind still swarming with new thoughts on the one eternal theme (like a lover's or a devotee's); that he had been sent at the last hour on a perilous mission, and performed it, not only with unflinching courage, but with a success which had no parallel in that era; and, above all, that he has been systematically slandered by the Jacobins to an extent that would have blackened a saint of God. Since he has been in America I have watched his career; and one thing it has never wanted, a fixed devotion to Irish interests. Who has served them with such a fascinating genius? His poetry and his essays touch me like the breath of Spring, and revive the buoyancy and chivalry of youth. I plunge into them like a refreshing stream 'of Irish undefiled.' What other man has the subtle charm to revoke our past history and make it live before us? If he has not loved and served his mistress, Ireland, with the fidelity of a true knight, I cannot name any man who has."—*C. G. Duffy's* "*Principles and Policy of the Irish Race.*"]

LONG, long ago, beyond the misty space
    Of twice a thousand years ;
In Erin old there dwelt a mighty race,
    Taller than Roman spears ;
Like oaks and towers they had a giant grace,
    Were fleet as deers,
With winds and waves they made their 'biding place,
    These western shepherd seers.

Their Ocean-God was Mân-â-nân,* M'Lir,
    Whose angry lips,
In their white foam, full often would inter
    Whole fleets of ships ;
Cromah† their Day-God, and their Thunderer
    Made morning and eclipse ;

* Mân-â-nân was the God of Waters, the Neptune of the ancient Irish. He was called Mac Lir, that is, Son of the Sea. The disposal of good or bad weather was said to be allotted to him, conjointly with the God of the Winds, and for this cause he was worshipped by mariners.

† Crom or Crom-eacha was the name given by the ancient and pagan Irish to their Fire-God, the Sun; the dispenser of vital heat, and the author of fecundity and prosperity. He was their Deus Optimus Maximus, from whom all other Deities descended. The name is derived from the Egyptian word Chrom,—*Ignis*, fire, which was the only *visible* object of devotion permitted, and that only as the symbol of the SUPREME. Consistently, however, with this view, they deified also the powers of Nature. The Irish Crom-Cruith,—God the Creator, was the same as that adored by Zoroaster and the Persians for more

Bride* was their Queen of song, and unto her
    They prayed with fire-touched lips.

Great were their deeds, their passions, and their sports;
    With clay and stone
They piled on strath and shore those mystic forts,
    Not yet o'erthrown;
On cairn-crown'd hills they held their council-courts;
    While youths alone,
With giant dogs, explored the elk resorts,
    And brought them down.

Of these was Fin, the father of the Bard,
    Whose ancient song
Over the clamour of all change is heard,
    Sweet-voic'd and strong.
Fin once o'ertook Granee, the golden-hair'd,
    The fleet and young;
From her the lovely, and from him the fear'd,
    The primal poet sprung.

Ossian! two thousand years of mist and change
    Surround thy name—
Thy Finian heroes now no longer range
    The hills of fame.
The very name of Fin and Gaul sound strange—
    Yet thine the same—
By miscalled lake and desecrated grange—
    Remains, and shall remain!

The Druid's altar and the Druid's creed
    We scarce can trace.
There is not left an undisputed deed
    Of all your race,
Save your majestic song, which hath their speed,
    And strength and grace;
In that sole song, they live and love, and bleed—
    It bears them on thro' space.

than five hundred years before Christ. Cruith is a derivative from Cruitham,
to form, to create, and hence the present Irish Cruithior,—the CREATOR.
  * Bridh or Bride was the daughter of the Fire-God, and was goddess of
Wisdom and Song. Her blessing was esteemed the richest and most valued
gift which man could receive from above; she therefore became the goddess of
Philosophers and Poets.

Oh, inspir'd giant! shall we e'er behold,
  In our own time,
One fit to speak your spirit on the wold,
  Or seize your rhyme?
One pupil of the past, as mighty soul'd
  As in the prime,
Were the fond, fair, and beautiful, and bold—
  They, of your song sublime!

SONG OF INNISFAIL.

BY THOMAS MOORE.

They came from a land beyond the sea,
  And now o'er the western main
Set sail, in their good ships, gallantly,
  From the sunny land of Spain.
"Oh, where's the Isle we've seen in dreams,
  Our destin'd home or grave?"*
Thus sung they as, by the morning's beams,
  They swept the Atlantic wave.

And, lo, where afar o'er ocean shines
  A sparkle of radiant green,
As though in that deep lay emerald mines,
  Whose light through the wave was seen.
"'Tis Innisfail—'tis Innisfail!"
  Rings o'er the echoing sea;
While, bending to heav'n the warriors hail
  That home of the brave and free.

Then turn'd they unto the Eastern wave,
  Where now their Day-God's eye
A look of such sunny omen gave
  As lighted up sea and sky.
Nor frown was seen through sky or sea,
  Nor tear o'er leaf or sod,
When first on their Isle of Destiny †
  Our great forefathers trod.

* "Milesius remembered the remarkable prediction of the principal Druid, who foretold that the posterity of Gadelus should obtain the possession of a Western Island (which was Ireland) and there inhabit."—*Keating.*
† The Island of Destiny, one of the ancient names of Ireland.

RURY AND DARVORGILLA.

(FROM THE IRISH.)

BY J. C. MANGAN.

[Ruaghri, Prince of Oriel, after an absence of two days and nights from his
own territories on a hunting expedition, suddenly recollects that he has forgotten his wedding day. He despairs of forgiveness from the bride whom he appears to have slighted, Dearbhorgilla, daughter of Prince Cairtre, but would
scorn her too much to wed her if she *could* forgive him. He accordingly pre-
pares for battle with her and her father, but unfortunately intrusts the command of his forces to one of his most aged *Ceanns*, or captains. He is probably incited to the selection of this chieftain by a wish to avoid provoking hostilities, which, however, if they occur, he will meet by defiance and conflict; but
his choice proves to have been a fatal one. His *Ceann* is seized with a strange
feeling of fear in the midst of the fray; and this, being communicated to his
troops, enlarges into a panic, and Ruaghri's followers are all slaughtered.
Ruaghri himself arrives next day on the battle-plain, and, perceiving the result
of the contest, stabs himself to the heart. Dearbhorgilla witnesses this sad
catastrophe from a distance, and, rushing towards the scene of it, clasps her
lover in her arms; but her stern father, following, tears her away from the
bleeding corpse, and has her cast in his wrath, it is supposed, into one of the
dungeons of his castle. But of her fate nothing certain is known afterwards;
though, from subsequent circumstances, it is conjectured that she perished, the
victim of her lover's thoughtlessness and her father's tyranny.]

KNOW ye the tale of the Prince of Oriel,
    Of Rury, last of his line of kings?
I pen it here as a sad memorial
    Of how much woe reckless folly brings.

Of a time that Rury rode woodwards, clothed
    In silk and gold on a hunting chase,
He thought like thunder* on his betrothed,
    And with clenched hand he smote his face.

"*Foreer!*† *Mo bhron!*‡ Princess Darvorgilla!
    Forgive she will not a slight like this;
But could she, dared she, I should be still a
    Base wretch to wed her for heaven's best bliss!

* *H-saoil se mar teoirneach;* he thought like thunder; *i. e.* the thought
came on him like a thunderbolt.
† Alas!
‡ Pronounced Mo vrone, and means My grief!

"*Forcer! Forcer!* Princess Darvorgilla!
　She has four hundred young bowmen bold;
But I—I love her, and would not spill a
　Drop of their blood for ten torques * of gold.

"Still, woe to all who provoke to slaughter!
　I count as nought, weighed with fame like mine,
The birth and beauty of Cairtre's daughter;
　So, judge the sword between line and line!

"Thou, therefore, Calbhach,† go, call a muster,
　And wind the bugle by fort and dun!
When stain shall tarnish our house's lustre,
　Then sets in darkness the noon-day sun!"

But Calbhach answered, "Light need to do so!
　Behold the noblest of heroes here!
What foe confronts us, I reck not whoso,
　Shall fly before us like hunted deer!"

Spake Rury then—"Calbhach, as thou willest!
　But see, old man, there be brief delay—
For this chill parle is of all things chillest,
　And my fleet courser must now away!

"Yet, though thou march with thy legions townwards,
　Well armed for ambush or treacherous fray,
Still shew they point their bare weapons downwards,
　As those of warriors averse to slay!"

Now, when the clansmen were armed and mounted,
　The aged Calbhach gave way to fears;
For, foot and horsemen, they barely counted
　A hundred cross-bows and forty spears.

And thus exclaimed he, "My soul is shaken!
　We die the death, not of men, but slaves;
We sleep the sleep from which none awaken,
　And scorn shall point at our tombless graves!"

---

* Royal neck-ornaments.
† Calbhach,—proper name of a man,—derived from Calb,—bald-pated

Then out spake Fergal—"A charge so weighty
 As this, O Rury, thou shouldst not throw
On a drivelling dotard of eight-and-eighty,
 Whose arm is nerveless for spear or bow!"

But Rury answered, "Away! To-morrow
 Myself will stand in Traghvally‖ town;
But, come what may come, this day I borrow
 To hunt through Glafna the brown deer down!"

So, through the night, unto grey Traghvally,
 The feeble *Ceann* led his hosts along;
But, faint and heart-sore, they could not rally,
 So deeply Rury had wrought them wrong.

Now, when the Princess beheld advancing
 Her lover's troops with their arms reversed,
In lieu of broadswords and chargers prancing,
 She felt her heart's hopes were dead and hearsed

And on her knees to her ireful father
 She prayed, "O father, let this pass by;
War not against the brave Rury! Rather
 Pierce this fond bosom, and let me die!"

But Cairtre rose in volcanic fury,
 And so he spake—"By the might of God,
I hold no terms with this craven Rury
 Till he or I lie below the sod!

"Thou shameless child! Thou, alike unworthy
 Of him, thy father, who speaks thee thus,
And her, my Mhearb,¶ who in sorrow bore thee;
 Wilt thou dishonour thyself and us?

"Behold! I march with my serried bowmen—
 Four hundred thine, and a thousand mine;
I march to crush these degraded foemen,
 Who gorge the ravens ere day decline!"

* Dundalk.   † Martha.

Meet now both armies in mortal struggle,
    The spears are shivered, the javelins fly:
But, what strange terror, what mental juggle,
    Be those that speak out of Calbhach's eye?

It is—it must be, some spell Satanic,
    That masters him and his gallant host.
Woe, woe the day! An inglorious panic
    O'erpowers the legions—and all is lost!

Woe, woe that day, and that hour of carnage!
    Too well they witness to Fergal's truth!
Too well in bloodiest appeal they warn Age
    Not lightly thus to match swords with Youth!

When Rury reached, in the red of morning,
    The battle-ground, it was he who felt
The dreadful weight of this ghastly warning,
    And what a blow had o'ernight been dealt!

So, glancing round him, and sadly groaning,
    He pierced his breast with his noble blade;
Thus all too mournfully mis-atoning
    For that black ruin his word had made.

But hear ye further! When Cairtre's daughter
    Saw what a fate had o'erta'en her Brave,
Her eyes became as twin founts of water,
    Her heart again as a darker grave.

Clasp now thy lover, unhappy maiden!
    But, see! thy sire tears thine arms away!
And in a dungeon, all anguish-laden,
    Shalt thou be cast ere the shut of day.

But what shall be in the sad years coming
    Thy doom? I know not, but guess too well
That sunlight never shall trace thee roaming
    Ayond the gloom of thy sunken cell!

This is the tale of the Prince of Oriel
    And Darvorgilla, both sprung of Kings;
I trace it here as a dark memorial
    Of how much woe thoughtless folly brings.

THE FATE OF KING DATHI.

BY THOMAS DAVIS.

["In the life-time of Niall of the Nine Hostages, Brian, his brother of the half-blood, became King of Connaught, and his second brother of the half-blood, Fiachra, the ancestor of the O'Dowds and all the Ui-Fiachrach tribes, became chief of the district extending from Carn Fearadhaigh, near Limerick, to Magh Mucroime, near Athenry. But dissensions soon arose between Brian and his brother Fiachra, and the result was that a battle was fought between them, in which the latter was defeated, and delivered as a hostage into the hands of his half-brother, Niall of the Nine Hostages. After this, however, Dathi, a very warlike youth, waged war on his uncle Brian, and challenged him to a pitched battle, at a place called Damh-cluain, not far from Knockmea-hill, near Tuam. In this battle, in which Dathi was assisted by Crimthann, son of Enna Cennseloch, King of Leinster. Brian and his forces were routed, and pursued from the field of battle to Fulcha Domhnaill, where he was overtaken and slain by Crimthann. * * * After the fall of Brian, Fiachra was set at liberty and installed King of Connaught, and enjoyed that dignity for twelve years, during which period he was general of the forces of his brother Niall. * * * According to the book of Lecan, this Fiachra had five sons, of which the most eminent were Dathi, and Amhalgaidh (vulgo Awley) King of Connaught, who died in the year 449. The seven sons of this Amhalgaidh, together with twelve thousand men, are said to have been baptized in one day by St. Patrick, at Forrach Mac n'Amhalgaidh, near Killala. On the death of his father Fiachra, Dathi became King of Connaught, and on the death of his uncle, Niall of the Nine Hostages, he became Monarch of Ireland, leaving the government of Connaught to his less warlike brother Amhalgaidh. King Dathi, following the example of his predecessor, Niall, not only invaded the coasts of Gaul, but forced his way to the very foot of the Alps, where he was killed by a flash of lightning, leaving the throne of Ireland to be filled by a line of Christian kings."—*Tribes and Customs of the Ui-Fiachrach.—Irish Archæological Society's Publications.*]

DARKLY their glibs o'erhang,
Sharp is their wolf-dog's fang,
Bronze spear and falchion clang—
    Brave men might shun them!
Heavy the spoil they bear—
Jewels and gold are there—
Hostage and maiden fair—
    How have they won them?

From the soft sons of Gaul,
Roman, and Frank, and thrall,
Borough, and hut, and hall,—
    These have been torn.

Over Britannia wide.
Over fair Gaul they hied,
Often in battle tried,—
    Enemies mourn !

Fiercely their harpers sing.·-
Led by their gallant king,
They will to ÉIRE bring
    Beauty and treasure.
Britain shall bend the knee—
Rich shall their households be—
When their long ships the sea
    Homeward shall measure.

Barrow and Rath shall rise,
Towers, too, of wondrous size,
Táiltin, they'll solemnize,
    Feis-Teamhrach assemble.
Samhain and Béal shall smile
On the rich holy isle—
Nay! in a little while
    Œtius shall tremble![*]

Up on the glacier's snow,
Down on the vales below,
Monarch and clansmen go—
    Bright is the morning.
Never their march they slack,
Jura is at their back,
When falls the evening black,
    Hideous, and warning.

Eagles scream loud on high ;
Far off the chamois fly ;
Hoarse comes the torrent's cry,
    On the rocks whitening.
Strong are the storm's wings ;
Down the tall pine it flings ;
Hail-stone and sleet it brings—
    Thunder and lightning.

* The consul Œtius, the shield of Italy, and terror of "the barbarian," was a cotemporary of King Dathi. *Feis-Teamhrach*, the Parliament of Tara. *Tailtin*, games held at Tailte, county Meath. *Samhain* and *Beal*, the moon and sun which Ireland worshipped.
                        E

Little these veterans mind
Thundering, hail, or wind;
Closer their ranks they bind—
    Matching the storm.
While, a spear-cast or more,
On, the front ranks before,
DATHI the sunburst bore—
    Haughty his form.

Forth from the thunder-cloud
Leaps out a foe as proud—
Sudden the monarch bowed—
    On rush the vanguard;
Wildly the king they raise—
Struck by the lightning's blaze—
Ghastly his dying gaze,
    Clutching his standard!

Mild is the morning beam,
Gently the rivers stream,
Happy the valleys seem;
    But the lone islanders—
Mark how they guard their king!
Hark, to the wail they sing!
Dark is their counselling—
    Helvetia's highlanders

Gather, like ravens, near—
Shall DATHI'S soldiers fear?
Soon their home-path they clear—
    Rapid and daring;
On through the pass and plain,
Until the shore they gain,
And, with their spoil, again,
    Landed in EIRINN.

Little does EIRE* care
For gold or maiden fair—
"Where is King DATHI?—where,
    Where is my bravest?"

* The true *ancient and modern* name of Ireland.

On the rich deck he lies,
O'er him his sunburst flies*—
Solemn the obsequies,
    EIRE! thou gavest.

See ye that countless train
Crossing Roscommon's plain,
Crying, like hurricane,
    Uile liú ai?—
Broad is his *carn's* base—
Nigh the "King's burial-place,"†
Last of the Pagan race,
    Lieth King DATHI!

THE EXPEDITION AND DEATH OF KING DATHY.

(FROM THE IRISH.)

BY J. C. MANGAN.

KING Dathy assembled his Druids and Sages,
And thus he spake them—"Druids and Sages!
    What of King Dathy?
What is revealed in Destiny's pages
    Of him or his? Hath he
Aught for the Future to dread or to dree?
Good to rejoice in, or Evil to flee?
    Is he a foe of the Gall—
Fitted to conquer, or fated to fall?"

And Beirdra, the Druid, made answer as thus—
    A priest of a hundred years was he—
"Dathy! thy fate is not hidden from us!
    Hear it through me!
Thou shalt work thine own will!
    Thou shalt slay—thou shalt prey—
And be Conqueror still!

* A Sunburst was the national standard of Ireland
† *Hibernice*, Roilig na Riogh, *vulgo*, Relignaree—"A famous burial-place near Cruachan, in Connaught, where the kings were usually interred, before the establishment of the Christian religion in Ireland."—*O'Brien's Ir. Dict.*

Thee the Earth shall not harm!
Thee we charter and charm
From all evil and ill!
Thee the laurel shall crown!
Thee the wave shall not drown!
Thee the chain shall not bind!
Thee the spear shall not find!
Thee the sword shall not slay!
Thee the shaft shall not pierce!
Thou, therefore, be fearless and fierce,
And sail with thy warriors away
    To the lands of the Gall,
    There to slaughter and sway,
    And be Victor o'er all!"

So Dathy he sailed away, away,
    Over the deep resounding sea;
Sailed with his hosts in armour grey
    Over the deep resounding sea,
Many a night and many a day,
    And many an islet conquered he—
He and his hosts in armour grey.
    And the billow drowned him not,
    And a fetter bound him not,
    And the blue spear found him not,
    And the red sword slew him not,
    And the swift shaft knew him not,
    And the foe o'erthrew him not.
Till, one bright morn, at the base
    Of the Alps, in rich Ausonia's regions,
His men stood marshalled face to face
    With the mighty Roman legions.
        Noble foes!
Christian and Heathen stood there among those,
Resolute all to overcome,
Or die for the Eagles of Ancient Rome!

When, behold! from a temple anear
    Came forth an aged priest-like man,
Of a countenance meek and clear,
    Who, turning to Eire's Ceann,*

           * Ceann,—Head, King.

Spake him as thus, "King Dathy! hear!
  Thee would I warn!
Retreat! retire! Repent in time
  The invader's crime,
Or better for thee thou hadst never been born!"
But Dathy replied, "False Nazarene!
  Dost thou, then, menace Dathy, thou?
  And dreamest thou that he will bow
To one unknown, to one so mean.
So powerless as a priest must be?
He scorns alike thy threats and thee!
On! on, my men, to victory!"

And, with loud shouts for Eire's King,
  The Irish rush to meet the foe,
And falchions clash and bucklers ring,—
      When, lo!
Lo! a mighty earthquake's shock!
And the cleft plains reel and rock;
Clouds of darkness pall the skies;
      Thunder crashes,
      Lightning flashes,
And in an instant Dathy lies
On the earth a mass of blackened ashes!
Then, mournfully and dolefully,
  The Irish warriors sailed away
  Over the deep resounding sea,
Till, wearily and mournfully,
They anchored in Eblana's Bay.
Thus the Seanachies* and Sages
Tell this tale of long-gone ages.

* Seanachies,—historians.

PRINCE ALDFRID'S ITINERARY THROUGH IRELAND.

(FROM THE IRISH.)

BY J. C. MANGAN.

[Amongst the Anglo-Saxon students resorting to Ireland was Prince Aldfrid, afterwards King of the Northumbrian Saxons. His having been educated there about the year 684 is corroborated by venerable Bede in his "Life of St. Cuthbert." The original poem, of which this is a translation, attributed to Aldfrid, is still extant in the Irish language.]

I FOUND in Innisfail the fair,
In Ireland, while in exile there,
Women of worth, both grave and gay men,
Many clerics and many laymen.

I travelled its fruitful provinces round,
And in every one of the five* I found,
Alike in church and in palace hall,
Abundant apparel and food for all.

Gold and silver I found, and money,
Plenty of wheat and plenty of honey;
I found God's people rich in pity,
Found many a feast and many a city.

I also found in Armagh, the splendid,
Meekness, wisdom, and prudence blended,
Fasting, as Christ hath recommended,
And noble councillors untranscended.

I found in each great church moreo'er,
Whether on island or on shore,
Piety, learning, fond affection,
Holy welcome and kind protection.

I found the good lay monks and brothers
Ever beseeching help for others,
And in their keeping the holy word
Pure as it came from Jesus the Lord.

* The two Meaths then formed a distinct province.

I found in Munster unfettered of any,
Kings, and queens, and poets a many —
Poets well skilled in music and measure,
Prosperous doings, mirth and pleasure.

I found in Connaught the just, redundance
Of riches, milk in lavish abundance;
Hospitality, vigour, fame,
In Cruachan's* land of heroic name.

I found in the country of Connall† the glorious,
Bravest heroes, ever victorious;
Fair-complexioned men and warlike,
Ireland's lights, the high, the starlike!

I found in Ulster, from hill to glen,
Hardy warriors, resolute men;
Beauty that bloomed when youth was gone,
And strength transmitted from sire to son.

I found in the noble district of Boyle
            (MS. here illegible.)
Brehons,‡ Erenachs, weapons bright,
And horsemen bold and sudden in fight.

I found in Leinster the smooth and sleek,
From Dublin to Slewmargy's§ peak;
Flourishing pastures, valour, health,
Long-living worthies, commerce, wealth.

I found, besides, from Ara to Glea,
In the broad rich country of Ossorie,
Sweet fruits, good laws for all and each,
Great chess-players, men of truthful speech.

I found in Meath's fair principality,
Virtue, vigour, and hospitality;
Candour, joyfulness, bravery, purity,
Ireland's bulwark and security.

---

* Cruachan, or Croghan, was the name of the royal palace of Connaught
† Tyrconnell, the present Donegal.
‡ Brehon,—a law judge; Erenach,—a ruler, an archdeacon.
§ Slewmargy, a mountain in the Queen's county, near the river Barrow

I found strict morals in age and youth,
I found historians recording truth;
The things I sing of in verse unsmooth,
I found them all—I have written sooth.*

THE "WISDOM-SELLERS" BEFORE CHARLEMAGNE.

BY T. D. M'GEE.

["When the illustrious Charles began to reign alone in the Western parts of the world, and Literature was everywhere almost forgotten, it happened that two Scots of Ireland came over with some British merchants to the coast of France—men incomparably skilled in human learning and in the Holy Scriptures. As they produced no merchandise for sale, they used to cry out to the crowds that flocked to purchase—'If any one is desirous of wisdom, let him come to us and receive it; for we have it to sell.' Their reason for saying that they had it for sale was, that, perceiving the people inclined to deal in saleable articles, and not to take anything gratuitously, they might rouse them to the acquisition of knowledge, as well as of objects for which they should give value; or, as the sequel showed, that by speaking in that manner they might excite their wonder and astonishment. They repeated this declaration so often, that an account of them was conveyed, either by their admirers, or by those who thought them insane, to King Charles, who, being a lover and very desirous of wisdom, had them conducted with all expedition before him, and asked them if they truly possessed wisdom, as had been reported to him. They answered that they did; and were ready, in the name of the Lord, to communicate it to such as would seek for it worthily. On his inquiring of them what compensation they would expect for it, they replied that they required nothing more than convenient situations, ingenious minds, and, as being in a foreign country, to be supplied with 'food and raiment.' This account was addressed to King Charles the Fat, grandson of Charlemagne, between the years 884 and 888. It was written by the Monk of St. Gall, by some called Monachus Sangallensis, whom Goidastres and Usher suppose to have been Notker Babulus, 'the celebrated.' But Mabillon and Muratori simply style him the Monk of St. Gall."—*Muratori Analia d'Italia*, year 781.—*Lanigan's Ecc. Hist. of Ireland*, vol. iii. p. 209.]

Monachus San-Gallensis Loquitur :—

" GRANDSON of Charlemagne! to tell
    Of exiled Learning's late return—

---

* " Bede assures us that the Irish were a harmless and friendly people. To them many of the Angles had been accustomed to resort in search of knowledge, and on all occasions had been received kindly and supported gratuitously. Aldfrid lived in spontaneous exile among the Scots (Irish) through his desire of knowledge, and was called to the throne of Northumbria after the decease of his brother Egfrid in 685."—*Lingard's England*, vol. i. chap. 3.

A task more grateful never fell
  To one still drinking at her urn;
      Of Force, O, King!
      Too many sing,
  Lauding mere sanguinary strength;
      But Wisdom's praise
      Our favoured days
  Have asked to hear at length.
When he whose sword and name you bear
  Reigned unopposed throughout the West,
And none would dream, or dreaming dare,
  Reject his high behest—
He found no peace, nor near, nor far,
  No spell to stay his swaying mind;
For Glory, like the sailor's star,
  Still left her votary far behind.
The wreck of Roman art remained,
  Casting dark lines of destiny;
The very roads they went proclaimed
  The modern man's degen'racy;
Our Charles wept like Philip's son,
Thinking Time's noblest wreaths were won.

" One morn upon his throne of state,
Crown'd and sad the Conqueror sate.
' What stirs without, my chiefs?' said he
' Do all things rest on land and sea?
Has France slept late, or has she lost
The love of being tempest tost?'
Spake an old soldier of his wars,
  One who had fought in Lombardy,
Whose breast beside bore Saxon scars—
  The Soldier-Emperor's friend was he!
' O, Carl, strange news your steward bears
  Of Merchants in the mart, who tell,
Standing amidst the mingled wares,
  That they bring *Wisdom* here to sell;
Tall men though strange they seem to be,
  And somewhere from ayont the sea.'
Quoth Charles —' 'Twere rare merchandise
That purchased could make Paris wise.
Fetch me those wisdom-sellers hither—
We fain would know their whence and whither.

" Of air erect, and full of grace,
  With bearded lip and arrowy eye
And signs no presence could efface
  Of learning's meek nobility,
The men appeared : Carl's lion front
  Was lifted as each bowed his head,
With words more gentle than his wont,
  To the two strangers thus he said—
' Merchants, what is the tale I hear ?
  That in the market-place you offer
Wisdom for sale ? Is Wisdom dear—
  Is't in the compass of our coffer ?'

" In accents such as seldom broke
The silence there, Albinus spoke :—
' O, Carl, illustrious Emperor,
We are but strangers on your shore,
From Erin's Isle, where every glen
  Is crowded with the sons of song,
And every port with learned men,
  We, venturing without the throng—
(And longing, not the least, to see
  The person of your Majesty,
Whose fame has reached the ends of ocean);
Forsook our native Isle, to bear
The lamps of wisdom everywhere,
Our heavenly Master's work to do—
And first we came, O King, to you ;
On Cormac's Cromleach you have gazed,
  And seen the prone strength of the past ;
You saw the piles the Cæsars raised—
  Saw Art his Empire-cause outlast ;
All scenes of war, all pomps of peace,
  Armies and harvests in array—
Your longing soul from sights like these
  To Time and Art oft turns away.

" ' Great hosts are bristling over earth,
  Like grain in harvest—till anon,
A wintry campaign, or a dearth
  Of valour, and your hosts are gone.
The soldier's pride is for a season,
  His day leads to a silent night ;

But sov'reign Power, inspired by reason,
  Creates a world of life and light;
We've rifled the departed ages,
  And bring their grave-gifts here to-day;
We sell the secrets of the sages—
  The code of Calvary and Sinai.
To Wisdom, King! we set no measure;
  For Wisdom's price—there is but one—
To value it above all treasure
  And spend it freely when 'tis won.
By every peaceful Gaelic river
  The Bookmen have a free abode,
They celebrate each Princely giver
  And teach the arts of Man and God.
All that we ask for, all we bring
  Is eager pupils round our cell,
And your protection, mighty King!
  While in the realms of France we dwell.'
          *   *   *   *   *   *

" Grandson of Carl! I need no more,
  The rest throughout the earth is known
How learning lost to us before
  Spread like a sun around his throne.
Till now in Saxon forests dim
New neophytes their love-lights trim—
How even my own Alpine heights
Are luminous through studious nights,
How Pavia's learned half regain
The glory of the Roman name—
How mind with mind and soul with soul
Press onward to the ancient goal—
How Faith herself smiles on the chase
Of Chimera and Reason's race—
How ' Wisdom-Sellers' one may meet
In every ship and every street—
Of how our Irish masters rest
In graves watched by th' grateful west—
How more than war or sanguine strength
        Of Wisdom's praise.
        Our favoured days
Have asked to hear at length."

BATTLE OF DUNDALK.

954.

BY NEIL M'DEVITT.

["CEALLACHAN, King of Munster, had on several occasions fought and routed the Danes under SITRICK, and had driven them completely from his territory. SITRICK, at length, professed a desire for peace, and in order to prove his sincerity, offered his sister in marriage to Ceallachan; and invited him to Dublin where he held his court, to have the marriage ceremony performed. CEALLACHAN and the few nobles who accompanied him were scarcely within sight of the city, when they were surrounded and attacked by SITRICK's army; they were seized and sent to Dundalk, where the Danish fleet lay at anchor, and was prepared to sail to Norway with the King and his nobles, as prisoners. Intelligence of this act of treachery having reached Mononia (Munster) the army and navy which could be brought together without delay, were despatched at once to Dundalk to rescue their King, whom they found tied with a rope to the mast of the Danish General's vessel. He being convinced that upon the loss of his own ship would in all probability follow the loss of all his fleet, exerted his skill and valour in order to save it: and that he might strike terror and dismay into the Irish, he caused the head of their admiral FAILBHE FIONN, King of Desmond, to be cut off, and exposed to view. FINGALL, the Admiral's second, being thus informed of his fate, resolved to avenge his death; and calling to his men to follow him, they boarded the Dane with an irresistible fury. The contest was hot and bloody: but there being so many fresh men to supply the place of the slaughtered or disabled Danes, the Irish had no prospect of obtaining the victory. Unable, however, as FINGALL was to possess himself of the Danish ship, he was too valiant an Irishman to think of retreating to his own; especially without the destruction of SITRICK, in revenge of the death of FAILBHE. He took a resolution therefore in this dilemma, which is not perhaps to be paralleled in any history. Making his way up to SITRICK, with his sword, against all that opposed him, he grasped him close in his arms and threw himself with him into the sea; where they both perished together. Two other Irish Captains, being fired with the glory of this action of FINGALL's, and being intent on securing the victory to their countrymen, made their way through the enemy with redoubled fury, and boarding the ship in which were TOR and MAGNUS, the surviving brothers of SITRICK, and then the chief commanders of the Danes, rushed violently upon them, caught them up in their arms, after the example of FINGALL, and jumping overboard with them, were all lost together. The Irish perceiving the enemy dispirited and giving way, pursued their success with so much the more ardour; and boarding most of the Danish fleet, a horrible slaughter ensued. The Danes, besides their numbers, had greatly the superiority in point of skill in naval encounters; and they not only fought for their present safety, but for their future peace and establishment in the island. On the other side the Irish contended not only for victory, but to redeem their king and country out of the hands of these treacherous and cruel enemies."— *Warner's History of Ireland,* vol. i. book 9.]

Lo, they come, they come; but all too late—their King is on the
      wave,
Bound to the mast of a Danish ship, the pirate Northman's slave.
Dundalk, thy shores have often heard the roar of the boiling sea,
But wilder far is the madd'ning shout that now is heard by thee;
The voice of the soldier's rage when the foe with the prize is fled,
And the bursting yell of pale despair when hope itself is dead;
Then o'er that warrior-band in wrath a death-like silence pass'd
As they gazed where Sitrick's sails unfurl'd swell'd proudly to
      the blast.

And must he go? Shall Mononia's King serve in a hostile land?
Oh for one ship! with Irish hearts, to crush that Danish band!
But hark! a cheer—and the list'ning hills give back the joyous
      sound.
A sail—a sail is seen away where the skies the waters bound.
There's a pause anew—each searching eye is on that sail afar;
Again the cheer rings loud and high—'tis Mononia's ships of war.
Boldly they come o'er the swelling tide, their men as wild and free.
As winds that play on the mountain's side, or waves that course
      the sea.

And well may they come to free their King from robbers of the
      main;
His sceptre ne'er a tyrant's rod, nor his rule a tyrant's chain.
And onwards towards the foe they steer—a sight sublimely grand—
War's stern array hath there an awe it never knows on land.
Soon many a sword salutes the sun, drawn in that deadly strife,
From many a heart that bounded high soon flows the tide of life.
The King—the King—to free the King bold Fionn hews his way,
And woe to him who meets his sword on this eventful day.

The King is won; but the lion heart that sets his master free
Is deeply pierced—as he cuts the cord his life-blood dyes the sea.
Brave Fionn's head is held on high, the Irish to appal,
But they rush more fiercely to the fight, led on by young Fingall.
Sternly, foot to foot and sword to sword, for death or life they meet,
And bravely, though few, they long withstand the hordes of
      Sitrick's fleet;
But slowly at last, o'er heaps of slain, the Irish yield apace,
The many have the few o'ercome, and defeat is no disgrace.

Oh, Fingall—Fingall, what dread resolve now seizes on your mind?
All, all is done that valour can—give way, and be resigned.

Swiftly he rush'd, as one possess'd, 'mid all that hostile train,
Seizing their King, with one wild bound, plung'd both into the
    main,
Then sudden, as if by frenzy sped, two Irish chiefs as brave,
The King's two brothers as quickly seized, and dash'd into the
    wave.
And Freedom smiled when she saw the deed—she knew the day
    was won;
But with that smile came a bitter tear—she had lost her favourite
    son.
With terror struck, the astonished Danes at ev'ry point gave way,
And few were left to tell the tale of that destructive fray.

There was joy that week o'er all the land, from Bann to Shannon's
    shore;
For they said those Danish chiefs will come to spoil our homes
    no more.
But ere the song of mirth went round, or toast in hut or hall,
A tear was shed, and a prayer was said, for Fionn and Fingall.
And thro' the wars of after years their name was the battle-cry,
And many a heart that else had quail'd, by them was taught to die;
And oft as Freedom broke a chain, or tyrants met their fall,
A tear was shed—a prayer was said for Fionn and Fingall.

———

VISION OF KING BRIAN,

THE NIGHT BEFORE THE BATTLE OF CLONTARF. *

The great old Irish houses, the proud old Irish names,
Like stars upon the midnight, to-day their lustre gleams—
Gone are the great old houses—the proud old names are low,
That shed a glory o'er the land a thousand years ago.
These were the great old houses o'er whom a spirit held
Mystic watching at life's closing, in the distant days of eld;
Oft foretold they of death's advent, in a slowly chaunted wail,
And often in the tones that glad a warrior in his mail.

And wheresoe'er a scion of those great old houses be,
In the country of his fathers, or the lands beyond the sea,

_____

* The battle of Clontarf was fought on Good Friday, 23d April, 1014.

In city, or in hamlet, by the valley, on the hill,
The spirit of his brave old sires is watching o'er him still.
'Twas thus before the battle, that freed the Irish land,
That crush'd the Dane for ever on Clontarf's empurpled strand.
'Twas thus that brave King Brian, at the midhour of the night,
Saw a vision as he slumbered, befitting kingly sight.

A woman pale and beautiful—a woman sad and fair—
Proud and stately was her stature, black and flowing was her hair;
White as snow the robe around her, floating shadow-like and free,
Whilst with a silver trumpet's tone, to the sleeper thus spoke she—
" King ! unto thee 'tis given, to triumph o'er the Dane—
To drive his routed army forth unto the northern main ,
But the palace of thy fathers, thou shalt never see again,
Thou, and the son thou lovest, shall sleep among the slain.

" Yet far into the future thy memory shall live,
And to the souls of men unborn a glorious impulse give ,
Thy dynasty shall perish before a factious band,
But thy spirit shall for ever dwell upon the Irish land.
Men yet unborn shall know thee as thy country's sword and shield,
Wise and prudent in the council, brave and skilful in the field,
When the factious and the spoilers shall trample on the free,
They will pray to God to raise them a Deliverer like thee.

" Thou shalt leave unto thy country, 'mid the nations, a proud
    name ;
Thou shalt leave it peace and freedom, and a bright and glorious
    fame ;
Thou shalt leave it upraised altars, happy homes, and smiling fields,
Where the sower shall be reaper of what Heaven's bounty yields.
Yet trampling on the country the spoiler's foot shall come,
Woo'd to conquest and to plunder by factious feud at home ;
Milesian with Milesian shall battle day by day,
Till the glory of the Irish land shall pass from it away.

" The fanatic and the bigot shall come with fire and brand,
With foreign swords and foreign laws, black heart and bloody hand,
They will trample on the altar, they will desecrate the shrine,
And pollute each holy relic that thy country holds divine.
But thy country shall stand firm thro' plunder and thro' scathe,
To that which thou shalt die for, her consecrated faith ;
Though her altar be in ruins, though her conquerors slay and rive,
Yet, despite of ban or guerdon, her faith shall still survive.

" Thy country's best and bravest shall struggle long in vain,
And some shall seek in distant lands to 'scape a conqueror's chain;
And some shall fall from princely hall, e'en to the peasant's shed,
And many on her hard fought fields shall slumber with the dead.
But the God whose hand is stretched forth, thy country to chastise,
In His own good time and fitting, will bid the prostrate rise;
For her faith He hath recorded where the mighty seal is set,
And His mercy, aye, it shall gush forth to vivify her yet.

" In her deepest hour of sorrow, in her hour of darkest shame,
Thy country still will treasure the glory of thy name.
In her greatest hour of triumph, when her history shall bear
To the future all her glory, thine shall still be foremost there."
No more spake she unto him, but passed like mist away,
As it floats up from the valley beneath the summer ray—
No more spake she unto him, but ever on the gale,
Until the hour of dawning, came a low and mystic wail.

    *   *   *   *   *   *   *

Next day, amid the foremost, brave Morrogh fighting fell,
The flower of Irish chivalry—the son he loved so well;
And from our shores for ever was swept that day the Dane—
But the old King and his valiant son were numbered with the
     slain!

BRIAN THE BRAVE.*

BY THOMAS MOORE.

REMEMBER the glories of Brian the brave,
    Tho' the days of the hero are o'er;
Tho' lost to Mononia† and cold in the grave,
    He returns to Kinkora‡ no more.
That star of the field which so often hath pour'd
    Its beam on the battle, is set;
But enough of its glory remains on each sword,
    To light us to victory yet.

---

   * Brian Boromhe, the great monarch of Ireland, who was killed at the battle
of Clontarf, in the beginning of the eleventh century, after having defeated the
Danes in twenty-five engagements.
   † Munster.
   ‡ The palace of Brian.

Mononia! when Nature embellish'd the tint
  Of thy fields, and thy mountains so fair,
Did she ever intend that a tyrant should print
  The footstep of slavery there?
No! Freedom, whose smile we shall never resign,
  Go, tell our invaders, the Danes,
That 'tis sweeter to bleed for an age at thy shrine,
  Than to sleep but a moment in chains.

Forget not our wounded companions, who stood *
  In the day of distress by our side;
While the moss of the valley grew red with their blood,
  They stirr'd not, but conquer'd and died.
That sun which now blesses our arms with his light,
  Saw them fall upon Ossory's plain;—
Oh! let him not blush, when he leaves us to-night,
  To find that they fell there in vain.

KING BRIAN BEFORE THE BATTLE.†

BY WILLIAM KENEALY.

STAND ye now for Erin's glory! Stand ye now for Erin's cau
Long ye've groaned beneath the rigour of the Northmen's sav.
   laws.

* This alludes to an interesting circumstance related of the Dalgais, the
favourite troops of Brian, when they were interrupted in their return from the
battle of Clontarf, by Fitzpatrick, prince of Ossory. The wounded men entreated that they might be allowed to fight with the rest.—*Let stakes* (they
said) *be stuck in the ground, and suffer each of us, tied to and supported by
one of these* stakes, to be placed in his rank by the side of a sound man."
" Between seven and eight hundred wounded men (adds O'Halloran) pale,
emaciated, and supported in this manner, appeared mixed with the foremost of
the troops;—never was such another sight exhibited."—*History of Ireland*,
book 12th, chap. i.
† The Annals of Innisfallen give an account of Brian's address to his forces
immediately before the battle of Clontarf. He rode through the ranks in the
twilight of morning, Good Friday, April 23d, 1014, accompanied by his son,
Morrogh; reminded the troops of the Bloody Sacrifice which was commemo-
rated on that day; and, holding up the Crucifix in his left hand, and his
golden-hilted sword in the right, declared he was willing to die in so just and
honourable a cause.

F

What though brothers league against us?*   What, though
    myriads be the foe?
Victory will be more honoured in the myriads' overthrow.

Proud Connacians! oft we've wrangled, in our petty feuds of yore:
Now we fight against the robber Dane, upon our native shore;
May our hearts unite in friendship, as our blood in one red tide,
While we crush their mail-clad legions, and annihilate their pride!

Brave Eugenians! Erin triumphs in the sight she sees to-day—
Desmond's homesteads all deserted for the muster and the fray!
Cluan's vale and Galtee's summit send their bravest and their best—
May such hearts be theirs for ever, for the Freedom of the West!

Chiefs and Kerne of Dalcassia! Brothers of my past career,
Oft we've trodden on the pirate-flag that flaunts before us here,
You remember Iniscattery,† how we bounded on the foe,
As the torrent of the mountain bursts upon the plain below!

They have razed our proudest castles—spoiled the Temples of the
    Lord—
Burnt to dust the sacred relics—put the Peaceful to the sword—
Desecrated all things holy—as they soon may do again,
If their power to-day we smite not—if to-day we be not men!

Slaughtered pilgrims is the story at St. Kevin's rocky cell,
And on the southern sea-shore, at Isle Helig's holy well;‡
E'en the anchorets are hunted, poor and peaceful though they be,
And not one of them left living, in their caves beside the sea!§

  * The Lagenians, under their king, Maelmordha, joined the Danes.
  † The Island of Iniscattery, in the mouth of the Shannon, made remarkable
by the sanctity of its eleven churches, and the tomb of St. Senanus, was seized
upon by the plundering horde, who used the sacred edifices as military stores.
Brian, with 1,200 of his Dalcassian heroes, landed here, and, after a fierce
struggle, succeeded in recovering possession of the sacred Isle.
  ‡ The Isles of Helig, on the coast of Kerry, famous for their monastery and
holy well.
  § The Monastery of Bangor, according to the "Annals of Munster," and
the "Annals of the Four Masters," was on one occasion attacked and plundered,
St. Comgall's shrine violated, and the abbot, with 900 monks, all murdered in
one day.—Monastery of the Emesh destroyed at Mayo.

Think of all your murder'd chieftains—all your rifled homes and
    shrines—
Then rush down, with whetted vengeance, like fierce wolves upon
    their lines!
Think of Bangor—think of Mayo—and Senanus' holy tomb*—
Think of all your past endurance—what may be your future doom!

On this day the God-man suffered—look upon the sacred sign—
May we conquer 'neath its shadow, as of old did Constantine!
May the heathen tribes of Odin fade before it like a dream,
And the triumph of this glorious day in future annals gleam!

God of Heaven, bless our banner—nerve our sinews for the strife!
Fight we now for all that's holy—for our altars, land, and life—
For red vengeance on the spoiler, whom the blazing temples trace—
For the honour of our maidens, and the glory of our race!

Should I fall before the foeman, 'tis the death I seek to-day;
Should ten thousand daggers pierce me, bear my body not away,
Till this day of days be over—till the field is fought and won—
Then the holy Mass be chaunted, and the funeral rites be done.

Curses darker than Ben Heder† light upon the craven slave
Who prefers the life of traitor to the glory of the grave!
Freedom's guerdon now awaits you, or a destiny of chains—
Trample down the dark oppressor while one spark of life remains!

Think not now of coward mercy—Heaven's curse is on their blood!
Spare them not, though myriad corses float upon the purple flood!
By the memory of great Dathi, and the valiant chiefs of yore,
This day we'll scourge the viper brood for ever from our shore!

Men of Erin! men of Erin! grasp the battle-axe and spear!
Chase these Northern wolves before you like a herd of frightened
    deer!
Burst their ranks, like bolts from heaven!   Down on the heathen
    crew,
For the glory of the Crucifix, and Erin's glory too!

---

* Moore states that these barbarians did not leave a hermit alive along the
coasts.
  † Ben Heder—the Mountain of Birds—now the Hill of Howth.

KINKORA.

1015.

(FROM THE IRISH.)

BY J. C. MANGAN.

[This poem is ascribed to the celebrated poet MAC LIAG, the secretary of the
renowned monarch BRIAN BORU, who, as is well known, fell at the battle of
Clontarf in 1014, and the subject of it is a lamentation for the fallen condition
of Kinkora, the palace of that monarch, consequent on his death.   The decease
of MAC LIAG is recorded in the "Annals of the Four Masters," as having
taken place in 1015.   A great number of his poems are still in existence, but
none of them have obtained a popularity so widely extended as his "Lament."
The palace of Kinkora, which was situated on the banks of the Shannon, near
Killaloe, is now a heap of ruins.]

Oh, where, Kinkora! is Brian the Great?
   And where is the beauty that once was thine?
Oh, where are the princes and nobles that sate
   At the feast in thy halls, and drank the red wine?
            Where, oh, Kinkora?

Oh, where, Kinkora! are thy valorous lords?
   Oh, whither, thou Hospitable! are they gone?
Oh, where are the Dalcassians of the golden swords?*
   And where are the warriors Brian led on?
            Where, oh, Kinkora?

And where is Morrogh, the descendant of kings;
   The defeater of a hundred—the daringly brave—
Who set but slight store by jewels and rings—
   Who swam down the torrent and laugh'd at its wave?
            Where, oh, Kinkora?

And where is Donogh, King Brian's worthy son?
   And where is Conaing, the beautiful chief?
And Kian and Core?   Alas! they are gone—
   They have left me this night alone with my grief!
            Left me, Kinkora!

* Colg n-or, or the Swords of Gold, i. e. of the Gold-hilted Swords.

And where are the chiefs with whom Brian went forth,
 The never-vanquish'd sons of Erin the brave,
The great King of Onaght, renowned for his worth,
 And the hosts of Baskinn from the western wave?
      Where, oh, Kinkora?

Oh, where is Duvlann of the Swift-footed Steeds?
 And where is Kian, who was son of Molloy?
And where is King Lonergan, the fame of whose deeds
 In the red battle-field no time can destroy?
      Where, oh, Kinkora?

And where is that youth of majestic height,
 The faith-keeping Prince of the Scots? Even he,
As wide as his fame was, as great as was his might,
 Was tributary, oh Kinkora, to thee!
      Thee, oh, Kinkora!

They are gone, those heroes of royal birth,
 Who plundered no churches, and broke no trust;
'Tis weary for me to be living on earth
 When they, oh Kinkora, lie low in the dust!
      Low, oh, Kinkora!

Oh, never again will Princes appear,
 To rival the Dalcassians* of the Cleaving Swords
I can never dream of meeting afar or anear,
 In the east or the west, such heroes and lords!
      Never, Kinkora!

Oh, dear are the images my memory calls up
 Of Brian Boru!—how he never would miss
To give me at the banquet, the first bright cup!
 Ah! why did he heap on me honour like this?
      Why, oh, Kinkora?

I am Mac Liag, and my home is on the Lake:
 Thither often, to that palace whose beauty is fled,
Came Brian, to ask me, and I went for his sake,
 Oh, my grief! that I should live, and Brian be dead
      Dead, oh, Kinkora!

* The Dalcassians were Brian's body-guard.

THE RETURN OF O'RUARK,

PRINCE OF BREFFNI.

BY THOMAS MOORE.

[This ballad is founded upon an event of most melancholy importance to Ireland; if, as we are told by our Irish historians, it gave England the first opportunity of profiting by our divisions and subduing us. The following are the circumstances as related by O'Halloran:—"The king of Leinster had long conceived a violent affection for Dearbhorgill, daughter to the King of Meath, and though she had been for some time married to O'Ruark, Prince of Breffni, yet it could not restrain his passion. They carried on a private correspondence, and she informed him that O'Ruark intended soon to go on a pilgrimage, (an act of piety frequent in those days,) and conjured him to embrace that opportunity of conveying her from a husband she detested to a lover she adored. Mac Murchad too punctually obeyed the summons, and had the lady conveyed to his capital of Ferns." The monarch Roderic espoused the cause of O'Ruark, while Mac Murchad fled to England, and obtained the assistance of Henry II. "Such," adds Giraldus Cambrensis, (as I find in an old translation,) "is the variable and fickle nature of woman, by whom all mischief in the world (for the most part) do happen and come, as may appear by Marcus Antonius, and by the destruction of Troy."]

THE valley lay smiling before me,
    Where lately I left her behind;
Yet I trembled, and something hung o'er me,
    That sadden'd the joy of my mind.
I look'd for the lamp which she told me
    Should shine when her Pilgrim return'd,
But, though darkness began to infold me,
    No lamp from the battlements burn'd!

I flew to her chamber—'twas lonely
    As if the lov'd tenant lay dead!
Ah! would it were death, and death only!
    But no—the young false one had fled.
And there hung the lute, that could soften
    My very worst pains into bliss,
While the hand, that had wak'd it so often,
    Now throbb'd to a proud rival's kiss.

There *was* a time, falsest of women!
    When BREFFNI's good sword would have sought
That man, through a million of foemen,
    Who dar'd but to wrong thee *in thought!*

While now—Oh degenerate daughter
   Of Erin, how fall'n is thy fame!
And thro' ages of bondage and slaughter,
   Our country shall bleed for thy shame.

Already the curse is upon her,
   And strangers her valleys profane;
They come to divide—to dishonour,
   And tyrants they long will remain!
But onward!—the green banner rearing,
   Go, flesh every sword to the hilt;
On *our* side is VIRTUE and ERIN!
   On *theirs* is the SAXON and GUILT.

THE BATTLE OF KNOCKTUAGH.*

1189.

BY THE AUTHOR OF "THE MONKS OF KILCREA."

[About this time (1189) the Anglo-Norman power in Ireland received a
severe check by the death of Sir Armoricus Tristram, brother-in-law, and, after
the chivalrous fashion of the day, sworn comrade of Sir John de Courcy.
Having gone with a strong force to Connaught on an expedition, he was attacked with a more numerous army by Cathal O'Connor, surnamed "The Red
Handed," and slain, with all his followers. This battle was fought by the Adventurers with a bravery unsurpassed in the annals of modern warfare. Of it
the historian says:—"Cathal, surnamed the bloody-handed, one of the sur-
vivors of the race of Roderick, was now received as King of Connaught, and
had united in a confederacy the chiefs of Thomond and Desmond, against the
new settlers, as the common enemy. Neither De Courcy nor De Lacy could
expect the support of each other. But De Courcy's trusty friend Armoric of
St. Lawrence, marched without delay to assist him in the defence of Ulster,
with a little band of two hundred foot and thirty cavalry. Cathal, to intercept
him on his march through his province, laid an ambuscade; and St. Lawrence
having fallen into it, found himself surrounded by an army, with which it
would be madness to contend in any hope of victory. In this emergency the
love of life so far prevailed over the cavalry, that they were on the point to
trust to the fleetness of their horses, leaving the foot to their fate. The infantry were informed of this resolution, and with the brother of Armoric at their
head, they gathered round their companions in arms, and reproached them for
so ignoble a purpose: then reminding them of the many toils and dangers in
which they had participated—the friendships and affinities they had mutually

---

* Knocktuadh, "The Hill of Axes," lies within a few miles of Galway.

formed; they conjured them, by every tender and affecting motive, not to disgrace their former prowess, by abandoning their fellow-soldiers and their
brethren to the fury of a barbarous and incensed enemy. Armoric and his
brave band could hear no more; he drew his sword and plunged it into his
horse; the rest of the troops followed his example, and with one voice all declared they would share the fate of their companions: that death was now
inevitable, and that they would meet it manfully with their weapons in their
hands, rather than stain their honour by submitting to the mercy of an enemy
they had so often vanquished. They proceeded to the execution of their purpose, with a truly Spartan resolution and composure. Two of the youngest of
their body were ordered to retire to a neighbouring eminence; there to view
the engagement, and to bear a faithful report to John de Courcy, of the conduct of his friends and countrymen in this last trying hour. The rest marched
forward with a confidence which struck the Irish army with amazement.
Cathal imagined they must have received a numerous reinforcement. Meanwhile, St. Lawrence and his band rushed desperately forward; they forced
their way with terrible havoc through the crowds of the enemy, of whom one
thousand are said to have fallen by their hands. As they were completely
armed, they sustained repeated onsets for a long time, without receiving a
wound. At length, overwhelmed by numbers, they sunk under a contest so
unequal: not one enduring to survive his companions. Cathal founded an
Abbey on the field of action, and named it *De Colle Victoriæ*."—*Liber
Munerum Publicorum Hiberniæ*, vol. i. part 1. page 13.]

CLOSE hemm'd by foes, in Ulster hills, within his castle pent,
For aid unto the west countrie Sir John de Courcy sent;
And for the sake of knightly vow, and friendship old and tried,
He prayed that Sir Armor Tristram would to his rescue ride.

Then grieved full sore that noble knight, when he those tidings
    heard,
And deep a vow he made, with full many a holy word—
That aid him Heaven and good St. Lawrence, full vengeance
    should await
The knaves who did De Courcy wrong, and brought him to this
    strait.

And a goodly sight it was, o'er Clare-Galway's glassy plain,
To see the bold Sir Tristram pass, with all his gallant train:
For thirty knights came with him there, all kinsmen of his blood,
And seven score spears and ten, right valiant men and good.

And clasping close, with sturdy arms, each horseman by the waist,
Behind each firm-fixed saddle there, a footman light was placed;
And fast they spurred in sweeping trot, as if in utmost need,
Their harness ringing loudly round, and foam upon each steed.

They cross the stream—they reach the wood—the bending
   boughs give way,
And fling upon their waving plumes light showers of sparkling
   spray;
But when they pass that leafy copse, and topp'd the hillock's crest,
Then jumped each footman down—each horseman laid his lance
   in rest.

For far and wide as eye could reach, a mighty host was seen
Of Irish kernes and gallowglass, with hobbelers between,
And proudly waving in the front fierce Cathal's standard flies,
With many more of Connaught's chiefs, and Desmond's tribes
   likewise.

Then to a knight Sir Tristram spake, with fearless eye and brow,
"Sir Hugolin, advance my flag, and do this errand now:
Go, seek the leader of yon host, and greet him fair from me,
And ask, why thus, with armed men, he blocks my passage free?"

Then stout Sir Hugolin prick'd forth, upon his gallant gray,
The banner in his good right hand, and thus aloud did say:—
"Ho! Irish chiefs! Sir Armor Tristram greets ye fair, by me.
And bids me ask, why thus in arms ye block his passage free?"

Then stept fierce Cathal to the front, his chieftains standing nigh:
"Proud stranger, take our answer back, and this our reason why:—
Our wolves are gaunt for lack of food—our eagles pine away,
And to glut them with your flesh, lo! we stop you here this day!"

"Now, gramercy for the thought!" calm Sir Hugolin replied,
And with a steadfast look and mien that wrathful chief he eyed:—
"Yet should your wild birds covet not the dainty fare you name,
Then, by the rood, our Norman swords shall carve them better
   game!"

Then turned his horse, and back he rode unto the little band
That, halted on the hill, in firm and martial order stand;
When told his tale, then divers knights began to counsel take,
How best they could their peril shun, and safe deliverance make.

"Against such odds, all human might is valueless!" they cried;
"And better 'twere at once to turn, and thro' the thicket ride."
When, high o'er all, Sir Tristram spake, in accents bold and free:—
"Let all depart who fear to fight this battle out with me;

" For never yet shall mortal say, I left him in his need,
Or brought him into danger's grasp—then trusted to my steed!
And, come what will, whate'er betide, let all depart who may,
I'll share my comrades' lot, and with them stand or fall this day!"

Then drooped with burning shame full many a knightly crest,
And nobler feelings answering swell'd throughout each throbbing
    breast ;
And stout Sir Hugolin spoke first :—" Whate'er our lot may be,
Come weal, come woe, 'fore Heaven, we'll stand or fall this day
    with thee!"

Then from his horse Sir Tristram lit, and drew his shining blade,
And gazing on the noble beast, right mournfully he said :—
" Thro' many a bloody field thou hast borne me safe and well,
And never knight had truer friend than thou, fleet Roancelle!

" When wounded sore, and left for dead, on far Knockgara's plain,
No friendly aid or vassal near—yet, thou didst still remain !
Close to thy master there thou mad'st thy rough and fearful bed,
And on thy side, that night, my steed, I laid my aching head !

" Yet now, my gallant horse, we part! thy proud career is o'er,
And never shalt thou bound beneath an armed rider more."
He spoke, and kist the blade—then pierced his charger's glossy
    side,
And madly plunging in the air, the noble courser died !

Then every horseman in his band, dismounting, did the same,
And in that company no steed alive was left, but twain ;
On one there rode De Courcy's squire. who came from Ulster wild,
Upon the other young Oswald sate, Sir Tristram's only child.

The father kist his son, then spake, while tears his eyelids fill :
" Good Hamo, take my boy, and spur with him to yonder hill ;
Go, watch from thence, till all is o'er ; then, northward haste in
    flight,
And say, that Tristram in his harness died, like a worthy knight."

Now pealed along the foeman's ranks a shrill and wild halloo !
While boldly back defiance loud the Norman bugles blew ;
And bounding up the hill, like hounds, at hunted quarry set,
The Irish kernes came fiercely on, and fiercely were they met.

Then rose the roar of battle loud—the shout—the cheer—the cry!
The clank of ringing steel, the gasping groans of those who die;
Yet onward still the Norman band, right fearless cut their way,
As move the mowers o'er the sward upon a summer's day.

For round them there, like shorn grass, the foe in hundreds bleed;
Yet, fast as e'er they fall, each side, do hundreds more succeed
With naked breasts, undaunted meet the spears of steel-clad men,
And sturdily, with axe and skein, repay their blows again.

Now crushed with odds, their phalanx broke, each Norman fights
    alone,
And few are left throughout the field, and they are feeble grown:
But, high o'er all, Sir Tristram's voice is like a trumpet heard,
And still, where'er he strikes, the foemen sink beneath his sword.

But once he raised his beaver up—alas! it was to try
If Hamo and his boy yet tarried on the mountain nigh;
When sharp an arrow from the foe, piercèd right thro' his brain,
And sank the gallant knight a corpse upon the bloody plain.

Then failed the fight, for gathering round his lifeless body there,
The remnant of his gallant band fought fiercely in despair;
And one by one they wounded fell—yet with their latest breath,
Their Norman war-cry shouted bold—then sank in silent death.

And thus Sir Tristram died; than whom no mortal knight could be
More brave in list or battle-field,—in banquet-hall more free;
The flower of noble courtesy—of Norman peers the pride;
Oh, not in Christendom's wide realms can be his loss supplied.

Sad tidings these to tell, in far Downpatrick's lofty towers,
And sadder news to bear to lone Ivora's silent bowers;
Yet shout ye not, ye Irish kernes—good cause have ye to rue;
For a bloody fight and stern was the battle of Knocktuagh.

THE MUNSTER WAR-SONG.*

1190.

BY R. D. WILLIAMS.

CAN the depths of the ocean afford you not graves,
That you come thus to perish afar o'er the waves;
To redden and swell the wild torrents that flow,
Through the valley of vengeance, the dark Aharlow?†

The clangour of conflict o'erburthens the breeze,
From the stormy Slieve Bloom to the stately Galtees;
Your caverns and torrents are purple with gore,
Slievenamon, Glencoloc, and sublime Galtymore!

The Sun-burst that slumbered embalmed in our tears,
Tipperary! shall wave o'er thy tall mountaineers!
And the dark hill shall bristle with sabre and spear,
While one tyrant remains to forge manacles here.

The riderless war-steed careers o'er the plain,
With a shaft in his flank and a blood-dripping mane,
His gallant breast labours, and glare his wild eyes;
He plunges in torture—falls—shivers—and dies.

Let the trumpets ring triumph! the tyrant is slain,
He reels o'er his charger deep-pierced through the brain;

---

* This ballad relates to the time when the Irish began to rally and unite
against their invaders. The union was, alas! brief, but its effects were great.
The troops of Connaught and Ulster, under Cathal Cruv-dearg (Cathal O'Connor of the Red Hand), defeated and slew Armoric St. Laurence, and stripped
De Courcy of half his conquests. But the ballad refers to Munster; and an
extract from Moore's book will show that there was solid ground for triumph:—
"Among the chiefs who agreed at this crisis to postpone their mutual feuds
and act in concert against the enemy, were O'Brian of Thomond, and Mac
Carthy of Desmond, hereditary rulers of North and South Munster, and chiefs
respectively of the two rival tribes, the Dalcassians and Eoganians. By a
truce now formed between those princes, O'Brian was left free to direct his
arms against the English; and having attacked their forces at Thurles, in
Fogarty's country, gave them A COMPLETE OVERTHROW, putting to the
sword, add the Munster Annals, a great number of knights."—*History of Ireland*, A. D. 1190.
   † Aharlow glen, County Tipperary.

And his myriads are flying like leaves on the gale,
But, who shall escape from our hills with the tale?

For the arrows of vengeance are show'ring like rain,
And choke the strong rivers with islands of slain,
Till thy waves, "lordly Shannon," all crimsonly flow,
Like the billows of hell with the blood of the foe.

Ay! the foemen are flying, but vainly they fly—
Revenge, with the fleetness of lightning, can vie;
And the septs of the mountains spring up from each rock,
And rush down the ravines like wolves on the flock.

And who shall pass over the stormy Slieve Bloom,
To tell the pale Saxon of tyranny's doom;
When, like tigers from ambush, our fierce mountaineers,
Leap along from the crags with their death-dealing spears?

They came with high boasting to bind us as slaves,
But the glen and the torrent have yawned for their graves—
From the gloomy Ardfinnan to wild Templemore—
From the Suir to the Shannon—is red with their gore.

By the soul of Heremon! our warriors may smile,
To remember the march of the foe through our isle;
Their banners and harness were costly and gay,
And proudly they flash'd in the summer sun's ray;

The hilts of their falchions were crusted with gold,
And the gems of their helmets were bright to behold,
By Saint Bride of Kildare! but they moved in fair show—
To gorge the young eagles of dark Aharlow!

DE COURCY'S PILGRIMAGE.

BY T. D. M'GEE.

["Sir John De Courcy under King Henry (the Second) was the chief conqueror of Ulster,—who about the getting of the same had seven battles with the Irish, five of which he won and lost two. Having at length reduced it to English rule and order, and occupied it for twenty years or more, King John hearing that De Courcy had boldly declared that the death of the rightful heir to the English crown, Prince Arthur, was effected through his commands, he instructed the brothers, Sir Walter and Sir Hugh De Lacy, to arrest De Courcy, and send him to England to be hanged. Sir Hugh went with his host from Meath and did battle with De Courcy in Down, and after many being slain on both sides the victory was in favour of De Courcy."—*Finglas's Breviate*—*Harris's Hibernica*, page 43.) Among the traditional heroes of Ireland John De Courcy occupies a prominent position. The exploits which fame ascribes to him entitle him to the character of an Irish Cid. The circumstance related in the following ballad, is popular in every homestead from Innishowen to Inisherkin.]

" I'm weary of your elegies, your keenings and complaints,
 .'e've heard no strain this blessed night, but histories of saints;
Sing us some deed of daring,—of the living or the dead !"
So Earl Gerald, in Maynooth, to the Bard Neelan, said

Answered the Bard Neelan,—" Oh, Earl, I will obey ;
And I will show you that you have no cause for what you say ;
A warrior may be valiant, and love holiness also,
As did the Norman Courcy, in this country long ago."

Few men could match De Courcy, on saddle or on sward,
The ponderous mace he valued more than any Spanish sword :
On many a field of slaughter scores of men lay smashed and stark,
And the victors as they saw them, said—" Lo ! John De Courcy's
    mark ! "

De Lacy was his deadly foe, through envy of his fame ;
He laid foul ambush for his life, and stigmatized his name ;
But the gallant John De Courcy, kept still his mace at hand,
And rode unfearing feint or force, across his rival's land.

He'd made a vow, for some past sins, a pilgrimage to pay,
At Patrick's tomb, and there to bide, a fortnight and a day ;
And now amid the cloisters, the disarmed giant walks,
And with the brown beads in his hand, from cross to cross he
    stalks.

News came to Hugo Lacy, of the penance of the Knight,
And he rose and sent his murderers, from Durrogh forth by night ;
A score of mighty Methian men, proof guarded for the strife,
And he has sworn them, man by man, to take De Courcy's life.

'Twas twilight in Downpatrick town, the pilgrim in the porch,
Sat, faint with fasting and with prayer, before the darkened church ;
When suddenly he heard a sound, upon the stony street—
A sound, familiar to his ears, of battle horses' feet.

He stepped forth to a hillock, where an oaken cross it stood,
And looking forth, he leaned upon the monumental wood.
"'Tis he, 'tis he!" the foremost cried—"'tis well you came to
  shrive,
For another sun, De Courcy, you shall never see alive!"

Then roused the softened heart within the pilgrim's sober weeds—
He thought upon his high renown, and all his knightly deeds,—
He felt the spirit swell within, his undefended breast,
And his courage rose the faster, that his sins had been confest.

"I am no dog to perish thus! no deer to couch at bay!
Assassins! ware* the life you seek, and stand not in my way!"
He pluck'd the tall cross from the root, and waving it around,
He dashed the master murderer, stark and lifeless to the ground.

As row on row, they pressed within the deadly ring he made,
Twelve of the score in their own gore within his reach he laid,
The rest in panic terror ran to horse and fled away,
And left the Knight De Courcy, at the bloody cross to pray.

"And now," quoth Neelan to the Earl, "I did your will obey,
Have I not shown, you had no cause—for what I heard you say?"
"Faith, Neelan," answered Gerald, "your holy man, Sir John,
Did bear his cross right manfully, so much we have to own.'"

———

CAHAL MOR OF THE WINE-RED HAND.

(A VISION OF CONNAUGHT IN THE THIRTEENTH CENTURY.)

BY J. C. MANGAN.

"Et moi, j'ai eté aussi en Arcadie."—And I, too, have been a dreamer.
—*Inscription on a Painting by Poussin.*

I WALKED entranced
    Through a land of morn;
The sun, with wondrous excess of light,
    Shone down and glanced
        Over seas of corn,
And lustrous gardens aleft and right.

* "Then ware a rising tempest on the main."—*Dryden.*

Even in the clime
Of resplendent Spain
Beams no such sun upon such a land;
But it was the time,
'Twas in the reign,
Of Cáhal Mór of the Wine-Red Hand. *

Anon stood nigh
By my side a man
Of princely aspect and port sublime.
Him queried I,
"O, my Lord and Khan,†
What clime is this, and what golden time?"
When he—"The clime
Is a clime to praise,
The clime is Erin's, the green and bland;
And it is the time,
These be the days,
Of Cáhal Mór of the Wine-red Hand!"

Then I saw thrones,
And circling fires,
And a dome rose near me, as by a spell,
Whence flowed the tones
Of silver lyres
And many voices in wreathed swell;
And their thrilling chime
Fell on mine ears
As the heavenly hymn of an angel-band —
"It is now the time,
These be the years,
Of Cáhal Mór of the Wine-red Hand!"

I sought the hall,
And, behold!—a change
From light to darkness, from joy to woe!
Kings, nobles, all,

* The Irish and Oriental poets both agree in attributing favourable or unfavourable weather and abundant or deficient harvests to the good or bad qualities of the reigning monarch. What the character of Cathal was will be seen
below. Mor means Great.
† Identical with the Irish *Ceann*, Head, or Chief; but I the rather gave him
the Oriental title, as really fancying myself in one of the regions of Araby the
Blest.

Looked aghast and strange;
The minstrel-group sate in dumbest show!
Had some great crime
Wrought this dread amaze,
This terror?   None seemed to understand!
'Twas then the time,
We were in the days,
Of Cáhal Mór of the Wine-red Hand.

I again walked forth;
But lo! the sky
Showed fleckt with blood, and an alien sun
Glared from the north,
And there stood on high,
Amid his shorn beams A SKELETON!*
It was by the stream
Of the castled Maine,
One autumn eve, in the Teuton's land,
That I dreamed this dream
Of the time and reign
Of Cáhal Mór of the Wine-red Hand!

BATTLE OF CREDRAN.

1257.

BY EDWARD WALSH.

[A brilliant battle was fought by Geoffrey O'Donnell, Lord of Tirconnell, against the Lord Justice of Ireland, Maurice Fitzgerald, and the English of Connaught, at Credran Cille, Roseede, in the territory of Carburry, north of Sligo, in defence of his principality. A fierce and terrible conflict took place, in which bodies were hacked, heroes disabled, and the strength of both sides exhausted. The men of Tirconnell maintained their ground, and completely overthrew the English forces in the engagement, and defeated them with great

* "It was but natural that these portentous appearances should thus be exhibited on this occasion, for they were the heralds of a very great calamity that befell the Connacians in this year—namely, the death of Cathal of the Red Hand, son of Torlogh Mor of the Wine, and King of Connaught, a prince of most amiable qualities, and into whose heart GOD had infused more piety and goodness than into the hearts of any of his contemporaries."—*Annals of the Four Masters*, A. D. 1224.

G

slaughter; but Geoffrey himself was severely wounded, having encountered in
the fight Maurice Fitzgerald, in single combat, in which they mortally wounded
each other.—*Annals of the Four Masters.*]

From the glens of his fathers O'Donnell comes forth,
With all Cinel-Conall,* fierce septs of the North—
O'Boyle and O'Daly, O'Dugan, and they
That own, by the wild waves, O'Doherty's sway.

Clan Connor, brave sons of the diadem'd Niall,
Has pour'd the tall clansmen from mountain and vale—
M'Sweeny's sharp axes, to battle oft bore,
Flash bright in the sunlight by high Dunamore.

Through Inis-Mac-Durin,† through Derry's dark brakes,
Glentocher of tempests, Slieve-snacht of the lakes,
Bundoran of dark spells, Loch-Swilly's rich glen,
The red deer rush wild at the war-shout of men!

O! why through Tir-Conall, from Cuil-dubh's dark steep,
To Samer's‡ green border the fierce masses sweep,
Living torrents o'er-leaping their own river shore,
In the red sea of battle to mingle their roar?

Stretch thy vision far southward, and seek for reply
Where blaze of the hamlets glares red on the sky—
Where the shrieks of the hopeless rise high to their God—
Where the foot of the Sassenach spoiler has trod!

Sweeping on like a tempest, the Gall-Oglach§ stern
Contends for the van with the swift-footed kern—
There's blood for that burning, and joy for that wail—
The avenger is hot on the spoiler's red trail!

The Saxon hath gather'd on Credran's far heights,
His groves of long lances, the flower of his knights—

* *Cinel-Conall*,—The descendants of Conall-Gulban, the son of Niall of the
Nine Hostages, Monarch of Ireland in the fourth century. The principality
was named Tir Chonaile, or Tyrconnell, which included the county Donegal,
and its chiefs were the O'Donnells.
† Districts in Donegal.
‡ *Samer*,—The ancient name of Loch Earne.
§ *Gall-Oglach* or *Gallowglass*,—The heavy armed foot soldier. *Kern* or
Ceithernach,—The light armed soldier.

His awful cross-bowmen, whose long iron hail
Finds through Cota* and Sciath, the bare heart of the Gael!

The long lance is brittle—the mailèd ranks reel
Where the Gall-Oglach's axe hews the harness of steel;
And truer to its aim in the breast of a foeman,
Is the pike of a Kern than the shaft of a bowman.

One prayer to St. Columb†—the battle-steel clashes—
The tide of fierce conflict tumultuously dashes;
Surging onward, high-heaving its billow of blood,
While war-shout and death-groan swell high o'er the flood!

As meets the wild billows the deep-centred rock,
Met glorious Clan-Conall the fierce Saxon's shock;
As the wrath of the clouds flash'd the axe of Clan-Conell,
Till the Saxon lay strewn 'neath the might of O'Donnell!

One warrior alone holds the wide bloody field,
With barbed black charger and long lance and shield—
Grim, savage, and gory he meets their advance,
His broad shield up-lifting, and couching his lance.

Then forth to the van of that fierce rushing throng
Rode a chieftain of tall spear and battle-axe strong,
His *bracca*,‡ and *geochal*, and *cochal's* red fold,
And war-horse's housings, were radiant in gold!

Say who is this chief spurring forth to the fray,
The wave of whose spear holds yon armed array?
And he who stands scorning the thousands that sweep,
An army of wolves over shepherdless sheep?

---

* *Cota*,—The saffron-dyed shirt of the kern, consisting of many yards o
yellow linen thickly plaited. *Sciath*,—The wicker shield, as its name imports.
† *St. Colum*, or *Colum-Cille, the dove of the Church.*—The patron saint of
Tyrconnell, descended from Conall Gulban.
‡ *Bracca*,—So called, from being striped with various colours, was the
tight-fitting Truis. It covered the ancles, legs, and thighs, rising as high as
the loins, and fitted so close to the limbs as to discover every muscle and motion
of the parts which it covered. *Geochal*,—The jacket made of gilded leather,
and which was sometimes embroidered with silk. *Cochal*,—A sort of cloak
with a large hanging collar of different colours. This garment reached to the
middle of the thigh, and was fringed with a border like shagged hair, and being
brought over the shoulders was fastened on the breast by a clasp, buckle, or
brooch of silver or gold. In battle, they wrapped the Cochal several times
round the left arm as a shield.— *Walker's Dress and Armour of the Irish.*

The shield of his nation, brave Geoffrey O'Donnell
(Clar-Fodhla's firm prop is the proud race of Conall)*
And Maurice Fitzgerald, the scorner of danger,
The scourge of the Gael, and the strength of the stranger

The launch'd spear hath torn through target and mail—
The couch'd lance hath borne to his crupper the Gael—
The steeds driven backwards all helplessly reel;
But the lance that lies broken hath blood on its steel!

And now, fierce O'Donnell, thy battle-axe wield—
The broad sword is shiver'd, and cloven the shield,
The keen steel sweeps griding through proud crest and crown—
Clar-Fodhla hath triumph'd—the Saxon is down!

THE BATTLE OF LOUGH SWILLY.

1258.

["O'Donnell Geoffrey was confined by his mortal wounds at Lough Beathach, for the space of a year, after the battle of Credrain. When Bryan O'Neill received intelligence of this, he collected his forces for the purpose of marching into Tyrconnell, and sent messengers to O'Donnell, demanding sureties, hostages, and submission, as they had no lord capable of governing them, after Geoffrey. The messengers, having delivered their commands, returned with all possible speed. O'Donnell summoned the Connellians from all quarters to wait on him, and having assembled at their lord's call, he ordered them, as he was not able to lead them, to prepare for him the coffin, in which his remains should be finally conveyed, to place him therein, and to carry him in the very midst of his people. He told them to fight bravely, as he was amongst them, and not to fear the power of their enemies. They then proceeded in battle array, at the command of their lord, to meet O'Neill's force, till both armies confronted each other on the shore of Lough Swilly. They attacked each other, without regard to friend or relative, till at length the Tyronians were defeated and driven back, leaving behind them many of their horses, men, and property. On the day of the return of the Connellian force from their victory, the coffin in which O'Donnell was borne was laid down on the place where the battle was fought, where his spirit departed, from the mortification of his wounds received in the battle of Credrain."—*Annals of the Four Masters.* A. D. 1258.]

* This is the translation of the first line of a poem of two hundred and forty-eight verses, written by Firgal og Mac-an-Bhaird on Dominick O'Donnell, in the year 1655. The original line is—
"Gaibhle Fodhla fuil Chonaill."—*O'Reilly's Irish Writers.*

ALL worn, and wan, and sore with wounds, from Credran's
    bloody fray,
In Donegal, for twelve long months, the proud O'Donnell lay;
Around his couch, in bitter grief, his trusty clansmen wait,
And silent watch, with aching hearts, his faint and feeble state.

Full sad it was, that gallant chief, thus stricken down to see,
The wise in hall, the brave in field, the fearless and the free;
Tyrowen's scourge, Tyrconnell's pride, now as an infant weak,
And wrung with pain his manly form, all sunk his pallid cheek.

His war-shield hangs above him there, his sword is by his bed;
And at the foot his henchman sits,—his bard is by its head;
And on his *clairseach* * wakes at times a soft and soothing strain,
And sings the songs of other days to lull his master's pain.

A light wind touched his banner there, and waved it to and fro,
And on his couch he raised him up all wearily and slow;
"Oh, bear me forth," the chieftain said, "and let me view once
    more,
The rustling woods of Gartan side, Lough Betagh's gentle shore.

" Methinks, upon this burning brow, right pleasant 'twere to feel
The fresh breeze from the waters sweep, and o'er it cooling steal;
And see the stag upon the hills, the white clouds drifting by,
And feel, upon my wasted cheek, God's sunshine ere I die."

It was a summer's evening, a glorious eve in June,
When bright the sun look'd back on hills, all purple in their bloom;
And blue the lake, and fair the sky when down his gillies bore
Their wounded chief, on litter soft, to Betagh's pleasant shore.

He looked upon the hills and lake—he gazed upon the sky;
The very harebell at his foot had beauty to his eye;
And o'er his brow, and features pale, a quiet calmness crept,
And, leaning back, he closed his eyes, all tranquilly, and slept.

But soon his slumber passed away, and suddenly he woke,
And thus, with kindling eye and cheek, the wounded warrior
    spoke :
" A war-steed's tramp is on the heath, and onward cometh fast,
And, by the Rood! a trumpet sounds!—Hark, 'tis the Red Hand's
    blast."

       * *Clairseach,*—Harp. *Skian,*—Short sword.

Nor hoof nor horn his vassals heard, nor echo from the hill ;
The lake was calm, the wood was hush'd, and all around was still;
But soon a kern all breathless ran, and told a stranger train
Across the heath was spurring fast, and then in sight it came.

"Now, bring me quick my father's sword," the noble chieftain
    said ;
" My mantle o'er my shoulders fling—place helmet on my head,
And raise me to my feet, for ne'er shall clansman of my foe
Go boasting tell in far Tyrone he saw O'Donnell low!"

They brought him there his father's sword, all goodly to behold,
His mantle o'er his shoulders cast—its clasp was twisted gold—
And on his brow a helmet placed, and then, tho' pale his face,
Yet circled by his chiefs he look'd the Monarch of his Race!

And thither came the messenger, O'Niall's henchman he,
And proudly o'er the heath he stept, with bearing bold and free,
His left hand grasps a sheathed sword—then spake O'Donnell
    brief,
" Stranger, you come from Clannaboy—what tidings from your
    chief?"

FYTTE II.

" High Chief of Donegal"—'twas thus the clansman back did say—
" O'Niall sends you greeting fair, as lord a vassal may,
And bids you render homage due, as did your sires before,
And unto him this tribute pay ere thrice three days are o'er:

" A hundred hawks from out your woods, all trained their prey to
    get ;
A hundred steeds from off your hills uncrost by rider yet ;
A hundred kine from off your plains, the best your land doth know;
A hundred hounds from out your halls, to hunt the stag and roe."

' Nor hawk, nor hound, nor steed, nor steer, O'Niall gets from me;
Nor homage yield, nor tribute send—no vassal clan are we !
And be he Lord of Clannaboy, and Chieftain at Tyrone,
Yet I am Prince in Donegal—let each man hold his own.

" We tread our hills as freeborn men ! nor Lord, nor Ruler, know;
We bend the knee to God alone—go tell your chieftain so !

Mac Carthan's rocks are hard to climb; Lough Swilly's sides are
  steep,
And what our fathers gave to us, our good right hands shall keep!"

The clansman heard in silent rage, then proud his sword he drew,
And boldly at O'Donnell's foot the scabbard down he threw;
And waved in air the blade aloft, and blew a trumpet blast—
Then folded stern his mantle wide, and o'er the hills he passed.

When out of sight, O'Donnell sank, all worn and weak with pain,
And from his wounded side, alas, the blood gush'd forth amain;
But still unquenched his spirit burned, as brightly as of old,
And thus he to his vassals spake, in accents calm and bold.

" Go, call around Tyrconnell's chiefs, my warriors tried and true;
Send fast a friend to Donal More, a scout to Lisnahue;
Light balefires quick on Easker's towers, that all the land may
  know
O'Donnell needeth help and haste, to meet his haughty foe.

" Oh, could I but my people head, or wield once more a spear,
Saint Angus! but we'd hunt their hosts like herds of fallow deer
But vain the wish, since I am now a faint and failing man,
Yet, ye shall bear me to the field, in centre of my clan!

" Right in the midst, and lest, perchance, upon the march I die,
In my coffin ye shall place me, uncovered let me lie;
And swear ye now, my body cold shall never rest in clay,
Until you drive from Donegal O'Niall's host away."

Then sad and stern, with hand on *skian*, that solemn oath they
  swore,
And in his coffin placed their chief, and on a litter bore;
Tho' ebbing fast his life-throbs came, yet dauntless in his mood,
He marshall'd well Tyrconnell's chiefs, like leader wise and good.

FYTTE III.

Lough Swilly's sides are thick with spears!—O'Niall's host is there,
And proud and gay their battle sheen, their banners flout the air;
And haughtily a challenge bold their trumpet bloweth free,
When winding down the heath-clad hills, O'Donnell's band
  they see.

No answer back those warriors gave, but sternly on they stept,
And in their centre, curtained black, a litter close is kept,
And all their host it guideth fair, as did in Galilee
Proud Judah's tribes the Ark of God, when crossing Egypt's sea.

"What pageant trick is this I see?" O'Niall sternly said;
"Do shaven priests, with stole and pall, Tyrconnell's rebels head?
Then shall they learn how scant I prize such mean and pompous
        show,
O'Hanlon! you have steeds and men, and yonder is the foe."

Then reined that chief his panting steed, his sword above him
        flash'd,
And "Forward! sons of Coll," he cried, and o'er the heath he
        dash'd;
And like a rock that thunders down some dried-up torrent's bed,
Clan Hanlon's horsemen bounded on, young Redmond at their head!

But M'Sweeny met them in the midst, and check'd their fierce
        career—
M'Sweeny, chief of Fanid broad, with many a mountain spear,
And he slew their gallant leader, and clove both crest and shield,
And wide Clan Hanlon's horsemen bold are scatter'd thro' the
        field!

Then rush'd like fire Clan Rory's race, with shouts that rend the
        skies,
And stricken by M'Gennis stern, the stout M'Sweeny dies;
But from the hills O'Cahan burst, with chiefs of Innishowen,
And falls the Tanist of Iveagh, for O'Niall and Tyrone!

Then rose the roar of battle loud, as clan met clan in fight,
And axe and *skian* grew red with blood, a sad and woful sight;
Yet, in the midst o'er all, unmoved, that litter black is seen,
Like some dark rock that lifts its head, o'er ocean's war serene!

Yet once, when blenching back fierce Bryan's charge before,
Tyrconnell waver'd in its ranks, and all was nearly o'er;
Aside those curtains wide were flung, and plainly to the view,
Each host beheld O'Donnell there, all pale and wan in hue.

And to his tribes he stretch'd his hands, and pointed to the foe,
And with a shout they rally round, and on Clan Hugh they go;

And back they beat their horsemen fierce, and in a column deep,
With O'Donnell in their foremost rank, in one fierce charge they
   sweep.

And on that host a panic came—a panic and a fear—
And then their hearts wax faint and low—their hands drop sword
   and spear;
And stricken by the ghastly sight, despite their leaders high,
They shrink before O'Donnell's face, and turn their steeds and fly!

In vain O'Niall dash'd along, with banner in his hand,
And for the honour of Tyrone, he bade them turn and stand;
In wild affright his squadrons flee, as ebbs the tide away,
Tho' the north wind strives to check it, in Dundrum's rocky bay!

Lough Swilly's banks are thick with spears!—O'Niall's host is there,
But rent and tost like tempest-clouds, Clan Donnell in the rere,
Lough Swilly's waves are red with blood, as madly in its tide
O'Niall's horsemen wildly plunge, to reach the other side!

And broken is Tyrowen's pride, and vanquish'd Clannaboy,
And there is wailing thro' the land, from Baun to Aughnacloy;
The Red Hand's crest is bent in grief, upon its shield a stain,
For its stoutest clans are broken—its bravest chiefs are slain.

But proud and high Tyrconnell shouts; but blending on the gale,
Upon the ear ascendeth now a sad and sullen wail;
For on that field, as back they bore, from chasing of the foe,
The spirit of O'Donnell fled!—oh, woe for Ulster, woe!

Yet died he there all gloriously—a victor in the fight—
A Chieftain at his people's head, a warrior in his might,
They dug him there a fitting grave, upon that field of pride—
And a lofty cairn raised above, by fair Lough Swilly's side.*
                                      * * *

   * We believe this ballad to be written by the author of "The Monks of Kilcrea."

THE BATTLE OF ARDNOCHER.

1328.

BY THE AUTHOR OF "THE MONKS OF KILCREA."

[A. D. 1328, MacGeoghegan gave a great overthrow to the English, in which three thousand five hundred of them, together with the D'Altons, were slain. This battle, in which the English forces met such tremendous defeat, was fought near Mullingar, on the day before the feast of St. Laurence—namely, the 9th August. The Irish clans were commanded by William MacGeoghegan, Lord of Kenil Feacha, in Westmeath, comprising the present baronies of Moycashel and Rathconrath. The English forces were commanded by Lord Thomas Butler, the Petits, Tuites, Nangles, Delemers, &c. The battle took place at the Hill of Ardnocher.—*Annals of the Four Masters.*]

ON the eve of St. Laurence, at the cross of Glenfad,
Both of chieftains and bonaghts what a muster we had,
Thick as bees, round the heather, on the side of Slieve Bloom,
To the trysting they gather by the light of the moon.

For The Butler from Ormond with a hosting he came,
And harried Moycashel with havoc and flame,
Not a hoof or a hayrick, nor corn blade to feed on,
Had he left in the wide land, right up to Dunbreedon.

Then gathered MacGeoghegan, the high prince of Donore,
With O'Connor from Croghan, and O'Dempsys *galore;* *
And, my soul, how we shouted, as dash'd in with their men,
Bold MacCoghlan from Clara, O'Mulloy from the glen.

And not long did we loiter where the four *toghers*† met,
But his saddle each tightened, and his spurs closer set,
By the skylight that flashes all their red burnings back,
And by black gore and ashes fast the rievers we track.

Till we came to Ardnocher, and its steep slope we gain,
And stretch'd there, beneath us, saw their host in the plain;
And high shouted our leader ('twas the brave William Roe)—
"By the Red Hand of Niall, 'tis the Sassenach foe!

"Now, low level your spears, grasp each battle-axe firm,
And for God and our Ladye strike ye downright and stern;

---

* *Galore,*—in abundance.   † *Toghers,*—roads.

For our homes and our altars charge ye steadfast and true,
And our watchword be vengeance, and *Lamh Dearg Aboo!*" *

Oh, then down like a torrent with a *farrah* we swept,
And full stout was the Saxon who his saddle-tree kept;
For we dash'd thro' their horsemen till they reel'd from the stroke,
And their spears, like dry twigs, with our axes we broke.

With our plunder we found them, our fleet garrons and kine,
And each chalice and cruet they had snatch'd from God's shrine.
But a red debt we paid them, the Sassenach raiders,
As we scatter'd their spearmen, slew chieftains and leaders.

In the Pale there is weeping and watchings in vain.
De Lacy and D'Alton, can ye reckon your slain?
Where's your chieftain, fierce Nangle? Has De Netterville fled?
Ask the Molingar eagles, whom their carcasses fed.

Ho! ye riders from Ormond, will ye brag in your hall,
How your lord was struck down with his mail'd knights and all?
Swim at midnight the Shannon, beard the wolf in his den,
Ere you ride to Moycashel on a foray again!

THE LIFE AND DEATH OF ART MACMURROGH.

BY WILLIAM PEMBROKE MULCHINOCK.

[W. P. Mulchinock was born in Tralee, county Kerry, and was formerly
partner in a respectable merchant firm, in his native town, which was favour-
ably known to the Woollen Merchants of Yorkshire. After the disturbances of
1848 he emigrated to America, where he is now reaping the fruits of his talents
and industry. He is loved and respected by every one who knows the genial
warmth of his heart, and his high and unbending principles.]

WHEN Dynasts and Tanists, array'd on the heather
For Erin, and vengeance, took counsel together,
Whose foot than the red deer's was freer and lighter?
Whose eye than the eagle's was keener and brighter?
Whose voice than the peal of the thunder was louder?
Whose bearing than that of a monarch's was prouder?

* *Lamh Dearg Aboc* —the Red Hand for ever. *Lamh* is pronounced *Lauv*

Whose plume was the haughtiest, air-borne, flying?
Whose sword flash'd the brightest o'er dead and o'er dying?
Though Saxons in herds should his person environ,
Whose grasp on the war-horse was rigid as iron?
Whose heart beat the lightest in trial and danger?
Whose hate was the blackest for Saxon and stranger?
Oh, whose but MacMurrogh's, the pride of his sireland,
The sword and the buckler, the war-god of Ireland :
The Pale's-men and Saxons like rabbits would burrow
In fastness and fortress, with fear of MacMurrogh!

When Fileas were chaunting where red wine was flowing—
When eyes sparkled brightly on cheeks hotly glowing—
Whom first did they laud, and to whom first give honour?——
The Calnach, O'Nolan, O'Brin, or O'Connor;—
Oh! who but MacMurrogh, the chieftain so glorious,
O'er Norman and Saxon for ever victorious.
At the gates of the Pale, on the banks of King's river,
Of Glory and Fame he made handmaids for ever.
When Ormond fled fast to the Pale, for a haven,
Leaving Mortimer's corpse to the wolf and the raven,
The castle of Wexford he gave to the burning,
Their ramparts and bulwarks in dust overturning.
At Atheroe, the ford of the blood-tarnish'd water,
Lord Thomas of England got pale for the slaughter;
By Butler and Perrers the tale was out-spoken,
Of all that Art did when his vengeance was woken.

The swords of the foemen he heap'd up to heaven,
Their owners lying near them, by thousands, unshriven—
E'en Richard of England confess'd him his master,
When blow follow'd blow, and disaster, disaster.
From forest and fastness, from hill-top and valley,
How bravely he'd dash—oh, how wildly he'd sally!
'Till Saxon blood flow'd like a stream from its fountain,
Then hie him again to his haunts in the mountain;
Oh! many the hearts, neither fickle nor hollow,
With joy, e'en to death, that loved leader to follow,
Would leave kine to starve, and untill'd leave the furrow,
When raised was your proud flag, thou dauntless MacMurrogh

As strong as an oak, and as tall as a cedar—
By birthright a Monarch, by Nature a Leader—

On self and his own gallant hosting reliant,
Of Richard and all his mailed nobles defiant—
Of large heart and loving, the foremost to rally
Around him the septs of the mountain and valley;
O'Brin, and MacDavid, O'Toole, and O'Connor,
All loved of green Erin, all spotless of honour—
Through gloom, and through danger would follow, and find him,
And peal in the fierce fight, their war-cries behind him.
Ah! woe for the day, when the hand of Death found him,
With his Maidens and Kerns, and Fileas around him.

With weeping and wailing, in sad Ross MacBruin,
The Bards and the Brehons foretold the land's ruin;
The folds of the flag of false Ormond were given
With joy to the free air, and breezes of heaven;
The heart of the Calvach with anguish was laden,
O'Toole of Imayle, wept aloud like a maiden,
O'Nolan, O'Brin, and MacDavid, in sorrow,
Looked down on their hostings, and thought on the morrow.
The sable-cowl'd friars the death mass were singing—
The maidens in anguish, their white hands were ringing,
By river, by lake, in each valley and high-land,
The Death Caoine was rais'd for the pride of the island—
The kine roam'd at large, and untill'd lay the furrow,
When death struck the haughty, and mighty MacMurrogh.

DEATH OF ART MACMURROGH.

BY T. D. M'GEE.

[Art M'Murrogh died at Ross in 1416, after having reigned over Leinster for
forty years. He was the greatest Irish soldier of his age, and the first, perhaps,
that overreached the Normans by tactics and strategy. His campaigns against
Roger Mortimer, Richard the Second, the Earl of Ormond, Sir John Stanley,
and Sir Stephen Scroope, Lord Thomas of Lancaster, and the first Earl of
Shrewsbury, the "British Achilles," have yet to claim the pen of an historian.
He took Ross, Carlow, Enniscorthy, and other fortified places from the English—exacted an annual tribute of 80 marks, which was paid to his descendants
until after the year 1603—and during his life, cost the English treasury, according to the statements of their own chronicles, about 1,200,000 marks. He
is spoken of by Caxton, Marlburgh, and Hollinshed, as "the chief captain of his
nation"—"the canker that lay in the heart of Leinster"—"M'Murgh, at whose
mighty prowess all Leinster trembled," and in the like phrases. Valour and
virtue sustained him through many trials, and victory shone like a sun round
his old age.]

FROM the King's home rose a hum
  Like the rising of a swarm,
And it spread round Ross and grew
  Loud and boding as a storm;
And from the many-gated town passed Easchlaghs* in affright,
Pale as the morning hours when rushing forth from night,
And north, east, south, and westward as they sped,
They cried, "The King is dead!"—"The King is dead!"

As the mountain echoes mimic
  The mort of the bugle-horn,
So far and farther o'er the land
  The deadly tale is borne;
Echo answers echo from wood, and rath, and stream—
Easchlagh follows Easchlagh, like horrors in a dream;
And, when entreated to repose, they only said,
In accents woe-begone and brief, "The King is dead!"

The news was brought to Offaly,
  To the Calvach† in his hall;
He said, "Still'd be the harp and flute—
  We now are orphans all."
The news was brought to O'Tuathal, in Imayle;
He said, "We have lost the bulwark of the Gael;"
And his chosen men a-south to the royal wake he led—
Sighing, "The King is dead!"—"The King is dead!

To O'Brin in Ballincor,
  To O'Nolan in Forth it came,
To MacDavid in Riavach,
  And all mourn'd the same;
They said, "We have lost the chief champion of our land,
The King of the stoutest heart and strongest hand;"
The hills of the four counties that night for joy were red,
And boastfully their Dublin bells chimed that the King was dead.

It was told in Kilkenny,
  And the Ormond flag flew out,

* *Easchlagh*,—a courier among the Gadelians, who was often a female.
The word is pronounced nearly as if it was written *asla*.
† The Calvach o'Connor Faily, was Morrogh O'Connor, a renowned warrior,
who beat the English in several battles; amongst others that of Killuchan,
fought in 1413.

That had hid among the cobwebs
    Since the Earl's Callan rout;
But the Friars of Irishtown, they grieved for him full sore,
And Innistioge and Jerpoint may long his loss deplore.
From Clones south to Bannow the holy bells they toll,
And all the monks are praying for the Benefactor's soul.

For ages, in the eastward
    Such a wake was never seen;
Since Brian's death, in Erin
    Such a mourning had not been;
And as the clans to St. Mullins bore the fleshly part
That was earthy and had perished of King Art—
The crying of the keeners was heard by the last man,
Though he was three miles off when the burial rite began.

"Mourn, mourn," they said, "ye chieftains,
    From Riavach* and from Forth;†
Mourn, ye Dynasts of the lowlands,
    And ye Tanists of the north;
The noblest man that was left us, here to-day
In the churchyard of his fathers we make his bed of clay—
Unlucky is this year above all years—
His life was more to us than ten thousand tested spears.

"No ash tree in Shillelah
    Was more comely to the eye—
And like the heavens above us,
    He was good as he was high.
The taker of rich tributes, the queller of our strife,
The open-handed giver, his life to us was life.
Oh! Art, why did you leave us? Oh! even from the grave,
Could you not come to live for them you would have died to save?

"When we think on your actions—
    How against you, all in vain,
The King's son, and the King himself
    Of London cross'd the main—
When we think of the battle at Athcroe, and the day
When Roger Mortimer, at Kells, fell in the fiery fray—
They chant the De Profundis, and we cannot help but cry—
'Defender of your nation, oh!—why did you die?'

---

* *Contœ Riavach*,—a name given to Wexford in the 14th and 15th centuries
† Forth, in Carlow. Shillelah, in Carlow.

"If death would have hostages,
        A million such as we
    To bring you back to Erin,
        O! a cheap exchange 'twould be;
But silent as the midnight, and white as your own hair,
With its sixty years of snow, noble King! you lie there—
Your lip at last is pale—at last is clos'd your eye—
Oh, terror of the Saxons, Art, why did you die?"

        Thus by the gaping grave,
            They moaned about his bier,
        Challenging with clamorous grief
            The dead that could not hear;
Then slowly and sorrowful they laid him down to rest,
His sword beside him laid, and his cross on his breast,
And each one took his way with drooping heart and head,
Sighing, "The King is dead!"—"The King is dead!"

                    AVRAN. *

        His grave is in St. Mullin's,
            But to Pilgrim eyes unknown—
        Unmarked by mournful yew,
            Unchronicled in stone;
His bones are with his people's, his clay with common clay,
His memory in the night that lies behind the hills of day,
Where hundreds of our gallant dead await
The long foretold, redeemed and honoured fate. †

                    ———

            THE TRUE IRISH KING. ‡

                BY THOMAS DAVIS.

The Cæsar of Rome has a wider demense,
    And the *Ard-Righ*§ of France has more clans in his train;

---

* A concluding stanza, generally intended as a recapitulation of the entire ballad.
    † The coming of an historian who shall liberate our illustrious dead from the bondage of neglect and calumny is foretold in our prophecies.
    ‡ See Appendix L to O'Donovan's "Hy-Fiachra," p. 425, &c.
    § *Ard-Righ*,—Great King.

The sceptre of Spain is more heavy with gems,
And our crowns cannot vie with the Greek diadems;
But kinglier far before heaven and man
Are the Emerald fields, and the fiery-eyed clan,
The sceptre, and state, and the poets who sing,
And the swords that encircle A True Irish King!

For, he must have come from a conquering race—
The heir of their valour, their glory, their grace;
His frame must be stately, his step must be fleet,
His hand must be trained to each warrior feat,
His face, as the harvest moon, steadfast and clear,
A head to enlighten, a spirit to cheer,
While the foremost to rush where the battle-brands ring,
And the last to retreat is A True Irish King!

Yet, not for his courage, his strength, or his name,
Can he from the clansmen their fealty claim.
The poorest, and highest, choose freely to-day
The chief, that to-night, they'll as truly obey;
For loyalty springs from a people's consent,
And the knee that is forced had been better unbent—
The Sassenach serfs no such homage can bring
As the Irishmen's choice of A True Irish King!

Come, look on the pomp when they "make an O'Neill;"
The muster of dynasts—O'Hagan, O'Sheil,
O'Cahan, O'Hanlon, O'Breslen, and all,
From mild Ardes and Orior to rude Donegal.
"St. Patrick's *comharba*,"* with bishops thirteen,
And ollaves,† and brehons,‡ and minstrels, are seen,
Round Tulach-Og Rath,§ like the bees in the spring,
All swarming to honour A True Irish King.

Unsandalled he stands on the foot-dinted rock,
Like a pillar-stone fix'd against every shock.
Round, round is the Rath on a far-seeing hill,
Like his blemishless honour, and vigilant will.

* Successor,—the Archbishop of Armagh.
† *Ollaves*,—Doctors or learned men.
‡ *Brehons*,—Judges.
§ Tulach-Og,—between Cookstown and Stewartstown, Co. Tyrone.

The grey-beards are telling how chiefs by the score
Have been crowned on "The Rath of the Kings" heretofore,
While, crowded, yet ordered, within its green ring,
Are the dynasts and priests round THE TRUE IRISH KING.

The chronicler read him the laws of the clan,
And pledged him to bide by their blessing and ban;
His *skian* and his sword are unbuckled to show
That they only were meant for a foreigner foe;
A white willow wand has been put in his hand—
A type of pure, upright, and gentle command—
While hierarchs are blessing, the slipper they fling,
And O'Cahan proclaims him A TRUE IRISH KING!

Thrice looked he to Heaven with thanks and with prayer—
Thrice looked to his borders with sentinel stare—
To the waves of Loch Neagh, the heights of Strabane;
And thrice on his allies, and thrice on his clan—
One clash on their bucklers!—one more!—they are still—
What means the deep pause on the crest of the hill?
Why gaze they above him?—a war-eagle's wing!
" 'Tis an omen!—Hurrah! for THE TRUE IRISH KING!"

God aid him!—God save him!—and smile on his reign—
The terror of England—the ally of Spain.
May his sword be triumphant o'er Sassenach arts!
Be his throne ever girt by strong hands, and true hearts!
May the course of his conquest run on till he see
The flag of Plantagenet sink in the sea!
May minstrels for ever his victories sing,
And saints make the bed of THE TRUE IRISH KING!

THE DESMOND.

BY THOMAS MOORE.

[Thomas, the heir of the Desmond family, had accidentally been so engaged
in the chase, that he was benighted near Tralee, and obliged to take shelter at
the Abbey of Feal, in the house of one of his dependants, called Mac Cormac.
Catherine, a beautiful daughter of his host, instantly inspired the earl with a
violent passion, which he could not subdue. He married her, and by this in-
ferior alliance alienated his followers, whose brutal pride regarded this indul-
gence of his love as an unpardonable degradation to his family. Thus perse-

ented, the unhappy young lord retired to Rouen, in Normandy, where he died in 1420, and was buried in a convent of Friars Preachers, at Paris—the King of England, it is said, attending his funeral.]

By the Feal's wave benighted, no star in the skies,
To thy door by Love blighted, I first saw those eyes,
Some voice whisper'd o'er me, as the threshold I crost,
There was ruin before me, if I lov'd, I was lost.

Love came, and brought sorrow too soon in his train;
Yet so sweet, that to-morrow 'twere welcome again.
Though misery's full measure my portion should be,
I would drain it with pleasure, if pour'd out by thee.

You, who call it dishonour to bow to this flame,
If you've eyes, look but on her, and blush while you blame.
Hath the pearl less whiteness because of its birth?
Hath the violet less brightness for growing near earth?

No—Man for his glory to ancestry flies;
But woman's bright story is told in her eyes.
While the Monarch but traces through mortals his line,
Beauty, born of the Graces, ranks next to Divine!

THE BRIDAL OF MALAHIDE.

BY GERALD GRIFFIN.

[Of the monuments most worthy of notice in the chapel of Malahide is an altar tomb surmounted with the effigy, in bold relief, of a female habited in the costume of the 14th century, and representing the Honourable Maude Plunket, wife of Sir Richard Talbot. She had been previously married to Mr. Hussey, son to the Baron of Galtrim, who was slain on the day of her nuptials, leaving her the singular celebrity of having been "A maid, wife, and widow, on the same day."—*Dalton's History of Drogheda.*]

The joy-bells are ringing in gay Malahide,
The fresh wind is singing along the sea-side;
The maids are assembling with garlands of flowers,
And the harpstrings are trembling in all the glad bowers.

Swell, swell the gay measure! roll trumpet and drum!
'Mid greetings of pleasure in splendour they come!
The chancel is ready, the portal stands wide
For the lord and the lady, the bridegroom and bride.

What years, ere the latter, of earthly delight
The future shall scatter o'er them in its flight!
What blissful caresses shall Fortune bestow,
Ere those dark-flowing tresses fall white as the snow!

Before the high altar young Maud stands array'd;
With accents that falter her promise is made—
From father and mother for ever to part,
For him and no other to treasure her heart.

The words are repeated, the bridal is done,
The rite is completed—the two, they are one;
The vow, it is spoken all pure from the heart,
That must not be broken till life shall depart.

Hark! 'mid the gay clangour that compass'd their car,
Loud accents in anger come mingling afar!
The foe's on the border, his weapons resound
Where the lines in disorder unguarded are found.

As wakes the good shepherd, the watchful and bold,
When the ounce or the leopard is seen in the fold,
So rises already the chief in his mail,
While the new-married lady looks fainting and pale.

"Son, husband, and brother, arise to the strife,
For the sister and mother, for children and wife!
O'er hill and o'er hollow, o'er mountain and plain,
Up, true men, and follow! let dastards remain!"

Farrah! to the battle! they form into line—
The shields, how they rattle! the spears, how they shine
Soon, soon shall the foeman his treachery rue—
On, burgher and yeoman, to die or to do!

The eve is declining in lone Malahide,
The maidens are twining gay wreaths for the bride;
She marks them unheeding—her heart is afar,
Where the clansmen are bleeding for her in the war

Hark! loud from the mountain 'tis Victory's cry!
O'er woodland and fountain it rings to the sky!
The foe has retreated! he flies to the shore;
The spoiler's defeated—the combat is o'er!

With foreheads unruffled the conquerors come—
But why have they muffled the lance and the drum?
What form do they carry aloft on his shield?
And where does he tarry, the lord of the field?

Ye saw him at morning how gallant and gay!
In bridal adorning the star of the day:
Now weep for the lover—his triumph is sped,
His hope it is over! the chieftain is dead!

But O for the maiden who mourns for that chief,
With heart overladen and rending with grief!
She sinks on the meadow in one morning-tide,
A wife and a widow, a maid and a bride!

Ye maidens attending, forbear to condole!
Your comfort is rending the depths of her soul.
True—true, 'twas a story for ages of pride;
He died in his glory—but, oh, he *has* died!

The war cloak she raises all mournfully now,—
And steadfastly gazes upon the cold brow.
That glance may for ever unaltered remain,
But the Bridegroom will never return it again.

The dead-bells are tolling in sad Malahide,
The death-wail is rolling along the sea-side;
The crowds, heavy-hearted, withdraw from the green,
For the sun has departed that brighten'd the scene!

Ev'n yet in that valley, though years have roll'd by,
When through the wild sally the sea-breezes sigh,
The peasant, with sorrow, beholds in the shade
The tomb where the morrow saw Hussey convey'd.

How scant was the warning, how briefly reveal'd,
Before on that morning death's chalice was fill'd!
The hero who drunk it there moulders in gloom,
And the form of Maud Plunket weeps over his tomb.

The stranger who wanders along the lone vale
Still sighs while he ponders on that heavy tale:
"Thus passes each pleasure that earth can supply—
Thus joy has its measure—we live but to die!"

LAMENT FOR EILEEN O'BRIN (OR O'BYRNE),

WHOM ROGER TYRREL, OF CASTLEKNOCK,[*] FORCIBLY CARRIED AWAY.

(FROM THE IRISH.)

SHE is gone—she is gone! where shall Dermod find rest,
From the grief of his spirit—the rage of his breast?
Since the child of his chieftain no more may he view,
As fair as the morning and pure as its dew.
She is gone! Now at eve, by the Liffey's gay tide,
Who shall lead the aged warrior and watch by his side?
Oh! hate to thee, Tyrrel, for black is thy sin,
Who hast nipp'd in its bloomhood the flow'r of O'Brin.

Young Armoric loved her, and once as she hung
O'er her harp, and the wrongs of green Erin she sung,
He vowed by her beauty, the strength of the land,
He would marshal for freedom, or forfeit her hand.
Poor Eileen was silent; still trembling she play'd,
While the tears in her dark eye her bosom betrayed:
Ah, madd'ning the thought! that the foes of her kin
And her country, should rob us of Eileen O'Brin.

As here in the depths of the dark tangled wood,
When the throstle, sweet bird, rears his promising brood,

---

[*] Castleknock (the castle hill), and from its green appearance sometimes called Glasteknue (the green hill), is a well-known locality, a short distance N.W. of the Phœnix Park—it was granted by Henry the Second to Hugh Tyrrell, together with a moiety of the river Liffey. In the early part of the 16th century the Tyrrell of Castleknock was also named Hugh, during whose absence with Skeffington in Ulster, his brother, Roger Tyrrell, seized Eileen O'Brin (or O'Byrne) near her father's residence, and carried her to that " stronghold of iniquity," where she died by her own hand. A part of a tower densely covered with ivy, and a wall some eight or ten feet in thickness, still stand to verify the site of the " stronghold." A treble line of circumvallation is nearly perfect where the writer of these lines, when freed from his task, has often gambolled in happy ignorance of the fate of Eileen O'Brin, and all the other "iniquities" of the place, *ferula* excepted.—O'Brin's residence was on a woody " rath " to the west of where Chapelizod now stands.—Turlogh O'Brin, one of the chiefs of Wicklow, had come down and fixed his residence in the Pale under the protection of the English government.—*Burton's Kilmainham* and *Dalton's Dublin.*

The spoiler, to mark them, is oft wont to come
Ere he, merciless, plunders their moss-covered home;
So Tyrrel, while ruin his heart had long plann'd,
Watch'd Eileen, to see all her beauties expand,
Then, fiend-like, that heart which he never could win
He tore from the homestead of Turlogh O'Brin.

How smooth was the Liffey—how blooming the lawn!
When she went forth as playful and light as a fawn;
Young Armoric greets her—no more could he say,
The ambush are on him—he falls—she's away!
We missed her at twilight, and swift in her track
Our kerns rush fiercely to conquer her back;
But in vain—she's secured the strong castle within,
And the accents of woe fill the home of O'Brin.

We trusted the stranger—we've dwelt on his plain,
Our safeguard his honour—'tis black with a stain;
Yet he recks not, but laughs in the face of our wail,
For they wrong, then insult us, those lords of the Pale.
Glendalough! O, thy deep sunny valleys for me,
And thy mountains that watch o'er the homes of the free,
Where chieftains, as brave as e'er battle did win,
Would bow to the beauty of Eileen O'Brin.

But we've lost her—up Cuallane,* thy warriors awake!
Glenduff, send thy bravest to fight for her sake—
O'Brin! see your name is dishonoured—repay
The tyrant whose minions forced Eileen away;
O'Tooles and O'Dempsies your weapons unsheath—
Come down, let your war-cry be "Vengeance or death,"
Nor cease ye one moment, when once ye begin,
Till the life-blood of Tyrrell atone to O'Brin.

                                                    MIRO.

* An ancient name of Wicklow.

THE SIEGE OF MAYNOOTH.

BY J. C. MANGAN.

*Crom, Crom-aboo!** The Geraldine rebels from proud Maynooth,
And with Him are leagued four hundred, the flower of Leinster's
youth.
Take heart once more, O, Erin! The great God gives thee hope;
And thro' the mists of Time and Woe thy true Life's portals ope!

Earl Thomas of the Silken Robes!—here doubtless burns thy soul?
Thou beamest here a Living Sun, round which thy planets roll?
O! would the Eternal Powers above that this were only so!
Then had our land, now scorned and banned, been saved a world
of woe!

No more!—no more!—it maddeneth so!—But rampart, keep, and
tower,
At least are still—long may they be—a part of Ireland's power!

---

* The war-cries of the principal Irish septs or families were the following:—
The FITZGERALDS', Earls of Kildare, *Crom-aboo! Crom for Ever!* or
Hurrah for Crom! This cry has been suggested by their stronghold of Cronm,
in the County Limerick. The FITZGERALDS', Knights of Kerry, *Farri-buidhe-
aboo! The Yellow Troop for Ever!* The O'NEILLS', Earls of Tyrone, *Lamh-
dearg-aboo! The Red Hand for Ever!* The Crest of the family is the Red
Hand. The O'BRIENS', *Lamh-laider-aboo! The Strong Hand for Ever!*
Crest, a dexter arm holding a naked sword. The M'CARTHYS' and FITZMAU-
RICES' was the same as the BRIENS'. But the M'CARTHYS', Earls of Des-
mond, took *Seun-ait-aboo! The Old Place for Ever!* The DE BURGOS' or
BOURKES', Earls of Clanricarde, *Gall-ruath-aboo! The Red Stranger for
Ever!* Richard De Burgo, the second Earl of Ulster, was red haired, and
hence he was called the Red Earl, and his descendants the Red Strangers.
The FITZPATRICKS' or MAC-GILLE-PATRICKS, *Geuir-laider-aboo! The
Sharp and Strong for Ever!* Crest, a Lion and a Dragon. The MAC-
SWEENEYS', *Battailah-aboo! The Noble Staff for Ever!*—in allusion to a part
of the family arms. The HEFFERNANS', *Ceart-na-Suas-aboo! The Right
from Above for Ever!* intimating that no justice was to be expected without
the aid of Heaven. The HUSSEYS,' Barons of Galtrim, *Cuir-direach-aboo!
Strict Justice for Ever!* These cries mean, Success to the cause of the family!
Hurrah for the family! or the family and cause for ever! Previously to at-
tacking an enemy it was customary among the Irish in former times to cry out,
Farrah! Farrah! which meant *Fall on! Fall on!* It is not unusual for the
Irish soldiers to-day to shout the cry of *Faug-a-ballagh! Clear the way!*
Napier, in his *History of the Peninsular War,* says,—" Nothing so startled the
French soldiery as the wild yell with which the Irish regiments sprung to the
charge."

But—who looks 'mid his warriors from the walls, as gleams a pearl
'Mid meaner stones?   'Tis Parez—foster-brother of the Earl.

Enough!—we shall hear more of him!   Amid the hundred shafts
Which campward towards the Saxon host the wind upbears and
    wafts,
One strikes the earth at Talbot's feet, with somewhat white—a
    scroll—
Impaled upon its barb—O! how exults the leader's soul!

He grasps it—reads—" Now, by St. George, the day at last is ours!
Before to-morrow's sun arise we hold yon haughty towers!
The craven traitor!—but, 'tis well!—he *shall* receive his hire,
And somewhat more to boot, God wot, than perchance he may
    desire !"

Alas! alas!—'tis all too true!   A thousand marks of gold
In Parez' hands, and Leinster's bands are basely bought and sold!
Earl Thomas loses fair Maynooth and a hundred of his clan—
But, worse! he loses half his hopes, for he loses trust in Man!

The morn is up: the gates lie wide; the foe pour in amain.
O! Parez, pride thee in thy plot, and hug thy golden chain!
There are cries of rage from battlements, and mellays beneath in
    court.
But Leinster's Brave, ere noon blaze high, shall mourn in donjon
    fort!

" Ho! Master Parez! thou?"   So spake in the hall the Saxon
    chief—
" How hast thou proved this tentless loon?   But, come, we will
    stanch thy grief!
Count these broad pieces over well!"   He flung a purse on the
    ground,
Which in wrathful silence Parez grasped, 'mid the gaze of all
    around.

" So!—right?"   " Yes, right, Sir John!   Enough!   I now depart
    for home!"
" *Home,* sayest thou, Master Parez?   Yes, and by my Halidome,
Mayest reach *that* sooner than thou dreamest.   But before we
    part,
I would a brief, blunt parle with thee.   Nay, man, why dost thou
    start?"

"A sudden spasm, Sir John."—"Ay, ay! those sudden spasms
    will shock,
As when, thou knowest, a traitor lays his head upon the block!"
"Sir John!"—"Hush, man, and answer me! Till then thou art
    in bale—
Till then mine enemy and thrall!" The fallen Chief turned pale.

"Say, have I kept good faith with thee?"—"Thou hast—good
    faith and true!"—
"I owe thee nought, then?"—"Nought, Sir John; the gold lies
    here to view."
"Thou art the Earl's own foster-brother?"—"Yes, and bosom-
    friend!"
"WHAT?"—"Nay, Sir John, I need those pieces, and ——"—
    "Come, there an end!"

"The Earl heaped favours on thee?"—"Never King heaped more
    on Lord!"
"He loved thee? honoured thee?"—"I was his heart, his arm,
    his sword!"
"He trusted thee?"—"Even as he trusted his own lofty soul!"
"AND THOU BETRAYEDST HIM? Base wretch! thou knowest
    the traitor's goal!

"Ho! Provost-Marshal, hither! Take this losel caitiff hence—
I mark, methinks, a scaffold under yonder stone defence.
Off with his head! By Heaven, the blood within me boils and
    seethes
To look on him! So vile a knave pollutes the air he breathes!"

'Twas but four days thereafter, of a stormy evening late,
When a horseman reared his charger in before the castle gate,
And gazing upwards, he descried by the light the pale moon shed,
Impaled upon an iron stake, a well-known gory head!

"So, Parez! thou hast met thy meed!" he said and turned away—
"And was it a foe that thus avenged me on that fatal day?
Now, by my troth, albeit I hate the Saxon and his land,
I could, methinks, for one brief moment press the Talbot's hand!"

PANEGYRIC OF BLACK THOMAS BUTLER,

EARL OF ORMOND, BETWEEN THE REIGNS OF HENRY VIII. AND
ELIZABETH.

(FROM THE IRISH.)

BY J. C. MANGAN.

STRIKE the loud lyre for Dark Thomas, the Roman,
　Roman in Faith, but Hibernian in Soul!
Him who, the idol of warrior and woman,
　Never feared peril, and never knew dole.
Who is the Man whom I name with such rapture?
　Who but our Ossory's and Ormond's Great Chief—
He whom his foes battled vainly to capture—
　He whom his friends loved beyond all belief!

Him the Great Henry* gave rubies and rings to—
　Him the King Edward for fleetness admired;
Even as his body, his spirit had wings, too,
　And defied efforts that Death alone tired.
Southwards this morn into deep Tipperary,
　Northward ere night on the shores of the Erne,
Always he showed his contempt of those chary
　Shifts of the Soul that no BUTLER could learn!

Oriel of Streams, and Duhallow of Harbours,
　Yielded him shorewards their silver and gold†—
All he despised!—as those greenwoods and arbours
　Girdling his towers from the ages of old.
Riches he loved not—his trust and his treasure
　Lay in the midst of his far-flaming sword;
War was his pastime and battle his pleasure,
　And his own glory the God he adored!

Thrice, and a fourth time, he humbled Clan Caura;‡
　His were the warriors that wasted Dunlo—
How his bands ravaged and fired Glen-na-Maura
　Who throughout green Inisfail doth not know?

* Henry VIII.　　　† Viz.:—Their white and yellow fish.
　　　‡ The MacCarthies.

Munster beheld his achievements of wonder,
   Connaught and Ulster his bands left bereaven ;
Wrath, like the wrath of his lightning and thunder,
   Cast into shade the high anger of Heaven !

Woe unto us ! This great man has departed !
   Quenched lies his lamp in the dust of the tomb !
He, the land's giant, the great Lion-hearted !
   He, even he, hath succumbed unto Doom !
Rest is his lot for whom Life yielded no rest—
   Darkling and lone is his dwelling to-night—
On the proud thousand-yeared Oak of the Forest
   Hath on a sudden come blastment and blight !

Toll ye his funeral dirge, ye dark waters,
   O'er which so often his fleets held their march !
Mourn for the Earl, thou Iërnà of Slaughters ;
   Build up his pillar and laurel his arch !
Thy foes were his, and with them he warred only—
   Weep for him, then, from the depths of thy core !
Weep for the Chief who hath left thee thus lonely—
   One like to him thou shalt never see more !

Oh ! for myself, my two eyes are as fountains—
   Flowing, o'erflowing, by night and by morn,
Gloomily roam I on Banba's * gray mountains,
   Feeling all wretched, all stricken and lorn.
Jewels and gold in profusion he gave me—
   Would they, not he, were now under the sod !
I shall soon follow him ; these cannot save me—
   Death is my guerdon, but, Glory to God !

Glory to God in the Highest—and Lowest !
   His are the Power and the Glory alone—
Pay Him, O, Man, the high homage thou owest,
   Whether thou rest on a footstool or throne !
Yet may His glory be mirrored in others—
   As in the waves the rich poop of the bark ;
And the mean man stands apart from his brothers,
   Who doth not trace it in Thomas the Dark !

---

* *Banba* (Banva) was one of the ancient names of Ireland.

SIR MORROGH'S RIDE TO THE DESMOND'S GATHERING.

1569.

BY G. H. SUPPLE.

[Gerald FitzGerald, the sixteenth and last Earl of Desmond, could bring into the field 600 knights of his own name, and 2,000 footmen, of his immediate following. His principality extended over the greater portion of four counties of Munster, and he kept sovereign state in his great castles of Mogeely and Adare. On the 2d November, 1569, he joined the national cause, and raised the standard of revolt against Elizabeth, and thence ensued, with varying success, a protracted and sanguinary war of years, until at last the Earl was overpowered, and South Munster reduced to a howling desert—without cow, sheep, goat, or living thing, save the wolf and the famine-stricken remnant of the broken clans. The Earl, hunted from fastness to fastness, was at length betrayed and murdered near Tralee, and his head carried to England, and spiked over the gates of London. This was the Chieftain, who, when, in the battle of Affane, taken prisoner, desperately wounded by the Ormond Butlers, on being tauntingly asked by his captors, bearing him away on a litter—"Where is the proud Earl of Desmond now?"—gave the haughty reply—"Where he ought to be—on the necks of the Butlers." Maurice, generally translated "Morrogh," was a favourite name among the Geraldines. The "Sir Shaune," alluded to below, was Sir John Desmond, who succeeded to the command of the national army on the death of the gallant Sir James Fitzmaurice Fitzgerald. Of terms in the ballad which may require explanation or translation, for the English reader, "Red Dog" is the literal rendering of *modhera ruadh*, the Gaelic for "Fox;" *Slua Shee* signifies the Fairy Host; *Betach*, the keeper of a house of hospitality. *Collough rue*, "Red Hag," was an Irish appellation of England's "Good Queen Bess." The *Phooka* was a demon-horse.]

THE Moon is bright on Muskerry—broad Muskerry's dark mountains;
Her beams are in its gliding streams and holy gushing fountains.
The gray wolf's howl is on the breeze—the red dog quits his cover;
But man is housed in hall and hut, all broad Muskerry over;
For on this night—All-hallows Night—no longer covert keeping,
By fairy moat, the *Slua Shee* o'er hill and dale are sweeping.
But who is he who spurs so late across the dreary highland?
And holds his path by bog and stream as boldly as on dry land.
A black plume in his *baradh** high, the red steel in his right hand,

---

* *Baradh*,—Head-dress.   *Seamus*,—James.   *Tomás*,—Thomas.   *Con Gurrue*,—Coarse, or pockmarked, Cornelius.   *Mavrone*,—My grief!

Less black, I trow, than his grim brow—than his fierce eye less
    bright, and
The moonbeams showed how, as he rode, like fiend's it glared
    and lightened.

On Ballyhowra side 'tis noon—on Awbeg's rushing water;
On many a crest of pride, and shield and spear of coming slaughter;
On many a long-locked, steel-clad knight, and mantled chieftain
    stern;
On galloglass, with axe in hand, and saffron-shirted kern.
Beneath the gray November sky, in the chill West wind curling,
O'er gathering bands and gleaming brands, a standard proud's
    unfurling—
The Desmond Flag! on whose broad fold is scroll'd heraldic story,
Of him, the knightly Geraldine, his clansmen's shield and glory:
" Earl Gerald of the open hand, and eye that scowls on danger—
The scourge of Sassenach, and stately *betach* of the stranger,
God and St. Coleman speed to-day the spears that round him
    ranged are!"

" The steed our chief so featly reins was bred by Guadalquiver,
And never bolder body-guard engirdled prince or riever.
Fourscore MacSheehies, stark and swart, in that grim troop
    assemble;
Now, soon at wild Clan-Gerralt's war-shout Youghal town will
    tremble;
And soon the *Collough-rue's* array by Cappoquin will scatter,
When yonder Imokilly axes casque and corslet shatter."
So sang the harper, as he strode the green hill-side before us,
While screamed from many a bagpipe round, a goodly battle-chorus.
He sang Earl Seamus, wise and great—Earl Tomàs, conquered
    never,
And him who tamed the Butler's pride by Nore's oak-shadow'd
    river,
And knightly deeds, the which, God wot, a bard might rhyme
    for ever.

The chief had turned his rein to greet some Condons tall and
    Roches,
When thro' the clan's dividing ranks a wounded knight approaches.
He lighted slowly down—good sooth! 'twas well his ride was
    ended,
And raised his black-plumed cap, and grasped the cordial hand
    extended.

"Brave kinsman, Morrogh! welcome to our hosting," quoth Earl
    Gerald—
"Thy tidings from Sir Shaune have fared but hardly with their
    herald:"
—"The Saxons barred my path ere I had crossed the Kerry border;
Con Gorrav fell, my henchman true! by false steel of marauder.
Dundarerk's lord purvey'd fresh steed, and escort thro' his passes,
And then the Barry More beset me with his galloglasses.
But here I am, and need thine ear far more than leech or masses.

"For, all along my devious path, by Araglin and Allo,
The *Banshee* of our clan danced ghastly in the moonbeam's halo—
Beside me, thro' the roaring flood, across the silent heather!
While shrilly rose her plaintive scream o'er wind and stream
    together.
'*Mavrone! mavrone!*' she wailed—'Mogeely's princely pride is
    ended!
Mavrone! mavrone! the Geraldine—the high and far-descended!
The oak is hewn—the flame is quenched; and who shall heir his
    glory?
Foes rend his spoil, and with his blood their bandog's maw is gory!'
My Chief! I pledge my knightly word, beside that apparition,
My charger sprang like *Phooka* steed, on Hell's own wrathful
    mission.
St. Bride befriend me! 'twas a ride might craze both brain and
    vision."

The Desmond's brow grew black as night—then red as stormy
    morning,
And curled his lip, and shook his long white locks in ireful
    scorning:—
"But that thy sword drank, at Affane, of Ormond blood so deeply,
I'd hold, Sir Morrogh! kinsman mine! thy manhood somewhat
    cheaply.
There rides the fierce O'Sullivan, from tempest-lash'd Ivèra!
There proud Clan Caura, and the sons of savage Iveleara!
Here wheel my haughty kindred, too, with plume and banner
    streaming!
'Twere well to greet such men to-day, with tale of brain-sick
    dreaming!
Less meet for ear of helmèd knight, than friar cowled and shaven.
If fall we must, Clan-London shall not vaunt us false or craven:
Their bandogs thirst, forsooth!—so do *our* Gaelic wolf and raven."

THE RAID OF FITZMAURICE.*

BY G. H. SUPPLE.

" St. Brigid, see yon gallant show along the green plain wending
Yon goodly troop of Habilars,† o'er rough-maned war-steeds
   bending—
Their glaives and lances flashing in the glorious noon-tide sun,
Their arms and laughter ringing blithe—oh, heavens! that I were
   one.
A *gorsoon-bo*, my chieftain's steers, I tend all idly here,
And save when fierce Clan-Brien came, I never grasped a spear.
And now careering nearer, are plainer given to view,
Full many a scar on sun-browned cheek, beneath the *baradh* blue,
And flashing eye and *crommeal* grim, and *coolun* turned to gray,
And hands on steel and rein, that speak a veteran array—
And out before them, prancing on a charger sleek and fair,
Rides one with eagle plume and eye, and noble knightly air.
But come they here in friendship, or bent for raid or fray—
No band so scant durst harry bold Clan-William's lands by day."

They halt—the fierce Fitzmaurice to the Shannon turns his eye,
To the pastures broad and castle there, to Castleconnell‡ high.
" Tho' bards invoke and priests beseech, and bleeding patriots call,
The lord of yon proud castle lounges listless in his hall—
His sword is in its scabbard and his charger in his stall ;
We've spurred a weary way, my men, since dawned the morning's
   light—
What say you if we sup on this De Burgo's beeves to-night?"

* Sir James Fitzmaurice Fitzgerald, a kinsman of the Earl of Desmond, was
the life and soul of the national cause against Elizabeth. He fell, as is related
above, before his heroic exertions came to a head, and the English Queen rewarded this Sir William De Burgo for ridding her of so formidable an enemy,
and consoled him for the loss of his son, by creating him Baron of Castleconnell, with a pension of 100 marks a-year from her exchequer—whereat, says
the chronicler, " he took so sudden joy that he swoned and seemed to be quite
dead "—an appreciation of English rewards which will not appear wonderful in
this generation.
  † The Irish cavalry were called Habilars, and Gallowglasses, the heavy
armed foot. *Gorsoon-bo*,—literally a Cow-boy. *Baradh*,—the conical cap,
or head dress. *Crommeal*,—the moustache. *Coolun*,—the flowing hair
Shanet aboo,—the war-cry of the Desmond Geraldines. *Gall ruadh aboo*,—
(the cause of the red stranger) the war-cry of the Burkes. *Creaght*,—a drove
of cattle.
  ‡ Castleconnell, within six miles of Limerick city.

So spake the bold Fitzmaurice—and his warriors with a shout
Broke forth and drove their *creaght* from the meads in joyous rout;
O'er the plain and thro' the leafy groves, and up the hill-side then,
Westward speed the low of oxen, and the urging shouts of men.

But see Clanwilliam, kith and kin, is mustering behind—
Ho!—bold raiders look and leave your prey, and ride ye like the
  wind;
Or as your knightly chief commands, array for combat now—
Brace tight each girth, and loose the axe that gleams at saddle-bow.
Now, as they come, Fitzmaurice spurs alone to meet their train,
And before his lordly glance and mien, their shouts of vengeance
  wane,
Then courteously he bendeth down, all to his charger's mane—
" Ho, Sir Chief of stout Clanwilliam, list, ere we join in fray,
For methinks despite my raid we may be brethren to-day—
Take back your kine, and let your strokes crush Saxon helm and
  mail,
For the sake of bleeding Eiré, and the black wrongs of the Gael,
Take back your kine—in sooth, Sir Knight, scant courtesy have I
When hungry men are round me, and when food is tempting nigh.

Fame says too, stout De Burgo, that you have sheathed your brand.
When this death-strife with the Sassenagh needs every heart and
  hand.
Ah!—felt ye but as I have felt,"—and here he dropped his rein,
And crossed his arms upon his breast, in dark and musing strain,
And drooped that haughty brow, deep bronzed by scorching
  foreign skies,
While an almost woman's wistfulness, grew sadly in his eyes.
" I strove in beauteous Italy, I strove in stately Spain,
And now I strive amongst mine own—are all my strivings vain?
The pleasures of their kings and courts, my wearied soul abhorr'd—
They'd feast me in their palace-halls, but would not aid my sword;
And he could give, the haughty prince, beside the Ebro's wave,
Small help to such ambassador, the Saxons' begging slave—
In our own hands this cause doth rest, and we are supine still,
And I'm forsaken, foiled, deceived, while England works her will.

This morning left I Holycross, a long and bootless ride—
The Leinster chiefs can gloze and whine, but durst not yet decide—
But come, De Burgo, here's my hand, and pledge your knightly
  word
To back this cause of native land, with head and heart and sword."

I

De Burgo silence held a space, then stroked his long grey hairs,
And said, "Sir Geraldine, a rash and fruitless strife but fares
Too harshly with its partisans; thou know'st I've suffered much
Betimes from Saxon war—I may not risk another such.
My counsel is yon flag to furl, and meeter time to bide;
And then perchance if"——"Hold!" Fitzmaurice fiercely cried—
"No, by my father's mouldering bones and ancient name I swear,
I'll keep the green flag flying, tho' they beard me in my lair;
I'll flaunt that flag o'er field and tower, thro' Eirè wide displayed,
Despite each dastard's treason and King Philip's niggard aid.

And God's red lightnings blast the slave that shuns such holy
        fray!
Accursed be the craven hand that lacks a brand to-day—
To-day's the time—none other—ha! thou wilt not then decide?
Well, hear, Sir Waverer, yonder herd must leave your Shannon
        side,
And more, tho' thrice my number stand so grimly round you now,
My true men's strokes ring somewhat sharp on traitors' crests, I
        trow."
He wheeled his charger, and regained his fierce, impatient band,
And leads them on with cheering shout and leader's guiding hand;
They burst upon Clan-William, and the foremost squadrons reel
Before their furious onset and wide-sweeping veteran steel.
"Shanet aboo!"—"Gall ruadh aboo!" shouts each opposing rank;
But soon some chosen gallowglass—men drawn from either flank,
And led by young De Burgo, on the rearmost forayers fell,
And their battle-axes quickly 'mongst the fewer horsemen tell.

Fitzmaurice turns his bloody sword, like a meteor in the fight,
Rearwards, where danger loometh, dealing death-strokes left and
        right;
Two Burkes, in steel from head to heel, their life-blood hath he
        spilt,
And a gallowglass in mail hath pierced up to his falchion's hilt;
He seeks the young De Burgo, Clanwilliam's stalwart pride.
And soon to meet right furiously the knightly foemen ride—
All reeling from their saddles, lifeless, down the warriors fall,
While aghast and spell-bound, breathless group, their grief-struck
        followers all.
The stillness of the grave usurps the fury of the strife,
As if all strength and enmity passed with each chieftain's life;
Then slowly raising each grim corpse upon its bloody shield,
They homeward wend, nor heed the herd that cost so dear a field.

There's man's grief and maid's lamenting, and the woe is Desmond
    wide
'Mongst the princes in Adare and in Mogeely's halls of pride—
The Caoiner's wail swells o'er each hill from many a chieftain's
    tower;
₊or of all Clan-Gerralt, stark and dead's the proudest knightli₊d
    flower;
"Seamus-eusal* of the brow of thought, and helmet-cleaving brand –
The scourge of the false Sassenach, and hope of lost Ireland.

THE RATH OF MULLAGHMAST.

BY R. D. WILLIAMS.

[In the year 1577 the English published a proclamation inviting the well-
affected Irish to an interview on the Rathmore at Mullaghmast, in the King'
County. A safe-conduct was given to those who accepted the invitation to return as they came,—for good and not evil was intended towards them. Some
hundreds of the most peaceable and well-affected came, and they were hardly
assembled when they found themselves surrounded by three or four lines of
English horse and foot completely accoutred, by whom they were treacherously
attacked and cut to pieces; not a single man escaped. Speaking of this massacre, Captain Lee in his Memorial to Queen Elizabeth says:—" They have
drawn unto them by protection, three or four hundred of these country people,
under colour to do your Majesty service, and brought them to a place of meeting, where your garrison soldiers were appointed to be, who have there met
dishonourably put them all to the sword; and this hath been *by the consent and
practice of the Lord Deputy for the time being.*"—*Desiderata Curiosa Hiber
nica*, vol. i. p. 91.]

O'ER the Rath of Mullaghmast,
On the solemn midnight blast,
What bleeding spectres past,
    With their gash'd breasts bare?
Hast thou heard the fitful wail
That o'erloads the sullen gale,
When the waning moon shines pale
    O'er the curs'd ground there?

Hark! hollow moans arise
Thro' the black tempestuous skies,
And curses, strife, and cries,
    From the lone Rath swell;

* *Seamus-eusal*,—means the cavalier, or nobleman.

For bloody Sydney there,
Nightly fills the lurid air
With the unholy pomp and glare
    Of the foul, deep hell.

He scorches up the gale,
With his knights, in fiery mail;
And the banners of the Pale
    O'er the red ranks rest.
But a wan and gory band
All apart and silent stand,
And they point th' accusing hand
    At that hell-hound's crest!

Red streamlets, trickling slow,
O'er their clotted *cuilins* flow,
And still and awful woe,
    On each pale brow weeps—
Rich bowls bestrew the ground,
And broken harps around,
Whose once enchanting sound
    In the bard's blood sleeps.

False Sydney! knighthood's stain,
The trusting brave in vain—
Thy guests—ride o'er the plain
    To thy dark cow'rd snare.
Flow'r of Offaly and Leix,
They have come thy board to grace—
Fools! to meet a faithless race
    Save with true swords bare.

While cup and song abound,
The triple lines surround
The closed and guarded mound,
    In the night's dark noon.
Alas! too brave O'More,
Ere the revelry was o'er
They have spill'd thy young heart's gore,
    Snatch'd from love too soon!

At the feast, unarmed all,
Priest, bard, and chieftain fall
In the treacherous Saxon's hall,
    O'er the bright wine-bowl;

And now nightly round the board,
With unsheath'd and reeking sword,
Strides the cruel felon lord
    Of the blood-stain'd soul.

Since that hour the clouds that pass'd
O'er the Rath of Mullaghmast,
One tear have never cast
    On the gore-dyed sod;
For the shower of crimson rain,
That o'erflowed that fatal plain,
Cries aloud, and not in vain,
    To the most high God.

Tho' the Saxon snake unfold
At thy feet his scales of gold,
And vow thee love untold,
    Trust him not, Green Land!
Touch not with gloveless clasp
A coil'd and deadly asp,
But with strong and guarded grasp
    In your steel-clad hand!

TYRRELL'S PASS.

1597.

BY THE AUTHOR OF "THE MONKS OF KILCREA."

[In the valuable notes to the *Annals of the Four Masters*, the following account of the battle of Tyrrell's-pass is given at page 621 :—" The Captain Tyrrell mentioned in the Annals was Richard Tyrrell, a gentleman of the Anglo-Norman family of the Tyrrells, Lords of Fertullagh, in Westmeath. He was one of the most valiant and celebrated commanders of the Irish in the war against Elizabeth, and during a period of twelve years had many conflicts with the English forces in various parts of Ireland; he was particularly famous for bold and hazardous exploits, and rapid expeditions. Copious accounts of him are given by Fynes Morrison, MacGeoghegan, and others. After the reduction of Ireland he retired to Spain. The battle of Tyrrell's-pass is described by MacGeoghegan, and mentioned by Leland, and other historians. It was fought in the summer of 1597, at a place afterwards called Tyrrell's-pass, now the name of a town in the Barony of Fertullagh, in Westmeath. When Hugh O'Neill, Earl of Tyrone, heard that the English forces were preparing to advance into Ulster, under the Lord Deputy Borrough, he detached Captain Tyr-

rell at the head of 400 chosen men, to act in Meath, and Leinster, and by thus
engaging some of the English forces, to cause a diversion, and prevent their
joining the Lord Deputy, or co-operate with Sir Conyers Clifford. The Anglo-
Irish of Meath, to the number of 1,000 men, assembled under the banner of
Barnwell, Baron of Trimleston, intending to proceed and join the Lord Deputy.
Tyrrell was encamped with his small force in Fertullagh, and was joined by
young O'Conor Faily of the King's County. The Baron of Trimleston, having heard where Tyrrell was posted, formed the project of taking him by surprise, and for that purpose despatched his son at the head of the assembled
troops. Tyrrell having received information of their advance, immediately put
himself in a posture of defence, and making a feint of flying before them as
they advanced, drew them into a defile covered with trees, which place has since
been called Tyrrell's-pass, and having detached half of his men, under the command of O'Conor, they were posted in ambush, in a hollow adjoining the road.
When the English were passing, O'Conor and his men sallied out from their
ambuscade, and with their drums and fifes played Tyrrell's march, which was
the signal agreed upon for the attack. Tyrrell then rushed out on them in
front, and the English being thus hemmed in on both sides, were cut to pieces,
the carnage being so great that out of their entire force only one soldier escaped,
and, having fled through a marsh, carried the news to Mullingar. O'Conor
displayed amazing valour, and being a man of great strength and activity,
hewed down many of their men with his own hand; while the heroic Tyrrell,
at the head of his men, repeatedly rushed into the thick of the battle. Young
Barnwell being taken prisoner, his life was spared, but he was delivered to
O'Neill. A curious circumstance is mentioned by MacGeoghegan, that from
the heat and excessive action of the sword-arm the hand of O'Conor became so
swelled that it could not be extricated from the guard of his sabre until the
handle was cut through with a file."]

THE Baron bold of Trimbleston hath gone in proud array,
To drive afar from fair Westmeath the Irish kerns away,
And there is mounting brisk of steeds and donning shirts of mail,
And spurring hard to Mullingar 'mong Riders of the Pale.

For, flocking round his banner there, from east to west there came,
Full many knights and gentlemen of English blood and name,
All prompt to hate the Irish race, all spoilers of the land,
And mustered soon a thousand spears that Baron in his band.

For trooping in rode Nettervilles and D'Altons not a few,
And thick as reeds pranced Nugent's spears, a fierce and godless
    crew;
And Nagle's pennon flutters fair, and, pricking o'er the plain,
Dashed Tuite of Sonna's mail-clad men, and Dillon's from Glen-
    Shane.

A goodly feast the Baron gave in Nagle's ancient hall,
And to his board he summons there his chiefs and captains all;

And round the red wine circles fast, with noisy boast and brag
How they would hunt the Irish kerns like any Cratloe stag.

But 'mid their glee a horseman spurr'd all breathless to the gate,
And from the warder there he crav'd to see Lord Barnwell
    straight;
And when he stept the castle hall, then cried the Baron, 'Ho!
You are De Petit's body-squire, why stops your master so?"

"Sir Piers De Petit ne'er held back," that wounded man replied,
" When friend or foeman called him on, or there was need to ride;
But vainly now you lack him here, for, on the bloody sod,
The noble knight lies stark and stiff—his soul is with his God.

" For yesterday, in passing through Fertullah's wooded glen,
Fierce Tyrrell met my master's band, and slew the good knight
    then;
And, wounded sore with axe and *skian*, I barely 'scaped with life.
To bear to you the dismal news, and warn you of the strife.

" MacGeoghegan's flag is on the hills! O'Reilly's up at Fore!
And all the chiefs have flown to arms, from Allen to Donore,
And as I rode by Granard's moat, right plainly might I see
O'Ferall's clans were sweeping down from distant Annalee."

Then started up young Barnwell there, all hot with Spanish wine—
" Revenge," he cries, " for Petit's death, and be that labour mine;
For, by the blessed rood I swear, when I Wat Tyrrell see,
I'll hunt to death the rebel bold, and hang him on a tree!"

Then rose a shout throughout the hall, that made the rafters ring,
And stirr'd o'erhead the banners there, like aspen leaves in spring;
And vows were made, and wine-cups quaft, with proud and bitter
    scorn,
To hunt to death Fertullah's clans upon the coming morn.

These tidings unto Tyrrell came, upon that selfsame day,
Where, camped amid the hazel boughs, he at Lough Ennel lay.
" And they will hunt us so," he cried—" why, let them if they
    will;
But first we'll teach them greenwood craft, to catch us, ere they
    kill."

And hot next morn the horsemen came, Young Barnwell at their
    head;
But when they reached the calm lake banks, behold! their prey
    was fled!
And loud they cursed, as wheeling round they left that tranquil
    shore,
And sought the wood of Garraclune, and searched it o'er and o'er.

And down the slopes, and o'er the fields, and up the steeps they
    strain,
And through Moylanna's trackless bog, where many steeds remain,
Till wearied all, at set of sun, they halt in sorry plight.
And on the heath, beside his steed, each horseman passed the night.

Next morn, while yet the white mists lay, all brooding on the hill,
Bold Tyrrell to his comrade spake, a friend in every ill—
"O'Conor, take ye ten score men, and speed ye to the dell,
Where winds the path to Kinnegad—you know that *togher* well.

"And couch ye close amid the heath, and blades of waving fern,
So glint of steel, or glimpse of man, no Saxon may discern,
Until ye hear my bugle blown, and up O'Conor, then,
And bid the drums strike Tyrrell's march, and charge ye with
    your men."

"Now by his soul who sleeps at Cong," O'Conor proud replied,
"It grieves me sore, before those dogs, to have my head to hide;
But lest, perchance, in scorn they might go brag it thro' the Pale,
I'll do my best that few shall live to carry round the tale."

The mist roll'd off, and "Gallants up!" young Barnwell loudly
    cries,
"By Bective's shrine, from off the hill, the rebel traitor flies;
Now mount ye all, fair gentlemen—lay bridle loose on mane,
And spur your steeds with rowels sharp—we'll catch him on the
    plain."

Then bounded to their saddles quick a thousand eager men,
And on they rushed in hot pursuit to Darra's wooded glen.
But gallants bold, tho' fair ye ride, here slacken speed ye may—
The chase is o'er!—the hunt is up!—the quarry stands at bay!

For, halted on a gentle slope, bold Tyrrell placed his band,
And proudly stept he to the front, his banner in his hand,

And plung'd it deep within the earth, all plainly in their view,
And waved aloft his trusty sword, and loud his bugle blew.

Saint Colman!' twas a fearful sight, while drum and trumpet
    played,
To see the bound from out the brake that fierce O'Conor made,
As waving high his sword in air he smote the flaunting crest
Of proud Sir Hugh De Geneville,* and clove him to the chest!

"On, comrades, on!" young Barnwell cries, "and spur ye to the
    plain,
Where we may best our lances use!"   That counsel is in vain,
For down swept Tyrrell's gallant band, with shout and wild halloo,
And a hundred steeds are masterless since first his bugle blew!

From front to flank the Irish charge in battle order all,
While pent like sheep in shepherd's fold the Saxon riders fall;
Their lances long are little use, their numbers block the way,
And mad with pain their plunging steeds add terror to the fray!

And of the haughty host that rode that morning through the dell,
But one has 'scaped with life and limb his comrades' fate to tell;
The rest all in their harness died, amid the thickets there,
Yet fighting to the latest gasp, like foxes in a snare!

The Baron bold of Trimbleston has fled in sore dismay,
Like beaten hound at dead of night from Mullingar away,
While wild from Boyne to Brusna's banks there spreads a voice
    of wail,
Mavrone! the sky that night was red with burnings in the Pale!

And late next day to Dublin town the dismal tidings came,
And Kevin's-Port and Watergate are lit with beacons twain,
And scouts spur out, and on the walls there stands a fearful crowd,
While high o'er all Saint Mary's bell tolls out alarums loud!

But far away beyond the Pale, from Dunluce to Dunboy,
From every Irish hall and rath there bursts a shout of joy,
As eager Asklas hurry past o'er mountain, moor, and glen,
And tell in each the battle won by Tyrrell and his men.

* The De Genevilles succeeded the De Lacys as Lords of Meath.

Bold Walter sleeps in Spanish earth; long years have passed away —
Yet Tyrrell's-pass is called that spot, ay, to this very day,
And still is told as marvel strange, how from his swollen hand,
When ceased the fight the blacksmith filed O'Conor's trusty brand!

THE PASS OF PLUMES.

1599.

BY R. D. WILLIAMS.

[To the pompous preparations of the Earl of Essex, the results of his government in Ireland formed a most lamentable sequel. Rarely, if ever, indeed, had
there been witnessed, in any military expedition, a more wretched contrast between the promises and performances of its leader; or a wider departure in the
field from the plans settled in the council. Provided with an army the largest
that Ireland had ever witnessed on her shores, consisting of 20,000 foot and
2,000 horse, his obvious policy, and at first his purpose, was to march directly
against Tyrone, and grapple at once with the strength of the rebellion in its
great source and centre, the north. Instead of pursuing this course of policy,
at once the boldest and most safe, he squandered both time and reputation on
a march of parade into Munster, and the sole result of his mighty enterprise
was the reduction of two castles and the feigned submission of three native
chiefs. When passing through Leinster, in his way back to Dublin, he was
much harassed by the O'Moores, who made an attack upon his rear-guard, in
which many of his men and several of his officers were killed; and among the
few traditional records we have of his visit, it is told that, from the quantity
of plumes of feathers of which his soldiers were despoiled, the place of action
long continued to be called the Pass of Plumes.—"Thus," says Moryson, in
describing the departure of Essex from London, "at the head of so strong an
army as did ominate nothing but victory and triumphs, yet with a sunshine
thunder happening (as Camden notes for an ominous ill token) this lord took
his journey."—*Moore's Ireland*, vol. iv. p. 112.]

"LOOK out," said O'Moore to his clansmen, "afar—
Is yon white cloud the herald of tempest or war?
Hark! know you the roll of the foreigners' drums?
By Heaven! Lord Essex in panoply comes,
With corslet, and helmet, and gay bannerol,
And the shields of the nobles with blazon and scroll;
And, as snow on the larch in December appears,
What a winter of plumes on that forest of spears!
To the clangour of trumpets and waving of flags
The clattering cavalry prance o'er the crags;
And their plumes—By St. Kyran! false Saxon, ere night,
You shall wish these fine feathers were wings for your flight.

Shall we leave all the blood and the gold of the Pale
To be shed at Armagh and be won by O'Neill?
Shall we yield to O'Ruark, to M'Guire, and O'Donnell,
Brave chieftains of Breffny, Fermanah,—Tyrconnell;
Yon helmets, that 'Erick'* thrice over would pay
For the Sassenach heads they'll protect not to-day?
No! By red Mullaghmast, fiery clansmen of Leix,
Avenge your sires' blood on their murderers' race.
Now, sept of O'Moore, fearless sons of the heather,†
Fling your scabbards away, and strike home and together!

> Then loudly the clang of commingled blows,
>   Upswell'd from the sounding fields,
> And the joy of a hundred trumps arose,
>   And the clash of a thousand shields
> And the long plumes danc'd, and the falchions rung,
>   And flash'd the whirl'd spear,
> And the furious barb through the wild war sprung,
>   And trembled the earth with fear;
> The fatal bolts exulting fled,
>   And hiss'd as they leap'd away;
> And the tortur'd steed on the red grass bled,
>   Or died with a piercing neigh.

I see their weapons crimson'd —I hear the mingled cries
Of rage and pain and triumph, as they thunder to the skies.
The Coolun'd kern rushes upon armour, knight, and mace,
And bone and brass are broken in his terrible embrace!
The coursers roll and struggle; and the riders, girt in steel,
From their saddles, crush'd and cloven, to the purple heather reel,
And shatter'd there, and trampled by the charger's iron hoof,
The seething brain is bursting thro' the crashing helmet's roof.
Joy! Heaven strikes for Freedom! and Elizabeth's array,
With her paramour to lead 'em, are sore beset to-day.

Their heraldry and plumery, their coronets and mail,
Are trampled on the battle field, or scatter'd on the gale!
As the cavalry of ocean, the living billows bound,
When lightnings leap above them, and thunders clang around,
And tempest-crested dazzlingly, caparison'd in spray,
They crush the black and broken rocks, with all their roots away

* Fine for manslaughter in the Irish code.
† The O'Moores wore a sprig of heather in their helmets.

So charg'd the stormy chivalry of Erin in her ire—
Their shock the roll of ocean, their swords electric fire—
They rose like banded billows that when wintry tempests blow,
The trembling shore, with stunning roar and dreadful wreck o'er-
flow,

And where they burst tremendously, upon the bloody groun',
Both horse and man, from rere to van, like shiver'd barques, went
down.
Leave your costly Milan hauberks, haughty nobles of the Pale,
And your snowy ostrich feathers as a tribute to the Gael.
Fling away gilt spur and trinket, in your hurry, knight and squire,
They will make our virgins ornaments or decorate the lyre.
Ho! Essex! how your vestal Queen will storm when she hears
The "Mere Irish" chased her minion and his twenty thousand
spears.

Go! tell the royal virgin that O'Moore, M'Hugh, O'Neill,
Will smite the faithless stranger while there's steel in Innisfail.
The blood you shed shall only serve more deep revenge to nurse,
And our hatred be as lasting as the tyranny we curse:
From age to age consuming, it shall blaze a quenchless fire,
And the son shall thirst and burn still more fiercely than his sire.
By our sorrows, songs, and battles—by our cromleachs, raths,
and tow'rs—
By sword and chain, by all our slain—between your race and ours
Be naked glaives and yawning graves, and ceaseless tears and gore,
Till battle's flood wash out in blood your footsteps from the shore!

———

THE CAPTURE OF RED HUGH O'DONNELL.

[The kidnapping of Red Hugh O'Donnell is perhaps better known than
any of the other family histories of Ireland. Red Hugh was born about
1571, and was fostered by his relative, the O'Doherty of Innishowen. From
youth upwards, the beauty of his person, his courage, and literary acquirements, were the subject of praise and admiration throughout Ireland. Jealousy
and fear of those qualities so early developed in the presumptive heir of the
Chief of Tyrconnell, alarmed Sir John Perrot, then Lord Justice of Ireland.
Under the sanction of Queen Elizabeth he determined upon getting Hugh into
his hands,—although at this very time Hugh's father was an ally of the English, against the O'Neill, Prince of Tirowen. To gain possession of young
Hugh, a ship was fitted up in the autumn of 1587, laden with some
Spanish wines and other liquors; she sailed for Lough Swilly, where she soon
cast anchor. Under the guise of a Spanish merchantman, the Captain de-

coyed young O'Donnell and a few of his friends on board to purchase some wines. Amongst these were Henry and Art, the sons of Con O'Neill. No sooner were they safely in the cabin, where they were invited to taste the wines, than the hatches were closed,—they were then heavily ironed, and brought up to Dublin Castle as prisoners. After more than three years' confinement they escaped one stormy winter's night. In making their way towards the Wicklow mountains, the blinding violence of a snow storm impeded their progress, until exhausted by fatigue and worn out by the toilsome journey, young Art O'Neill laid down and died in his bed of snow. O'Donnell and Henry O'Neill were found by the O'Byrnes in Glenmalure beside their dead companion, so benumbed and frostbitten that they were unable to walk. Having been treated hospitably by the head of the clan, they pursued their way through Meath, Drogheda, Dundalk, and Dungannon, to the castle of Hugh O'Neill, Earl of Tyrone, who kindly but privately, for fear of the vengeance of the English government, entertained them for four nights and days. On the arrival of Red Hugh in his father's territory, he was elected Chief, and upon the request of his father, who was advanced in years, he was solemnly inaugurated and proclaimed "The O'Donnell" on 3d May 1592. He entered at once into a solemn league with the Earl of Tyrone to extirpate the English root and branch. After the defeat of the Spaniards at Kinsale under Don Juan in 1602, he went to Spain to urge the immediate fulfilment of the King's promise to send another army to aid the Irish. In travelling from Corunna to have a personal interview with the King who was at Valladolid, he reached only as far as Simanca where he died of a broken heart on the 21st September 1602. Thus perished a great captain, the flower of Irish chivalry, and the most dangerous and uncompromising foe of English rule in Ireland.]

ON the calm ocean's purple breast the kindling sunbeams sleep,
And scarce a ripple mars the picture mirrored on the deep;
The iron cliffs of Donegal like bristling armies stand,
With nature's rough-hewn battlements, to sentinel the land.

No hand hath carved those giant rocks, the tempest and the wave
Shaped, in their maddening revelry, the column, arch, and cave;
Where foot of man hath never trod, the eagle's famished brood
Rush from their eyrie in the cleft, above the threatening flood.

Upon the horizon's distant verge, a stately ship appears,
Right onward to the welcome shore, her course she proudly steers,
Her white sails glow like silken sheets, her spars like shafts of
    gold,
Her freight—a store of Spanish wine—deep hidden in the hold.

Beneath the noon-day radiance, her cables brightly gleam,
In the dim lessening distance, like silver cords they seem—
She cleaves the waters gallantly, through the white path of spray,—
Some mermaid's hand hath surely strewn, with pearls her glitter-
    ing way.

'Mid the cold waters struggling, the fleet ship hastens on;
The stranded rocks and shoals are passed, the land is safely won;
Beneath O'Donnell's castle towers in wild Tirconnell's bay,
The Saxons furl the sails, and quick the ponderous anchor weigh.

The chieftain, from the ramparts, hails the good ship's trusty band,
And, with an Irish greeting, bids them welcome to the land :
" Oh, tarry here, the night comes on, no farther shall ye roam,
For, ever in Tirconnell's halls, the stranger finds a home!"

They may not stay—the wind blows fair, and, ere the morrow rise,
Their bark must spread her swelling sails 'neath colder, darker
    skies ;
Mayhap the Prince would graciously their simple banquet share,
For royalty hath oftentimes partook their frugal fare.

No need to press the warm appeal, the generous prince, Red Hugh,
Unguarded, quits the fortress walls, and stands amid the crew:
" Down with the hatches, set the sails, we've won the wished-for
    prize,
Above the rebel's prison cell to-morrow's sun shall rise."

Untasted foams the Spanish wine—the board is spread in vain,
The hand that waved a welcome forth is shackled by a chain.
Yet faster, faster through the deep, the vessel glideth on ;
Tirconnell's towers, like phantoms fade, the last faint trace is gone.

Oh ! trusting prince, betrayed and lost, through Saxon treachery,
Let those who mourn thy fate take heed, for they may fall like thee;
The flowers they tender to our grasp, but veil the hidden thorn,
And 'neath the smiling mask of love, the frown of hatred's worn.

FINOLA.

THE O'NEILL.

[Hugh O'Neill, representative and chief of the powerful family of that name,
in the year 1587, accepted of a patent from Queen Elizabeth, creating him Earl
of Tir-owen ; in the eyes of his kinsmen and followers this acceptance was an
act of submission, and the title itself a degradation; The O'Neill being a royal
name, and conferring on its holder kingly authority. The mark of favour bestowed by Elizabeth, was held by the Earl until 1595, in the spring of which
year he suddenly called an assembly of the chiefs of his country, formally renounced the act of submission, and resumed the original distinguishing appellation of his forefathers—The O'Neill. The cause of this alteration in his con-

duct has been variously accounted for; but an old tradition, which is still current in the country where he flourished, attributes it wholly to the interference
of a supernatural agent. After relating in a simple style what is stated above,
it tells that for three nights previous to the calling of the assembly, the Banshee, or guardian spirit of the family, was heard in his castle of Dungannon,
upbraiding him with his submission, conjuring him to throw off the odious epi-
thet with which his enemies had branded him, rousing him to a sense of his
danger by describing the sufferings of some of the neighbouring chiefs, charging
him to arm, and promising him assistance.]

"CAN ought of glory or renown,
     To thee from Saxon titles spring?
Thy name a kingdom and a crown,
     Tir-owen's chieftain, Ulster's king!"

These were the sounds that on the ear
     Of Tir-owen's startled Earl arose,
That blanch'd his alter'd cheek with fear,
     And from his pillow chas'd repose.

In vain was closed his weary eye,
     In vain his prayer for peaceful sleep,
Still from a viewless spirit nigh,
     Broke forth in accents loud and deep.

"Can ought of glory or renown,
     To thee from Saxon titles spring?
Thy name a kingdom and a crown,
     Tir-owen's chieftain, Ulster's king!

"Oft did thy eager youthful ear,
     Bend to the tale of Thomond's shame,*
And in thy pride of blood didst swear
     To hold with life thy glorious name!

"Yet thou didst leave thy native land,
     For honours on a foreign shore,
And for submission's purchas'd brand,
     Barter'd the name thy fathers bore!

---

* In the reign of Henry the Eighth, the palace of Cluan-road, near Ennis,
in the county of Clare, the magnificent mansion of the chief of the O'Briens,
was burned to the ground by those of his own blood, in revenge for his having
accepted of the comparatively degrading title of Earl of Thomond.

" Where are those fathers' glories gone?
    The pride of ages that have been!
While tamely bows their traitor son,
    The vassal of a Saxon queen:

" While still within a dungeon's walls,
    Ardmira's fetter'd prince reclines, *
While Imayle for her chieftain calls, †
    Who in a distant prison pines:

" While from that corse, yet reeking warm,
    O'er his own fields the life-streams flow,
Well mayst thou start! that mangled form
    Once was thy friend, Mac Mahon Roe. ‡

" Forget'st thou that a vessel came
    To Cineal's strand, in gaudy pride,
Fraught with each store of valued name,
    That nature gave or art supplied:

" No voice to bid the youth beware,
    Of banquets by the Saxon spread;
He tasted, and the treacherous snare
    Clos'd o'er the young O'Donnell's head. §

" Hopeless, desponding, still he lies,
    No aid his griefs to soothe or end;
And oft in vain his languid eyes
    Turn bright'ning on his father's friend:

" Who was that friend?—a chief of power,
    The guardian of a kingdom's weal,
Tir-owen's pride and Ulster's flower,
    A prince, a hero, THE O'NEILL!

* O'Dogherty of Ardmir, who was seized and thrown into prison by the lord
deputy Fitzwilliam.
    † O'Toole of I'Maoile, father to the wife of O'Neill, also imprisoned by Fitz-
william.
    ‡ Hugh Roe Mac Mahon, chief of Monaghan, who was tried before Fitz-
william, by a jury of common soldiers, and butchered at his castle door.
    § O'Donnell, son of the chief of Tyrconnell, who was decoyed on board a
vessel and carried prisoner to Dublin, where he was detained nearly four years.

" He at whose war-horn's potent blast,
　　Twice twenty chiefs in battle tried,
Unsheath'd the sword in warlike haste,
　　And rang'd their thousands on his side.

" But now he dreads the paths to tread,
　　That lead to honours, power, and fame;
And stands, each nobler feeling dead,
　　Nameless, who own'd a monarch's name.

" Shall Ardmir's prince for ever groan,
　　And Imayle's chief still fetter'd lie?
None for Mac Mahon's blood atone?
　　Nought cheer O'Donnell's languid eye?

" To thee they turn, on thee they rest:
　　Release the chain'd, revenge the dead,
Or soon the halls thy sires possest,
　　Shall echo to a stranger's tread !

" And in the sacred chair of stone,*
　　The base Ne Gaveloc † shalt thou see
Receive the name, the power, the throne,
　　That once was dear as life to thee !

" Arise ! for on his native plains
　　His father's warriors marshall'd round, —
O'Donnell, freed from Saxon chains,
　　Shall soon the signal trumpet sound :

" And soon, thy sacred cause to aid,
　　The brave O'Cahan,‡ at thy call,
Shall brandish high the flaming blade,
　　That filled the grasp of Cuie-na-gall :

" Resume thy name, in arms arise,
　　Tear from thy breast the Saxon star,

* The chair of stone on which the chiefs of the O'Neills were solemnly invested
with the power and titles of chief of Tir-owen, and paramount prince of Ulster.
　† Hugh O'Nial, illegitimate son of John, formerly chief of Tir-owen, surnamed *Ne Gaveloc*, or the fettered, from his having been born during the captivity of his mother.
　‡ O'Cahan of *Cinachta*, descended from the famous *Cuie-na-gall*, or the " Terror of the Stranger," who was celebrated for his exploits against the English.

K

And let the coming midnight skies
Be crimson'd with thy fires of war!

"And bid around the echoing land
The war-horn raise thy vassal powers;
And, once again, the Bloody Hand
Wave on Dungannon's royal towers!"

LAMENT FOR THE PRINCES,

OF TYRONE AND TYRCONNELL.

(FROM THE IRISH.)

BY J. C. MANGAN.

[This is an Elegy on the death of the princes of Tyrone and Tyrconnell, who having fled with others from Ireland in the year 1607, and afterwards dying at Rome, were interred on St. Peter's Hill, in one grave. The poem is the production of O'Donnell's bard, Owen Roe Mac an Bhaird, or Ward, who accompanied the family in their exile, and is addressed to Nuala, O'Donnell's sister, who was also one of the fugitives. As the circumstances connected with the flight of the Northern Earls, which led to the subsequent confiscation of the six Ulster Counties by James I., may not be immediately in the recollection of many of our readers, it may be proper briefly to state, that it was caused by the discovery of a letter directed to Sir William Ussher, Clerk of the Council, dropped in the Council-chamber on the 7th of May, and which accused the Northern chieftains generally of a conspiracy to overthrow the government. The charge is now totally disbelieved. As an illustration of the poem, and as an interesting piece of hitherto unpublished literature in itself, we extract the account of the flight as recorded in the Annals of the Four Masters, and translated by Mr. O'Donovan:—
" Maguire (Cuconnaught) and Donogh, son of Mahon, who was son of the Bishop O'Brien, sailed in a ship to Ireland, and put in at the harbour of Swilly. They then took with them from Ireland the Earl O'Neill (Hugh, son of Fedoragh) and the Earl O'Donnell (Rory, son of Hugh, who was son of Magnus) and many others of the nobles of the province of Ulster. These are the persons who went with O'Neill, namely, his Countess, Catherina, daughter of Magennis, and her three sons; Hugh, the Baron, John and Brian; Art Oge, son of Cormac, who was son of the Baron; Ferdoragh, son of Con, who was son of O'Neill; Hugh Oge, son of Brian, who was son of Art O'Neill; and many others of his most intimate friends. These were they who went with the Earl O'Donnell, namely, Caffer, his brother, with his sister Nuala; Hugh, the Earl's child, wanting three weeks of being one year old; Rose, daughter of O'Doherty and wife of Caffer, with her son Hugh, aged two years and three months; his (Rory's) brother son Donnell Oge, son of Donnel, Naghtan son of Calvach, who was son of Donogh Cairbreach O'Donnell, and many others of his intimate friends. They embarked on the Festival of the Holy Cross in autumn. This was a distinguished company; and it is certain that the sea has not borne and the wind

has not wafted in modern times a number of persons in one ship more eminent, illustrious, or noble, in point of genealogy, heroic deeds, valour, feats of arms, and brave achievements, than they. Would that God had but permitted them to remain in their patrimonial inheritances until the children should arrive at the age of manhood! Woe to the heart that meditated, woe to the mind that conceived, woe to the council that recommended the project of this expedition, without knowing whether they should, to the end of their lives, be able to return to their native principalities or patrimonies." The Earl of Tyrone, was the illustrious Hugh O'Neill, the Irish leader in the wars against Elizabeth.]

O, WOMAN of the Piercing Wail,
  Who mournest o'er yon mound of clay
    With sigh and groan,
Would God thou wert among the Gael!
  Thou would'st not then from day to day
    Weep thus alone.
'Twere long before, around a grave
  In green Tirconnell, one could find
    This loneliness;
Near where Beann-Boirche's banners wave
  Such grief as thine could ne'er have pined
    Companionless.

Beside the wave, in Donegal,
  In Antrim's glens, or fair Dromore,
    Or Killillee,
Or where the sunny waters fall,
  At Assaroe, near Erna's shore,
    This could not be.
On Derry's plains—in rich Drumclieff—
  Throughout Armagh the Great, renowned
    In olden years,
No day could pass but woman's grief
  Would rain upon the burial-ground
    Fresh floods of tears!

O, no!—from Shannon, Boyne, and Suir,
  From high Dunluce's castle-walls,
    From Lissadill,
Would flock alike both rich and poor,
  One wail would rise from Cruachan's halls
    To Tara's hill;
And some would come from Barrow-side,
  And many a maid would leave her home
    On Leitrim's plains,

And by melodious Banna's tide,
  And by the Mourne and Erne, to come
    And swell thy strains!

O, horses' hoofs would trample down
  The Mount whereon the martyr-saint *
    Was crucified.
From glen and hill, from plain and town,
  One loud lament, one thrilling plaint,
    Would echo wide.
There would not soon be found, I ween,
  One foot of ground among those bands
    For museful thought,
So many shriekers of the *keen* †
  Would cry aloud, and clap their hands,
    All woe-distraught!

Two princes of the line of Conn
  Sleep in their cells of clay beside
    O'Donnell Roe:
Three royal youths, alas! are gone,
  Who lived for Erin's weal, but died
    For Erin's woe!
Ah! could the men of Ireland read
  The names these noteless burial stones
    Display to view,
Their wounded hearts afresh would bleed,
  Their tears gush forth again, their groans
    Resound anew!

The youths whose relics moulder here
  Were sprung from Hugh, high Prince and Lord
    Of Aileach's lands;
Thy noble brothers, justly dear,
  Thy nephew, long to be deplored
    By Ulster's bands.
Theirs were not souls wherein dull Time
  Could domicile Decay or house
    Decrepitude!

* St. Peter. This passage is not exactly a blunder, though at first it may
seem one: the poet supposes the grave itself transferred to Ireland, and he
naturally includes in the transference the whole of the immediate locality around
the grave.—Tr.
† *Keen,* or *Caoine,* the funeral-wail.

They passed from Earth ere Manhood's prime,
  Ere years had power to dim their brows
      Or chill their blood.

And who can marvel o'er thy grief,
  Or who can blame thy flowing tears,
      That knows their source?
O'Donnell, Dunnasava's chief,
  Cut off amid his vernal years,
      Lies here a corse
Beside his brother Cathbar, whom
  Tirconnell of the Helmets mourns
      In deep despair—
For valour, truth, and comely bloom,
  For all that greatens and adorns,
      A peerless pair.

O, had these twain, and he, the third,
  The Lord of Mourne, O'Niall's son,
      Their mate in death—
A prince in look, in deed, and word—
  Had these three heroes yielded on
      The field their breath,
O, had they fallen on Criffan's plain,
  There would not be a town or clan
      From shore to sea,
But would with shrieks bewail the Slain,
  Or chant aloud the exulting *rann**
      Of jubilee!

When high the shout of battle rose,
  On fields where Freedom's torch still burned
      Through Erin's gloom,
If one, if barely one of those
  Were slain, all Ulster would have mourned
      The hero's doom!
If at Athboy, where hosts of brave
  Ulidian horsemen sank beneath
      The shock of spears,
Young Hugh O'Neill had found a grave,
  Long must the north have wept his death
      With heart-wrung tears!

* Song.

If on the day of Ballachmyre
　　The Lord of Mourne had met, thus young,
　　　　A warrior's fate,
In vain would such as thou desire
　　To mourn, alone, the champion sprung
　　　　From Niall the Great!
No marvel this—for all the Dead,
　　Heaped on the field, pile over pile,
　　　　At Mullach-brack,
Were scarce an *eric*＊ for his head,
　　If Death had stayed his footsteps while
　　　　On victory's track!

If on the Day of Hostages
　　The fruit had from the parent bough
　　　　Been rudely torn
In sight of Munster's bands—Mac-Nee's—
　　Such blow the blood of Conn, I trow,
　　　　Could ill have borne.
If on the day of Balloch-boy
　　Some arm had laid, by foul surprise,
　　　　The chieftain low,
Even our victorious shout of joy
　　Would soon give place to rueful cries
　　　　And groans of woe!

If on the day the Saxon host
　　Were forced to fly—a day so great
　　　　For Ashanee †—
The Chief had been untimely lost,
　　Our conquering troops should moderate
　　　　Their mirthful glee.
There would not lack on Lifford's day,
　　From Galway, from the glens of Boyle,
　　　　From Limerick's towers,
A marshalled file, a long array,
　　Of mourners to bedew the soil
　　　　With tears in showers!

If on the day a sterner fate
　　Compelled his flight from Athenree,
　　　　His blood had flowed,

＊ A compensation or fine.　　　　　　† Ballyshannon.

What numbers all disconsolate
 Would come unasked, and share with thee
   Affliction's load!
If Derry's crimson field had seen
 His life-blood offered up, though 'twere
   On Victory's shrine,
A thousand cries would swell the *keen*,
 A thousand voices of despair
   Would echo thine!

O, had the fierce Dalcassian swarm
 That bloody night on Fergus' banks
   But slain our Chief,
When rose his camp in wild alarm—
 How would the triumph of his ranks
   Be dashed with grief!
How would the troops of Murbach mourn
 If on the Curlew Mountains' day,
   Which England rued,
Some Saxon hand had left them lorn,
 By shedding there, amid the fray,
   Their prince's blood!

Red would have been our warriors' eyes
 Had Roderick found on Sligo's field
   A gory grave,
No Northern Chief would soon arise
 So sage to guide, so strong to shield,
   So swift to save.
Long would Leith-Cuinn have wept if Hugh
 Had met the death he oft had dealt
   Among the foe;
But, had our Roderick fallen too,
 All Erin must, alas! have felt
   The deadly blow!

What do I say? Ah, woe is me!
 Already we bewail in vain
   Their fatal fall!
And Erin, once the Great and Free,
 Now vainly mourns her breakless chain,
   And iron thrall!

Then, daughter of O'Donnell! dry
  Thine overflowing eyes, and turn
      Thy heart aside,
For Adam's race is born to die,
  And sternly the sepulchral urn
      Mocks human pride!

Look not, nor sigh, for earthly throne,
  Nor place thy trust in arm of clay—
      But on thy knees
Uplift thy soul to God alone,
  For all things go their destined way
      As He decrees.
Embrace the faithful Crucifix,
  And seek the path of pain and prayer
      Thy Saviour trod;
Nor let thy spirit intermix
  With earthly hope and worldly care
      Its groans to God!

And Thou, O mighty Lord! whose ways
  Are far above our feeble minds
      To understand,
Sustain us in these doleful days,
  And render light the chain that binds
      Our fallen land!
Look down upon our dreary state,
  And through the ages that may still
      Roll sadly on,
Watch Thou o'er hapless Erin's fate,
  And shield at least from darker ill
      The blood of Conn!

"'The Saturday before the flight, the Earl of Tyrone was with the lord-deputy
at Slane, where he had spoken with his lordship of his journey into England,
and told him he would be there about the beginning of Michaelmas term, according to his Majesty's directions. He took leave of the lord-deputy in a
more sad and passionate manner than was usual with him. From thence he
went to Mellifont and Garret Moore's house, where he wept abundantly when
he took his leave, giving a solemn farewell to every child and every servant in
the house, which made them all marvel, because in general it was not his manner to use such compliments. On Monday he went to Dungarvan, where he
rested two whole days, and on Wednesday night they say he travelled all
night. It is likewise reported that the countess, his wife, being exceedingly
weary, slipped down from her horse, and weeping, said, 'she could go no further.' Whereupon the earl drew his sword, and swore a great oath that 'he

would kill her on the spot if she would not pass on with him, and put on a
more cheerful countenance.' When the party, which consisted (men, women,
and children) of fifty or sixty persons, arrived at Loch Foyle, it was found that
their journey had not been so secret but that the governor there had notice of
it, and sent to invite Tyrone and his son to dinner. Their haste, however, was
such that they accepted not his courtesy, but hastened on to Rathmulla a
town on the west side of Lough Swilly, where the Earl of Tyrconnell and his
company met with them. From thence the whole party embarked, and, landing on the coast of Normandy, proceeded through France to Brussels. DAVIES
concludes his curious narrative with a few pregnant words, in which the difficulties that England had to contend with in conquering Tyrone are thus acknowledged with all the frankness of a generous foe:—'As for us that are
here,' he says, 'we are glad to see the day wherein the countenance and majesty of the law and civil government hath banished Tyrone out of Ireland,
which the best army in Europe, and the expense of two millions of sterling
pounds had not been able to bring to pass.'"—*Moore's Ireland.*

THE BATTLE OF BEAL-AN-ATHA-BUIDH. *

1598.

BY WILLIAM DRENNAN.

["The Irish Kerne were at the first rude souldiers, so as two or three of them
were employed to discharge one peece—but now they were growne ready in
managing their peeces, and bold to skirmish in boggss and wooddy passages;
they became so disasterous to the English, as they shaked the gouernement in
this kingdome, till it tottered, and wanted little of fatall ruine. Captaine
Williams (who occupied the Fort of the Blackwater which Hugh O'Neill had
vigorously besieged) and his few warders did with no lesse courage suffer hunger, and having eaten the few horses they had, lined vpon hearbes growing in
the ditches and wals, suffering all extremities, till the Lord Lieutenant in the
moneth of August sent *Sir Henry Bagnell*, Marshall of Ireland, with the most
choice companies of foote and horse troopes of the English army, to victuall
this Fort and to raise the Rebels siege. When the English entered the Pace,
and thicke woods beyond *Armagh*, on the east side, *Tyrone* with all the Rebels
forces assembled to him, pricked forward with the rage of enuy and settled
rancour against the Marshal, assayled the English, and turning his full force
against the Marshals person, had the successe to kill him, valiantly fighting
among the thickest of the Rebels. Whereupon the English being dismaied
with his death, the Rebels obtained a great victory against them; the English
from their first arriual in that Kingdome, never had received so great an overthrow. Thirteen valiant Captaines, and 1,500 common souldiers, whereof many
were of the old companies which had serued in *Brittany* vnder Generall *Nor-
reys*, were slain in the field; and the yeelding of the Fort of *Blackwater* fol-

---

* Beal-an-atha-buidhe literally means "The Mouth of the Yellow Ford,"
and is pronounced *Beal-un-ath-buie.*

lowed this disaster. By this victory the rebels got plenty of armes and
victuals,—*Tyrone* was among the Irish, celebrated as the Deliuerer of his Country from thraldome, and the combined Traytors on all sides were puffed up
with intolerable pride. The rebels of Leinster swarmed into the English pale,
while the English lay in their garrisons, so farre from assailing the Rebels, as
they rather liued in continuall feare to be surprised by them. After the de-
feate of *Blackwater*, Tyrone sent *Owen Mac Rory O'More*, and one Captaine
Tyrel of English race, but a bold and vnnatural enemy to his countrie and the
English, to trouble the prouince of Mounster."—*Fynes Moryson's Itinerary,*
part ii. book i.]

By O'NEILL close beleaguer'd, the spirits might droop
Of the Saxon—three hundred shut up in their coop,
Till Bagenal drew forth his Toledo, and swore,
On the sword of a soldier to succour Portmore.

His veteran troops, in the foreign wars tried—
Their features how bronz'd, and how haughty their stride—
Stept steadily on; it was thrilling to see
That thunder-cloud brooding o'er BEAL-AN-ATHA-BUIDH.

The flash of their armour, inlaid with fine gold,—
Gleaming matchlocks and cannons that mutteringly roll'd—
With the tramp and the clank of those stern cuirassiers,
Dyed in blood of the Flemish and French cavaliers.

And are the mere Irish, with pikes and with darts—
With but glibb-cover'd heads, and but rib-guarded hearts—
Half-naked, half-fed, with few muskets, no guns—
The battle to dare against England's stout sons?

Poor Bonnochts,* and wild Gallowglasses, and Kern—
Let them war with rude brambles, sharp furze. and dry fern;
Wirrastrue for their wives—for their babes *ochanie,*
If they wait for the Saxon at BEAL-AN-ATHA-BUIDH.

Yet O'Neill standeth firm—few and brief his commands—
" Ye have hearts in your bosoms, and pikes in your hands;
Try how far ye can push them, my children, at once;
Fag-a-Bealach!—and down with horse, foot, and great guns.

* *Bonnocht,*—a billeted soldier. *Wirrastrue, A Mhuire as truagh,*—Oh!
Mary, what sorrow! *Fag-a-Bealach.*—Clear the way. *Go leor,*—in abundance. *Fuilleluah.*—joyous exclamation. *Ceud mile failte go,*—a hundred
thousand welcomes to.

They have gold and gay arms—they have biscuit and bread;
Now, sons of my soul, we'll be found and be fed;"
And he clutch'd his claymore, and—"look yonder," laughed he,
" What a grand commissariat for BEAL-AN-ATHA-BUIDH."

Near the chief, a grim tyke, an O'Shanaghan stood,
His nostril dilated seemed snuffing for blood;
Rough and ready to spring, like the wiry wolf-hound
Of Ierne, who, tossing his pike with a bound,

Cried, "My hand to the Sassenach! ne'er may I hurl
Another to earth if I call him a churl!
He finds me in clothing, in booty, in bread—
My Chief, won't O'Shanaghan give him a bed?"

" Land of Owen, aboo!" and the Irish rush'd on—
The foe fir'd but one volley—their gunners are gone;
Before the bare bosoms the steel-coats have fled,
Or, despite casque or corslet, lie dying and dead.

And brave Harry Bagenal, he fell while he fought
With many gay gallants—they slept as men ought:
Their faces to Heaven—there were others, alack!
By pikes overtaken, and taken aback.

And my Irish got clothing, coin, colours, great store,
Arms, forage, and provender—plunder *go leor!*
They munch'd the white manchets—they champ'd the brown chin'
Failleluah! for that day, how the natives did dine!

The Chieftain looked on, when O'Shanaghan rose,
And cried, hearken O'Neill! I've a health to propose—
" To our Sassenach hosts!" and all quaff'd in huge glee.
With *Cead mile failte go*, BEAL-AN-ATHA-BUIDH!"

THE RUINS OF DONEGAL CASTLE. *

(FROM THE IRISH.)

BY J. C. MANGAN.

O MOURNFUL, O forsaken pile,
  What desolation dost thou dree !
How tarnished is the beauty that was thine ere while,
  Thou mansion of chaste melody !

Demolished lie thy towers and halls ;
  A dark, unsightly, earthen mound
Defaces the pure whiteness of thy shining walls,
  And solitude doth gird thee round.

Fair fort ! thine hour has come at length,
  Thine older glory has gone by.
Lo ! far beyond thy noble battlements of strength,
  Thy corner-stones all scattered lie !

Where now, O rival of the gold
  Emania, be thy wine-cups all ?
Alas ! for these thou now hast nothing but the cold,
  Cold stream that from the heavens doth fall !

Thy clay-choked gateways none can trace,
  Thou fortress of the once bright doors !
The limestones of thy summit now bestrew thy base
  Bestrew the outside of thy floors.

Above thy shattered window-sills
  The music that to-day breaks forth
Is but the music of the wild winds from the hills,
  The wild winds of the stormy North !

What spell o'ercame thee, mighty fort,
  What fatal fit of slumber strange,
O palace of the wine !—O many-gated court !
  That thou should'st undergo this change ?

* This fine old castle of his ancestors was razed to the ground by Hugh Roe
O'Donnell, previously to his journey to Spain, lest it should fall into the hands
of the English.

Thou wert, O bright-walled, beaming one,
  Thou cradle of high deeds and bold,
The Tara of Assemblies to the sons of Con,
  Clan-Connell's Council-hall of old!

Thou wert a new Emania, thou!
  A northern Cruachan in thy might—
A dome like that which stands by Boyne's broad water now,
  Thou Erin's Rome of all delight!

In thee were Ulster's tributes stored,
  And lavished like the flowers in May;
And into thee were Connaught's thousand treasures pour'd,
  Deserted though thou art to-day!

How often from thy turrets high,
  Thy purple turrets, have we seen
Long lines of glittering ships, when summer time drew nigh,
  With masts and sails of snow-white sheen!

How often seen, when gazing round,
  From thy tall towers, the hunting trains,
The blood-enlivening chase, the horseman and the hound,
  Thou fastness of a hundred plains!

How often to thy banquets bright
  We have seen the strong-armed Gaels repair,
And when the feast was over, once again unite
  For battle, in thy bass-court fair!

Alas, for thee, thou fort forlorn!
  Alas, for thy low, lost estate!
It is my woe of woes, this melancholy morn,
  To see thee left thus desolate!

O! there hath come of Connell's race
  A many and many a gallant chief,
Who, if he saw thee now, thou of the once glad face!
  Could not dissemble his deep grief.

Could Manus of the lofty soul
  Behold thee as this day thou art,
Thou of the regal towers! what bitter, bitter dole,
  What agony would rend his heart!

Could Hugh Mac Hugh's imaginings
   Portray for him thy rueful plight,
What anguish, O, thou palace of the northern kings,
   Were his through many a sleepless night!

Could even the mighty Prince whose choice
   It was to o'erthrow thee—could Hugh Roe
But view thee now, methinks he would not much rejoice
   That he had laid thy turrets low!

Oh! who could dream that one like him,
   One sprung of such a line as his,
Thou of the embellished walls, would be the man to dim
   Thy glories by a deed like this!

From Hugh O'Donnell, thine own brave
   And far-famed sovereign, came the blow!
By him, thou lonesome castle o'er the Esky's wave,
   By him was wrought thine overthrow!

Yet not because he wished thee ill
   Left he thee thus bereaven and void;
The prince of the victorious tribe of Dalach still
   Loved thee, yea, thee whom he destroyed!

He brought upon thee all his woe,
   Thou of the fair-proportioned walls,
Lest thou shouldst ever yield a shelter to the foe,
   Shouldst house the black ferocious Galls!

Should'st yet become in saddest truth
   A *Dun-na-Gall* *—the stranger's own.
For this cause only, stronghold of the Gaelic youth,
   Lie thy majestic towers o'erthrown.

It is a drear, a dismal sight,
   This of thy ruin and decay,
Now that our kings, and bards, and men of mark and might
   Are nameless exiles far away!

Yet, better thou shouldst fall, meseems,
   By thine own King of many thrones,

        * Fort of the foreigner.

Than that the truculent Galls should rear around thy streams
   Dry mounds and circles of great stones.

As doth in many a desperate case
   The surgeon by the malady,
So hath, O shield and bulwark of great Coffey's race,
   Thy royal master done by thee!

The surgeon, if he be but wise,
   Examines till he learns and sees
Where lies the fountain of his patient's health, where lies
   The germ and root of his disease;

Then cuts away the gangrened part,
   That so the sounder may be freed
Ere the disease hath power to reach the sufferer's heart,
   And so bring death without remead.

Now, thou hast held the patient's place,
   And thy disease hath been the foe;
So he, thy surgeon, O proud house of Dalach's race,
   Who should he be if not Hugh Roe?

But he, thus fated to destroy
   Thy shining walls, will yet restore
And raise thee up anow in beauty and in joy,
   So that thou shalt not sorrow more.

By God's help, he who wrought thy fall
   Will reinstate thee yet in pride;
Thy variegated halls shall be rebuilded all,
   Thy lofty courts, thy chambers wide.

Yes! thou shalt live again, and see
   Thine youth renewed! Thou shalt outshine
Thy former self by far, and Hugh shall reign in thee,
   The Tirconnellian's king and thine!

OH! BLAME NOT THE BARD.*

BY THOMAS MOORE.

Oh! blame not the bard, if he fly to the bowers,
  Where Pleasure lies carelessly smiling at Fame;
He was born for much more, and in happier hours
  His soul might have burn'd with a holier flame.
The string that now languishes loose o'er the lyre,
  Might have bent a proud bow to the warrior's dart;
And the lip, which now breathes but the song of desire,
  Might have pour'd the full tide of a patriot's heart.

But alas for his country!—her pride is gone by,
  And that spirit is broken, which never would bend;
O'er the ruin her children in secret must sigh,
  For 'tis treason to love her, and death to defend.
Unpriz'd are her sons, till they've learned to betray;
  Undistinguish'd they live, if they shame not their sires;
And the torch that would light them thro' dignity's way,
  Must be caught from the pile, where their country expires

Then blame not the bard, if in pleasure's soft dream,
  He should try to forget what he never can heal:
Oh! give but a hope—let a vista but gleam
  Through the gloom of his country, and mark how he'll feel!
That instant, his heart at her shrine would lay down
  Every passion it nurs'd, every bliss it ador'd;
While the myrtle, now idly entwin'd with his crown,
  Like the wreath of Harmodius, should cover his sword. †

But tho' glory be gone, and tho' hope fade away,
  Thy name, loved Erin,‡ shall live in his songs;

---

* We may suppose this apology to have been uttered by one of those wandering bards, whom Spenser so severely, and, perhaps, truly, describes in his State of Ireland, and whose poems, he tells us, "were sprinkled with some pretty flowers of their natural device, which have good grace and comeliness unto them, the which it is great pity to see abused to the gracing of wickedness and vice, which, with good usage, would serve to adorn and beautify virtue."

† See the Hymn attributed to Alcæus:—"I will carry my sword, hidden in myrtles, like Harmodius, and Aristogiton," &c.

‡ It is conjectured by Wormius, that the name of Ireland is derived from Yr, the Runic for a bow, in the use of which weapon the Irish were once very

Not ev'n in the hour, when his heart is most gay,
  Will he lose the remembrance of thee and thy wrongs.
The stranger shall hear thy lament on his plains;
  The sigh of thy harp shall be sent o'er the deep,
Till thy masters themselves, as they rivet thy chains,
  Shall pause at the song of their captive, and weep!

THE LAST O'SULLIVAN BEARE.

BY THOMAS D'ARCY M'GEE.

[Philip O'Sullivan Beare, a brave captain, and the author of many works
relating to Ireland, commanded a ship-of-war for Philip IV. of Spain. In his
"Catholic History," published at Lisbon in 1609, he has preserved the sad
story of his family. It is in brief thus:—In 1602 his father's castle of Dun-
buidhe, being demolished by cannonade, his family—consisting of a wife, son,
and two daughters—emigrated to Spain, where his youngest brother, Donald,
joined him professionally, but was soon after killed in an engagement with the
Turks. The old chief, at the age of one hundred, died at Corunna, and was
soon followed by his long-wedded wife. One daughter entered a convent and
took the veil; the other, returning to Ireland, was lost at sea. In this version
the real names have been preserved.]

ALL alone—all alone, where the gladsome vine is growing—
All alone by the bank of the Tagus darkly flowing,
No morning brings a hope for him, nor any evening cheer,
To O'Sullivan Beare thro' the seasons of the year.

He is thinking—ever thinking of the hour he left Dunbuie,
His father's staff fell from his hand, his mother wept wildly;
His brave young brother hid his face, his lovely sisters twain,
How they wrung their maiden hands to see him sail away for Spain.

They were Helen bright and Norah staid, who in their father's hall,
Like sun and shadow, frolicked round the grave armorial wall;
In Compostella's cloisters he found many a pictured saint,
But the Spirits boyhood canonised no human hand can paint.

expert. This derivation is certainly more creditable to us than the following:
"So that Ireland, called the land of *Ire*, from the constant broils therein for
400 years, was now become the land of concord."—*Lloyd's State Worthies*, art.
The Lord Grandison.

L

All alone—all alone, where the gladsome vine is growing—
All alone by the bank of the Tagus darkly flowing—
No morning brings a hope for him, nor any evening cheer,
To O'Sullivan Beare thro' the seasons of the year.

Oh! sure he ought to take a ship and sail back to Dunbuie—
He ought to sail back, back again to that castle o'er the sea;
His father, mother, brother, his lovely sisters twain,
'Tis they would raise the roof with joy to see him back from Spain.

Hush! hush! I cannot tell it—the tale will make me wild—
He left it, that grey castle, in age almost a child;
Seven long years with Saint James's Friars he conned the page of
      might—
Seven long years for his father's roof was sighing every night.

Then came a caravel from the north, deep freighted, full of wo,
His houseless family it held, their castle it lay low,
Saint James's shrine, thro' ages famed as pilgrim haunt of yore,
Saw never wanderers so wronged upon its scalloped shore.

Yet it was sweet—their first grief past—to watch those two fond
      girls
Sit by the sea, as mermaiden hold watch o'er hidden pearls—
To see them sit and try to sing for that sire and mother old
O'er whose heads five score winters their thickening snows had
      rolled.

To hear them sing and pray in song for *them* in deadly work,
Their gallant brothers battling for Spain against the Turk—
Corunna's port at length they reach, and seaward ever stare,
Wondering what belates the ship their brothers home should bear.

Joy! joy!—it comes—their Philip lives!—ah! Donald is no more:
Like half a hope one son kneels down the exiled two before;
They spoke no requiem for the dead, nor blessing for the living;
The tearless heart of parentage has broken with its grieving.

Two pillars of a ruined pile—two old trees of the land—
Two voyagers on a sea of grief, long suff'rers hand in hand.
Thus at the woful tidings told left life and all its tears.
So died the wife of many a spring, the chief of an hundred years.

One sister is a black veiled nun of Saint Ursula, in Spain,
And one sleeps coldly far beneath the troubled Irish main ;
'Tis Helen bright who ventured to the arms of her true lover,
But Cleena's* stormy waves now roll the radiant girl over.

All alone—all alone, where the gladsome vine is growing—
All alone by the bank of the Tagus darkly flowing,
No morning brings a hope for him, nor any evening cheer,
To O'Sullivan Beare thro' the seasons of the year.

DIRGE OF O'SULLIVAN BEARE.

BY J. J. CALLANAN.

[In 1756 one of the Sullivans of Bearhaven, who went by the name of
Morty Oge, fell under the vengeance of the law. He had long been a very popular character in the wild district which he inhabited, and was particularly
obnoxious to the local authorities, who had good reason to suspect him of en-
listing men for the Irish brigade in the French service, in which it was said he
held a captain's commission. Information of his raising these "wild geese,"
(the name by which such recruits were known,) was given by a Mr. Puxly, on
whom, in consequence, O'Sullivan vowed revenge, which he executed by shoot-
ing him on Sunday while on his way to church. This called for the interposi-
tion of the higher powers, and accordingly a party of military was sent round
from Cork to attack O'Sullivan's house. He was daring and well armed ; and
the house being fortified, he made an obstinate defence. At last, a confi-
dential servant of his, named Scully, was bribed to wet the powder in the guns
and pistols prepared for his defence, which rendered him powerless. He attempted to escape, but while springing over a high wall in the rear of his house,
he received a mortal wound in the back. They tied his body to a boat, and
dragged it in that manner through the sea from Bearhaven to Cork, where his
head was cut off, and fixed on the county jail, where it remained for several
years. Such is the story current among the people about Beerhaven. In the
version given of it in the rude chronicle of the local occurrences of Cork, there
is no mention made of Scully's perfidy ; and perhaps that circumstance might
have been added by those to whom O'Sullivan was deemed a hero, in order to
save his credit as much as possible. The dirge was composed by his nurse, who
has made no sparing use of the peculiar energy of cursing, which the Irish
language is by all allowed to possess. In the following song, Morty, in Irish,
Muiertach, is a name very common among the old families of Ireland. It signifies *expert at sea*. Oge, is *young*. Where a whole district is peopled, in a
great measure, by a sept of one name, such distinguishing titles are necessary,
and in some cases even supersede the original appellative. I-vera, or Aoi-vera,
is the original name of *Bearhaven* ; Aoi, or I, signifying an *island*.]

* The waves off the coast of Cork, so called.

THE sun on Ivera
  No longer shines brightly;
The voice of her music
  No longer is sprightly;
No more to her maidens
  The light dance is dear,
Since the death of our darling,
  O'Sullivan Beare.

Scully! thou false one,
  You basely betrayed him,
In his strong hour of need,
  When thy right hand should aid him.
He fed thee—he clad thee—
  You had all could delight thee:
You left him—you sold him—
  May heaven requite thee!

Scully! may all kinds
  Of evil attend thee!
On thy dark road of life
  May no kind one befriend thee!
May fevers long burn thee,
  And agues long freeze thee!
May the strong hand of God
  In his red anger seize thee!

Had he died calmly,
  I would not deplore him;
Or if the wild strife
  Of the sea-war closed o'er him:
But with ropes round his white limbs
  Through ocean to trail him,
Like a fish after slaughter,
  'Tis therefore I wail him.

Long may the curse
  Of his people pursue them;
Scully, that sold him,
  And soldier that slew him!
One glimpse of heaven's light
  May they see never!
May the hearth-stone of hell
  Be their best bed for ever!

In the hole, which the vile hands
    Of soldiers had made thee;
Unhonour'd, unshrouded,
    And headless they laid thee.
No sigh to regret thee,
    No eye to rain o'er thee,
No dirge to lament thee,
    No friend to deplore thee!

Dear head of my darling,
    How gory and pale
These aged eyes see thee,
    High spiked on their gaol!
That cheek in the summer sun
    Ne'er shall grow warm;
Nor that eye e'er catch light,
    But the flash of the storm.

A curse, blessed ocean,
    Is on thy green water,
From the haven of Cork,
    To Ivera of slaughter:
Since thy billows were dyed
    With the red wounds of fear,
Of Muiertach Oge,
    Our O'Sullivan Beare!

SIR CAHIR O'DOHERTY. *

BY EVA. (MISS MARY EVA KELLY.)

By the Spanish plum'd hat, and the costly attire,
And the dark eye that's blended of midnight and fire,
And the bearing and stature so princely and tall,
Sir Cahir you'll know in the midst of them all.

* Sir Cahir was the son of Sir John O'Doherty, Chief of Innishowen, and
was born in 1587. At that time, and during his whole life, Ireland was
the arena of the most sanguinary warfare between the native princes and
the armies of Queen Elizabeth. When about twenty years of age he was described as " a man to be marked amongst a thousand,—a man of the loftiest
and proudest bearing in Ulster; his Spanish hat with the heron's plume was
too often the terror of his enemies and the rallying-point of his friends not to

Like an oak on the land, like a ship on the sea,
Like the eagle above, strong and haughty is he,
In the greenness of youth—yet he's crowned as his due,
With the fear of the false, and the love of the true.

Right fiercely he swoops on their plundering hordes,
Right proudly he dares them, the proud English lords!
And darkly you'll trace him by many a trail,
From the hills of the North to the heart of the Pale.

By red field, ruined keep, and fire-shrouded hall,
By the tramp of the charger o'er buttress and wall;
By the courage that springs in the breach of despair,
Like the bound of the lion erect from his lair!

O'Neill and O'Donnell, Maguire and the rest,
Have sheathed the sabre, and lowered the crest;
O'Cahan is crushed, and Macmahon is bound,
And Magennis slinks after the foe like his hound.

But high and untrimm'd, o'er the valley and height,
Soars the proud sweeping pinion so young in its flight;
The toil and the danger are brav'd all alone,
By the fierce-taloned falcon of old Innishowen!

And thus runs his story—he fought and he fell,
Young, honour'd and brave—so the *seanachies* tell;
The foremost of those who have guarded "the green,"
When men wrote their names with the sword and the *skian!*

bespeak the O'Doherty." Like most of the Irish chiefs, Sir Cahir was plundered of his castle and lands, which were given to the Chichesters of Belfast and other English adventurers. He was killed in 1608 by a random shot, after having held Ulster for five months against the armies of England. He was brave and chivalrous,—faithful to his engagements,—firm and prompt in the execution of his designs, but implacable in his resentments,]

O'HUSSEY'S ODE TO THE MAGUIRE.*

BY J. C. MANGAN.

[O'Hussey, the last hereditary bard of the great sept of Maguire, of Fermanagh, who flourished about 1630, possessed a fine genius. He commenced his vocation when quite a youth, by a poem celebrating the escape of the famous Hugh Roe O'Donnell from Dublin Castle, in 1591, into which he had been treacherously betrayed, as already noticed. The noble ode which O'Hussey addressed to Hugh Maguire, when that chief had gone on a dangerous expedition, in the depth of an unusually severe winter, is as interesting an example of the devoted affection of the bard to his chief, and as vivid a picture of intense desolation, as could be well conceived.]

WHERE is my Chief, my Master, this bleak night, *marrone!*
O, cold, cold, miserably cold is this bleak night for Hugh,
Its showery, arrowy, speary sleet pierceth one through and
    through,
Pierceth one to the very bone!

Rolls real thunder? Or, was that red livid light
Only a meteor? I scarce know; but, through the midnight dim
The pitiless ice-wind streams. Except the hate that persecutes *him*,
Nothing hath crueller venomy might.

An awful, a tremendous night is this, meseems!
The floodgates of the rivers of heaven, I think, have been burst
    wide—
Down from the overcharged clouds, like unto headlong ocean's
    tide,
Descends grey rain in roaring streams.

* Mr. Ferguson, in a fine piece of criticism on this poem, remarks: "There is a vivid vigour in these descriptions, and a savage power in the antithetical climax, which claim a character almost approaching to sublimity. Nothing can be more graphic, yet more diversified, than his images of unmitigated horror—nothing more grandly startling than his heroic conception of the glow of glory triumphant over frozen toil. We have never read this poem without recurring, and that by no unworthy association, to Napoleon in his Russian campaign. Yet, perhaps O'Hussey has conjured up a picture of more inclement desolation, in his rude idea of northern horrors, than could be legitimately employed by a poet of the present day, when the romance of geographical obscurity no longer permits us to imagine the Phlegrean regions of endless storm, where the snows of Hæmus fall mingled with the lightnings of Etna, amid Bistonian wilds or Hyrcanian forests."—*Dublin University Magazine*, vol. iv.

Though he were even a wolf ranging the round green woods,
Though he were even a pleasant salmon in the unchainable sea,
Though he were a wild mountain eagle, he could scarce bear he,
This sharp sore sleet, these howling floods.

O, mournful is my soul this night for Hugh Maguire!
Darkly, as in a dream, he strays! Before him and behind
Triumphs the tyrannous anger of the wounding wind,
The wounding wind, that burns as fire!

It is my bitter grief—it cuts me to the heart—
That in the country of Clan Darry this should be his fate!
Oh, woe is me, where is he? Wandering, houseless, desolate,
Alone, without or guide or chart!

Medreams I see just now his face, the strawberry-bright,
Uplifted to the blackened heavens, while the tempestuous winds
Blow fiercely over and round him, and the smiting sleet-shower
        blinds
The hero of Galang to-night!

Large, large affliction unto me and mine it is,
That one of his majestic bearing, his fair, stately form,
Should thus be tortured and o'erborne—that this unsparing storm
Should wreak its wrath on head like his!

That his great hand, so oft the avenger of the oppressed,
Should this chill, churlish night, perchance, be paralyzed by frost,
While through some icicle-hung thicket—as one lorn and lost—
He walks and wanders without rest.

The tempest-driven torrent deluges the mead,
It overflows the low banks of the rivulets and ponds—
The lawns and pasture-grounds lie locked in icy bonds,
So that the cattle cannot feed.

The pale bright margins of the streams are seen by none.
Rushes and sweeps along the untameable flood on every side—
It penetrates and fills the cottagers' dwellings far and wide—
Water and land are blent in one.

Through some dark woods, 'mid bones of monsters, Hugh now
        strays,
As he confronts the storm with anguished heart, but manly brow—

Oh! what a sword-wound to that tender heart of his were now
A backward glance at peaceful days!

But other thoughts are his—thoughts that can still inspire
With joy and an onward-bounding hope the bosom of Mac Nee—
Thoughts of his warriors charging like bright billows of the sea,
Borne on the wind's wings, flashing fire!

And though frost glaze to-night the clear dew of his eyes,
And white ice-gauntlets glove his noble fine fair fingers o'er,
A warm dress is to him that lightning-garb he ever wore,
The lightning of the soul, not skies.

AVRAN. *

Hugh marched forth to the fight—I grieved to see him so depart;
And lo! to-night he wanders frozen, rain-drenched, sad, betrayed—
*But the memory of the limewhite mansions his right hand hath laid
In ashes warms the hero's heart!*

O'BRIEN OF ARRA.

BY THOMAS DAVIS, M.R.I.A.

[This was a branch of the old family of that name, well celebrated in the Annals of Munster,—and descended from Brian Roe O'Brien, prince of Thomond, who was expelled from his own territory in the early part of the fourteenth century, and settled in the district of Arra in the north-west of the county Tipperary. It is a small mountain tract north of the *Camailte*, or Keeper Hills. *Cead Mile Failte* means a hundred thousand welcomes.

TALL are the towers of O'Kennedy—
    Broad are the lands of MacCaura—
Desmond feeds five hundred men a-day;
    Yet, here's to O'Brien of Arra!
        Up from the castle of Drumineer,
            Down from the top of Camailte,
        Clansmen and kinsmen are coming here
            To give him the CEAD MILE FAILTE.

* A concluding stanza, generally intended as a recapitulation of the entire poem.

See you the mountains look huge at eve—
  So is our chieftain in battle—
Welcome he has for the fugitive,
  Usquebaugh, fighting, and cattle!
      Up from the Castle of Drumineer,
        Down from the top of Camailte,
      Gossip and ally are coming here
        To give him the CEAD MILE FAILTE.

Horses the valleys are tramping on,
  Sleek from the Sassenach manger—
Creaghts the hills are encamping on,
  Empty the bawns of the stranger!
      Up from the Castle of Drumineer,
        Down from the top of Camailte,
      Kern and bonaght are coming here
        To give him the CEAD MILE FAILTE.

He has black silver from Killaloe—
  Ryan and Carroll are neighbours—
Nenagh submits with a fuililiú—
  Butler is meat for our sabres!
      Up from the Castle of Drumineer,
        Down from the top of Camailte,
      Ryan and Carroll are coming here
        To give him the CEAD MILE FAILTE.

'Tis scarce a week since through Ossory
  Chased he the Baron of Durrow—
Forced him five rivers to cross, or he
  Had died by the sword of Red Murrough!
      Up from the Castle of Drumineer,
        Down from the top of Camailte,
      All the O'Briens are coming here
        To give him the CEAD MILE FAILTE.

Tall are the towers of O'Kennedy—
  Broad are the lands of MacCaura—
Desmond feeds five hundred men a-day;
  Yet, here's to O'Brien of Arra!
      Up from the Castle of Drumineer,
        Down from the top of Camailte,
     Clansman and kinsman are coming here
        To give him the CEAD MILE FAILTE.

THE SACK OF BALTIMORE.

BY THOMAS DAVIS.

[Baltimore is a small seaport in the barony of Carbery, in South Munster.
It grew up round a castle of O'Driscoll's, and was, after his ruin, colonized by
the English. On the 20th of June, 1631, the crew of two Algerine galleys
landed in the dead of the night, sacked the town, and bore off into slavery all
who were not too old, or too young, or too fierce for their purpose. The pirates
were steered up the intricate channel by one Hackett, a Dungarvan fisherman,
whom they had taken at sea for the purpose. Two years after he was convicted and executed for the crime. Baltimore never recovered this. To the
artist, the antiquary, and the naturalist, its neighbourhood is most interesting.
—See "*Smith's Ancient and Present State of the County and City of Cork*"
vol. i. p. 270.]

THE summer sun is falling soft on Carb'ry's hundred isles—
The summer's sun is gleaming still through Gabriel's rough defiles—
Old Inisherkin's crumbled fane looks like a moulting bird;
And in a calm and sleepy swell the ocean tide is heard;
The hookers lie upon the beach; the children cease their play;
The gossips leave the little inn; the households kneel to pray—
And full of love, and peace, and rest—its daily labour o'er—
Upon that cosy creek there lay the town of Baltimore.

A deeper rest, a starry trance, has come with midnight there;
No sound, except that throbbing wave, in earth, or sea, or air.
The massive capes, and ruined towers, seem conscious of the calm,
The fibrous sod and stunted trees are breathing heavy balm.
So still the night, these two long barques, round Dunashad that
    glide,
Must trust their oars—methinks not few—against the ebbing tide—
Oh! some sweet mission of true love must urge them to the shore—
They bring some lover to his bride, who sighs in Baltimore!

All, all asleep within each roof along that rocky street,
And these must be the lover's friends, with gently gliding feet—
A stifled gasp! a dreamy noise! "the roof is in a flame!"
From out their beds, and to their doors, rush maid, and sire, and
    dame—
And meet, upon the threshold stone, the gleaming sabre's fall,
And o'er each black and bearded face the white or crimson shawl—
The yell of "Allah!" breaks above the pray'r, and shriek, and
    roar—
Oh, blessed God! the Algerine is lord of Baltimore!

Then flung the youth his naked hand against the shearing sword;
Then sprung the mother on the brand with which her son was gor'd;
Then sunk the grandsire on the floor, his grand-babes clutching
   wild;
Then fled the maiden moaning faint, and nestled with the child;
But see, yon pirate strangled lies, and crushed with splashing heel,
While o'er him in an Irish hand there sweeps his Syrian steel—
Though virtue sink, and courage fail, and misers yield their store,
There's *one* hearth well avengèd in the sack of Baltimore!

Mid-summer morn, in woodland nigh, the birds begin to sing—
They see not now the milking maids—deserted is the spring!
Mid-summer day—this gallant rides from distant Bandon's town—
These hookers crossed from stormy Skull, that skiff from Affadown;
They only found the smoking walls, with neighbours' blood besprent,
And on the strewed and trampled beach awhile they wildly went—
Then dashed to sea, and passed Cape Cléir, and saw five leagues
   before
The pirate galleys vanishing that ravaged Baltimore.

Oh! some must tug the galley's oar, and some must tend the steed—
This boy will bear a Scheik's chibouk, and that a Bey's jerreed.
Oh! some are for the arsenals, by beauteous Dardanelles;
And some are in the caravan to Mecca's sandy dells.
The maid that Bandon gallant sought is chosen for the Dey—
She's safe—she's dead—she stabbed him in the midst of his Serai;
And, when to die a death of fire, that noble maid they bore,
She only smiled—O'Driscoll's child—she thought of Baltimore.

'Tis two long years since sunk the town beneath that bloody band,
And all around its trampled hearths a larger concourse stand,
Where, high upon a gallows tree, a yelling wretch is seen—
'Tis Hackett of Dungarvan—he, who steered the Algerine!
He fell amid a sullen shout, with scarce a passing prayer,
For he had slain the kith and kin of many a hundred there—
Some muttered of M'Morrogh, who had brought the Norman o'er—
Some cursed him with Iscariot, that day in Baltimore.

RORY O'MOORE.

AN ULSTER BALLAD.

ANON.

[Roger, or Rory O'Moore, is one of the most honoured and stainless names in Irish history. Writers, who concur in nothing else, agree in representing him as a man of the loftiest motives and the most passionate patriotism. In 1640, when Ireland was weakened by defeat and confiscation, and guarded with a jealous care constantly increasing in strictness and severity, O'Moore, then a private gentleman with no resources beyond his intellect and his courage, conceived the vast design of rescuing her from England; and accomplished it. In three years England did not retain a city in the island but Dublin and Drogheda. For eight years her power was barely nominal; the land was possessed and the supreme authority exercised by the Confederation created by O'Moore. History contains no stricter instance of the influence of an individual mind. Before the insurrection broke out, the people had learned to know and expect their Deliverer, and it became a popular proverb and the burden of national songs, that the hope of Ireland was in "God, the Virgin, and Rory O'Moore." It is remarkable that O'Moore, in whose courage and resources this great insurrection had its birth, was a descendant of the chieftains of Leix, massacred by English troops at Mullaghmast, a century before. But if he took a great revenge, it was a magnanimous one: none of the excesses which stained the first rising in Ulster are charged upon him. On the contrary, when he joined the Northern Army, the excesses ceased, and strict discipline was established, as far as it was possible, among men unaccustomed to control, and wild with wrongs and sufferings.]

On the green hills of Ulster the white cross waves high,
And the beacon of war throws its flames to the sky;
Now the taunt and the threat let the coward endure,
Our hope is in God and in Rory O'Moore!

Do you ask why the beacon and banner of war
On the mountains of Ulster are seen from afar?
'Tis the signal our rights to regain and secure,
Through God and our Lady and Rory O'Moore.

For the merciless Scots, with their creed and their swords,
With war in their bosoms, and peace in their words,
Have sworn the bright light of our faith to obscure,
But our hope is in God and in Rory O'Moore.

Oh! lives there the traitor who'd shrink from the strife—
Who, to add to the length of a forfeited life,
His country, his kindred, his faith would abjure?—
No! we'll strike for our God and for Rory O'Moore.

UNA PHELIMY.

AN ULSTER BALLAD, A.D. 1641.

BY SAMUEL FERGUSON, M.R.I.A.

[This ballad was intended to illustrate the same period in Irish History as
the last, but the author looks at it from a different and more unfavourable point
of view. Together, they furnish another evidence of how infallibly truth sooner
or later comes to be recognized.—Two Northern Protestants, writing of a civil
war, where the strife lay between their ancestors and the plundered Catholics
(fighting for their lands and their lives,) one of them vehemently sympathises
with the Insurgents, the other speaks bitterly to be sure, but not uncharitably
of the contest.]

"AWAKEN, Una Phelimy,
   How canst thou slumber so?
How canst thou dream so quietly
   Through such a night of woe?
Through such a night of woe," he said,
   "How canst thou dreaming lie,
When the kindred of thy love lie dead,
   And he must fall or fly?"

She rose and to the casement came;
   "Oh, William dear, speak low;
For I should bear my brothers' blame
   Did Hugh or Angus know."
"Did Hugh or Angus know, Una?
   Ah, little dreamest thou
On what a bloody errand bent
   Are Hugh and Angus now."

"Oh, what has chanced my brothers dear?
   My William, tell me true!
Our God forbode that what I fear
   Be that they're gone to do!"
"They're gone on bloody work, Una,
   The worst we feared is done;
They've taken to the knife at last,
   The massacre's begun!

"They came upon us while we slept
   Fast by the sedgy Bann;
In darkness to our beds they crept,
   And left me not a man!

Bann rolls my comrades even now
   Through all his pools and fords;
And their hearts' best blood is warm, Una,
   Upon thy brothers' swords!

" And mine had borne them company,
   Or the good blade I wore,
Which ne'er left foe in victory
   Or friend in need before;
In theirs as in their fellows' hearts
   Also had dimmed its shine,
But for these tangling curls, Una,
   And witching eyes of thine!

" I've borne the brand of flight for these,
   For these, the scornful cries
Of loud insulting enemies;
   But busk thee, love, and rise;
For Ireland's now no place for us;
   'Tis time to take our flight,
When neighbour steals on neighbour thus,
   And stabbers strike by night.

" And black and bloody the revenge
   For this dark midnight's sake,
The kindred of my murdered friends
   On thine and thee will take,
Unless thou rise and fly betimes,
   Unless thou fly with me,
Sweet Una, from this land of crimes
   To peace beyond the sea.

" For trustful pillows wait us there,
   And loyal friends beside,
Where the broad lands of my father are,
   Upon the banks of Clyde;
In five days hence a ship will be
   Bound for that happy home:
Till then we'll make our sanctuary
   In sea-cave's sparry dome:
Then busk thee, Una Pheliny,
   And o'er the waters come!"

   *   *   *   *   *   *

The midnight moon is wading deep;
  The land sends off the gale;
The boat beneath the sheltering steep
  Hangs on a seaward sail;
And, leaning o'er the weather-rail,
  The lovers hand in hand,
Take their last look of Innisfail;
  " Farewell, doomed Ireland !"

" And art thou doomed to discord still?
  And shall thy sons ne'er cease
To search and struggle for thine ill,
  Ne'er share thy good in peace?
Already do thy mountains feel
  Avenging Heaven's ire?
Hark—hark—this is no thunder peal,
  That was no lightning fire !"

It was no fire from heaven he saw,
  For, far from hill and dell,
O'er GOBBIN's brow the mountain flaw
  Bears musquet-shot and yell,
And shouts of brutal glee, that tell
  A foul and fearful tale,
While over blast and breaker swell
  Thin shrieks and woman's wail.

Now fill they far the upper sky,
  Now down mid air they go,
The frantic scream, the piteous cry,
  The groan of rage and woe;
And wilder in their agony
  And shriller still they grow—
Now cease they, choking suddenly,
  The waves boom on below.

" A bloody and a black revenge !
  Oh, Una, blest are we
Who this sore-troubled land can change
  For peace beyond the sea;
But for the manly hearts and true
  That Antrim still retain,

> Or be their banner green or blue,
> For all that there remain,
> God grant them quiet freedom too,
> And blithe homes soon again!"

THE MUSTER OF THE NORTH.

1641.

BY CHARLES GAVAN DUFFY, M.P.

[The Irish Pale resembled the borders between Scotland and England so closely in its general character, that it is no extravagant assumption to suppose that it must have given birth to a host of poems of the same class, as the Border Ballads collected by Sir Walter Scott in his own country. The same incessant feuds, the same daring adventures, the same deadly hatred, and an equally poetic people to sing their own achievements, existed in both countries; and if there are few remains of our legendary and local ballads, the disuse of the Irish language in which they were written, and the neglect of our national literature since the Elizabethan war, will account for their loss without throwing the smallest doubt on their former existence. In fact, they may be deduced as plainly from the physical and intellectual condition of the country, without any other evidence, as the use of weapons for war or castles for defence, which it needs no ruins and no museums to establish. If they are as completely lost as the ballads on which the early history of Rome was founded they as surely existed; and we have in lieu of a better, that remedy for our loss which Macaulay has so successfully adopted in the case of his "Lays of Ancient Rome"—to sing for our ancestors such ballads as they probably sung for themselves. Historical songs and ballads are the best nutriment for the nationality and public spirit of a country—the recollection of the men and achieveme... ... celebrate act on its youth like a second conscience—they become ashamed to disgrace a land that was the mother of such men. The memory of Wallace does more for Scotland than the sermons of ten Dr. Chalmers, and Kosciusko makes every Pole respectable throughout the world. Scott's own legendary ballads and poems did a thousand times more for Scotland than all he ever collected, and Burns's "Scots wha hae" was worth a hundred "Minstrelsies of the Border" in its national influence. The present ballad is founded on the rising of Ulster in 1641, at the commencement of the ten years' war. We have always denied the alleged massacre of that era, and the atrocious calumnies on Sir Phelim O'Neill; but that the natives, in ejecting the English from their towns and castles, committed various excesses is undeniable—as is equally the bitter provocation—in the plunder of their properties by James I., and the long persecution that ensued. The object of the ballad is not to excuse these excesses, which we condemn and deplore, but to give a vivid picture of the feelings of an outraged people in the first madness of successful resistance.]

Joy! joy! the day is come at last, the day of hope and pride,
And see! our crackling bonfires light old Bann's rejoicing tide,

M

And gladsome bell, and bugle-horn from Newry's captured Tower,
Hark! how they tell the Saxon swine, this land is ours, is ours!

Glory to God! my eyes have seen the ransomed fields of Down,
My ears have drunk the joyful news, " Stout Phelim hath his own."
Oh! may they see and hear no more, oh! may they rot to clay,
When they forget to triumph in the conquest of to-day.

Now, now we'll teach the shameless Scot to purge his thievish maw,
Now, now the Courts may fall to pray, for Justice is the Law,
Now, shall the Undertaker* square, for once, his loose accounts,
We'll strike, brave boys, a fair result, from all his false amount.

Come, trample down their robber rule, and smite its venal spawn,
Their foreign laws, their foreign church, their ermine and their
        lawn;
With all the specious fry of fraud that robbed us of our own,
And plant our ancient laws again beneath our lineal throne.

Our standard flies o'er fifty towers. o'er twice ten thousand men,
Down have we pluck'd the pirate Red never to rise agen;
The Green alone shall stream above our native field and flood—
The spotless Green, save where its folds are gemmed with Saxon
        blood!

Pity!† no, no, you dare not, Priest—not you our Father, dare
Preach to us now that godless creed—the murderer's blood to
        spare;
To spare his blood, while tombless still our slaughter'd kin implore,
" Graves and revenge" from Gobbin-Cliffs and Carrick's bloody
        shore!‡

Pity! could we "forget—forgive," if we were clods of clay,
Our martyr'd priests, our banish'd chiefs, our race in dark decay,
And worse than all—you know it, Priest—the daughters of our
        land,
With wrongs we blushed to name until the sword was in our hand!

* The Scotch and English adventurers planted in Ulster by James I. were
called Undertakers.
† Leland the Protestant Historian states that the Catholic Priests " laboured
zealously to moderate the excesses of war;" and frequently protected the English by concealing them in their places of worship, and even under their altars.
‡ The scene of the massacre of the unoffending inhabitants of Island Magee
by the garrison of Carrickfergus.

Pity! well, if you needs must whine, let pity have its way,
Pity for all our comrades true, far from our side to-day;
The prison-bound who rot in chains, the faithful dead who poured
Their blood 'neath Temple's lawless axe or Parson's ruffian sword.

They smote us with the swearer's oath, and with the murderer's
    knife,
We in the open field will fight, fairly for land and life;
But, by the Dead and all their wrongs, and by our hopes to-day,
One of us twain shall fight their last, or be it we or they—

They bann'd our faith, they bann'd our lives, they trod us into earth,
Until our very patience stirred their bitter hearts to mirth;
Even this great flame that wraps them now, not *we* but *they* have
    bred,
Yes, this is their own work, and now, THEIR WORK BE ON THEIR
    HEAD.

Nay, Father, tell us not of help from Leinster's Norman Peers,
If we but shape our holy cause to match their selfish fears,—
Helpless and hopeless be their cause who brook a vain delay,
Our ship is launched, our flag's afloat, whether they come or stay

Let Silken Howth, and savage Slane still kiss their tyrant's rod,
And pale Dunsany still prefer his Master to his God,
Little we'd miss their fathers' sons, the Marchmen of the Pale,
If Irish hearts and Irish hands had Spanish blade and mail?

Then, let them stay to bow and fawn, or fight with cunning words;
I fear me more their courtly acts than England's hireling swords,
Nathless their creed they hate us still, as the Despoiler hates,
Could they love us, and love their prey, our kinsmen's lost estates!

Our rude array's a jaggèd rock to smash the spoiler's power,
Or need we aid, His aid we have who doomed this gracious hour;
Of yore he led his Hebrew host to peace through strife and pain,
And us he leads the self-same path, the self-same goal to gain.

Down from the sacred hills whereon a SAINT* commun'd with God,
Up from the vale where Bagnall's blood manured the reeking sod,
Out from the stately woods of Truagh, M'Kenna's plundered home,
Like Malin's waves, as fierce and fast, our faithful clansmen come.

* St. Patrick, whose favourite retreat was Lecale, in the County Down.

Then, brethren, *on!*—O'Neill's dear shade would frown to see you
    pause—
Our banished Hugh, our martyred Hugh, is watching o'er your
    cause—
His generous error lost the land—he deemed the Norman true,
Oh! forward! friends, it must not lose the land again in you!

BATTLE OF BENBURB.

1646.

[About the end of May, 1646, Owen Roe O'Neill, at the head of five thousand foot and five hundred horse, approached Armagh. Monroe, who was
then stationed within ten miles of the city, marched thither on the 4th of June,
at midnight, with eight hundred horse and six thousand foot. Meanwhile,
O'Neill, aware of his advance, had encamped his troops at Benburb, betwixt
two small hills. The rear of his army was protected by a wood, and the right
by the river Blackwater. Here Monroe determined to attack him, and for this
purpose marched thither on the 5th of June, at the head of his troops. He
had ordered his brother, George Monroe, to proceed expeditiously with his
corps from Coleraine, and to join him at Glasslough or Benburb. O'Neill, aware
of this movement, had despatched Colonel Bernard M'Mahon and Patrick Mac
Neny, with their regiments, to prevent this force from joining with Monroe.
Monroe himself had passed the river, at a ford near Kinard (now Caledon) and
marched towards Benburb. As he advanced, he was met by Colonel Richard
O'Farrell, who occupied a strait through which it was necessary for him to
pass; but the fire of his cannon compelled that commander, after a short ren-
contre, to retreat. And now the two armies met in order of battle. The wary
O'Neill amused his enemy, during several hours, with various manœuvres and
trifling skirmishes, until the sun, which at first had been favourable to the
Scots, began to descend in the rear of the Irish troops, and shed a dazzling
glare on their enemies. The detachment which O'Neill had sent against George
Monroe, was seen returning towards the hostile armies. The Scottish general
at first imagined that this was the expected reinforcement from Coleraine; but
when he perceived his error, he prepared instantly to retreat. O'Neill, however, seized the opportunity with the promptitude of an experienced commander, and charged the Scots and British with the most determined valour.
The gallant Lord Blaney, at the head of an English regiment, made a noble
defence. He fell combating with the most undaunted resolution, and his men
maintained their ground till they were hewn to pieces, fighting around their
beloved commander. Meanwhile the Scottish cavalry was broken by O'Neill's
horse, and a general rout ensued. One regiment indeed, commanded by Colonel
Montgomery, retreated with some regularity, but the rest of the British troops
fled in total disorder. Lord Montgomery, twenty-one officers, and one hundred
and fifty soldiers were taken prisoners; three thousand two hundred and forty-
three men were slain on the field of battle, and many perished the succeeding
day in the rout. Monroe himself fled with the utmost precipitation, leaving his
artillery, tents, and baggage, with the greater part of his arms, booty, and pro-

visions to the enemy. Colonel Conway, accompanied by Captain Burke, also escaped to Newry, after having two horses slain under him in his flight. The loss of O'Neill in this decisive battle was only seventy men killed and two hundred wounded.—*Moore's Ireland*, vol. iv. page 284.]

GIVE praise to the Virgin Mother! O'Neill is at Benburb,
The Chieftain of the martial soul, who scorns the Saxon curb;
Between two hills his camp is pitch'd, and in its front upthrown,
The "Red Hand" points to victory from the standard of Tyrone;
Behind him rise the ancient woods, while on his flank anear him,
The deep Blackwater calmly glides and seems to greet and cheer
    him.

'Tis a glorious morn in glowing June! Against the sapphire sky,
Bright glancing in the golden light the adverse banners fly;
With godly boast the Scottish host, led on by stout Monroe,
Have crossed the main with venal swords to aid our ruthless foe.
And never in sorer need than now, the steel of the hireling fenc'd
    him,
For a dauntless Chief, and mighty host, stand in array against him!

By all the Saints they are welcome! across the crested wave,
For few who left Kinard this morn, ere night shall lack a grave.
The hour—the man, await them now, and retribution dire
Shall sweep their ranks from front to rear, by our avenging fire;
Yet on they march in pride of heart—the hell-engendered gloom
Of the grim, predestin'd Puritan impels them to their doom.

A thrilling charge their trumpets blow, but the shout—"O'Neill
    aboo!"
Is heard above the clarion call,—ringing the wild woods through!
"On," cries Lord Ardes, "On, Cunninghame! Forward with
    might and main."
And the flower of Scottish chivalry come swooping down the plain—
Fiercely they dash and thunder on,—as the wrathful waves come
    leaping
Toward Rathlin gray on a wild March day, when western winds
    are sweeping.

Now, where are thy hardy kerne O'Neill? oh, whither have they
    fled?
Hurrah! that volley from out the brakes hath covered the sward
    with dead.
The horses rear, and in sudden fear, the Scottish warriors flee,
And the field is dyed with a crimson tide from their bravest cavalry!

All praise to the Right-protecting God, who guards his own in
    danger,
None fell save one of the Irish host by the guns of the baffled
    stranger.

"On to the charge!" cries fierce Monroe,—"Fear not the bush
    and scrog—
Nor that the river bound your right, and your left be flanked with
    bog."
And on they come right gallantly,—but the Fabius of the West
Receives the shock, unmoved as a rock, and calm as a lion at rest.
The red artillery flashes in vain, or standeth spent and idle.
While the war-steeds bound across the plain, and foaming champ
    the bridle.

From the azure height of his realm of light the sun is sinking low,
And the blinding gleams of his parting beams dazzle the chafing
    foe ;
And Owen's voice like a trumpet note, rings clear through his
    serried ranks—
"Brave brothers in arms, the hour has come, give God and the
    Virgin thanks,
Strike home to-day, or heavier woes will crush our homes and
    altars,
Then trample the foeman in his blood, and curst be the slave who
    falters!"

A wild shout rends the lurid air, and at once from van to rear,
Of the Irish troops each soldier grasps his matchlock, sword, or
    spear ;
The chieftains haste their steeds to loose, and spring upon their feet,
That every chance be thus cut off, of a coward's base retreat.
And, "Onward! Forward!" swells the cry, in one tumultuous
    chorus,
By God and the Virgin's help we'll drive these hireling Scots be-
    fore us!"

'Tis body to body with push of pike—'tis foe confronting foe,
'Tis gun to gun and blade to blade—'tis blow returning blow.
Fierce is the conflict,—fell the strife,—but Heaven defends the
    right,—
The Puritan's sword is broken, and his army put to flight.
They break away in wild dismay, while some to escape the slaughter
Plunge panting into the purple tide that dyes the dark Blackwater

May Mary our Mother be ever praised, for the battle fought and won!
By Irish hearts and Irish hands, beneath that evening sun;
Three thousand two hundred and forty foes lay dead upon the plain,
And the Scots bewailed of their noble chiefs, Lord Blaney among
 the slain;
And ever against a deadly foe no weaponed hand should falter,
But strike as the valiant Owen Roe, for home, and shrine, and altar'

THE RED HAND FOR EVER.

(LAMH'-DEARG-ABOO. *)

BY THE AUTHOR OF "THE MONKS OF KILCREA."

HIGH race of O'Neill! will no Feardan bring thee
His *clearsach* of power to honour and sing thee?
From the hills of the North hath thy glory departed?
Are the bards of Tyr-Owen grown false and cold-hearted?
That when wine cups are fill'd and true hearts are meeting,
All silent, they pay thee nor homage nor greeting?—
No' though sad is my soul that thy house, once the greatest,
Hath left but one minstrel, the meanest and latest.
The broken in spirit, the weigh'd down by sorrow—
And, oh! how unlike to the bard of MacCnura,
Yet weak though his harp, as the reed by the river,
Its chords are his heart-strings—The Red Hand for ever!

Proud Lords of Tirowen! high chiefs of Lough Neagh,
How broad stretch'd the lands that were ruled by your sway
What eagle would venture to wing them right through,
But would droop on his pinion o'er half ere he flew.
From the hills of MacCarthan, and waters that ran
Like steeds down Glen Swilly to soft flowing Bann—
From Clannaboy's heather to Carrick's sea-shore,
And high Armagh of Saints to wild Innismore—
From the cave of the hunter on Tyrconnel hills
To the dells of Glenarm, all gushing with rills—
From Antrim's bleak rocks to the woods of Rosstrevor—
All echoed thy war-shout—The Red Hand for ever!

* Pronounced *Lauv-dearg-aboo!*—The Red or Bloody Hand for ever; the war-cry of the O'Neills.

Ah! show me on earth coronation so splendid
As when the *Lia-fail** thy chieftain ascended—
His Brehons around him—the blue heavens o'er him—
His true clan behind, and his broad lands before him;
While grouped far below him on moor and on heather
His tanists and chiefs are assembled together;
They give him a sword, and he swears to protect them;
A slender white wand, and he vows to direct them;
And then, in GOD's sunshine, O'NEILL they proclaim him,
Through life, unto death, ne'er to flinch from or fail him;
And earth hath no spell that can shatter or sever
That bond from their true hearts—The Red Hand for ever!

When the Saxon, with slaughter, swept fierce from the Pale,
Who arose, in their might, with their flag on the gale?—
Unconquer'd and strong met the foe in their pride,
And, as Rathlin the sea, dash'd their billows aside,
Who, like straw in the stubble, trod down Nugent's spears,
And MacAlister tore from his stout mountaineers?
Who humbled proud Essex? stern Bagnall, and bore
His flag, without check, from Armagh to Dunmore?—
Who conquer'd at *Baelbreac*,† made Munroe to flee,
Like a stag from the deer-hounds, on high Clan-hugh-bwee?—
Who scatter'd the Saxons, by plain, ford, and river?
Hark! answers Benburb with—The Red Hand, for ever!

And, oh! what a time for the scorner and scoffer,
When the Saxons to *Shane*‡ their poor coronet offer—
He, son of Great Nial, brave Owen's descendant,
And heir to a line through long centuries splendant—
Whose vassals were princes—O'Donnell, MacMahon,
O'Hanlon, MacSweeney, Maguire, and O'Cahan!—
Full well it became him, proud chief, back to hurl
In the teeth of the braggarts their title of *Earl*,
When the *Calliagh*,§ their Queen, all shame be upon her!
Strove the crest of his sires to lessen in honour—
When she gave to each Knight, from Loch Lene to Dunkever,
To blazon his shield with—The Red Hand for ever!

  * *Lia-fail*,—the stone of destiny, and the chair on which the O'Neills were crowned.
  † *Beal-breac*,—the spotted mouth, in allusion to the Battle of Beal-an-atha-buidh.
  ‡ *Shane*.—John O'Neill.
  § *Calliagh*,—an old woman.

And yet, gallant the sight, when thy proud chieftain came
To the halls of the Tudor, with nobles and train,
All brave men and true, young and goodly withal,
As ere charged in the battle, or paced within hall;
Apparel'd in saffron, all 'broidered with gold,
With banner and brand, like a monarch of old;
And many fair dames, as they bent to the tale
Of the greenwoods and bowers that bloom'd 'cross the Pale,
In secret soft murmur'd—"How happy 'twould be
With those strangers to dwell in their Isle o'er the sea,"
And the proud Queen herself, despite her endeavour,
In love as in war own'd—The Red Hand for ever!

High race of O'Neill! thy splendour has faded,
And the star of thy line sets, all altered and shaded;
From Dungannon no more thy proud chieftains sally,
And burst on the Pale from each mountain and valley.
The horn of thy hunters hath no lip to sound it,
And the hearth of thy halls hath no joy twin'd round it;
The Saxons have conquer'd—thy glories are over—
And darkness descends on the house of Ceancover!
Yet—yet, though the Fate-Stone be loos'd on Shane Tower,*
It totters, 'twill fall soon—oh, woe for the hour.
Some chief may arise with a soul to inherit
The fame of his sires with their freedom and spirit.
What, though the old tree may be worn out and drooping,
And each time-honoured branch all leafless and stooping,
There are saplings abroad by mountain and river,
And Tyr-Owen shall yet shout—The Red Hand for ever!

                                                             * * *

   * A head carved in stone, is pointed out upon one of the old walls at Shane's Castle, concerning which there is a tradition that when it falls the race will be extinct—it is already tottering.

LAMENT FOR OWEN ROE O'NEILL.

1649.

BY THOMAS DAVIS.

[Thomas Osborne Davis was born in Mallow, county Cork, in 1814, and died in September 1845 in Dublin. In early youth he was distinguished for the ardour and severe discipline with which he pursued his studies, and this closeness of application he steadily continued till the twenty-sixth year of his age, when he had accumulated an amount of knowledge rarely possessed by a man of his years. He finished his education in Trinity College, Dublin, and in 1840 was called to the Irish Bar. Upon the dismissal of Chancellor Plunket in that year, Davis first directed his mind to politics; he and his friend John Dillon, becoming contributors to one of the Dublin papers. Some time after, this Journal having changed its independent tone (the proprietor was looking for place which he subsequently obtained), they withdrew their support, and transferred their services to the silent but practical work of the Committee of the Repeal Association,—of which they were both members. The want of a thoroughly independent and national Journal being felt by the young men of the country,—Thomas Davis, John Dillon, and Charles Gavan Duffy determined in 1842 to establish the *Nation*, as a political and literary Journal, under the editorial management of Mr. Duffy, who had previously conducted the *Belfast Vindicator*. The *Nation's* principal aim was to teach the people that in education and industrial pursuits their true dignity consisted, and to impress upon them the importance of temperance and self-reliance as the means best calculated to secure the nationality and independence of the country. It was then that Davis became a man of great and noble purposes; he threw his whole heart and soul into the new undertaking,—and possessing the rare power of imbuing others with his own burning spirit, the *Nation* was supported by a staff of writers never equalled before in Irish journalism. To promote the object for which this journal was established, the editor held it to be indispensable that songs and ballads for the people should form a prominent feature. He knew their stirring and fascinating influence upon the Irish heart. A poet who could produce such national ballads as would find a ready acceptance with the people was required; and though Davis had previously never attempted verse, he did not hesitate in this emergency to undertake to supply this great *desideratum*. The following vigorous and highly dramatic ballad was his first contribution; this, and his other productions in these volumes, will amply prove that he did not mistake his vocation. He not only wrote himself but incited others to do the like, until the *Nation* became the medium of giving to the world some of the finest ballads of modern times. A more earnest or sincere man than Davis never lived. In his total abnegation of self,—in his unwearied industry which no obstacles could abate,—in his fiery genius and generous impulses, he was "his own parallel." The characteristics of his nature were a strict love of truth and right, and an exuberant, joyous spirit; and though confident of his power and influence, as a poet and essayist, his ambition was to rank beside Owen Roe and Grattan, rather than beside Moore and Goldsmith. He estimated talents and fame, however brilliant and dazzling, and liberty, however broad and secure, in proportion only as they promoted solid virtue and permanent happiness. Acting upon these principles he effected during his short career, more than most others in a long life could accomplish. His devoted love for Ireland knew no bounds, his fidelity to her interests has rarely been equalled; and he served her with intense zeal, without stint or reserve, for the sole gratification of doing good to his kind. His simplicity and almost womanly tenderness of nature were beautifully blended with the severe integrity of his principles. His masculine understanding, his high enthusiasm, his marvellous energy and unconquerable resolution preeminently fitted him for the achievement of any noble or patriotic enterprize. He bore nature's impress of a great man,—and she had marked him as the faithful champion of his country's rights and freedom.]

Time—10th Nov. 1649. Scene—Ormond's Camp, County Waterford. Speakers—A Veteran of Owen O'Neill's clan, and one of the horsemen, just arrived with an account of his death.

"DID they dare, did they dare, to slay Owen Roe O'Neill?"
'Yes, they slew with poison him they feared to meet with steel.'
"May God wither up their hearts! May their blood cease to flow!
May they walk in living death, who poisoned Owen Roe!

Though it break my heart to hear, say again the bitter words."
'From Derry, against Cromwell, he marched to measure swords;
But the weapon of the Saxon met him on his way,
And he died at Clough-Oughter, upon St. Leonard's Day.'

Wail, wail ye for The Mighty One! Wail, wail ye for the Dead,
Quench the hearth, and hold the breath—with ashes strew the head.
How tenderly we loved him! How deeply we deplore!
Holy Saviour! but to think we shall never see him more.

Sagest in the council was he,—kindest in the hall,
Sure we never won a battle—'twas Owen won them all.
Had he lived—had he lived—our dear country had been free;
But he's dead, but he's dead, and 'tis slaves we'll ever be.

O'Farrell and Clanrickarde, Preston and Red Hugh,
Audley and MacMahon—ye are valiant, wise, and true;
But—what, what are ye all to our darling who is gone?
The Rudder of our Ship was he, our Castle's corner stone!

Wail, wail him through the Island! Weep, weep for our pride!
Would that on the battle-field our gallant chief had died!
Weep the Victor of Benburb—weep him, young man and old;
Weep for him, ye women—your Beautiful lies cold!

We thought you would not die—we were sure you would not go,
And leave us in our utmost need to Cromwell's cruel blow—
Sheep without a shepherd, when the snow shuts out the sky—
Oh! why did you leave us, Owen?   Why did you die?

Soft as woman's was your voice, O'Neill! bright was your eye,
Oh! why did you leave us Owen? why did you die?
Your troubles are all over, you're at rest with God on high;
But we're slaves, and we're orphans, Owen!—why did you die!"

THE WEXFORD MASSACRE.

1649.

BY MICHAEL JOSEPH BARRY.

[" The Mayor and Governor offered to capitulate; but whilst their commis-
sioners were treating with Cromwell,—Strafford, the Governor of the Castle,
perfidiously opened it to the enemy; the adjacent wall was immediately scaled,
and, after a stubborn but unavailing resistance in the Market-place, Wexford
was abandoned to the mercy of the assailants.   The tragedy so recently acted
at Drogheda was renewed.   No distinction was made between the defenceless
inhabitant and the armed soldier; nor could the shrieks and prayers of three
hundred females, who had gathered round the Great Cross, preserve them from
the swords of these ruthless barbarians."—*Lingard's England,* vol. viii. p. 276.
Under date of 19th October 1649, Cromwell says:—"I meddle not with any
man's conscience; but if by liberty of conscience be meant a liberty to exercise
the MASS, I judge it best to use plain dealing: where the Parliament of England have power. *that* will not be allowed of."—*Cromwell's Letters and Speeches
by Carlyle,* vol. ii. p. 228.]

THEY knelt around the Cross divine,
     The matron and the maid—
They bow'd before redemption's sign
     And fervently they prayed—
Three hundred fair and helpless ones,
     Whose crime was this alone—
Their valiant husbands, sires, and sons,
     Had battled for their own.

Had battled bravely, but in vain—
     The Saxon won the fight,
And Irish corses strewed the plain
     Where Valour slept with Right.

And now, that Man of demon guilt,
    To fated Wexford flew—
The red blood reeking on his hilt,
    Of hearts to Erin true!

He found them there—the young, the old—
    The maiden and the wife;
Their guardian Brave in death were cold,
    Who dared for *them* the strife.
They prayed for mercy—God on high!
    Before *thy* cross they prayed,
And ruthless Cromwell bade them die
    To glut the Saxon blade!

Three hundred fell—the stifled prayer
    Was quenched in woman's blood;
Nor youth nor age could move to spare
    From slaughter's crimson flood.
But nations keep a stern account
    Of deeds that tyrants do;
And guiltless blood to Heaven will mount,
    And Heaven avenge it, too!

"IN-FELIX FELIX."

BY T. D. M'GEE.

[Sir Phelim O'Neill was executed by Cromwell's order, at Dublin, in 1652,
as a punishment for the alleged "great Popish Massacre" of 1641. He was
offered his life, on the scaffold, if he would consent to inculpate King Charles.
He "stoutly refused," and was instantly executed.]

WHY is his name unsung, oh! Minstrel host?
Why do you pass his memory like a ghost?
Why is no rose, no laurel, on his grave?
Was he not constant, vigilant, and brave?
Why, when that hero-age you deify,
Why do you pass "*In-felix Felix*" by?

He rose the first—he looms the morning star
Of the long, glorious, unsuccessful war.
England abhors him! Has she not abhorr'd
All who for Ireland ventured life or word?

What memory would she not have cast away,
That Ireland hugs in her heart's-heart to-day?

He rose in wrath to free his fettered land,
"There's blood—there's English blood—upon his hand."
Ay, so they say!—three thousand less or more,
He sent untimely to the Stygian shore—
They were the keepers of the prison-gate—
He slew them, his whole race to liberate.

Oh! clear-eyed Poets, ye who can descry,
Through vulgar heaps of dead, where heroes lie—
Ye to whose glance the primal mist is clear—
Behold there lies a trampled Noble here.
Shall we not leave a mark? shall we not do
Justice to one so hated and so true?

If ev'n his hand and hilt were so distained,
If he was guilty, as he has been blamed,
His death redeemed his life—he chose to die,
Rather than get his freedom with a lie;
Plant o'er his gallant heart a laurel tree,
So may his head within the shadow be.

I mourn for thee, oh, hero of the North—
God judge thee gentler than we do on earth!
I mourn for thee, and for our Land, because
She dare not own the Martyrs in her cause.
But they, our Poets, they who justify—
They will not let thy memory rot or die.

————

OLIVER'S ADVICE.

AN ORANGE BALLAD.

BY COLONEL BLACKER.

The night is gathering gloomily, the day is closing fast—
The tempest flaps his raven wings in loud and angry blast;

The thunder clouds are driving athwart the lurid sky—
But, "put your trust in God, my boys, and keep your powder
   dry."*

There *was* a day when loyalty was hail'd with honour due,
Our banner the protection wav'd to all the good and true—
And gallant hearts beneath its folds were link'd in honour's tie,
We put our trust in God, my boys, and kept our powder dry.

When Treason bar'd her bloody arm, and madden'd round the land,
For king, and laws, and order fair, we drew the ready brand ;
Our gathering spell was William's name—our word was, " do or die,"
And still we put our trust in God, and kept our powder dry.

But now, alas ! a wondrous change has come the nation o'er,
And worth and gallant services remember'd are no more,
And, crush'd beneath oppression's weight, in chains of grief we lie—
But put your trust in God, my boys, and keep your powder dry.

Forth starts the spawn of Treason, the 'scap'd of Ninety-Eight,
To bask in courtly favour, and seize the helm of state—
E'en *they* whose hands are reeking yet with murder's crimson dye—
But put your trust in God, my boys, and keep your powder dry.

They come, whose deeds incarnadin'd the Slaney's silver wave—
They come, who to the foreign foe the hail of welcome gave ;
He comes, the open rebel fierce—he comes the Jesuit sly ;
But put your trust in God, my boys, and keep your powder dry.

They come, whose counsels wrapp'd the land in foul rebellious flame,
Their hearts unchastened by remorse, their cheeks unting'd by
   shame.
Be still, be still, indignant heart—be tearless, too, each eye,
And put your trust in God, my boys, and keep your powder dry.

The Pow'r that led his chosen, by pillar'd cloud and flame,
Through parted sea and desert waste, that Pow'r is still the same.
He fails not—He, the loyal hearts that firm on him rely—
So put your trust in God, my boys, and keep your powder dry.

---

* There is a well-authenticated anecdote of Cromwell. On a certain occasion, when his troops were about crossing a river to attack the enemy, he con-
cluded an address, couched in the usual fanatic terms in use among them, with
these words—" put your trust in God; but mind to keep your powder dry."

The Pow'r that nerv'd the stalwart arms of Gideon's chosen few,
The Pow'r that led great William, Boyne's reddening torrent thro',—
In his protecting aid confide, and every foe defy—
Then put your trust in God, my boys, and keep your powder dry.

Already see the star of hope emits its orient blaze,
The cheering beacon of relief it glimmers thro' the haze.
It tells of better days to come, it tells of succour nigh,
Then put your trust in God, my boys, and keep your powder dry.

See, see along the hills of Down its rising glories spread,
But brightest beams its radiance from Donard's lofty head.
Clanbrassil's vales are kindling wide, and "Roden" is the cry—
Then put your trust in God, my boys, and keep your powder dry.

Then cheer, ye hearts of loyalty, nor sink in dark despair,
Our banner shall again unfold its glories to the air.
The storm that raves the wildest, the soonest passes by;
Then put your trust in God, my boys, and keep your powder dry.

For "happy homes," for "altars free," we grasp the ready sword,
For freedom, truth, and for our God's unmutilated word,
These, these the war-cry of our march, our hope the Lord on high;
Then put your trust in God, my boys, and keep your powder dry.
        1834.

THE DEATH OF SCHOMBERG.

1690.

BY DIGBY PILOT STARKEY, M.R.I.A.

(AUTHOR OF "THEORIA.")

["Frederick Schonberg, or Schomberg, first developed his warlike talents under the command of Henry and William II. of Orange; afterwards obtained several victories over the Spaniards; reinstated on the throne the house of Braganza; defeated in England the last hopes of the Stuarts; and finally died at the advanced age of eighty-two, at the battle of the Boyne, in 1690."]

'Twas on the day when Kings did fight beside the Boyne's dark
        water,
And thunder roar'd from every height, and earth was red with
        slaughter,—

That morn an aged chieftain stood apart from mustering bands,
And, from a height that crown'd the flood, surveyed broad Erin's
    lands.

His hand upon his sword-hilt leant, his war-horse stood beside,
And anxiously his eyes were bent across the rolling tide:
He thought of what a changeful fate had borne him from the land
Where frown'd his father's castle-gate,* high o'er the Rhenis
    strand,

And plac'd before his opening view a realm where strang
Where he, a leader, scarcely knew the tongue of those
He looked upon his chequered life, from boyhood's ea
Through scenes of tumult and of strife, endur'd in e

To where the snows of eighty years usurped tl
And still the din was in his ears, the broads
He turn'd him to futurity, beyond the bat
But then a shadow from on high, hung

And through the darkness of the clou
Beheld, with winding-sheet and shr
He quail'd not, as he felt him nea
But, dashing off one rising tear,

"God of my fathers! death i
My hour is come, and I wou
For thee, for freedom, hav
Give me but victory for n

"Forbid the future to r
Or that, by freemen dr
From either curse, let
Acknowledge what a

He said : fate grante
    strode,
And fell, as on the

* Schonberg, or " th
the many now ruinous
dence of the chiefs of a
the time of Charlemag

He sleeps in a cathedral's gloom,* amongst the mighty dead,
And frequent, o'er his hallow'd tomb, redeedful pilgrims tread.
The other half, though fate deny, we'll strive for, one and all,
And William's—Schomberg's spirits nigh, we'll gain—or, fighting,
    fall !
      1833.

THE BATTLE OF THE BOYNE.

1690.

BY COLONEL BLACKER.

mer's morn, unclouded rose the sun,
waving corn their way the breezes won ;
orient beam, 'mid banks of verdure gay,
er stream held smilingly away.

a monarch camp'd around,
ide their white pavilions crowned ;
how'd, nor long beneath the ray
ed, to meet the new-born day.

, from out that dark ravine, †
the gleam of arms is seen ;
ong you verdant banks,
'd the martial ranks.

he echoing vales along,
ves on the gallant throng;
rdless all of life,
e deadly strife.

h glowing heart beats

'Death or Liberty !"
ith sounds unwonted

rd the mighty clang;

The silver stream is crimson'd wide, and clogg'd with many a corse,
As floating down its gentle tide come mingled man and horse.
Now fiercer grows the battle's rage, the guarded stream is cross'd,
And furious, hand to hand engage each bold contending host ;

He falls—the veteran hero falls,* renowned along the Rhine—
And *he*, whose name, while Derry's walls endure, shall brightly
shine.†
Oh! would to heav'n that churchman bold, his arms with triumph
blest,
The soldier spirit had controll'd that fir'd his pious breast.

And he, the chief of yonder brave and persecuted band,‡
Who foremost rush'd amid the wave, and gain'd the hostile strand ;
He bleeds, brave Caillemotte—he bleeds—'tis clos'd, his bright
career,
Yet still that band to glorious deeds his dying accents cheer.

And now that well contested strand successive columns gain,
While backward James's yielding band are borne across the plain.
In vain the sword green Erin draws, and life away doth fling—
Oh! worthy of a better cause and of a bolder king.

In vain thy bearing bold is shown upon that blood-stain'd ground ;
Thy tow'ring hopes are overthrown, thy choicest fall around.
Nor, shamed, abandon thou the fray, nor blush, though conquer'd
there,
A power against thee fights to-day no mortal arm may dare.

Nay, look not to that distant height in hope of coming aid—
The dastard thence has ta'en his flight, and left thee all betray'd.
Hurrah! hurrah! the victor shout is heard on high Donore ;
Down Platten's vale, in hurried rout, thy shatter'd masses pour.

But many a gallant spirit there retreats across the plain,
Who, change but kings, would gladly dare that battle field again.§
Enough! enough! the victor cries ; your fierce pursuit forbear,
Let grateful prayer to heaven arise, and vanquished freemen spare.

* Duke Schomberg.
† Walker, the gallant defender of Derry.
‡ Caillemotte, who commanded a regiment of French Protestants.
§ This alludes to the expression attributed to Sarsfield — "Only change
kings, and we will fight the battle over again."

Hurrah! hurrah! for liberty, for her the sword we drew,
And dar'd the battle, while on high our Orange banners flew;
Woe worth the hour—woe worth the state, when men shall cease
    to join
With grateful hearts to celebrate the glories of the Boyne!

THE BOYNE WATER.

(FROM W. R. WILDE'S "BEAUTIES OF THE BOYNE AND THE
BLACKWATER.)

'TWAS bright July's first morning clear,
    Of unforgotten glory,
That made this stream, through ages dear,
    Renown'd in song and story.
Yet, not her charms on history's page—
    For Nature's own I sought her;
And took my pleasant pilgrimage,
    To see the sweet Boyne water.

Here, musing on these peaceful banks,
    The mind looks back in wonder;
And visions rise of hostile ranks,
    Impatient, kept asunder:
From every land a warrior band—
    For Europe owns the quarrel—
His hand shall clench no barren branch,
    That snatches this day's laurel.

All-conquering William—great Nassau!
    Her crown a realm decreed him;
And here he vindicates her law,
    And champions here her freedom.
And ne'er let valour lose its meed—
    A foe right nobly banded,
Though changeless love for king and creed
    With treason's stain be branded.

Ah, wherefore cannot kings be great,
    And rule with man approving?
Or why should creeds enkindle hate,
    And all their precepts, loving?

Here, on a cast, land, life, and fame,
    Faith, freedom,—all abide it :
A glorious stake ! play out the game,
    Let war's red die decide it !

Now strike the tents—the rolling drums,
    Their loud defiance beating,
Right for the ford brave Schomberg comes,
    And Sarsfield gives him greeting.
Grenade and musket—hut and hedge
    In flame unintermitting ;
I' the very sedge, by the water's edge,
    The angry fuse is spitting.

The banks are steep, the stream is deep,
    The cannon deadly knelling ;
On man and horse, o'er many a corse,
    Th' impeded tide is swelling ;
Yet firm, as 'twere some pageant brave,
    To their trumpets' notes advancing.
And plumes and pennons proudly wave,
    And their eager swords are glancing.

With arms held high, and powder dry,
    Fast on the bank they're forming :—
Shame on those Kerne ! the steeps they fly,
    Should baffle England's storming.
But stand together—firmly stand !
    Down the defile, and crushing
Like loosen'd rocks, to the crowded strand,
    Come headlong squadrons rushing.

Gallantly done, bold Hamilton !
    The scared Dane flies before him ;
What can the Huguenot's pikeless gun
    'Gainst the sabres flashing o'er him ?
Their leader down—down in his blood—
    And William at a distance
Unhors'd, but toiling through the flood
    To back their brave resistance.

And back they go, the unsated foe,
    Still threatening, though retreating.

Away! the Walloon broadsword's blow
  Will never need repeating.
And away together, hilt to hilt,
  Through the frighted hamlet going;
The lavish blood, like water spilt,
  In its narrow street-way flowing.

The heights are carried : far and wide
  Are battle-lines extended ;
Morass and mound—on every side,
  And at every point defended ;
A moment well might William halt,
  In front a force so shielded ;
But prompt th' impetuous assault,
  And post on post is yielded.

But still the rattle and the roar,
  And flight, and hot pursuing ;
And Berwick rallies on Donore,
  The conflict fierce renewing.
No toil too great that wins renown ;
  The fight seems still beginning ;
Proud valour's meed is fortune's crown,
  And that crown is William's winning.

But where is James? What? urged to fly
  Ere quailed his brave defenders!
Their dead in Oldbridge crowded lie,
  But not a sword surrenders :
Again they've found the 'vantage ground ;
  Their zeal is still untiring ;
As slowly William hems them round
  In narrowing ring still firing.

O'Neill's upon the English front
  With whirlwind fury wheeling ;
And, flank or front, where'er the brunt,
  Their stoutest columns reeling :
Up, Brandenburg! the bravest yield,
  The hoof they're trodden under ;
On Inniskillings! and the field
  Shakes to their tramp of thunder !

And through and through the stubborn spears
  Such awful gaps they're cleaving—
Though Hamilton, still charging, cheers,
  The field's beyond retrieving.
Oh, Hamilton! a hero now
  O'er prostrate foemen riding:
A moment more, and where art thou?
  A foe thy rein is guiding.

Thy routed comrades crowd the pass:
  The weak impede the stronger;
And terror strikes the yielding mass,
  And the brave are bold no longer.
'Tis done: that beacon of the fight—
  That hope—the crown redeeming!
In heaven's sight, in victory's light,
  The English Banner's gleaming!

Now, Drogheda, undo thy gate—
  Saint Mary's bells are ringing;
The Mill-Mount captives, snatch'd from fate,
  Their grateful hymns are singing:
From dale and down, from field and fell,
  The sulphurous clouds are clearing;
The Boyne, with full but gentle swell,
  In beauty re-appearing.

But search the field, what friends are lost
  May claim our brief lamenting:
No victory wanting victory's cost
  Its scenic show presenting.
Schomberg, the silver-hair'd, is down—
  Caillemotte no trump awaketh—
And Walker, with his mural crown,
  His last, deep slumber taketh!

Well—honour'd be the graves that close
  O'er every bold and true heart!
And sorrows sanctified repose
  Thy dust, discrownèd Stuart!
O'er scenes like these our hearts may ache,
  When calmly we review them—
Yet each awake its part to take,
  If time should e'er renew them.

Here from my hand as from a cup
I pour this pure libation;
And ere I drink, I offer up
One fervent aspiration—
Let man with man—let kin with kin
Contend through fields of slaughter—
Whoever fights, may FREEDOM win!
As then at the Boyne water.

THE TREATY STONE OF LIMERICK.

ANON.

[The large stone which served Sarsfield for a chair and writing desk, when signing the articles of the treaty of Limerick, is still shown as an object of historic interest to the stranger visiting that city. It stands on the right bank of the Shannon, at the foot of Thomond Bridge.]

THE Treaty Stone of Limerick! what mem'ries of the past
Flash'd through my soul, when first on it mine eyes I fondly cast!
To see it proudly standing by the lordly Shannon's flood,
And think that there for centuries the grey old stone had stood!
How breathless did I listen while my fancy heard it tell,
Of all that, erst, 'mid strife and storm, the olden town befell;
Since proud Le Gros' * bold kinsman crossed the azure stream
        alone,
Till Chateau Renaud's † frigates weighed, beside the Treaty Stone.

The Treaty Stone of Limerick! the monument unbuilt,
Of Irish might, and Irish right—and Saxon shame and guilt—
That saw the Prince of Orange the siege obliged to raise,
And leave his wounded Brandenburghs to perish in the blaze,
When the storied maids and matrons rushed fearless on the foe,
At the breach where fell their kinsmen, by the side of Boisseleau—
That saw the vet'ran conqueror of Aughrim and Athlone
Forced to comply with D'Usson's terms—the aged Treaty Stone!

* Raymond Le Gros, one of the earliest of the Anglo-Norman invaders. His nephew, David Walsh, was the first to swim his horse across the river, in the attack made on Limerick by Raymond.
† The French Admiral, whose squadron conveyed Tesse, D'Usson and near five thousand Irish Brigadiers from Limerick.

The Treaty Stone of Limerick ! the ancient city's pride,
That oft rang loud with clash of steel, and oft with blood was dyed ;
That saw the hope of Lucan's Earl—his own unconquer'd band—
With stern resolve, but broken hearts, around it take their stand.
That saw him sign the Treaty, and saw him sign in vain ;
For shamefully 'twas broken, ere the Wild Geese reach'd the main;
That witnessed the departure and heard the wild *Ochone,*
As Louis's ships dropp'd down the tide that washed the Treaty
    Stone.

The Treaty Stone of Limerick !—that oft, with magic charm,
Lit up in wrath the Irish heart, and nerv'd the Irish arm.
What hewed, in scores, at Fontenoy, King George's cohorts down,
But burning thoughts of thee, and home—the treaty-riven town ?
And oh ! how Sarsfield's great heart throbb'd, on Landen's bloody
    field,
That fast for thee, for fatherland, his life-stream he could yield.
Thrice holier than the treasure * robb'd, by England's King from
    Scone,
Is the glory of old *Luimeneach*—the hallowed Treaty Stone !

————

THE PENAL TIMES.

["In Scotland what a work have the four-and-twenty letters to show for
themselves ! The natural enemies of vice, and folly, and slavery ; the great
sowers, but the still greater weeders of the human soil."—*John Philpot Curran.*]

IN that dark time of cruel wrong, when on our country's breast,
A dreary load, a ruthless code, with wasting terrors prest—
Our gentry stript of land and clan, sent exiles o'er the main,
To turn the scales on foreign fields for foreign monarchs' gain—
Our people trod like vermin down, all fenceless flung to sate
Extortion, lust, and brutal whim, and rancorous bigot hate—
Our priesthood tracked from cave to hut, like felons chased and
    lashed,
And from their ministering hands the lifted chalice dashed ;
In that black time of law-wrought crime, of stifling woe and thrall,
There stood supreme one foul device, one engine worse than all:

* The "stone of destiny" on which the old Scottish kings were wont to be
crowned—said to be removed from the Abbey of Scone, by Edward the First,
in one of his predatory excursions through Scotland.

Him whom they wished to keep a slave, they sought to make a
    brute—
They banned the light of heaven—they bade instruction's voice
    be mute.

God's second priest—the Teacher—sent to feed men's mind with
    lore—
They marked a price upon his head, as on the priest's before.
Well—well they knew that never, face to face beneath the sky,
Could tyranny and knowledge meet, but one of them should die:
That lettered slaves will link their might until their murmurs grow
To that imperious thunder-peal which despots quail to know;
That men who learn will learn their strength—the weakness of
    their lords—
Till all the bonds that gird them round are snapt like Samson's
    cords.
This well they knew, and called the power of ignorance to aid:
So might, they deemed, an abject race of soulless serfs be made—
When Irish memories, hopes, and thoughts, were withered, branch
    and stem—
A race of abject, soulless serfs, to hew and draw for them.

Ah, God is good and nature strong—they let not thus decay
The seeds that deep in Irish breasts of Irish feeling lay;
Still sun and rain made emerald green the loveliest fields on earth,
And gave the type of deathless hope, the little shamrock, birth;
Still faithful to their Holy Church, her direst straits among,
To one another faithful still, the priests and people clung,
And Christ was worshipped, and received with trembling haste
    and fear,
In field and shed, with posted scouts to warn of blood-hounds near;
Still, crouching 'neath the sheltering hedge, or stretched on moun-
    tain fern,
The teacher and his pupils met, feloniously—to learn;
Still round the peasant's heart of hearts his darling music twined,
A fount of Irish sobs or smiles in every note enshrined;
And still beside the smouldering turf were fond traditions told
Of heavenly saints and princely chiefs—the power and faith of old.

Deep lay the seeds, yet rankest weeds sprang mingled—could
    they fail?
For what were freedom's blessed worth, if slavery wrought not bale?
As thrall, and want, and ignorance, still deep and deeper grew,
What marvel weakness, gloom, and strife fell dark amongst us too,

And servile thoughts, that measure not the inborn wealth of man—
And servile cringe, and subterfuge to 'scape our master's ban !—
And drunkenness—our sense of woe a little while to steep—
And aimless feud, and murderous plot—oh, one could pause and
 weep !
'Mid all the darkness, faith in Heaven still shone, a saving ray,
And Heaven o'er our redemption watched, and chose its own
 good day.
Two men were sent us—one for years, with Titan strength of soul,
To beard our foes, to peal our wrongs, to band us and control.
The other at a later time, on gentler mission came,
To make our noblest glory spring from out our saddest shame !
On all our wondrous, upward course hath Heaven its finger set,
And we—but, oh, my countrymen, there's much before us yet !

How sorrowful the useless powers our glorious Island yields—
Our countless havens desolate, our waste of barren fields,
The all unused mechanic-might our rushing streams afford,
The buried treasures of our mines, our sea's unvalued hoard !
But, oh, there is one piteous waste whence all the rest have grown,
One worst neglect, the mind of man left desert and unsown.
Send KNOWLEDGE forth to scatter wide, and deep to cast its
 seeds,
The nurse of energy and hope, of manly thoughts and deeds.
Let it go forth : right soon will spring those forces in its train
That vanquish Nature's stubborn strength, that rifle earth and
 main—
Itself a nobler harvest far than Autumn tints with gold,
A higher wealth, a surer gain than wave and mine enfold ;
Let it go forth unstained, and purged from Pride's unholy leaven,
With fearless forehead raised to Man, but humbly bent to Heaven.

Deep let it sink in Irish hearts the story of their isle,
And waken thoughts of tenderest love, and burning wrath the
 while;
And press upon us, one by one, the fruits of English sway,
And blend the wrongs of bygone times with this our fight to-day;
And show our Fathers' constancy by truest instinct led,
To loathe and battle with the power that on their substance fed :
And let it place beside our own the world's vast page, to tell
That never lived the nation yet could rule another well.
Thus, thus our cause shall gather strength ; no feeling vague and
 blind,
But stamped by passion on the heart, by reason on the mind.

Let it go forth—a mightier foe to England's power than all
The rifles of America—the armaments of Gaul!
It *shall* go forth, and woe to them that bar or thwart its way;
'Tis God's own light—all heavenly bright—we care not who says
    nay!

THE PENAL DAYS.

BY THOMAS DAVIS.

Oh ! weep those days, the penal days,
    When Ireland hopelessly complained.
Oh ! weep those days, the penal days,
    When godless persecution reigned ;
        When, year by year,
        For serf and peer,
    Fresh cruelties were made by law,
        And, filled with hate,
        Our senate sate
    To weld anew each fetter's flaw.
Oh ! weep those days, those penal days—
Their mem'ry still on Ireland weighs.

They bribed the flock, they bribed the son,
    To sell the priest and rob the sire ;
Their dogs were taught alike to run
    Upon the scent of wolf and friar.
        Among the poor,
        Or on the moor,
    Were hid the pious and the true—
        While traitor knave,
        And recreant slave,
    Had riches, rank, and retinue ;
And, exiled in those penal days,
Our banners over Europe blaze.

A stranger held the land and tower
    Of many a noble fugitive ;
No Popish lord had lordly power,
    The peasant scarce had leave to live :
        Above his head
        A ruined shed,

No tenure but a tyrant's will—
    Forbid to plead,
    Forbid to read,
Disarm'd, disfranchis'd, imbecile—
What wonder if our step betrays
The freedman, born in penal days?

They're gone, they're gone, those penal days!
  All creeds are equal in our isle;
Then grant, O Lord, thy plenteous grace,
  Our ancient feuds to reconcile.
    Let all atone
    For blood and groan,
  For dark revenge and open wrong;
    Let all unite
    For Ireland's right,
And drown our griefs in Freedom's song;
Till time shall veil in twilight haze,
The memory of those Penal days.

THE PARALLEL.

BY THOMAS MOORE.

YES, sad one of Sion,* if closely resembling,
  In shame and in sorrow, thy wither'd-up heart—
If drinking deep, deep, of the same "cup of trembling"
  Could make us thy children, our parent thou art.

Like thee doth our nation lie conquer'd and broken,
  And fall'n from her head is the once royal crown;
In her streets, in her halls, Desolation hath spoken,
  And "while it is day yet, her sun hath gone down."†

Like thine doth her exile, 'mid dreams of returning,
  Die far from the home it were life to behold;
Like thine do her sons, in the day of their mourning,
  Remember the bright things that bless'd them of old.

---

* These verses were written after the perusal of a treatise by Mr. Hamilton, professing to prove that the Irish were originally Jews.
† "Her sun is gone down while it was yet day." *Jeremiah* xv. 9.

Ah, well may we call her, like thee, "The Forsaken," *
Her boldest are vanquish'd, her proudest are slaves;
And the harps of her minstrels, when gayest they waken,
Have tones 'mid their mirth like the wind over graves!

Yet hadst thou thy vengeance—yet came there the morrow,
That shines out, at last, on the longest dark night,
When the sceptre, that smote thee with slavery and sorrow,
Was shiver'd at once, like a reed in thy sight.

When that cup, which for others the proud Golden City †
Had brimm'd full of bitterness, drench'd her own lips;
And the world she had trampled on heard, without pity,
The howl in her halls, and the cry from her ships.

When the curse Heaven keeps for the haughty came over
Her merchants rapacious, her rulers unjust,
And a ruin, at last, for the earthworm to cover, ‡
The Lady of Kingdoms lay low in the dust. §

THE IRISH RAPPAREES.

A PEASANT BALLAD OF 1691.

BY CHARLES GAVAN DUFFY, M.P.

[When Limerick was surrendered, and the bulk of the Irish army took service with Louis XIV., a multitude of the old soldiers of the Boyne, Aughrim,
and Limerick, preferred remaining in the country at the risk of fighting for
their daily bread; and with them some gentlemen, loath to part from their
estates or their sweethearts, among whom REDMOND O'HANLON is perhaps
the most memorable. The English army and the English law drove them by
degrees to the hills, where they were long a terror to the new and old settlers
from England, and a secret pride and comfort to the trampled peasantry who
loved them even for their excesses. It was all they had left to take pride in.]

RIGH SHEMUS ‖ he has gone to France, and left his crown behind:—
Ill luck be theirs, both day and night, put runnin' in his mind!

* "Thou shalt no more be termed Forsaken." *Isaiah* lxii. 4.
† "How hath the oppressor ceased! the golden city ceased!" *Isaiah* xiv. 4.
‡ "Thy pomp is brought down to the grave . . . and the worms cover
thee." *Isaiah* xiv. 11.
§ "Thou shalt no more be called the Lady of Kingdoms." *Isaiah* xlvii. 5.
‖ *Righ Shemus,*—King James II.

Lord Lucan* followed after, with his Slashers brave and true,
And now the doleful keen is raised—" What will poor Ireland do?
   What must poor Ireland do?
Our luck," they say, "has gone to France—what *can* poor Ire-
   land do?"

O, never fear for Ireland, for she has so'gers still,
For Rory's boys are in the wood, and Remy's on the hill;
And never had poor Ireland more loyal hearts than these—
May God be kind and good to them, the faithful Rapparees!
         The fearless Rapparees!
The jewel were you, Rory, with your Irish Rapparees!

Oh, black's your heart, Clan Oliver, and coulder than the clay!
Oh, high's your head, Clan Sassenach, since Sarsfield's gone away!
It's little love you bear to us, for sake of long ago,
But howld your hand, for Ireland still can strike a deadly blow—
         Can strike a mortal blow—
Och! *dhar-a-Chreesth!* 'tis she that still could strike the deadly
   blow!

The Master's bawn, the Master's seat, a surly *bodagh*† fills;
The Master's son, an outlawed man, is riding on the hills.
But, God be praised, that round him throng, as thick as summer
   bees,
The swords that guarded Limerick wall—his loyal Rapparees!
         His lovin' Rapparees!
Who dare say *no* to Rory Oge, with all his Rapparees?

Black Billy Grimes of Latnamard, he racked us long and sore—
God rest the faithful hearts he broke!—we'll never see them more!
But I'll go bail he'll break no more, while Truagh has gallows-trees,
For why?—he met, one lonesome night, the fearless Rapparees!
         The angry Rapparees!
They never sin no more, my boys, who cross the Rapparees!

Now, Sassenach and Cromweller, take heed of what I say—
Keep down your black and angry looks, that scorn us night and
   day;

---

* After the Treaty of Limerick, Patrick Sarsfield, Lord Lucan, sailed with
the brigade to France, and was killed whilst leading his countrymen to victory
at the battle of Landen, in the Low Countries, on 29th July 1693.
† *Bodagh*,—a severe and inhospitable man.

For there's a just and wrathful Judge, that every action sees,
And He'll make strong, to right our wrong, the faithful Rapparees;
     The fearless Rapparees!
The men that rode at Sarsfield's side, the roving Rapparees!

THE CLAN OF MAC CAURA.*

BY D. F. M'CARTHY,

AUTHOR OF "BALLADS, POEMS AND LYRICS," AND PROFESSOR OF POETRY
IN THE CATHOLIC UNIVERSITY OF IRELAND.

Oh! bright are the names of the chieftains and sages,
That shine like the stars through the darkness of ages,
Whose deeds are inscribed on the pages of story,
There for ever to live in the sunshine of glory—
Heroes of history, phantoms of fable,
Charlemagne's champions, and Arthur's Round Table—
Oh! but they all a new lustre could borrow
From the glory that hangs round the name of Mac Caura!

Thy waves, Manzanares, wash many a shrine,
And proud are the castles that frown o'er the Rhine,
And stately the mansions whose pinnacles glance
Through the elms of Old England and vineyards of France;
Many have fallen, and many will fall—
Good men and brave men have dwelt in them all—
But as good and as brave men, in gladness and sorrow,
Have dwelt in the halls of the princely Mac Caura!

Montmorency, Medina, unheard was thy rank
By the dark-eyed Iberian and light-hearted Frank,
And your ancestors wandered, obscure and unknown,
By the smooth Guadalquiver, and sunny Garonne—
Ere Venice had wedded the sea, or enrolled
The name of a Doge in her proud "Book of Gold;†

---

* Mac Carthy—Mac Cartha (the correct way of spelling the name in Román characters) is pronounced in Irish Mac Caura, the *th* or dotted *t* having in that language, the soft sound of *h*.

† *Montmorency* and *Medina* are respectively at the head of the French and Spanish nobility —The first Doge elected in Venice in 709. Voltaire consid-

When her glory was all to come on like the morrow,
There were chieftains and kings of the clan of Mac Caura!

Proud should thy heart beat, descendant of Heber,*
Lofty thy head as the shrines of the Guebre,
Like *them* are the halls of thy forefathers shattered,
Like *theirs* is the wealth of thy palaces scattered.
Their fire is extinguished—*your* flag long unfurled—
But how proud were ye both in the dawn of the world!
And should both fade away, oh! what heart would not sorrow
O'er the towers of the Guebre—the name of Mac Caura!

What a moment of glory to cherish and dream on,
When far o'er the sea came the ships of Heremon,
With Heber, and Ir, and the Spanish patricians,
To free Inis-Fail from the spells of magicians,
Oh! reason had these for their quaking and pallor,
For what magic can equal the strong sword of valour?
Better than spells are the axe and the arrow,
When wielded or flung by the hand of Mac Caura!†

From that hour a Mac Caura had reigned in his pride
O'er Desmond's green valleys and rivers so wide,
From thy waters, Lismore, to the torrents and rills
That are leaping for ever down Brandon's brown hills;
The billows of Bantry, the meadows of Bear,
The wilds of Evaugh, and the groves of Glancare—
From the Shannon's soft shores to the banks of the Barrow—
All owned the proud sway of the princely Mac Caura!

In the house of Miodchuart,‡ by princes surrounded,
How noble his step when the trumpet was sounded,

---

ered the families whose names were inscribed in *The Book of Gold* at the
founding of the city as entitled to the first place in European nobility.—*Burke's
Commoners.*
* The Mac Carthys trace their origin to Heber Fionn, the eldest son of
Milesius, King of Spain, through Oilioll Olium, King of Munster, in the third
century.—*Shrines of the Guebre*—THE ROUND TOWERS.
† Heremon and Ir were also the sons of Milesius.—The people who were in
possession of the country when the Milesians invaded it, were the Tuatha de
Danaans, so called, says Keating, "from their skill in necromancy, of whom
some were so famous as to be called gods."
‡ The house of *Miodchuart* was an apartment in the palace of Tara, where
the provincial kings met for the dispatch of public business, at the Feis (pronounced as one syllable), or parliament of Tara, which assembled then once in

And his clansmen bore proudly his broad shield before him,
And hung it on high in that bright palace o'er him:
On the left of the monarch the chieftain was seated.
And happy was he whom his proud glances greeted;
'Mid monarchs and chiefs at the great Feis of Tara—
Oh! none was to rival the princely Mac Caura!

To the halls of the Red Branch, when conquest was o'er,
The champions their rich spoils of victory bore,*
And the sword of the Briton, the shield of the Dane,
Flashed bright as the sun on the walls of Eamhain—
There Dathy and Niall bore trophies of war,
From the peaks of the Alps and the waves of the Loire;†
But no knight ever bore from the hills of Ivaragh
The breast-plate or axe of a conquered Mac Caura!

In chasing the red deer what step was the fleetest,
In singing the love song what voice was the sweetest—
What breast was the foremost in courting the danger—
What door was the widest to shelter the stranger—
In friendship the truest, in battle the bravest—
In revel the gayest, in council the gravest—
A hunter to-day and a victor to-morrow?
Oh! who but a chief of the princely Mac Caura!

But, oh! proud Mac Caura, what anguish to touch on
The one fatal stain of thy princely escutcheon—
In thy story's bright garden the one spot of bleakness—
Through ages of valour the one hour of weakness!
Thou, the heir of a thousand chiefs, sceptred and royal—
Thou, to kneel to the Norman and swear to be loyal!
Oh! a long night of horror, and outrage, and sorrow,
Have we wept for thy treason, base Diarmid Mac Caura!

Oh! why, ere you thus to the foreigner pandered,
Did you not bravely call round your Emerald standard,

every three years—the ceremony alluded to is described in detail by Keating
See Petrie's "Tara."
    * The house of the Red Branch was situated in the stately palace of Eam-
hain (or Emania), in Ulster; here the spoils taken from the foreign foe were
hung up, and the chieftains who won them were called Knights of the Red
Branch.
    † Dathy was killed at the Alps by lightning, and Niall (his uncle and prede-
cessor), by an arrow fired from the opposite side of the river by one of his own
generals as he sat in his tent on the banks of the Loire in France.

The chiefs of your house of Lough Lene and Clan Awley,
O'Donogh, MacPatrick, O'Driscoll, MacAwley,
O'Sullivan More, from the towers of Dunkerron,
And O'Mahon, the chieftain of green Ardinterran?
As the sling sends the stone, or the bent bow the arrow,
Every chief would have come at the call of Mac Caura?

Soon, soon, didst thou pay for that error in woe—*
Thy life to the Butler—thy crown to the foe—
Thy castles dismantled, and strewn on the sod—
And the homes of the weak, and the abbeys of God!
No more in thy halls is the wayfarer fed—
Nor the rich mead sent round, nor the soft heather spread—
Nor the *clairsech's* sweet notes, now in mirth, now in sorrow—
All, all have gone by, but the name of Mac Caura!

Mac Caura, the pride of thy house is gone by,
But its name cannot fade, and its fame cannot d'e—
Though the Arigideen, with its silver waves, shine †
Around no green forests or castles of thine—
Though the shrines that you founded no incense doth hallow,
Nor hymns float in peace down the echoing Allo— ‡
One treasure thou keepest—one hope for the morrow—
True hearts yet beat of the clan of Mac Caura!

* Diarmid Mac Carthy, King of Desmond, and Daniel O'Brien, King of Thomond, were the first of the Irish princes to swear fealty to Henry the Second.
† ‡ The *Arigideen* means the little silver stream, and *Allo* the echoing river. By these rivers and many others in the South of Ireland, castles were erected and monasteries founded by the Mac Carthys.

THE DEATH OF O'CAROLAN.

BY T. D. M'GEE.

[Turlogh O'Carolan, born at Nobber, A.D. 1670, became blind at the age of manhood, and then the harp which had been his amusement became his profession. The lady of the Mac Dermott of Aldersford, in Roscommon, equipped him with horse, harp, and *gossoon*. At every house he was a welcome guest, and for half-a-century he wandered from mansion to mansion, improvising words and airs. Roscommon, the native county of Goldsmith, was his favourite district, where he died in 1731, at the house of his first patroness. One of Gold-

smith's most touching essays is on "Carolan the Blind," and his musical influence can certainly be traced not only in Goldsmith's Poems, but also in Sheridan,
Moore, and Gerald Griffin.]

THERE is an empty seat by many a Board,
  A Guest is missed in hostelry and hall—
There is a Harp hung up in Alderford
  That was in Ireland, sweetest harp of all.
The hand that made it speak, woe's me, is cold,
  The darkened eyeballs roll inspired no more;
The lips—the potent lips—gape like a mould,
  Where late the golden torrent floated o'er.

In vain the watchman looks from Mayo's towers
  For him whose presence filled all hearts with mirth;
In vain the gathered guests outsit the hours,
  The honoured chair is vacant by the hearth.
From Castle-Archdall, Moneyglass, and Trim,
  The courteous messages go forth in vain,
Kind words no longer have a joy for him
  Whose final lodge is in Death's dark demesne.

Kilronan Abbey is his Castle now,
  And there till Doomsday peacefully he'll stay;
In vain they weave new garlands for his brow,
  In vain they go to meet him by the way;
In kindred company he does not tire,
  The native dead and noble lie around,
His life-long song has ceased, his wood and wire
  Rest, a sweet harp unstrung, in holy ground.

Last of our ancient Minstrels! thou who lent
  A buoyant motive to a foundering Race—
Whose saving song, into their being blent,
  Sustained them by its passion and its grace.
God rest you! May your judgment dues be light,
  Dear Turlogh! and the purgatorial days
Be few and short, till clothed in holy white,
  Your soul may come before the Throne of rays.

BATTLE OF FONTENOY.

1745.

BY THOMAS DAVIS.

[Upon the death of Charles VI., Emperor of Austria, in 1740, his daughter Maria Theresa discovered that the sovereigns of Europe, instead of being true to their oaths and to her, made immediate claims upon her territories, and prepared to enforce them by open hostilities. In a short time the question became an European quarrel, to be settled only by the doubtful issue of war. Louis XV of France, and Frederick the Great opposed her, whilst England, Holland, Hungary, Bavaria, and Hanover, aided her in the protection of those rights which had been guaranteed to her. In prosecution of this war, an army of 79,000 men, commanded by Marshal Saxe, and encouraged by the presence of both King and Dauphin, laid siege to Tournay, early in May 1745. The Duke of Cumberland advanced at the head of 55,000 men, chiefly English and Dutch, to relieve the town. At the Duke's approach, Saxe and the King advanced a few miles from Tournay with 45,000 men, leaving 18,000 to continue the siege, and 6,000 to guard the Scheld. Saxe posted his army along a range of slopes thus: his centre was on the village of Fontenoy, his left stretched off through the wood of Barri, his right reached to the town of St. Antoine, close to the Scheld. He fortified his right and centre by the villages of Fontenoy and St. Antoine, and redoubts near them His extreme left was also strengthened by a redoubt in the wood of Barri, but his left centre, between that wood and the village of Fontenoy, was not guarded by any thing save slight lines. Cumberland had the Dutch, under Waldeck, on his left, and twice they attempted to carry St. Antoine, but were repelled with heavy loss. The same fate attended the English in the centre, who thrice forced their way to Fontenoy, but returned fewer and sadder men. Ingoldsby was then ordered to attack the wood of Barri with Cumberland's right. He did so, and broke into the wood, when the artillery of the redoubt suddenly opened on him, which, assisted by a constant fire from the French tirailleurs (light infantry), drove him back. The Duke resolved to make one great and final effort. He selected his best regiments, veteran English corps, and formed them into a single column of 6,000 men. At its head were six cannon, and as many more on the flanks, which did good service. Lord John Hay commanded this great mass. Every thing being now ready, the column advanced slowly and evenly, as if on the parade ground. It mounted the slope of Saxe's position, and pressed on between the wood of Barri and the village of Fontenoy. In doing so, it was exposed to a cruel fire of artillery and sharp-shooters; but it stood the storm, and got behind Fontenoy. The moment the object of the column was seen, the French troops were hurried in upon them. The cavalry charged; but the English hardly paused to offer the raised bayonet, and then poured in a fatal fire. They disdained to rush at the picked infantry of France. On they went till within a short distance, and then threw in their balls with great precision, the officers actually laying their canes along the muskets, to make the men fire low. Mass after mass of infantry was broken, and on went the column, reduced, but still apparently invincible. Duc Richelieu had four cannon hurried to the front, and he literally battered the head of the column, while the household cavalry surrounded them, and, in repeated charges, wore down their

strength: but these French were fearful sufferers. Louis was about to leave
the field. In this juncture Saxe ordered up his last reserve—the Irish Brigade.
It consisted that day of the regiments of Clare, Lally, Dillon, Berwick, Roth,
and Buckley, with Fitzjames's horse. O'Brien, Lord Clare, was in command.
Aided by the French regiments of Normandy and Vaisseany, they were ordered
to charge upon the flank of the English with fixed bayonets without firing.
Upon the approach of this splendid body of men, the English were halted on
the slope of a hill, and up that slope the Brigade rushed rapidly and in fine order.
"They were led to immediate action, and the stimulating cry of ' *Cuimhnigidh
ar Luimneac agus ar fheile na Sacsanach,*' [' Remember Limerick and British
faith,'] was re-echoed from man to man. The fortune of the field was no
longer doubtful, and victory the most decisive crowned the arms of France."
The English were weary with a long day's fighting, cut up by cannon, charge
and musketry, and dispirited by the appearance of the Brigade—fresh, and
consisting of young men in high spirits and discipline—still they gave their fire
well and fatally; but they were literally stunned by the shout and shattered
by the Irish charge. They broke before the Irish bayonets, and tumbled down
the far side of the hill, disorganized, hopeless, and falling by hundreds. The
Irish troops did not pursue them far: the French cavalry and light troops
pressed on till the relics of the column were succoured by some English cavalry,
and got within the batteries of their camp. The victory was bloody and complete. Louis is said to have ridden down to the Irish bivouac, and personally
thanked them; and George II., on hearing it, uttered that memorable impre-
cation on the Penal Code, "Cursed be the laws which deprive me of such subjects." The one English volley, and the short struggle on the crest of the hill,
cost the Irish dear. One fourth of the officers, including Colonel Dillon, were
killed, and one third of the men. The capture of Ghent, Bruges, Ostend, and
Oudenarde followed the victory of Fontenoy.]

THRICE, at the huts of Fontenoy, the English column failed,
And, twice, the lines of Saint Antoine, the Dutch in vain assailed:
For town and slope were filled with fort and flanking battery,
And well they swept the English ranks, and Dutch auxiliary.
As vainly, through De Barri's wood, the British soldiers burst,
The French artillery drove them back, diminished, and dispersed.
The bloody Duke of Cumberland beheld with anxious eye,
And ordered up his last reserve, his latest chance to try.
On Fontenoy, on Fontenoy, how fast his generals ride!
And mustering come his chosen troops, like clouds at eventide.

Six thousand English veterans in stately column tread,
Their cannon blaze in front and flank, Lord Hay is at their head;
Steady they step adown the slope—steady they climb the hill;
Steady they load—steady they fire, moving right onward still,
Betwixt the wood and Fontenoy, as through a furnace blast,
Through rampart, trench, and palisade, and bullets showering fast;
And on the open plain above they rose, and kept their course,
With ready fire and grim resolve, that mocked at hostile force:

Past Fontenoy, past Fontenoy, while thinner grow their ranks—
They break, as broke the Zuyder Zee through Holland's ocean
    banks.

More idly than the summer flies, French tirailleurs rush round ;
As stubble to the lava tide, French squadrons strew the ground ;
Bomb-shell, and grape, and round-shot tore, still on they marched
    and fired—
Fast, from each volley, grenadier and voltigeur retired.
" Push on, my household cavalry !" King Louis madly cried ;
To death they rush, but rude their shock—not unavenged they
    died.
On through the camp the column trod—King Louis turns his rein :
" Not yet, my liege," Saxe interposed, " the Irish troops remain ;"
And Fontenoy, famed Fontenoy, had been a Waterloo,
Were not these exiles ready then, fresh, vehement, and true.

" Lord Clare," he says, " you have your wish, there are your
    Saxon foes !"
The Marshal almost smiles to see, so furiously he goes !
How fierce the look these exiles wear, who're wont to be so gay,
The treasured wrongs of fifty years are in their hearts to-day—
The treaty broken, ere the ink wherewith 'twas writ could dry,
Their plundered homes, their ruined shrines, their women's part-
    ing cry,
Their priesthood hunted down like wolves, their country over-
    thrown,—
Each looks, as if revenge for all were staked on him alone.
On Fontenoy, on Fontenoy, nor ever yet elsewhere,
Rushed on to fight a nobler band than these proud exiles were.

O'Brien's voice is hoarse with joy, as, halting, he commands,
" Fix bay'nets "—" charge,"—Like mountain-storm, rush on these
    fiery bands !
Thin is the English column now, and faint their volleys grow,
Yet, must'ring all the strength they have, they make a gallant
    show.
They dress their ranks upon the hill to face that battle wind—
Their bayonets the breakers' foam ; like rocks, the men behind !
One volley crashes from their line, when, through the surging
    smoke,
With empty guns clutched in their hands, the headlong Irish broke.
On Fontenoy, on Fontenoy, hark to that fierce huzza !
" Revenge ! remember Limerick ! dash down the Sassenagh !"

Like lions leaping at a fold, when mad with hunger's pang,
Right up against the English line the Irish exiles sprang:
Bright was their steel, 'tis bloody now, their guns are filled with
    gore;
Through shattered ranks, and severed files, and trampled flags
    they tore;
The English strove with desperate strength, paused, rallied, stag-
    gered, fled—
The green hill-side is matted close with dying and with dead;
Across the plain, and far away passed on that hideous wrack,
While cavalier and fantassin dash in upon their track.
On Fontenoy, on Fontenoy, like eagles in the sun,
With bloody plumes the Irish stand—the field is fought and won!

"THE BRIGADE" AT FONTENOY.

11TH MAY, 1745.

BY BARTHOLOMEW DOWLING.

[Mr. Dowling is a native of Limerick, and was clerk to the Treasurer of the
Corporation of that city, when he wrote the following spirited ballad. He
emigrated to the United States in 1851, and has there obtained that position
to which his talents and his industry so justly entitle him.]

BY our camp fires rose a murmur,
    At the dawning of the day,
And the tread of many footsteps
    Spoke the advent of the fray;
And as we took our places,
    Few and stern were our words,
While some were tightening horse-girths,
    And some were girding swords.

The trumpet blast has sounded
    Our footmen to array—
The willing steed has bounded,
    Impatient for the fray—
The green flag is unfolded,
    While rose the cry of joy—
" Heaven speed dear Ireland's banner
    To-day at Fontenoy."

We looked upon that banner,
  And the memory arose
Of our homes and perished kindred,
  Where the Lee or Shannon flows;
We looked upon that banner,
  And we swore to God on high
To smite to-day the Saxons' might—
  To conquer or to die.

Loud swells the charging trumpet—
  'Tis a voice from our own land—
God of battles—God of vengeance,
  Guide to-day the patriot's brand;
There are stains to wash away—
  There are memories to destroy,
In the best blood of the Briton
  To-day at Fontenoy.

Plunge deep the fiery rowels
  In a thousand reeking flanks—
Down, chivalry of Ireland,
  Down on the British ranks—
Now shall their serried columns
  Beneath our sabres reel—
Through their ranks, then, with the war-horse—
  Through their bosoms with the steel.

With one shout for good King Louis,
  And the fair land of the vine,
Like the wrathful Alpine tempest,
  We swept upon their line—
Then rang along the battle-field
  Triumphant our hurrah,
And we smote them down, still cheering
  "*Erin, slanthagal go bragh.*"*

As prized as is the blessing
  From an aged father's lip—
As welcome as the haven
  To the tempest-driven ship—
As dear as to the lover
  The smile of gentle maid—

_____
  * Ireland, the bright toast for ever!

Is this day of long-sought vengeance
  To the swords of the Brigade.

See their shattered forces flying,
  A broken, routed line—
See England, what brave laurels
  For your brow to-day we twine.
Oh, thrice blessed the hour that witnessed
  The Briton turn to flee
From the chivalry of Erin,
  And France's "*fleur de lis.*"

As we lay beside our camp fires,
  When the sun had passed away,
And thought upon our brethren,
  Who had perished in the fray—
We prayed to God to grant us,
  And then we'd die with joy,
One day upon our own dear land
  Like this of Fontenoy.

KATHALEEN NY-HOULAHAN.*

(A JACOBITE RELIC—FROM THE IRISH.)

BY J. C. MANGAN.

LONG they pine in weary woe, the nobles of our land,
Long they wander to and fro, proscribed, alas! and banned;
Feastless, houseless, altarless, they bear the exile's brand:
    But their hope is in the coming-to of Kathaleen Ny-Hou-
      lahan!

Think her not a ghastly hag, too hideous to be seen,
Call her not unseemly names, our matchless Kathaleen;
Young she is, and fair she is, and would be crowned a queen,
    Were the king's son at home here with Kathaleen Ny-
      Houlahan!

* *Anglice*, Catherine Holohan, a name by which Ireland was allegorically
known.

Sweet and mild would look her face, O none so sweet and mild,
Could she crush the foes by whom her beauty is reviled;
Woollen plaids would grace herself and robes of silk her child.
> If the king's son were living here with Kathaleen Ny-
> Houlahan!

Sore disgrace it is to see the Arbitress of thrones,
Vassal to a *Saxoneen* of cold and sapless bones!
Bitter anguish wrings our souls—with heavy sighs and groans
> We wait the Young Deliverer of Kathaleen Ny-Houlahan!

Let us pray to Him who holds Life's issues in his hands—
Him who formed the mighty globe, with all its thousand lands;
Girding them with seas and mountains, rivers deep, and strands,
> To cast a look of pity upon Kathaleen Ny-Houlahan!

He, who over sands and waves led Israel along—
He, who fed, with heavenly bread, that chosen tribe and throng—
He, who stood by Moses, when his foes were fierce and strong—
> May He show forth His might in saving Kathaleen Ny-
> Houlahan!

WELCOME TO THE PRINCE.

(A JACOBITE RELIC—FROM THE IRISH.)

BY J. C. MANGAN.

[This was written about the period of the Battle of Culloden (27th April 1746) by William Heffernan, surnamed Dall, or the Blind, of Shronehill, county Tipperary.

> LIFT up the drooping head,
>> Meehal Dubh Mac-Giolla-Kierin!*
> Her blood yet boundeth red
>> Through the myriad veins of Erin.
> No! no! she is not dead
>> Meehal Dubh Mac-Giolla-Kierin!
> Lo! she redeems
> The lost years of bygone ages—

* Dark Michael M'Gilla Kerin, prince of Ossory.

New glory beams
Henceforth on her History's pages!
Her long penitential Night of Sorrow
Yields at length before the reddening morrow!

You heard the thunder-shout
    Meehal Dubh Mac-Giolla-Kierin!
Saw the lightning streaming out
    O'er the purple hills of Erin!
And, bide you yet in doubt,
    Meehal Dubh Mac-Giolla-Kierin?
  O! doubt no more!
Through Ulidia's voiceful valleys,
  On Shannon's shore,
Freedom's burning spirit rallies.
Earth and Heaven unite in sign and omen *
Bodeful of the downfall of our foemen.

Thurot commands the North,
    Meehal Dubh Mac-Giolla-Kierin!
Louth sends her heroes forth,
    To hew down the foes of Erin!
Swords gleam in field and *gorth*, †
    Meehal Dubh Mac-Giolla-Kierin!
  Up! up! my friend!
There's a glorious goal before us;
  Here will we blend
Speech and soul in this grand chorus :—
" By the Heaven that gives us one more token,
We will die, or see our shackles broken!"

Charles leaves the Grampian hills,
    Meehal Dubh Mac-Giolla-Kierin!
Charles, whose appeal yet thrills,
    Like a clarion-blast, through Erin.
Charles, he whose image fills
    Thy soul, too, Mac-Giolla-Kierin!
  Ten thousand strong,
His clans move in brilliant order,

---

* This is an allusion to that well-known atmospherical phenomenon of the
" cloud armies," which is said to have been so common about this period in
Scotland.
  † *Gorth*, literally means Garden.

Sure that ere long
He will march them o'er the Border,
While the dark-haired daughters of the Highlands
Crown with wreaths the Monarch of three islands!

Fill, then, the ale-cup high,
    Mechal Dubh Mac-Giolla-Kierin!
Fill! the bright hour is nigh
    That shall give her own to Erin!
Those who so sadly sigh,
    Even as you, Mac-Giolla-Kierin,
  Henceforth shall sing.
Hark!—O'er heathery hill and dell come
  Shouts for the King!
Welcome, our Deliverer! Welcome!
Thousands this glad night, ere turning bedward,
Will, with us drink "Victory to Charles Edward!"

IRISH EMIGRANTS.

1776.

BY CARROLL MALONE.

OH! how she ploughed the ocean, the good ship Castle Down,
The day we hung our colours out, the Harp *without* the Crown!
A gallant barque, she topped the wave; and fearless hearts were we,
With guns, and pikes, and bayonets, a stalwart company.
'Twas a sixteen years from THUROT;* and sweeping down the bay,
The "Siege of Carrickfergus" so merrily we did play;
By the old Castle's foot we went, with three right hearty cheers;
And waved our green cockades aloft, for we were Volunteers,
            Volunteers,
Oh! we were in our prime that day, stout Irish Volunteers.

'Twas when we waved our anchor on the breast of smooth Gar-
    moyle,
Our guns spoke out in thunder: "Adieu, sweet Irish soil!"

  * The landing of Thurot at Carrickfergus, in 1760, was long used as an
epoch by the people in the North, and is known to have occasioned the first
formation of the Irish Volunteers.

At Whiteabbey, and Greencastle, and Holywood so gay,
Were hundreds waving handkerchiefs, with many a loud huzza.
Our voices o'er the water went to the hollow mountains round;
Young Freedom struggling at her birth, might utter such a sound.
But one green slope beside Belfast, we cheered, and cheered it still:
The people had changed its name that year, and called it
    Bunker's Hill;*
                Bunker's Hill,
Oh! that our hands, like our hearts, had been in the trench at
    Bunker's Hill!

Our ship cleared out for Quebec port; but thither little bent,
Up some New England river, to run her keel we meant.
We took our course due North as out round old Blackhead we
    steered,
Till Ireland bore south-west by south, and Fingal's rock appeared.
Then on the poop stood Webster, while the ship hung flutteringly,
About to take her tack across the wide, wide ocean sea.
He pointed to the Atlantic—" Yonder's no place for slaves;
Haul down these British badges; for Freedom rules the waves,
            Rules the waves!"
Three hundred strong men answered, shouting, " Freedom rules
    the waves!"

Then all together rose, and brought the British ensign down;
And up we raised our island Green, without the British Crown:
Emblazoned there a golden harp, like maiden undefiled,
A shamrock wreath around its head, looked o'er the sea and smiled.
A hundred days, with adverse winds, we kept our course afar;
On the hundredth day, came bearing down, a British sloop-of-war.
When they spied our flag they fired a gun; but as they neared
    us fast,
Old Andrew Jackson went aloft, and nailed it to the mast,
            To the mast.
A soldier was that old Jackson; he made our colours fast.

Patrick Henry was our Captain, as brave as ever sailed:
" Now we must do or die," said he, " for our green flag is nailed."
Silently came the sloop along; and silently we lay
Till with ringing cheers and cannonade the foe began the fray:

  * Bunker's Hill on the shore of Down, opposite Belfast, was so called in
honour of the famous hill at Boston.

Then, their boarders o'er the bulwarks, like shuttlecocks we cast,
One broadside volley from our guns swept down the tapering
 mast :—
"Now, British Tars! St. George's cross is trailing in the sea;
How do you like the greeting, and the handsel of the Free?
   Of the Free?
These are the terms and tokens of men who will be free."

They answer'd us with cannon, their honour to redeem:
To shoot away our Irish flag, each gunner took his aim;
They ripped it up in ribbons, till it fluttered in the air,
And filled with shot-holes, till no trace of golden Harp was there;
But the ragged holes did glance and gleam, in the sun's golden
 light,
Even as the twinkling stars adorn God's unfurled flag at night.
With drooping fire we sung—"Good night, and fare-ye-well,
 brave Tars!"
Our Captain looked aloft :—"By Heaven! the flag is stripes and
 stars,
   Stripes and stars."
Right into Boston port we sailed, below the Stripes and Stars.

THE VOLUNTEERS.

" Mother—dear mother, tell me what meant the proud array
Of armed men and prancing steeds which passed yon mountain
 way?
And who was he of noble mien and brow of lordly pride,
Who rode, like warrior chief of old, that gallant band beside?

" Marked you how lighted up his eye, as in the noonday sun
Their silken banners flutter'd wide and flash'd each polish'd gun,
And how with gentle courtesy he oft and lowly bowed,
As rang the brazen trumpets out, and cheer'd th' assembled crowd?

" Methinks the Spartan chief who fell at famed Thermopylæ,
Of whom we read but yesternight was such a man as he—
The same proud port and eagle eye—the same determined frown,
And supple arm to shield a friend or strike a foeman down.

" And then those troops as on they passed, in proud and glittering
    show,
Seemed worthy of the chief who led—'twere pity of the foe
Who roused to wrath their slumbering might, or wronged our
    own green land—
I'd promise them a scattered host with many a shivered brand."

" You're right, dear Mabel, for the chief who leads that warrior
    host
Is Grattan—high and honoured name—thy country's proudest
    boast ;
And they whose closely marshalled ranks the people hailed with
    cheers,
Thy country's soldier-citizens—the gallant Volunteers."

" Then why, dear mother—tell me why those Volunteers arose ?
Was it to guard some sacred right, or to repel our foes ?
For I have heard my father say he dreaded England's word
And English perfidy far more than foreign foeman's sword."

" They rose to guard from foreign foes—as well from British guile—
Thy liberties and mine, my child, and all within this Isle ;
To make this glorious land of ours—those hills we love so well,
A fitting home and resting place where freedom's foot might dwell.

" They rose and swore by Freedom's name, by kindred and by
    kind,
No foreign rule, no foreign guile, their country's limbs should bind—
That she should stand erect and fair, as in the olden time,
The loveliest 'mong the nations—of Ocean's Isles the prime.

" That they have nobly kept this pledge, bear witness one and all,
The bootless plots of England, the baffled hosts of Gaul.
That they may long be spared to guard our country's rights divine,
Should be your prayer at night and morn, my child, as it is mine."
                                        M. O'B.

•

SONG OF THE VOLUNTEERS OF 1782.

BY THOMAS DAVIS.

HURRAH ! 'tis done—our freedom's won—
   Hurrah for the Volunteers !
No laws we own, but those alone
   Of our Commons, King, and Peers.
The chain is broke—the Saxon yoke
   From off our neck is taken ;
Ireland awoke--Dungannon spoke—
   With fear was England shaken.

When Grattan rose, none dared oppose
   The claim he made for Freedom :
They knew our swords, to back his words,
   Were ready, did he need them.
Then let us raise, to Grattan's praise,
   A proud and joyous anthem ;
And wealth, and grace, and length of days,
   May God, in mercy grant him!

Bless Harry Flood, who nobly stood
   By us, through gloomy years !
Bless Charlemont, the brave and good,
   The Chief of the Volunteers
The North began ; the North held on
   The strife for native land ;
Till Ireland rose, and cowed her foes—
   God bless the Northern land !

And bless the men of patriot pen —
   Swift, Molyneux, and Lucas ;
Bless sword and gun, which " Free Trade " won—
   Bless God ! who ne'er forsook us .
And long may last, the friendship fast,
   Which binds us all together ;
While we agree, our foes shall flee
   Like clouds in stormy weather.

Remember still, through good and ill,
   How vain were prayers and tears—

P

How vain were words, till flashed the swords
Of the Irish Volunteers.
By arms we've got the rights we sought
Through long and wretched years—
Hurrah! 'tis done, our Freedom's won—
Hurrah for the Volunteers!

———

WAKE OF WILLIAM ORR.

1798.

BY DR. DRENNAN.

[The case of William Orr involves one of the most ruthless acts of tyranny that preceded the insurrection of 1798. Orr, who was a young Presbyterian farmer of Antrim, and a man of great personal popularity, was tried and convicted in October '97 of administering the United Irish oath to a private soldier, named Whitly. But, on the same day, four of his jury made affidavits stating that whisky had been introduced into the jury room, and the verdict agreed to under the joint influence of drunkenness and intimidation. Next day Whitly, the crown witness, confessed that his evidence was false or distorted in essential particulars. Under these strange circumstances Orr was reprieved by government; and the reprieve twice renewed. But, ultimately, when the nation confidently awaited the commutation of his sentence, *he was ordered for execution.* A storm of indignation followed this arbitrary and merciless decision. The most moderate men were outraged by its injustice; the most timid were stung to resistance by its naked tyranny. Orr died with unshaken courage, exhorting his countrymen " to be true and faithful to each other as he had been true to them." His fortitude increased popular enthusiasm to a passion. He was universally regarded as a martyr to Liberty; and " Remember Orr! " became the most popular and stimulating watch-word of the national party. His death was celebrated in innumerable elegies, of which these noble and affecting verses are the best.]

HERE our murdered brother lies;
Wake him not with women's cries:
Mourn the way that manhood ought;
Sit in silent trance of thought.

Write his merits on your mind;
Morals pure and manners kind;
In his head as on a hill,
Virtue plac'd her citadel.

Why cut off in palmy youth?
Truth he spoke, and acted truth.
Countrymen UNITE, he cried,
And died—for what his Saviour died.

God of Peace, and God of Love,
Let it not thy vengeance move,
Let it not thy lightnings draw;
A nation guillotin'd by law.

Hapless Nation! rent, and torn,
Thou wert early taught to mourn,
Warfare of six hundred years!
Epochs marked with blood and tears!

Hunted thro' thy native grounds,
Or flung *reward* to human hounds;
Each one pull'd and tore his share,
Heedless of thy deep despair.

Hapless Nation—hapless Land,
Heap of uncementing sand!
Crumbled by a foreign weight;
And by worse, domestic hate.

God of mercy! God of peace!
Make the mad confusion cease;
O'er the mental chaos move,
Through it SPEAK the light of love.

Monstrous and unhappy sight!
Brothers' blood will not unite;
Holy oil and holy water,
Mix, and fill the world with slaughter.

Who is she with aspect wild?
The widow'd mother with her child,
Child new stirring in the womb!
Husband waiting for the tomb!

Angel of this sacred place
Calm her soul and whisper peace,
Cord, or axe, or Guillotin'
Make the sentence—not the sin.

Here we watch our brother's sleep;
Watch with us, but do not weep;
Watch with us thro' dead of night,
But expect the morning light.

Conquer fortune—persevere!—
Lo! it breaks, the morning clear!
The cheerful COCK awakes the skies,
The day is come—arise!—arise!

[Dr. Drennan, the author of this ballad, was one of the ablest writers among the United Irishmen. His *Letters of Orellana* contributed powerfully to enlist Ulster in "the Union." His songs and ballads, which were chiefly directed to the same object, are vigorous and graceful beyond any political poetry of the period. His song commencing "When Erin first rose from the dark swelling flood," which fixed upon Ireland the title of "the Emerald Isle," Moore esteems among the most perfect of modern songs. A little volume of his poems was published in 1815, but is now very scarce. In 1794 he was brought to trial for his political principles; but then, or throughout a long and honoured life, he never abandoned them. He died in Belfast in 1820, aged sixty-three years.]

THE UNITED BROTHERS.

(HENRY AND JOHN SHEARES).

1798.

BY DR. R. R. MADDEN.

[These two brave and gifted men were arrested on 21st May 1798, tried on 12th, and executed on the 14th of July following. John Warnford Armstrong, a Lieutenant in the King's County Militia, wormed himself into their confidence, and then betrayed them for the informer's bribe. He pretended to become a member of the United Irish Society, and took the oath of fidelity to that body,—he even visited the happy family of Henry Sheares, and nursed his only child upon his knee; whilst at the same time, he was in daily communication with the Law Officers of the Crown,—retailing to them the results of his treachery. This man is still alive, in the 85th year of his age.]

THE brothers in love are united in death,
    And they sealed with their blood that alliance;
The ties of one cause, of one kindred, and faith,
    And affliction, bid despots defiance.

They joined, heart and hand, in one struggle, and gave
  Their young blood to maintain it; while others,
Who urged on the strife, soon abandoned the brave,
  But they—stood by their country like brothers!

When Freedom, by treachery foully betrayed,
  Found the friends fall away who had plighted
Their faith to her cause, still one spirit prevailed
  In the hearts of the brothers united—
They clung to that cause in the midst of despair,
  When the tempest had terrified others;
And, like comrades in danger, endeared, as they were,
  They went down with the wreck like true brothers!

THE BROTHERS.

BY SPERANZA (MRS. W. R. WILDE).

'Tis midnight, falls the lamp-light dull and sickly
  On a pale and anxious crowd,
Through the court, and round the judges thronging thick!
  With prayers, they dare not speak aloud.
Two youths, two noble youths, stand prisoners at the bar
  You can see them through the gloom—
In the pride of life and manhood's beauty, there they are
  Awaiting their death-doom.

All eyes an earnest watch on them are keeping,
  Some sobbing turn away,
And the strongest men can hardly see for weeping,
  So noble and so loved were they.
Their hands are lock'd together, these young brothers,
  As before the judge they stand—
They feel not the deep grief that moves the others,
  For they die for Fatherland.

They are pale, but it is not fear that whitens
  On each proud high brow,
For the triumph of the martyr's glory brightens
  Around them even now.

They sought to free their land from thrall of stranger,
    Was it treason? Let them die;
But their blood will cry to Heaven—the Avenger
    Yet will hearken from on high.

Before them, shrinking, cowering, scarcely human,
    The base *Informer* bends,
Who, Judas-like, could sell the blood of true men,
    While he clasp'd their hand as friends.
Ay, could fondle the young children of his victim—
    Break bread with his young wife,
At the moment that for gold his perjured dictum
    Sold the husband and the father's life.

There is silence in the midnight—eyes are keeping
    Troubled watch till forth the jury come;
There is silence in the midnight—eyes are weeping—
    Guilty!—is the fatal uttered doom.
For a moment o'er the brothers' noble faces
    Came a shadow sad to see,
Then silently they rose up in their places,
    And embraced each other fervently.

Oh! the rudest heart might tremble at such sorrow,
    The rudest cheek might blanch at such a scene:
Twice the judge essayed to speak the word—To-morrow—
    Twice faltered, as a woman he had been.
To-morrow!—Fain the elder would have spoken,
    Prayed for respite, though it is not Death he fears;
But thoughts of home and wife his heart hath broken,
    And his words are stopped by tears.

But the youngest—oh! he spake out bold and clearly:
    "I have no ties of children or of wife;
Let me die—but spare the brother who more dearly
    Is loved by me than life."
—Pale martyrs, ye may cease, your days are numbered-
    Next noon your sun of life goes down—
One day between the sentence and the scaffold—
    One day between the torture and the *Crown*.

A hymn of joy is rising from creation—
    Bright the azure of the glorious summer sky;
But human hearts weep sore in lamentation,
    For the brothers are led forth to die.

Ay, guard them with your cannon and your lances—
  So of old came martyrs to the stake ;
Ay, guard them—see the people's flashing glances,
  For those noble two are dying for their sake.

Yet none spring forth their bonds to sever :
  Ah ! methinks, had I been there,
I'd have dared a thousand deaths ere ever
  The sword should touch their hair.
It falls !—there is a shriek of lamentation
  From the weeping crowd around ;
They're still'd—the noblest hearts within the nation—
  The noblest heads lie bleeding on the ground.

Years have pass'd since that fatal scene of dying,
  Yet life-like to this day
In their coffins * still those sever'd heads are lying,
  Kept by angels from decay.
Oh ! they preach to us, those still and pallid features—
  Those pale lips yet implore us from their graves,
To strive for our birthright as God's creatures,
  Or die, if we can but live as slaves.

EDWARD MOLLOY.

1798.

A REMINISCENCE OF TROUBLED TIMES.

BY J. FRAZER.

" WHAT use in delaying for vengeance to strike ?
Has each bosom a heart ?—has each shoulder a pike ?
On, on, to Rathangan—'tis full to the gorge,
With the red-handed ruffians of black-hearted George ;
Who stabbed with their bayonets, in search of pike-heads,
The thatch of our cabins, and ticks of our beds ;
Who lashed us, like hounds, till we reddened our tracks
From triangle to threshold, with blood from our backs ;
The cruel destroyer 'tis just to destroy—
What says our young captain, brave Edward Molloy ?"

---

  * They were buried in St. Michan's Church. The singular preservative
quality which the vaults there possess is well known.

Six feet to the forehead, with muscle and limb
To match, had made out his commission for him;
But a spirit in danger more recklessly brave,
True men never followed to glory, or grave—
Though heart never beat in the breast of a dove,
With gentler affections for woman to love;—
His wisdom withal, and his rough, honest pride
In the people their tyrants both robbed and belied,
Confirmed to the man, what he won as a boy—
An empire of friendship for Edward Molloy.

Then forward he strode to the first in the van—
Laid his arm, like a bar, on the breast of the man;
And cried (with an energy deep'ning his tone,
As if a vex'd prophet's combined with his own)—
" Return, I command you; there is not a chance
Of holding Rathangan, unaided by France.
Ay, call me a traitor, though *traitorous rogue*
Is below me as much as the nails in my brogue:
But ye shall not be led, our good cause to destroy,
And ourselves for a tilly, by Edward Molloy.

In hurry is ruin—in prudence is power—
Sure the gains of this day will be lost in an hour,
Though the bosom in hearts, and the shoulder in pikes,
Outnumbered the barley in grains, and in spikes;
For, morning or midnight, the battle may come,
And *red-coat* is ready at tap of a drum;
But *frieze-coat* is never prepared to break out,
Till battle to battle may chorus the shout;
Await but *that* moment, and earth has no joy
Like heading your onslaught, for Edward Molloy."

Alas! for his counsel—their wounds were too fresh,
And the goad had been driven too deep in their flesh.
Brave fellows! they measured the pike with the gun,
And Rathangan was theirs, ere the set of the sun;
" All lost!" he exclaimed, as they rushed to the town—
' Our cause, with the day, will to darkness go down."
Yet he dashed to the front, for his heart would not yield
To his own weighty reasons for quitting the field,
While friends to his country had need to employ
The wisdom, or weapon, of Edward Molloy.

Woe--woe to the victors!—the daylight had sunk—
The routed had rallied—the victors were drunk ;
Disordered, and scattered—but tyrants may thank
Their vanity more than the liquor they drank ;
The sleepers were butchered—the stragglers were slain,
While searching for weapons to grapple again ;
Yet fierce were the flashings of courage, that then
Had nothing to fire it, but *dying like men;*
Till wearied and wounded, alone, to employ
A score of " Black Horse," stood brave Edward Molloy.

There rose in Rathangan a lamp-post—but fail
The powers of my purpose to finish the tale.
The curse of a widow condemned it to rot,
Ere the tears of her orphans were dried on the spot.
Men showed me that post—and I wandered, until
No marvel seems strange—yet it haunteth me still :
For I swore at its foot that my land should be free,
Or tyrants should find such a lamp-post for me ;
Though I listened in silence—and wept when a boy,
For the failure, and fate, of brave Edward Molloy.

TONE'S GRAVE.

BY THOMAS DAVIS.

In Bodenstown Churchyard there is a green grave,
And wildly along it the winter winds rave ;
Small shelter, I ween, are the ruined walls there,
When the storm sweeps down on the plains of Kildare.

Once I lay on that sod—it lies over Wolfe Tone—
And thought how he perished in prison alone,
His friends unavenged, and his country unfreed—
" Oh, bitter," I said, " is the patriot's meed.

For in him the heart of a woman combined
With a heroic life, and a governing mind—
A martyr for Ireland—his grave has no stone—
His name seldom named, and his virtues unknown."

I was woke from my dream by the voices and tread
Of a band, who came into the home of the dead ;
They carried no corpse, and they carried no stone,
And they stopped when they came to the grave of Wolfe Tone.

There were students and peasants, the wise and the brave,
And an old man who knew him from cradle to grave,
And children who thought me hard-hearted ; for they,
On that sanctified sod, were forbidden to play.

But the old man, who saw I was mourning there, said.
"We come, sir, to weep where young Wolfe Tone is laid,
And we're going to raise him a monument, too—
A plain one, yet fit for the simple and true."

My heart overflowed, and I clasped his old hand,
And I blessed him, and blessed every one of his band ;
"Sweet! sweet! 'tis to find that such faith can remain
To the cause, and the man so long vanquished and slain."

In Bodenstown Churchyard there is a green grave,
And freely around it let winter winds rave—
Far better they suit him—the ruin and gloom,—
TILL IRELAND, A NATION, CAN BUILD HIM A TOMB.

———

ARTHUR M'COY.

1798.

WHILE the snow-flakes of Winter are falling
    On mountain, and housetop, and tree,
Come olden weird voices recalling
    The homes of Hy-Faly to me ;
The ramble by river and wild wood,
    The legends of mountain and glen,
When the bright, magic mirror of childhood
    Made heroes and giants of men.

Then I had my dreamings ideal,
    My prophets and heroes sublime,
Yet I found one, true, living, and real,
    Surpass all the fictions of time :

Whose voice thrilled my heart to its centre,
   Whose form tranced my soul and my eye;
A temple no treason could enter;
   My hero was Arthur M'Coy.

For Arthur M'Coy was no bragger,
   No bibber, nor blustering clown,
'Fore the club of an alehouse to swagger,
   Or drag his coat-tail through the town;
But a veteran, stern and steady,
   Who felt for his land and her ills;
In the hour of her need ever ready
   To shoulder a pike for the hills.

As the strong mountain tower spreads its arms,
   Dark, shadowy, silent, and tall,
In our tithe-raids and midnight alarms,
   His bosom gave refuge to all—
If a mind clear, and calm, and expanded,
   A soul ever soaring and high,
'Mid a host—gave a right to command it—
   A hero was Arthur M'Coy.

While he knelt, with a Christian demeanour,
   To his priest, or his Maker, alone,
He scorned the vile slave, or retainer,
   That crouched round the castle, or throne,
The Tudor—The Guelph, The Pretender,
   Were tyrants, alike, branch and stem;
But who'd free our fair land, and defend her,
   A nation, were monarchs to him.

And this faith in good works he attested,
   When Tone linked the true hearts, and brave,
Every billow of danger he breasted—
   His sword-flash, the crest of its wave;
A standard he captured in Gorey,
   A sword-cut and ball through the thigh,
Were among the mementoes of glory
   Recorded of Arthur M'Coy.

Long the *quest* of the law and its beagles,
   His covert the cave and the tree;

Though his home was the home of the eagles,
  His soul was the soul of the free.
No toil, no defeat, could enslave it,
  Nor franchise, nor " Amnesty Bill "—
No lord. but the Maker who gave it,
  Could curb the high pride of his will.

With the gloom of defeat ever laden—
  Seldom seen at the hurling or dance,
Where through blushes, the eye of the maiden
  Looks out for her lover's advance ;
And whenever he stood to behold it,
  A curl of the lip, or a sigh,
Was the silent reproach that unfolded
  The feelings of Arthur M'Coy.

For it told him of freedom o'ershaded—
  That the iron had entered their veins—
When beauty bears manhood degraded
  And manhood's contented in chains.
Yet he loved that fair race, as a martyr,
  And if his own death could recall
The blessings of liberty's charter,
  His bosom had bled for them all.

And he died for his love.—I remember,
  On a mound by the Shannon's blue wave,
On a dark snowy eve in December,
  I knelt at the patriot's grave.
The aged were all heavy-hearted—
  No cheek in the churchyard was dry :
The Sun of our hills had departed—
  God rest you, old Arthur M'Coy !

                                    PONTIAC.

THE CROPPY BOY.

A BALLAD OF '98.

BY CARROLL MALONE.

" Good men and true! in this house who dwell,
To a stranger *bouchal*, I pray you tell
Is the priest at home? or may he be seen?
I would speak a word with Father Green."

"The Priest's at home, boy, and may be seen;
'Tis easy speaking with Father Green;
But you must wait, till I go and see
If the holy father alone may be."

The youth has entered an empty hall—
What a lonely sound has his light footfall!
And the gloomy chamber's chill and bare,
With a vested Priest in a lonely chair.

The youth has knelt to tell his sins:
" *Nomine Dei*," the youth begins;
At " *mea culpa*" he beats his breast,
And in broken murmurs he speaks the rest.

" At the siege of Ross did my father fall,
And at Gorey my loving brothers all;
I alone am left of my name and race,
I will go to Wexford and take their place.

" I cursed three times since last Easter day--
At mass-time once I went to play;
I passed the churchyard one day in haste,
And forgot to pray for my mother's rest.

" I bear no hate against living thing;
But I love my country above my King.
Now, Father! bless me, and let me go
To die, if God has ordained it so."

The Priest said nought, but a rustling noise
Made the youth look up in wild surprise;
The robes were off, and in scarlet there
Sat a yeoman captain with fiery glare.

With fiery glare and with fury hoarse,
Instead of blessing, he breathed a curse:—
" 'Twas a good thought boy, to come here and shrive,
For one short hour is your time to live.

" Upon yon river three tenders float,
The Priest's in one, if he isn't shot—
We hold his house for our Lord the King,
And, amen say I, may all traitors swing!"

At Geneva Barrack that young man died,
And at Passage they have his body laid.
Good people who live in peace and joy,
Breathe a prayer and a tear for the Croppy Boy.

•——

EMMET'S DEATH.

" HE dies to-day," said the heartless judge,
    Whilst he sate him down to the feast,
And a smile was upon his ashy lip
    As he uttered a ribald jest;
For a demon dwelt where his heart should be,
    That lived upon blood and sin,
And oft as that vile judge gave him food
    The demon throbbed within.

" He dies to-day," said the gaoler grim,
    Whilst a tear was in his eye;
" But why should I feel so grieved for *him?*
    Sure, I've seen many die!
Last night I went to his stony cell,
    With the scanty prison fare—
He was sitting at a table rude,
    Plaiting a lock of hair!

And he look'd so mild, with his pale, pale face,
   And he spoke in so kind a way,
That my old breast heav'd with a smothering feel,
   And I knew not what to say!"

" He dies to-day," thought a fair, sweet girl—
   She lacked the life to speak,
For sorrow had almost frozen her blood,
   And white were her lip and cheek—
Despair had drank up her last wild tear,
   And her brow was damp and chill,
And they often felt at her heart with fear,
   For its ebb was all but still.

                                    S. F. C.

LAMENT FOR GRATTAN.

(WHO DIED IN 1820.)

BY THOMAS MOORE.

SHALL the Harp then be silent, when he who first gave
   To our country a name, is withdrawn from all eyes?
Shall a Minstrel of Erin stand mute by the grave,
   Where the first—where the last of her Patriots lies?

No—faint tho' the death-song may fall from his lips,
   Tho' his Harp, like his soul, may with shadows be crost,
Yet, yet shall it sound, 'mid a nation's eclipse,
   And proclaim to the world what a star hath been lost;—

What a union of all the affections and powers
   By which life is exalted, embellish'd, refined,
Was embraced in that spirit—whose centre was ours,
   While its mighty circumference circled mankind.

Oh, who that loves Erin, or who that can see,
   Through the waste of her annals, that epoch sublime—
Like a pyramid raised in the desert—where he
   And his glory stand out to the eyes of all time;

That *one* lucid interval, snatch'd from the gloom
   And the madness of ages, when fill'd with his soul,
A Nation o'erleap'd the dark bounds of her doom,
   And for *one* sacred instant, touch'd Liberty's goal?

Who, that ever hath heard him—hath drank at the source
   Of that wonderful eloquence, all Erin's own,
In whose high-thoughted daring, the fire, and the force,
   And the yet untamed spring of her spirit are shown?

An eloquence rich, wheresoever its wave
   Wander'd free and triumphant, with thoughts that shone thro',
As clear as the brook's "stone of lustre," and gave,
   With the flash of the gem, its solidity too.

Who, that ever approach'd him, when free from the crowd,
   In a home full of love, he delighted to tread
'Mong the trees which a nation had giv'n, and which bow'd,
   As if each brought a new civic crown for his head—

Is there one, who hath thus, through his orbit of life
   But at distance observed him—through glory, through blame,
In the calm of retreat, in the grandeur of strife,
   Whether shining or clouded, still high and the same,—

Oh no, not a heart, that e'er knew him, but mourns
   Deep, deep o'er the grave, where such glory is shrined—
O'er a monument Fame will preserve, 'mong the urns
   Of the wisest, the bravest, the best of mankind!

THE BURIAL.*

BY THOMAS DAVIS.

Why rings the knell of the funeral bell from a hundred village
      shrines?
Through broad Fingall, where hasten all those long and ordered
      lines?

* Written on the funeral of the Rev. P. J. Tyrrell, P. P. of Lusk; one of
those indicted with O'Connell in the government prosecutions of 1843.

With tear and sigh they're passing by,—the matron and the
  maid—
Has a hero died—is a nation's pride in that cold coffin laid?
With frown and curse, behind the hearse, dark men go tramping on—
Has a tyrant died, that they cannot hide their wrath till the rites
  are done?

THE CHAUNT.

"*Ululu! ululu!* high on the wind,
There's a home for the slave where no fetters can bind.
Woe, woe to his slayers"—comes wildly along,
With the trampling of feet and the funeral song.

    And now more clear
    It swells on the ear;
    Breathe low, and listen, 'tis solemn to hear.

"*Ululu! ululu!* wail for the dead.
Green grow the grass of Fingall on his head;
And spring-flowers blossom, ere elsewhere appearing,
And shamrocks grow thick on the Martyr for Erin.
Ululu! ululu! soft fall the dew
On the feet and the head of the martyr'd and true."

    For awhile they tread
    In silence dread—
    Then muttering and moaning go the crowd,
    Surging and swaying like mountain cloud,
    And again the wail comes fearfully loud.

THE CHAUNT.

"*Ululu! ululu!* kind was his heart!
Walk slower, walk slower, too soon we shall part.
The faithful and pious, the Priest of the Lord,
His pilgrimage over, he has his reward.
By the bed of the sick, lowly kneeling,
To God with the raised cross appealing—
He seems still to kneel, and he seems still to pray,
And the sins of the dying seem passing away.

Q

"In the prisoner's cell, and the cabin so dreary,
Our constant consoler, he never grew weary;
But he's gone to his rest,
And he's now with the blest,
Where tyrant and traitor no longer molest—
Ululu! ululu! wail for the dead!
Ululu! ululu! here is his bed."

Short was the ritual, simple the prayer,
Deep was the silence and every head bare;
The Priest alone standing, they knelt all around,
Myriads on myriads, like rocks on the ground.
Kneeling and motionless—"Dust unto dust."
"He died as becometh the faithful and just—
Placing in God his reliance and trust;"

Kneeling and motionless—"ashes to ashes"—
Hollow the clay on the coffin-lid dashes;
Kneeling and motionless, wildly they pray,
But they pray in their souls, for no gesture have they—
Stern and standing—oh! look on them now,
Like trees to one tempest the multitude bow;
Like the swell of the ocean is rising their vow:

THE VOW.

"We have bent and borne, though we saw him torn from his
      home by the tyrant's crew—
And we bent and bore, when he came once more, though suffering
      had pierced him through:
And now he is laid beyond our aid, because to Ireland true—
A martyr'd man—the tyrant's ban, the pious patriot slew.

"And shall we bear and bend for ever,
And shall no time our bondage sever,
And shall we kneel, but battle never,
                  For our own soil?

"And shall our tyrants safely reign
On thrones built up of slaves and slain,
And nought to us and ours remain
                  But chains and toil?

" No! round this grave our oath we plight,
To watch, and labour, and unite,
Till banded be the nation's might—
                    Its spirit steeled,

" And then, collecting all our force,
We'll cross oppression in its course,
And die—or all our rights enforce,
                    On battle field."

Like an ebbing sea that will come again,
Slowly retired that host of men;
Methinks they'll keep some other day
The oath they swore on the martyr's clay.

THE IRISH CHIEFS.

BY CHARLES GAVAN DUFFY, M.P.

OH! to have lived like an IRISH CHIEF, when hearts were fresh
    and true,
And a manly thought, like a pealing bell, would quicken them
    through and through;
And the seed of a gen'rous hope right soon to a fiery action grew,
And men would have scorned to talk and talk, and never a deed
    to do.
            Oh! the iron grasp,
            And the kindly clasp,
        And the laugh so fond and gay;
            And the roaring board,
            And the ready sword,
        Were the types of that vanished day.

Oh! to have lived as Brian lived, and to die as Brian died;
His land to win with the sword, and smile,* as a warrior wins his
    bride.
To knit its force in a kingly host, and rule it with kingly pride,
And still in the girt of its guardian swords over victor fields to ride;

* Our great Brian is called a usurper, inasmuch as he combined, by force
and policy, the scattered and jealous powers of the island into one sovereignty,
and ruled it himself, by the true Divine right of being the fittest ruler.

And when age was past,
And when death came fast,
To look with a softened eye
On a happy race
Who had loved his face,
And to die as a king should die.

Oh! to have lived dear Owen's life—to live for a solemn end,
To strive for the ruling strength and skill God's saints to the
    Chosen send;
And to come at length with that holy strength, the bondage of
    fraud to rend,
And pour the light of God's freedom in where Tyrants and Slaves
    were denned;
            And to bear the brand
            With an equal hand,
        Like a soldier of Truth and Right,
            And, oh! Saints, to die,
            While our flag flew high,
        Nor to look on its fall or flight.

Oh! to have lived as Grattan lived, in the glow of his manly years,
To thunder again those iron words that thrill like the clash of
    spears;
Once more to blend for a holy end, our peasants, and priests, and
    peers,
Till England raged, like a baffled fiend, at the tramp of our
    Volunteers.
            And, oh! best of all,
            Far rather to fall
        (With a blesseder fate than he,)
            On a conqu'ring field,
            Than one right to yield,
        Of the Island so proud and free!

Yet, scorn to cry on the days of old, when hearts were fresh and
    true,
If hearts be weak, oh! chiefly *then* the Missioned their work
    must do;
Nor wants our day its own fit way, the want is in *you* and *you*;
For these eyes have seen as kingly a King as ever dear Erin knew.
            And with Brian's will,
            And with Owen's skill,
        And with glorious Grattan's love,

He had freed us soon—
But death darkened his noon,
And he sits with the saints above.

Oh! could you live as Davis lived—kind Heaven be his bed!
With an eye to guide, and a hand to rule, and a calm and kingly
    head,
And a heart from whence, like a Holy Well, the soul of his land
    was fed,
No need to cry on the days of old that your holiest hope be sped.
    Then scorn to pray
    For a by-past day—
The whine of the sightless dumb!
    To the true and wise
    Let a king arise,
And a holier day is come!

THE GERALDINES.

BY THOMAS DAVIS.

THE Geraldines! the Geraldines!—'tis full a thousand years
Since, 'mid the Tuscan vineyards, bright flashed their battle-spears;
When Capet seized the crown of France, their iron shields were
    known,
And their sabre-dint struck terror on the banks of the Garonne;
Across the downs of Hastings they spurred hard by William's
    side,
And the grey sands of Palestine with Moslem blood they dyed;—
But never then, nor thence, till now, has falsehood or disgrace
Been seen to soil Fitzgerald's plume, or mantle in his face.

The Geraldines! the Geraldines!—'tis true in Strongbow's van,
By lawless force, as conquerors, their Irish reign began;
And, oh! through many a dark campaign they proved their
    prowess stern,
In Leinster's plains, and Munster's vales, on king, and chief, and
    kerne:
But noble was the cheer within the halls so rudely won,
And gen'rous was the steel-gloved hand that had such slaughter
    done;

How gay their laugh, how proud their mien, you'd ask no herald's
    sign—
Among a thousand you had known the princely Geraldine.

These Geraldines! these Geraldines!—not long our air they breath'd;
    Not long they fed on venison, in Irish water seethed ;
    Not often had their children been by Irish mothers nursed,
When from their full and genial hearts an Irish feeling burst!
The English monarchs strove in vain, by law, and force, and bribe,
To win from Irish thoughts and ways this " more than Irish " tribe;
For still they clung to fosterage, to brehon, cloak, and bard :
What king dare say to Geraldine, " Your Irish wife discard ?"

Ye Geraldines ! ye Geraldines !—how royally ye reigned
O'er Desmond broad, and rich Kildare, and English arts disdained;
Your sword made knights, your banner waved, free was your
    bugle call
By Glyn's green slopes, and Dingle's tide, from Barrow's banks
    to Youghal.
What gorgeous shrines, what brehon lore, what minstrel feasts
    there were
In and around Maynooth's gray keep, and palace-filled Adare !
But not for rite or feast ye stay'd, when friend or kin were press'd;
And foeman fled, when " *Crom abo* " bespoke your lance in rest.

Ye Geraldines ! ye Geraldines !—since Silken Thomas flung
King Henry's sword on council board, the English thanes among,
Ye never ceased to battle brave against the English sway,
Though axe and brand and treachery your proudest cut away.
Of Desmond's blood, through woman's veins passed on th' ex-
    hausted tide ;
His title lives—a Saxon churl usurps the lion's hide :
And, though Kildare tower haughtily, there's ruin at the root,
Else why, since Edward fell to earth, had such a tree no fruit ?

True Geraldines ! brave Geraldines !—as torrents mould the earth,
You channelled deep old Ireland's heart by constancy and worth:
When Ginckle 'leagured Limerick, the Irish soldiers gazed
To see if in the setting sun dead Desmond's banner blazed !
And still it is the peasant's hope upon the Curragh's mere,
" They live, who'll see ten thousand men with good Lord Edward
    here "—
So let them dream till brighter days, when, not by Edward's shade,
But by some leader true as he, their lines shall be arrayed !

These Geraldines! these Geraldines!—rain wears away the rock,
And time may wear away the tribe that stood the battle's shock,
But ever, sure, while one is left of all that honoured race,
In front of Ireland's chivalry is that Fitzgerald's place:
And, though the last were dead and gone, how many a field and
    town,
From Thomas Court to Abbeyfeale, would cherish their renown,
And men would say of valour's rise, or ancient power's decline,
" 'Twill never soar, it never shone, as did the Geraldine."

The Geraldines! the Geraldines!—and are there any fears
Within the sons of conquerors for full a thousand years?
Can treason spring from out a soil bedewed with martyr's blood?
Or has that grown a purling brook, which long rushed down a
    flood?—
By Desmond swept with sword and fire,—by clan and keep laid
    low,—
By Silken Thomas and his kin,—by Sainted Edward! No!
The forms of centuries rise up, and in the Irish line
COMMAND THEIR SON TO TAKE THE POST THAT FITS THE
    GERALDINE!

THE IMPRISONED CHIEF.

TO C. G. D.

BY T. D. M'GEE.

'TWAS but last night I traversed the Atlantic's furrowed face,
The stars but thinly colonized the wilderness of space—
A white sail glinted here and there, and sometimes o'er the swell
Rung the seaman's song of labour or the silvery night-watch bell;
I dreamt I reached the Irish shore, and felt my heart rebound
From wall to wall within my breast, as I trod that holy ground;
I sat down by my own hearth-stone, beside my love again—
I met my friends, and Him, the first of friends, and Irishmen.

I saw once more the dome-like brow, the large and lustrous eyes;
I marked upon the sphynx-like face the clouds of thought arise;
I heard again the clear quick voice, that as a trumpet thrill'd
The souls of men, and wielded them even as the speaker will'd;

I felt the cordial-clasping hand that never feigned regard,
Nor ever dealt a muffled blow, nor nicely weighed reward.
My friend! my friend—oh, would to God that you were here
    with me,
A-watching in the starry west for Ireland's libertie!

Oh, Brothers, I can well declare, who read it like a scroll,
What Roman characters were stamp'd upon that Roman soul,
The courage, constancy and love—the old time, faith and truth—
The wisdom of the sages—the sincerity of youth.
Like an oak upon our native hills. a host might camp thereunder,
Yet it bare the song-birds in its core above the storm and thunder;
It was the gentlest, firmest soul, that ever lamp-like showed
A young race seeking freedom up her misty mountain-road.

Like a convoy from a flag-ship, our fleet is scattered far,
And you, the valiant Admiral, chained and imprisoned are—
Like a royal galley's precious freight, flung on sea-sundered strands,
The diamond wit and golden worth are far cast on the lands,
And I, whom most you loved, am here, and I can but indite
My yearnings and my heart-hopes, and curse *them* while I write;
Alas! alas! ah what are prayers, and what are moans and sighs,
When the heroes of the land are lost—of the land that will not
    RISE.

But I swear to you, dear CHARLES, by my honour and my faith,
As I hope for stainless name, and salvation after death—
By the green grave of my mother, beneath Seskar's ruined wall—
By the birthland of my mind and love, of you, my bride, and all—
That my days are dedicated to the ruin of the power,
That holds you fast and libels you in your defenceless hour—
Like an Indian of the wild woods. I'll dog their track of slime,
And I'll shake the Gaza-pillars yet, of their godless mammon shrine.

They will bring you in their manacles, beneath their bloody rag—
They will chain you like the Conqueror to some sea-moated crag;
To their fiends it will be given, your great spirit to annoy—
To fling falsehood in your cup. and to break your martyr joy;
But you will bear it nobly as Regulus did of eld,
The oak will be the oak, and honour'd e'en when fell'd.
Change is brooding over earth—it will find you mid the main,
And throned between its wings you'll reach, your native land again.

THE IRISH PEASANT TO HIS MISTRESS.

BY THOMAS MOORE.

[This is an allegorical ballad, embodying the address of the Irish Catholic to Holy Mother Church.]

THROUGH grief and through danger, thy smile hath cheered my way,
Till hope seem'd to bud from each thorn that round me lay;
The darker our fortune, the brighter our pure love burn'd,
Till shame into glory, till fear into zeal was turn'd;
Yes, slave as I was, in thy arms my spirit felt free,
And bless'd even the sorrows that made me more dear to thee.

Thy rival was honour'd, while thou wert wrong'd and scorn'd,
Thy crown was of briers, while gold her brows adorn'd;
She woo'd me to temples, while thou lay'st hid in caves,
Her friends were all masters, while thine, alas! were slaves;
Yet cold in the earth, at thy feet, I would rather be,
Than wed what I lov'd not, or turn one thought from thee.

They slander thee sorely, who say thy vows are frail—
Hadst thou been a false one, thy cheek had look'd less pale.
They say, too, so long thou hast worn those lingering chains,
That deep in thy heart they have printed their servile stains—
Oh! foul is the slander,—no chain could that soul subdue—
Where shineth *thy* spirit, there liberty shineth too!*

LAMENT FOR BANBA.†

(FROM THE IRISH.)

BY J. C. MANGAN.

OH, my land! oh, my love!
What a woe, and how deep,

---

* " Where the Spirit of the Lord is, there is liberty."—St. PAUL, 2 Cor. i. 17.
† Banba (*Banva*) was one of the most ancient names given by the Bards to Ireland.

Is thy death to my long mourning soul!
God alone, God above,
  Can awake thee from sleep,
Can release thee from bondage and dole!
    Alas, alas, and alas,
        For the once proud people of Banba!

As a tree in its prime,
  Which the axe layeth low,
Didst thou fall, oh, unfortunate land!
  Not by Time, nor thy crime,
  Came the shock and the blow.
They were given by a false felon hand!
    Alas, alas, and alas,
        For the once proud people of Banba!

Oh, my grief of all griefs
  Is to see how thy throne
Is usurped, whilst thyself art in thrall!
  Other lands have their chiefs,
  Have their kings, thou alone
Art a wife, yet a widow withal!
    Alas, alas, and alas,
        For the once proud people of Banba!

The high house of O'Neill
  Is gone down to the dust,
The O'Brien is clanless and banned;
  And the steel, the red steel,
  May no more be the trust
Of the Faithful and Brave in the land!
    Alas, alas, and alas,
        For the once proud people of Banba!

True, alas! Wrong and Wrath
  Were of old all too rife.
Deeds were done which no good man admires;
  And perchance Heaven hath
  Chastened us for the strife
And the blood-shedding ways of our sires!
    Alas, alas, and alas,
        For the once proud people of Banba!

But, no more! This our doom,
　　While our hearts yet are warm,
Let us not over-weakly deplore!
　For the hour soon may loom
　　When the Lord's mighty hand
Shall be raised for our rescue once more!
　　　And our grief shall be turned into joy
　　　For the still proud people of Banba!

THE CELTIC TONGUE.

'TIS fading, oh, 'tis fading! like leaves upon the trees!
In murmuring tone 'tis dying, like the wail upon the breeze!
'Tis swiftly disappearing, as footprints on the shore
Where the Barrow, and the Erne, and Loch Swilly's waters roar—
Where the parting sunbeam kisses Loch Corrib in the West,
And Ocean, like a mother, clasps the Shannon to her breast!
The language of old Erin, of her history and name—
Of her monarchs and her heroes—her glory and her fame—
The sacred shrine where rested, thro' sunshine and thro' gloom,
The spirit of her martyrs, as their bodies in the tomb,
The time-wrought shell, where murmur'd, 'mid centuries of wrong.
The secret voice of Freedom, in annal and in song—
Is slowly, surely sinking, into silent death at last,
To live but in the memories of those who love the Past.

The olden tongue is sinking like a patriarch to rest,
Whose youth beheld the Tyrian* on our Irish coasts a guest;
Ere the Roman or the Saxon, the Norman or the Dane,
Had first set foot in Britain, o'er trampled heaps of slain;
Whose manhood saw the Druid rite at forest-tree and rock—
And savage tribes of Britain round the shrines of Zernebock;†
And for generations witnessed all the glories of the Gael,
Since our Celtic sires sung war-songs round the sacred fires of Baal;
The tongues that saw its infancy are ranked among the dead,
And from their graves have risen those now spoken in their stead.

---

* An old Irish tradition says that during the commerce of the Tyrians with
Ireland, one of the Princes of Tyre was invited over by the Monarch of Ireland,
and got married to one of the Irish princesses during his sojourn there.
　† Zernebock and Odin were two of the gods of the early Britons

The glories of old Erin, with her liberty have gone,
Yet their halo linger'd round her, while the Gaelic speech liv'd on;
For 'mid the desert of her woe, a monument more vast
Than all her pillar-towers, it stood—that old Tongue of the Past!

'Tis leaving, and for ever, the soil that gave it birth,
Soon,—very soon, its moving tones shall ne'er be heard on earth,
O'er the island dimly fading, as a circle o'er the wave—
Receding, as its people lisp the language of the slave,*
And with it too seem fading as sunset into night
The scattered rays of liberty that lingered in its light,
For ah! tho' long, with filial love, it clung to motherland,
And Irishmen were Irish still, in language, heart and hand;
T' instal its Saxon Rival,† proscribed it soon became,
And Irishmen are Irish now in nothing but in name;
The Saxon chain our rights and tongues alike doth hold in thrall,
Save where amid the Connaught wilds and hills of Donegal—
And by the shores of Munster, like the broad Atlantic blast,
The olden language lingers yet and binds us to the Past.

Thro' cold neglect 'tis dying now; a stranger on our shore!
No Tara's hall re-echoes to its music as of yore—
No Lawrence‡ fires the Celtic clans round leagured Athaclee §—
No Shannon wafts from Limerick's towers their war-songs to the sea.
Ah! magic Tongue, that round us wove its spells so soft and dear!
Ah! pleasant Tongue, whose murmurs were as music to the ear!
Ah! glorious Tongue, whose accents could each Celtic heart enthral!
Ah! rushing Tongue, that sounded like the swollen torrent's fall!
The Tongue, that in the Senate was lightning flashing bright,—
Whose echo in the battle was the thunder in its might!
That Tongue, which once in chieftain's hall poured loud the
  . minstrel lay,
As chieftain, serf, or minstrel old is silent there to-day!   .

---

* Tacitus says,—" The language of the conqueror in the mouth of the conquered, is ever the language of the slave."—*Germania.*
† Acts of Parliament were enacted to destroy the Irish, and to encourage the growth of the English language.
‡ St. Lawrence O'Toole, Archbishop of Dublin, succeeded in organizing the Irish chieftains under Roderick O'Connor, King of Connaught, against the first band of adventurers under Strongbow.
§ Athaclee, *Athacleith,* the Irish name of Dublin. *Baile-ath-cliath,* literally means the *Town of the ford of hurdles.*

That Tongue whose shout dismayed the foe at Kong and
    Mullaghmast, *
Like those who nobly perished there is numbered with the Past!

The Celtic Tongue is passing, and we stand coldly by—
Without a pang within the heart, a tear within the eye—
Without one pulse for Freedom stirred, one effort made to save
The Language of our Fathers from dark oblivion's grave!
Oh, Erin! vain your efforts—your prayers for Freedom's crown,
Whilst offered in the language of the foe that clove it down;
Be sure that tyrants ever with an art from darkness sprung,
Would make the conquered nation slaves alike in limb and tongue;
Russia's great Czar ne'er stood secure o'er Poland's shatter'd frame,
Until he trampled from her heart the tongue that bore her name.
Oh, Irishmen, be Irish still! stand for the dear old tongue
Which as ivy to a ruin, to your native land has clung!
Oh, snatch this relic from the wreck! the only and the last,
And cherish in your heart of hearts, the language of the Past!

THE CELTIC CROSS.

BY T. D. M'GEE.

THROUGH storm, and fire, and gloom, I see it stand,
    Firm, broad, and tall—
The Celtic Cross that marks our Fatherland,
    Amid them all!
Druids, and Danes, and Saxons vainly rage
    Around its base;
It standeth shock on shock, and age on age,
    Star of our scattered race.

O, Holy Cross! dear symbol of the dread
    Death of our Lord,
Around thee long have slept our Martyr-dead,
    Sward over sward!
An hundred Bishops I myself can count
    Among the slain;

* "Nothing so affrighted the enemy at the raid of Mullaghmast, as the
unintelligible password in the Irish tongue, with which the Irish troops burst
upon the foe."—Green Book.

Chiefs, Captains, rank and file, a shining mount
Of God's ripe grain.

The Recreant's hate, the Puritan's claymore,
Smote thee not down;
On headland steep, on mountain summit hoar,
In mart and town;
In Glendalough, in Ara, in Tyrone,
We find thee still,
Thy open arms still stretching to thine own,
O'er town, and lough and hill.

And they would tear thee out of Irish soil,
The guilty fools!
How Time must mock their antiquated toil
And broken tools!
Cranmer and Cromwell from thy grasp retired,
Baffled and thrown;
William and Anne to sap thy site conspired—
The rest is known!

Holy Saint Patrick, Father of our Faith,
Beloved of God!
Shield thy dear church from the impending scaith,
Or, if the rod
Must scourge it yet again, inspire and raise
To emprise high,
Men like the heroic race of other days,
Who joyed to die!

Fear! Wherefore should the Celtic people fear
Their Church's fate?
The day is not—the day was never near—
Could desolate
The Destined Island, all whose seedy clay
Is holy ground—
Its cross shall stand till that predestined day,
When Erin's self is drowned!

Political Ballads.

IRISH NATIONAL HYMN.

BY J. C. MANGAN.

O, Ireland! Ancient Ireland!
   Ancient! yet for ever young!
Thou our mother, home and sireland—
   Thou at length hast found a tongue—
     Proudly thou, at length,
     Resistest in triumphant strength.
Thy flag of freedom floats unfurled;
   And as that mighty God existeth,
Who giveth victory when and where He listeth,
Thou yet shalt wake and shake the nations of the world.

   For this dull world still slumbers,
     Weetless of its wants or loves,
   Though, like Galileo, numbers
     Cry aloud, "It moves! it moves!"
       In a midnight dream,
       Drifts it down Time's wreckful stream—
All march, but few descry the goal,
   O, Ireland! be it thy high duty
To teach the world the might of Moral Beauty,
And stamp God's image truly on the struggling soul.

   Strong in thy self-reliance,
     Not in idle threat or boast,
Hast thou hurled thy fierce defiance
     At the haughty Saxon host—

Thou hast claimed, in sight
Of high Heaven, thy long-lost right.
Upon thy hills—along thy plains—
In the green bosom of thy valleys,
The new-born soul of holy freedom rallies,
And calls on thee to trample down in dust thy chains!

Deep, saith the Eastern story,
Burns in Iran's mines a gem,
For its dazzling hues and glory
Worth a Sultan's diadem.
But from human eyes
Hidden there it ever lies!
The aye-travailing Gnomes alone,
Who toil to form the mountain's treasure,
May gaze and gloat with pleasure without measure
Upon the lustrous beauty of that wonder-stone.

So is it with a nation
Which would win for its rich dower
That bright pearl, Self-Liberation—
It must labour hour by hour.
Strangers, who travail
To lay bare the gem, shall fail;
Within itself, must grow, must glow—
Within the depths of its own bosom
Must flower in living might, must broadly blossom,
The hopes that shall be born ere Freedom's Tree can blow.

Go on, then, all-rejoiceful!
March on thy career unbowed!
IRELAND! let thy noble, voiceful
Spirit cry to God aloud!
Man will bid thee speed—
God will aid thee in thy need—
The Time, the Hour, the Power are near—
Be sure thou soon shalt form the vanguard
Of that illustrious band whom Heaven and Man guard:—
And these words come from *one whom some have called a Seer.*

LIFE AND LAND.

BY T. D. M'GEE.

DEATH reapeth in the fields of Life, and we cannot count the
    corpses :
Black and fast before our eyes march the biers and hearses ;
In loneways, and in highways, the stark skeletons are lying,
And daily unto Heaven their living kin are crying—
"Must the slave die for the tyrant—the sufferer for the sin—
And a wide inhuman desert be, where Ireland has been ;
Must the billows of oblivion over all our hills be rolled,
And our land be blotted out, like the accursed lands of old?"

Oh ! hear it, friends of France—hear it, our cousin Spain,
Hear it, our kindly kith and kin across the western main—
Hear it, ye sons of Italy—let Turk and Russian hear it—
Hear Ireland's sentence registered, and see how we can bear it—
Our speech must be unspoken, our rights must be forgot,
Our land must be forsaken—submission is our lot—
We are beggars, we are cravens, and vengeful England feels
Us at her feet, and tramples us with both her iron heels.

These the brethren of Gonsalvo, these the cousins of the Cid—
They are Spaniels and not Spaniards, born but to be bid—
They of that Celtic war-race who made the storied rally
Against the Teuton lances in the lists of Roncesvalles—
They, kindred to the mariner, whose soul's sublime devotion
Led his caravel like a star to new worlds through the Ocean.
No ! no ! they were begotten by fathers in their chains,
Whose valiant blood refused to flow along the vassal veins.

"Ho! ho!" the Devils are merry in the farthest vaults of night,
This England so out-Lucifers the prime arch-hypocrite ;
Friend of Peace, and friend of Freedom—yea, divine Religion's
    friend,
She is feeding on our hearts like a sateless nether fiend—
"Ho! ho!" for now the vultures are black on the four winds—
No purveyor like England that foul camp-follower finds—
Do you not mark them flitting between you and the sun ?
They are come to reap the booty, for the battle has been won.

R

Lo! what other shape is this self-poised in upper air,
With wings like trailing comets, and face darker than despair?
See! see! the bright sun sickens into saffron in its shade,
And the poles are shaken at their ends, infected and afraid—
It is the Spirit of the Plague, and round and round the shore
It circles on its course, shedding bane for evermore—
And the slave falls for the tyrant, and the suff'rer for the sin,
And a wide inhuman desert *is*, where Ireland has been.

'Twas a vision—'tis a fable—I did but tell my dream—
Yet twice, yea thrice, I saw it, and still it seemed the same.
Ah! my soul is with this darkness, nightly, daily overcast—
And I fear me, God permitting, it may fall out true at last.
God permitting, man decreeing! What, and shall man so will,
And our unsealed lips be silent and our unbound hands be still?
Shall we look upon our fathers, and our daughters, and our wives,
Slain, ravished, in our sight, and be paltering for our lives?

Oh! countrymen and kindred, make yet another stand—
Plant your flag upon the common soil—be your motto, Life and Land!
From the charnel shore of Cleena to the sea-bridge of the Giant
Let the sleeping souls awake—the supine rise self-reliant—
And arouse thee up, oh! City, that sits furrowed and in weeds,
Like the old Egyptian ruins amid the sad Nile's reeds—
Up, Mononia, land of heroes, and bounteous mother of song—
And Connaught, like thy rivers, come unto us swift and strong
Oh! countrymen and kindred, make yet another stand—
Plant your flag upon the common soil—be your motto, Life and
    Land!

THE KNIGHT OF THE SHAMROCK.

BY J. FRAZER.

My Lady-love, hadst thou not broken
  The spirit of thy sacred vow,
The burning words would be unspoken,
  That sear thy guilty bosom now.
In fealty, faith—and hope, I followed—
  Wooed—waited—watched thy steps for years;
At last, my very heart was hollowed,
  By scorching thoughts and scalding tears.

My fortunes by thy house were blighted—
   And full revenge I ne'er forgot ;
Until thy queenly word was plighted
   To love me—why redeem it not ?
It waked a passion that betrayed me
   From vengeance, till the chance was gone: -
Thy truth itself had scarce repaid me—
   Thy falsehood left me more undone.

Wert thou of cold, repelling nature—
   Unkind to suitors, one and all—
I could forgive the heartless creature,
   Who recked not for my rise, or fall:
But I for scoff and scorn was singled ;
   And all the treacheries of thy race,
In thy deceitful smile were mingled,
   To ruin—wrong me—and debase.

Thy quarrel found me ever ready—
   Thy bidding set my lance in rest—
My arm and heart, how strong and steady,
   Thy friends and foes have both confess'd ;
And if, as oft, in general gladness,
   My prowess was forgotten—then
It was my strange escape from sadness,
   To dare, and do, for thee again.

Away with thy new burst of kindness—
   I feel it like a weary load :
Thy smile had dazzled me to blindness—
   Thy frown has let me see my road.
My heart is to thy hate adjusted,
   And thou may'st hate me to the end ;
Thou wert untrue, when tried and trusted,
   And treacherous natures never mend.

The more and more my brain remembers
   Thy deep deceit and my deep shame,
The more I turn me to the embers,
   Yet living, of my father's fame !
A blade may yet, amid the ashes,
   Be temper'd to such dangerous edge,
Thy haughty house may fear its flashes,
   And wish thou hadst redeem'd thy pledge.

Although no maiden of the many
   May smile a gentle smile on me—
Though I may ne'er expect from any
   The faith I did not find in thee;
Yet, to thy proud imperial beauty
   I bow'd myself the latest time;
The homage—once a knightly duty—
   Were now a sordid *villein's* crime!

THE WARNING VOICE.

BY J. C. MANGAN.

" Il me semble que nous sommes à la veille d'une grande bataille humaine.
Les forces sont là ; mais je n'y vois pas de général."
                    BALZAC: *Livre Mystique.*

YE Faithful!—ye Noble!
   A day is at hand
Of trial and trouble,
   And woe in the land!
O'er a once greenest path,
   Now blasted and sterile,
     Its dusk shadows loom—
It cometh with Wrath,
   With Conflict and Peril,
     With Judgment and Doom!

False bands shall be broken,
   Dead systems shall crumble,
     And the Haughty shall hear
Truths yet never spoken,
       Though smouldering like flame
    Through many a lost year
  In the hearts of the Humble;
For, Hope will expire
As the Terror draws nigher,
     And, with it, the Shame
Which so long overawed
   Men's minds by its might—
And the Powers abroad

Will be Panic and Blight,
And phrenetic Sorrow—
Black Pest all the night,
And Death on the morrow!

Now, therefore, ye True,
Gird your loins up anew!
By the good you have wrought!
By all you have thought,
    And suffered, and done!
        By your souls! I implore you,
            Be leal to your mission—
    Remembering that *one*
        Of the *two* paths before you
            Slopes down to perdition!
To you have been given,
    Not granaries and gold,
But the Love that lives long,
    And waxes not cold;
And the Zeal that hath striven
    Against Error and Wrong,
And in fragments hath riven
    The chains of the Strong!
Bide now, by your sternest
Conceptions of earnest
Endurance for others,
Your weaker-souled brothers!
Your true faith and worth
    Will be History soon,
And their stature stand forth
    In the unsparing Noon!

You have dreamed of an era
    Of Knowledge and Truth,
        And Peace—the *true* glory!
Was this a chimera?
    Not so!—but the childhood and youth
        Of our days will grow hoary
Before such a marvel shall burst on their sight!
    On *you* its beams glow not—
    For *you* its flowers blow not!
You cannot rejoice in its light,
    But in darkness and suffering instead
    You go down to the place of the Dead!

To *this* generation
The sore tribulation,
The stormy commotion,
And foam of the Popular Ocean,
    The struggle of class against class;
The Dearth and the Sadness,
    The Sword and the War-vest;
To the *next*, the Repose and the Gladness,
    " The sea of clear glass," *
    And the rich Golden Harvest!

Know, then, your true lot,
    Ye Faithful, though Few!
        Understand your position,
        Remember your mission,
And vacillate not,
    Whatsoever ensue!
Alter not! Falter not!
    Palter not now with your own living souls,
    When each moment that rolls
        May see Death lay his hand
On some new victim's brow!
Oh! let not your vow
    Have been written in sand!
    Leave cold calculations
Of Danger and Plague
    To the slaves and the traitors
Who cannot dissemble
    The dastard sensations
That now make them tremble
    With phantasies vague!
The men without ruth—
    The hypocrite haters
Of Goodness and Truth,
Who at heart curse the race
    Of the sun through the skies;
And would look in God's face
    With a lie in their eyes!
To the last do your duty,
    Still mindful of this—
That Virtue is Beauty,
    And Wisdom, and Bliss;

* Apoc. iv. 6.

So, howe'er, as frail men, you have erred on
    Your way along Life's throngèd road,
Shall your consciences prove a sure guerdon
       And tower of defence,
      Until Destiny summon you hence
    To the Better Abode!

THE PEOPLE'S CHIEF.

BY EVA. (MISS MARY EVA KELLY.)

COME forth, come forth, O Man of Men! to the cry of the
    gathering nations,
We watch on the tow'r, we watch on the hill, pouring our
    invocations—
Our souls are sick of sounds and shades, that mock our shame
    and grief,
We hurl the Dagons from their seats, and call the lawful Chief!

Come forth, come forth, O Man of Men! to the frenzy of our
    imploring,
The winged despair that no man can bear, up to the Heavens
    soaring—
Come! Faith and Hope, and love and trust, upon their centre
    rock,
The wailing Millions summon thee amid the earthquake shock!

We've kept the weary watch of years, with a wild and heart-
    wrung yearning,
But the star of the Advent we sought in vain, calmly and purely
    burning;
False meteors flash'd across the sky, and falsely led us on;
The parting of the strife is come—the spell is o'er and gone!

The storms of enfranchised passions rise as the voice of the eagle's
    screaming,
And we scatter now to the earth's four winds the memory of our
    dreaming!
The clouds but veil the lightning's bolt—Sibylline murmurs ring,
In hollow tones from out the depths—the People seek their King!

Come forth, come forth, Anointed One! nor blazon nor honours
    bearing—
No "ancient line" be thy seal or sign, the crown of Humanity
    wearing—
Spring out, as lucent fountains spring exulting from the ground
Arise, as Adam rose from God, with strength and knowledge crown'd!

The leader of the world's wide host guiding our aspirations,
Wear thou the seamless garb of Truth sitting among the nations!
Thy foot is on the empty forms around in shivers cast—
We crush ye with the scorn of scorn, exuvial of the past!

The Future's close gates are now on their ponderous hinges jarring,
And there comes a sound as of winds and waves each with the
    other warring:
And forward bends the list'ning world, as to their eager ken
From out that dark and mystic land appears the Man of Men!

RECRUITING SONG FOR THE IRISH BRIGADE

BY MAURICE O'CONNELL.

Is there a youthful gallant here
On fire for fame—unknowing fear—
Who in the charge's mad career
On Erin's foes would flesh his spear?
    Come, let him wear the White Cockade,
    And learn the soldier's glorious trade,
    'Tis of such stuff a hero's made,
    Then let him join the Bold Brigade.

Who scorns to own a Saxon Lord,
And toil to swell a stranger's hoard?
Who for rude blow or gibing word
Would answer with the Freeman's sword?
    Come, let him wear the White Cockade, &c.

Does Erin's foully slandered name
Suffuse thy cheek with generous shame—
Would'st right her wrongs—restore her fame?—
Come, then, the soldier's weapon claim—
    Come, then, and wear the White Cockade, &c.

Come, free from bonds your father's faith,
Redeem its shrines from scorn and scathe,
The Hero's fame, the Martyr's wreath,
Will gild your life or crown your death.
  Then, come, and wear the White Cockade, &c.

To drain the cup—with girls to toy,
The serf's vile soul with bliss may cloy,
But would'st thou taste a manly joy?—
Oh! it was ours at Fontenoy!
  Come, then, and wear the White Cockade, &c.

To many a fight thy fathers led,
Full many a Saxon's life-blood shed;
From thee, as yet, no foe has fled—
Thou wilt not shame the glorious dead?
  Then, come, and wear the White Cockade, &c.

Oh! come—for slavery, want, and shame,
We offer vengeance, freedom, fame,
With Monarchs, comrade rank to claim,
And, nobler still, the Patriot's name!
  Oh! come and wear the White Cockade,
  And learn the soldier's glorious trade;
  'Tis of such stuff a hero's made—
  Then come and join the Bold Brigade.

THE VOICE OF LABOUR.

A CHAUNT OF THE CITY MEETINGS. A. D. 1843.

BY CHARLES GAVAN DUFFY, M.P.

YE who despoil the sons of toil, saw ye this sight to-day,
When stalwart trade in long brigade, beyond a king's array,
Marched in the blessed light of heaven, beneath the open sky,
Strong in the might of sacred RIGHT, that none dare ask them why?
These are the slaves, the needy knaves, ye spit upon with scorn—
The spawn of earth, of nameless birth, and basely bred as born;
Yet know, ye soft and silken lords, were we the thing ye say,
Your broad domains, your coffered gains, your lives were ours
  to-day!

Measure that rank, from flank to flank ; 'tis fifty thousand strong;
And mark you here, in front and rear, brigades as deep and long;
And know that never blade of foe, or Arran's deadly breeze,
Tried by assay of storm or fray, more dauntless hearts than these;
The sinewy smith, little he recks of his own child—the sword ;
The men of gear, think you they fear *their* handiwork—a Lord?
And undismayed, yon sons of trade might see the battle's front,
Who bravely bore, nor bowed before, the deadlier face of want.

What lack we here of show or form that lures your slaves to death?
Not serried bands, nor sinewy hands, nor music's martial breath ;
And if we broke the bitter yoke our suppliant race endure,
No robbers we—but chivalry—the Army of the Poor.
Shame on ye now, ye Lordly crew, that do your betters wrong—
We are no base and braggart mob, but merciful and strong.
Your henchmen vain, your vassal train, would fly our first defiance;
In us—in our strong, tranquil breasts—abides your sole reliance.

Ay! keep them all, castle and hall, coffers and costly jewels—
Keep your vile gain, and in its train the passions that it fuels.
We envy not your lordly lot—its bloom or its decayance ;
But ye *have* that we claim as ours—our right in long abeyance :
Leisure to live, leisure to love, leisure to taste our freedom—
Oh! suff'ring poor, oh! patient poor, how bitterly you need them !
" Ever to moil, ever to toil," that is your social charter,
And city slave or peasant serf, the TOILER is its martyr.

Where Frank and Tuscan shed their sweat the goodly crop is
        theirs—
If Norway's toil make rich the soil, she eats the fruit she rears—
O'er Maine's green sward there rules no lord, saving the Lord on
        high ;
But we are slaves in our own land—proud masters, tell us why?
The German burgher and his men, brother with brothers live,
While toil must wait without *your* gate what gracious crusts you give.
Long in your sight, for our own right, we've bent, and still we
        bend ;–
Why did we bow? why do we now?—proud masters, this must end.

Perish the past—a generous land is this fair land of ours,
And enmity may no man see between its Towns and Towers.
Come, join our bands—here take our hands—now shame on him
        that lingers,
Merchant or Peer, you have no fear from labour's blistered fingers.

Come, join at last—perish the past—its traitors, its seceders—
Proud names and old, frank hearts and bold, come join and be
our Leaders,
But know, ye lords, that be your swords with us or with our
Wronger,
Heaven be our guide, for we shall bide this lot of shame no longer !

THE BATTLE OF THE DIAMOND.

In the good old times when royalty
    Was loved with right and reason;
When truth might honour loyalty
    Without a charge of treason—
        In those old days, rebellion's throng,
        Stung by despair, once mustered strong
        To trample right, and lift up wrong,
            Near the village of the Diamond.

But though they muster'd thousands strong,
    And thought no power could shake them;
And though they swore both loud and long
    That nought but blood should slake them—
        Yet there were met a faithful few—
        Undoubting, for they fully knew
        That hands wax strong when hearts are true—
            In the green fields of the Diamond.

They closed—and then the echoes woke
    With musketry hoarse roaring;
But o'er the strife and clouding smoke,
    Our flag was onward soaring;
        And when the sword its work had done,
        And silent was the rattling gun,
        That fearless few the day had won,
            In the green fields of the Diamond.

Then think of those who steadily
    Fought for the truth in season,
And even now for truth would die—
    Though truth were construed treason.

And faithfully from year to year,
Though lordlings frown we'll never fear
To fill the cup, and raise the cheer
    To the heroes of the Diamond.

A SALUTATION.

BY T. D. M'GEE.

DAUNTLESS voyagers who venture out upon the wreck-pav'd deep,
Who can sail with hearts unfailing o'er the ages sunk in sleep;
There is outlet—ye shall know it by the tide's deep conscious flow;
There is offing—may ye show it to the convoy following slow.

Gallant champions, whose long labours file away in vista'd space,
Lost the fitful hour of sabres—not the Archimedean place;
In the future realm before ye down the vale of labour looms
Your new Athens, oh! pine benders reared above the robbers' tombs.

Be ye therefore calm in council, Patience is the heart of Hope—
Never wrangle with the brambles when with old oaks ye must cope;
William, Walpole, Pitt and Canning, ye shall smite and overthrow,
Not by practising with pigmies can ye giant warfare know.

Whoso ye find fittest, wisest, he your suzerain shall be,
Yield him following and affection, stand like sons around his knee;
Make his name a word of honour, make him feel you as a fence,
Trust not even him too blindly, build your faith on evidence.

Brothers, ye have drained the chalice, late replenished by defeat,
Unto brethren bear no malice, put the past beneath your feet—
For the love of God whose creatures ye see daily crucified,
For your martyrs—for your teachers, shun the selfish paths of
    pride.

Then, by all our pure immortals, ye, true champions, shall be blest,
By St. Patrick and St. Columb, by St. Brendan of the west,
By St. Molling and St. Bridget, and our myriad martyr bands,
And your land shall be delivered, yea! delivered by your hands.

A RIGHT ORANGE BALLAD.

1825.

YE gentlemen of Ireland, in country and in town,
Whose honour'd flag in Ninety-Eight put foul rebellion down;
That glorious standard raise again to face the Tricolor,
Where it waves on their graves who put it down before—
Oh, face it as your fathers did, 'twill shame your skies no more.

The glories of your fathers shall start from every fold,
Of the fair and ample banner in orange and in gold:
The British Lions rampant, and the golden Harp, shall soar
Through the black stormy track of treason gathering o'er
The Isle of evil destiny, to burst in rain of gore.

You need no frantic orators, no riots in the cause;
Your strength is in the sacred might of Truth's eternal laws.
With lessons from God's living Word, you need no other lore,
Though lies should arise from traitors by the score;
When they yell their noon day blasphemies, and ruffians round
    them roar.

Did not your flag of honour around the welkin burn,
Till the gathering storm be scared and gone, and skies of blue
    return!
Then, then, ye loyal Orangemen, the wine-cup shall run o'er,
When ye fill, as ye will, to the manly hearts who bore
The rampant Lion of the North first o'er the Tricolor!

THE MEMORY OF THE DEAD.

WHO fears to speak of Ninety-Eight?
    Who blushes at the name?
When cowards mock the patriot's fate,
    Who hangs his head for shame?
He's all a knave, or half a slave,
    Who slights his country thus;
But a *true* man, like you, man,
    Will fill your glass with us.

We drink the memory of the brave,
  The faithful and the few—
Some lie far off beyond the wave—
  Some sleep in Ireland, too;
All—all are gone—but still lives on
  The fame of those who died—
All true men, like you, men,
  Remember them with pride.

Some on the shores of distant lands
  Their weary hearts have laid,
And by the stranger's heedless hands
  Their lonely graves were made;
But, though their clay be far away
  Beyond the Atlantic foam—
In true men, like you, men,
  Their spirit's still at home.

The dust of some is Irish earth,
  Among their own they rest;
And the same land that gave them birth
  Has caught them to her breast;
And we will pray that from their clay
  Full many a race may start,
Of true men, like you, men,
  To act as brave a part.

They rose in dark and evil days
  To right their native land;
They kindled here a living blaze
  That nothing shall withstand.
Alas! that Might can vanquish Right—
  They fell and pass'd away;
But true men, like you, men,
  Are plenty here to-day.

Then here's their memory—may it be
  For us a guiding light,
To cheer our strife for liberty,
  And teach us to unite.
Through good and ill, be Ireland's still,
  Though sad as theirs your fate;
And true men be you, men,
  Like those of Ninety-Eight.

THE WEARING OF THE GREEN.

1798.

FAREWELL, for I must leave thee, my own, my native shore,
And doom'd in foreign lands to dwell, may never see thee more;
For laws, our tyrant laws have said, that seas must roll between
Old Erin and her faithful sons, that love to wear the Green.
Oh, we love to wear the Green! oh, *how* we love the Green,
Our native land we cannot stand, for wearing of the Green;
Yet wheresoe'er the exile lives though oceans roll between,
Thy faithful sons will fondly sing, "The wearing of the Green."

My father lov'd his country, and sleeps within her breast,
While I, that would have died for her, must never so be blest;
Those tears my mother shed for me, how bitter had they been,
If I had prov'd a traitor to "The wearing of the Green."
There were some who wore the Green, who *did* betray the Green,
Our native land we cannot stand, through traitors to the Green
Yet whatsoe'er our fate may be, when oceans roll between,
Her faithful sons will ever sing, "The wearing of the Green."

My own, my native island, where'er I chance to roam,
Thy lonely hills shall ever be my own beloved home;
And brighter days must surely come, than those that we have seen,
When Erin's sons may boldly sing, "The wearing of the Green."
For we love to wear the Green, oh, *how* we love the Green!
Our native land we cannot stand, for wearing of the Green;
But brighter days must surely come, than those that we have seen,
When all her sons may proudly sing, "The wearing of the Green"

THE MAIDEN CITY.

BY CHARLOTTE ELIZABETH,

AUTHORESS OF THE "SIEGE OF DERRY," &c.

[This truly spirited song in memory of the gallant stand made by the
"Prentice Boys" of Derry against James's army, well deserves a place in an
Irish national collection. Our history might surely be read with a better object

than that of perpetuating factious animosities; and Derry, Limerick, Aughrim, and the Boyne, should serve for nobler purposes than to be made the watchwords of party.]

WHERE Foyle his swelling waters rolls northward to the main,
Here, Queen of Erin's daughters, fair Derry fixed her reign :
A holy temple crowned her, and commerce graced her street,
A rampart wall was round her, the river at her feet ;
And here she sate alone, boys, and, looking from the hill,
Vow'd the Maiden on her throne, boys, would be a Maiden still.

From Antrim crossing over, in famous Eighty-Eight,
A plumed and belted lover came to the Ferry Gate :
She summon'd to defend her, our sires—a beardless race—
Who shouted No SURRENDER ! and slamm'd it in his face.
Then, in a quiet tone, boys, they told him 'twas their will
That the Maiden on her throne, boys, should be a Maiden still.

Next, crushing all before him, a kingly wooer came,
(The royal banner o'er him, blush'd crimson deep for shame ;)
He showed the Pope's commission, nor dream'd to be refused,
She pitied his condition, but begg'd to stand excused.
In short, the fact is known, boys, she chased him from the hill,
For the Maiden on her throne, boys, would be a Maiden still.

On our brave sires descending. 'twas then the tempest broke,
Their peaceful dwellings rending, 'mid blood, and flame, and smoke.
That hallow'd grave-yard yonder, swells with the slaughter'd dead —
Oh, brothers ! pause and ponder, it was for us they bled ;
And while their gift we own, boys—the fane that tops our hill,
Oh, the Maiden on her throne, boys, shall be a Maiden still.

Nor wily tongue shall move us, nor tyrant arm affright,
We'll look to One above us who ne'er forsook the right ;
Who will, may crouch and tender the birthright of the free,
But, brothers, No SURRENDER, no compromise for me !
We want no barrier stone, boys, no gates to guard the hill,
Yet the Maiden on her throne, boys, shall be a Maiden still.

ERIN.

BY DR. DRENNAN.

WHEN Erin first rose from the dark swelling flood,
God bless'd the green island, and saw it was good;
The em'rald of Europe, it sparkled and shone,
In the ring of the world, the most precious stone.
In her sun, in her soil, in her station thrice blest,
With her back towards Britain, her face to the West,
Erin stands proudly insular, on her steep shore,
And strikes her high harp mid the ocean's deep roar.

But when its soft tones seem to mourn and to weep,
The dark chain of silence is thrown o'er the deep;
At the thought of the past the tears gush from her eyes,
And the pulse of her heart makes her white bosom rise.
O! sons of green Erin, lament o'er the time,
When religion was war, and our country a crime,
When man, in God's image, inverted his plan,
And moulded his God in the image of man.

When the int'rest of state wrought the general woe,
The stranger a friend, and the native a foe;
While the mother rejoic'd o'er her children oppressed,
And clasp'd the invader more close to her breast.
When with pale for the body and pale for the soul,
Church and state joined in compact to conquer the whole;
And as Shannon was stained with Milesian blood,
Ey'd each other askance and pronounced it was good.

By the groans that ascend from your forefathers' grave,
For their country thus left to the brute and the slave,
Drive the Demon of Bigotry home to his den,
And where Britain made brutes now let Erin make men.
Let my sons like the leaves of the shamrock unite,
A partition of sects from one footstalk of right,
Give each his full share of the earth and the sky,
Nor fatten the slave where the serpent would die.

Alas! for poor Erin that some are still seen,
Who would dye the grass red from their hatred to Green;

S

Yet, oh! when you're up and they're down, let them live,
Then yield them that mercy which they would not give.
Arm of Erin be strong! but be gentle as brave!
And uplifted to strike, be still ready to save!
Let no feeling of vengeance presume to defile
The cause of, or men of, the Emerald Isle.

The cause it is good, and the men they are true,
And the green shall outlive both the Orange and Blue!
And the triumphs of Erin her daughters shall share,
With the full swelling chest, and the fair flowing hair.
Their bosom heaves high for the worthy and brave,
But no coward shall rest in that soft-swelling wave;
Men of Erin! awake, and make haste to the blest,
Rise—Arch of the Ocean, and Queen of the West!

THE ORANGEMAN'S SUBMISSION.

BY CHARLOTTE ELIZABETH.

[These verses were written and published anonymously when the Orange
Institution was disbanded.]

WE'VE furled the banner that wav'd so long
    Its sunny folds around us;
We've still'd the voice of our ancient song,
    And burst the tie that bound us.
No, no, that tie, that sacred tie,
    Cannot be loos'd or broken;
And thought will flash from eye to eye,
    Though never a word be spoken.

Go raze old Derry's tell-tale wall—
    Bid Enniskillen perish;
Choke up the Boyne—abolish all
    That we too fondly cherish;
'Twill be but as the pruning knife
    Used by a skilful master,
To concentrate the sap of life,
    And fix the strong root faster.

We love the throne—oh, deep you plann'd
  The hateful wile to prove us!
But firm in loyal truth we stand—
  The Queen shall know and love us.
When William came to free the isle
  From galling chains that bound her,
Our fathers built, beneath his smile,
  This living rampart round her.

Ye've taken the outer crust away,
  But, secret strength supplying,
A spirit shrined within the clay,
  Lives quenchless and undying—
A sparkle from the hallow'd flame
  Of our insulted altars,
Pure as the source whence first it came
  Our love nor fades nor falters.

Our love to thee, dear injured land,
  By mocking foes derided;
Our duteous love to the Royal hand,
  By trait'rous craft misguided.
Banner, and badge, and name alone,
  At our monarch's call we tender;
The loyal truth that guards the throne
  We'll keep, and—No Surrender!

ORANGE AND GREEN.

BY GERALD GRIFFIN.

THE night was falling dreary,
  In merry Bandon town,
When in his cottage weary,
  An Orangeman lay down.
The summer sun in splendour
  Had set upon the vale,
And shouts of "No surrender!"
  Arose upon the gale.

Beside the waters, laving
    The feet of aged trees,
The Orange banners waving,
    Flew boldly in the breeze —
In mighty chorus meeting,
    A hundred voices join,
And fife and drum were beating
    The *Battle of the Boyne.*

Ha ! tow'rd his cottage hieing,
    What form is speeding now,
From yonder thicket flying,
    With blood upon his brow ?
" Hide—hide me, worthy stranger,
    Though green my colour be,
And in the day of danger
    May heaven remember thee !

" In yonder vale contending
    Alone against that crew,
My life and limbs defending,
    An Orangeman I slew.
Hark ! hear that fearful warning,
    There's death in every tone—
Oh, save my life till morning,
    And heaven prolong your own !"

The Orange heart was melted
    In pity to the Green;
He heard the tale and felt it,
    His very soul within.
" Dread not that angry warning
    Though death be in its tone—
I'll save your life till morning,
    Or I will lose my own."

Now, round his lowly dwelling
    The angry torrent press'd,
A hundred voices swelling,
    The Orangeman addressed—
" Arise, arise, and follow
    The chase along the plain !
In yonder stony hollow
    Your only son is slain !"

With rising shouts they gather
　Upon the track amain,
And leave the childless father
　Aghast with sudden pain.
He seeks the righted stranger,
　In covert where he lay—
" Arise!" he said, " all danger
　Is gone and past away!

" I had a son—one only,
　One loved as my life,
Thy hand has left me lonely,
　In that accursed strife.
I pledged my word to save thee
　Until the storm should cease,
I keep the pledge I gave thee—
　Arise, and go in peace!"

The stranger soon departed,
　From that unhappy vale;
The father, broken-hearted,
　Lay brooding o'er that tale.
Full twenty summers after
　To silver turned his beard;
And yet the sound of laughter
　From him was never heard.

The night was falling dreary,
　In merry Wexford town,
When in his cabin weary,
　A peasant laid him down.
And many a voice was singing
　Along the summer vale,
And Wexford town was ringing
　With shouts of " Granua Uile."

Beside the waters, laving
　The feet of aged trees,
The green flag, gaily waving,
　Was spread against the breeze—
In mighty chorus meeting,
　Loud voices filled the town,
And fife and drum were beating,
　" Down, Orangemen, lie down!"

Hark ! 'mid the stirring clangour
    That woke the echoes there,
Loud voices, high in anger,
    Rise on the evening air.
Like billows of the ocean,
    He sees them hurry on—
And, 'mid the wild commotion,
    An Orangeman alone.

" My hair," he said, " is hoary,
    And feeble is my hand,
And I could tell a story
    Would shame your cruel band.
Full twenty years and over
    Have changed my heart and brow,
And I am grown a lover
    Of peace and concord now.

" It was not thus I greeted
    Your brother of the Green;
When fainting and defeated
    I freely took him in.
I pledged my word to save him,
    From vengeance rushing on,
I kept the pledge I gave him,
    Though he had killed my son."

That aged peasant heard him,
    And knew him as he stood,
Remembrance kindly stirr'd him,
    And tender gratitude.
With gushing tears of pleasure,
    He pierced the listening train,
" I'm here to pay the measure
    Of kindness back again !"

Upon his bosom falling,
    That old man's tears came down;
Deep memory recalling
    That cot and fatal town.
" The hand that would offend thee,
    My being first shall end ;
I'm living to defend thee,
    My saviour and my friend !"

He said, and slowly turning,
  Address'd the wondering crowd,
With fervent spirit burning,
  He told the tale aloud.
Now pressed the warm beholders,
  Their aged foe to greet ;
They raised him on their shoulders
  And chaired him through the street.

As he had saved that stranger,
  From peril scowling dim,
So in his day of danger
  Did Heav'n remember him.
By joyous crowds attended,
  The worthy pair were seen,
And their flags that day were blended
  Of Orange and of Green.

DEAR LAND.

WHEN comes the day, all hearts to weigh,
  If stanch they be, or vile,
Shall we forget the sacred debt
  We owe our mother isle ?
My native heath is brown beneath,
  My native waters blue ;
But crimson red o'er both shall spread,
  Ere I am false to you,
                    Dear land—
  Ere I am false to you.

When I behold your mountains bold—
  Your noble lakes and streams—
A mingled tide of grief and pride
  Within my bosom teems.
I think of all, your long, dark thrall—
  Your martyrs brave and true ;
And dash apart the tears that start—
  We must not *weep* for you,
                    Dear land—
  We must not weep for you.

My grandsire died, his home beside,
  They seized and hanged him there;
IIis only crime, in evil time,
  Your hallowed green to wear.
Across the main his brothers twain
  Were sent to pine and rue;
And still they turn'd, with hearts that burned,
  In hopeless love to you,
                    Dear land—
  In hopeless love to you.

My boyish ear still clung to hear
  Of Erin's pride of yore,
Ere Norman foot had dared pollute
  Her independent shore;
Of chiefs, long dead, who rose to head
  Some gallant patriot few,
Till all my aim on earth became
  To strike one blow for you,
                    Dear land—
  To strike one blow for you.

What path is best your rights to wrest
  Let other heads divine;
By work or word, with voice or sword,
  To follow them be mine.
The breast that zeal and hatred steel,
  No terrors can subdue;
If death should come, that martyrdom
  Were sweet, endured for you,
                    Dear land—
  Were sweet, endured for you.

THE LONGING.

AH, my heart is weary waiting,
  Waiting for the fray—
Waiting for the sunlight dancing,
Where the bristling pikeheads glancing,

With the rifles alternating,
  Ranks in green and grey.
Ah, my heart is weary waiting,
  Waiting for the fray.

Ah, my heart is weary longing,
  Longing for the fray—
Longing to escape from speeching,
Reading, writing, and beseeching,
  Longing for the stormy thronging
  Round our banners gay.
  Ah, my heart is weary longing,
    Longing for the fray.

Ah, my heart is pained with throbbing,
  Throbbing for the fray,
Throbbing for the time of starting,
Wives and sisters fondly parting,
  Kisses from the loved one robbing,
  "Love, I cannot stay."
  Ah, my heart is pained with throbbing,
    Throbbing for the fray.

Ah, my heart's athirst with burning,
  Burning for the fray—
Burning for the roar and rattle,
For the crimson stream of battle.
  Squadrons round me wildly turning,
  Fear far, far, away.
  Ah, my heart's athirst with burning,
    Burning for the fray.

Waiting, calm, determined, steady,
  Waiting for the fray.
Spring goes by with preparations,
Baffled law and stern ovations—
  Summer comes. That we be ready,
  God of hosts, I pray.
  Ah, my heart is weary waiting,
    Waiting for the fray.

THE LIVING AND THE DEAD.

BY T. D. M'GEE.

BRIGHT is the Spring time, Erin, green and gay to see;
But my heart is heavy, Erin, with thoughts of thy sons and thee;
Thinking of your dead men lying as thick as grass new mown—
Thinking of your myriads dying, unnoted and unknown—
Thinking of your myriads flying beyond the abysmal waves—
Thinking of your magnates sighing, and stifling their thoughts
    like slaves!

Oh! for the time, dear Erin, the fierce time long ago,
When your men felt, dear Erin, and their hands could strike a
    blow!
When your Gaelic chiefs were ready to stand in the bloody breach—
Danger but made *them* steady; they struck, and saved their speech!
But where are the men to head ye, and lead you face to face,
To trample the powers that tread ye, men of the fallen race?

The yellow corn, dear Erin, waves plenteous o'er the plain;
But where are the hands, dear Erin, to gather in the grain?
The sinewy man is sleeping in the crowded churchyard near,
And his young wife is keeping his lonesome company there,
His brother shoreward creeping, has begged his way abroad,
And his sister—tho' for weeping, she scarce could see the road.

No other nation, Erin, but only you would bear
A yoke like yours, oh! Erin, a month, not to say a year;
And will you bear it for ever, writhing and sighing sore,
Now learn—learn now, or never, to dare, not to deplore—
Learn to join in one endeavour your creeds and people all—
'Tis only thus can you sever your tyrant's iron thrall.

Then call your people, Erin, call with a Prophet's cry—
Bid them link in union, Erin, and do like men or die—
Bid the hind from the loamy valley, the miller from the fall—
Bid the craftsman from his alley, the lord from his lordly hall—
Bid the old and the young man rally, and trust to work—not
    words,
And thenceforth ever shall ye be free as the forest birds.

COURAGE.

1848.

BY SPERANZA (MRS. W. R. WILDE).

LIFT up your pale faces, ye children of sorrow,
The night passes on to a glorious to-morrow.
Hark! hear you not sounding glad Liberty's pæan
From the Alps to the Isles of the tideless Ægean?
And the rythmical march of the gathering nations,
And the crashing of thrones 'neath their fierce exultations,
And the cry of Humanity cleaving the ether,
With hymns of the conquering rising together—
God, Liberty, Truth! How they burn heart and brain—
These words shall they burn—shall they waken in vain?

No—soul answers soul—steel flashes on steel,
And land wakens land with a grand thunder peal—
Shall we, oh! my brothers, but weep, pray, and groan
When France reads her rights by the flames of a throne—
Shall we fear and falter to join the grand chorus?
When Europe has trod the dark pathway before us;
Oh, courage! and we, too, will trample them down—
The minions of power, the serfs of a crown.
Oh, courage, but courage, if once to the winds
Ye fling Freedom's banner, no tyranny binds.

At the voice of the people the weak symbols fall,
And humanity marches o'er purple and pall,
O'er sceptre and crown with a glorious disdain,
For the symbol must fall and humanity reign.
Onward, then onward ye brave to the vanguard,
Gather in glory round Liberty's standard.
Like France, lordly France, we shall sweep from their station
All, all who oppose the stern will of a nation;
Like Prussia's brave children we'll stoop to no lord,
But demand our just rights at the point of the sword.

We'll conquer, we'll conquer. No tears for the dying,
The portal to Heaven be the field where they're lying;
We'll conquer, we'll conquer. No tears for the slain,
God's angels will smile on their death-hour of pain.

On, on in your masses dense, resolute, strong,
To war against treason, oppression, and wrong;
On, on with your chieftains, and Him we adore most,
Who strikes with the bravest and leads with the foremost,
Who brings the proud light of a name great in story
To guide us through danger unconquered to glory.

With faith like the Hebrews we'll stem the Red Sea—
God! smite down the Pharaohs—our trust is in thee;
Be it blood of the tyrant or blood of the slave,
We'll cross it to Freedom, or find there a grave.
Lo! a throne for each worker, a crown for each brow,
The palm for each martyr that dies for us now;
Spite the flash of their muskets, the roar of their cannon,
The assassins of Freedom shall lower their pennon;
For the will of a nation what foe dare withstand?
Then patriots, heroes, strike! God for our land!

MY BETROTHED.

BY FRANCIS DAVIS.

[Mr. Davis, a muslin-weaver of Belfast, is the author of this noble lyric, which gushes with such tenderness and sublimity. He is an earnest and manly workman, who throws off during his hours of labour at his loom, amid the monotonous din of his workshop, such brave and racy ballads as this. He is one of the people,—hopes, fears, hates, and labours with them; and is a man of tolerant mind, of great faith, and noble purposes. He has published two small volumes of poems in Belfast, from which we have taken those ballads of his, which appear in this collection.]

Oh! come, my betrothed, to thine anxious bride,
Too long have they kept thee from my side;
Sure I sought thee by meadow and mountain, *asthore*,
And I watch'd and I wept till my heart was sore,
    While the false to the false did say:
We will lead her away by the mound and the rath,
And we'll nourish her heart in its worse than death,
Till her tears shall have traced a pearly path,
    For the work of a future day.

Ah! little they knew what their guile could do—
It has won me a host of the stern and true,

Who have sworn by the eye of the yellow sun,
That my home is their hearts till thy hand be won;
   And they've gathered my tears and sighs;
And they've woven them into a cloudy frown,
That shall gird my brow like an ebony crown,
Till these feet, in my wrath, shall have trampled down
    All, all that betwixt us rise.

Then come, my betrothed, to thine anxious bride!
Thou art dear to my breast as my heart's red tide;
And a wonder it is you can tarry so long,
And your soul so proud, and your arm so strong,
   And your limb without a chain;
And your feet in their flight like the midnight wind,
When he laughs at the flash that he leaves behind;
And your heart so warm, and your look so kind—
   Oh! come to my arms again!

Oh, my dearest has eyes like the noontide sun;
So bright that my own dare scarce look on;
And the clouds of a thousand years gone by,
Brought back, and again on the crowded sky,
   Heaped haughtily pile o'er pile,
Then all in a boundless blaze outspread,
Rent, shaken, and tossed o'er their flaming bed,
Till each heart by the light of the heavens was read,
   Were as nought to his softest smile!

And to hear my love in his wild mirth sing
To the flap of the battle-god's fiery wing!
How his chorus shrieks through the iron tones
Of crashing towers and creaking thrones,
   And the crumbling of bastions strong!
Yet, sweet to my ear as the sigh that slips
From the nervous dance of a maiden's lips,
When the eye first wanes in its love eclipse,
   Is his soul-creating song!

Then come, my betrothed, to thine anxious bride!
Thou hast tarried too long, but I may not chide;
For the prop and the hope of my home thou art,
Ay, the vein that suckles my growing heart:
   Oh, I'd frown on the world for thee!

And it is not a dull, cold, soulless clod,
With a lip in the dust at a tyrant nod,
Unworthy one glance of the Patriot's God,
  That you ever shall find in me!

———

THE PARTING FROM IRELAND.

BY T. D. M'GEE.

On! dread Lord of Earth and Heaven! hard and sad is it to go,
From the land I loved and cherished into outward gloom and woe;
Was it for this, Guardian Angel, when to manly years I came,
Homeward as a light you led me—light that now is turned to flame!

I am as a shipwrecked sailor, by one wave flung on the shore,
By the next torn struggling seaward, without hope for evermore:
I am as a sinner toiling onward to Redemption Hill,
By the rising sands environed—by the Simoom baffled still.

How I loved this nation ye know, gentle friends, who share my fate;
And you, too, heroic comrades, loaded with the fetter's weight—
How I coveted all knowledge that might raise her name with men—
How I sought her secret beauties with an all-insatiate ken.

God! it is a maddening prospect thus to see this storied land,
Like some wretched culprit writhing, in a strong avenger's hand,
Kneeling, foaming, weeping, shrieking, woman-weak and woman-
  loud;
Better, better, Mother Ireland, we had laid you in your shroud!

If an end were made, and nobly, of this old centennial feud—
If, in arms outnumbered, beaten, less, oh! Ireland, had I rued;
For the scattered sparks of valour might re-light thy darkness yet,
And thy long chain of Resistance to the Future had been knit.

Now *their* Castle sits securely on its old accursèd hill,
And their motley pirate standard taints the air of Ireland still;
And their titled paupers clothe them with the labour of our hands,
And their Saxon greed is glutted from our plundered fathers' lands.

But our faith is all unshaken, though our present hope is gone :
England's lease is *not* for ever—Ireland's warfare is *not* done.
God in Heaven, He is immortal—Justice is his sword and sign—
If Earth will not be our ally, we have One who is Divine.

Though my eyes no more may see thee, Island of my early love !
Other eyes shall see thy Green Flag flying the tall hills above ;
Though my ears no more may listen to thy rivers as they flow
Other ears shall hear a Pæan closing thy long *keen* of woe.

RUINS.

BY SPERANZA (MRS. W. R. WILDE.)

SHALL we tread the dust of ages,
    Musing dream-like on the past ;
Seeking on the broad earth's pages
    For the shadows Time hath cast ;
Waking up some ancient story,
    From each prostrate shrine or hall,
Old traditions of a glory
    Earth may never more recall !

Poet thoughts of sadness breathing,
    For the temples overthrown ;
Where no incense now is wreathing,
    And the gods are turned to stone.
Wandering by the graves of heroes,
    Shrouded deep in classic gloom,
Or the tombs where Egypt's Pharaohs
    Wait the trumpet and the doom.

By the city, desert-hidden, *
    Which Judea's mighty king
Made the Geni, at his bidding,
    Raise by magic of his ring ;
By the Lake Asphaltian wander,
    While the crimson sunset glow
Flings its radiance as we ponder
    On the buried towns below.

* Palmyra, or Tadmor.

By the Cromleach sloping downward,
  Where the Druid's victim bled:
By those towers pointing sunward,
  Hieroglyphics none have read.
In their mystic symbols seeking
  Of past rites and creeds o'erthrown,
If the truths they shrined are speaking
  Yet, in Litanies of Stone.

By the temple of the Muses,
  Where the climbers of the mount
Learned the soul's diviner uses
  From the Heliconian fount.
By the banks of dark Illyssus,
  Where the Parcæ walked of old,
In their crowns of white narcissus,
  And their garments starred with gold.

By the tomb of queenly Isis,
  Where her fallen prophets wail,
Yet no hand has dared the crisis
  Of the lifting of the vail.
By the altar which the Grecian
  Raised to God without a name;
By the stately shrine Ephesian,
  Erostratus burned for fame.

By the Libyan shrine of Ammon,
  Where the sands are trod with care,
Lest we, bending to examine,
  Start the lion from his lair.
Shall we tread the halls Assyrian,
  Where the Arab tents are set,
Seek the glory of the Tyrian,
  Where the fisher spreads his net?

Shall we seek the " Mene, mene,"
  Wrote by God upon the wall,
While the proud son of Mandane
  Strode across the fated hall?
Shall we mourn the Loxian's lyre,
  Or the Pythian priestess mute;
Shall we seek the Delphic fire,
  Though we've lost Apollo's lute?

Ah, the world has sadder ruins
  Than these wrecks of things sublime ;
For the touch of man's misdoings
  Leaves more blighted tracks than Time.
Ancient lore gives no examples
  Of the ruins here we find—
Prostrate souls for fallen temples,
  Mighty ruins of the mind.

We had hopes that rose as proudly
  As each sculptured marble shrine ;
And our prophets spake as loudly
  As their oracles divine.
Grand resolves of giant daring,
  Such as Titans breathed of old,
Brilliant aims their front uprearing,
  Like a temple roofed with gold.

Souls of fire, like columns pointing,
  Flame-like upward to the skies ;
Glorious brows which God's anointing
  Consecrated altar wise.
Stainless hearts, like temples olden,
  None but priest hath ever trod ;
Hands as pure as were the golden
  Staves which bore the ark of God.

Oh, they built up radiant visions,
  Like an iris after rain ;
How all paradise traditions
  Might be made to live again.
Of humanity's sad story,
  How their hand should turn the page,
And the ancient primal glory,
  Fling upon this latter age.

How with God-like aspirations,
  Up the souls of men would climb,
Till the fallen, enslaved nations
  Trod in rhythmic march sublime :
Reaching heights the people knew not,
  Till their prophet Leaders led—
Bathed in light that mortals view not,
  While the spirit life lies dead.

                              T

How the pallid sons of labour,
  They should toil and toil to raise,
Till a glory, like to Tabor,
  Once again should meet earth's gaze.
How the poor, no longer keeping
  Count of life alone by groans,
With the strong cry of their weeping,
  Start the angels on their thrones.

Ah, that vision's bright ideal,
  Must it fade and perish thus?
Must its fall alone be real,
  Are its ruins trod by us?
Ah, they dream'd an Eldorado,
  Given not to mortal sight;
Yet the souls that walk in shadow,
  Still bend forward to its light.

Earnest dreamers, sooth we blame not
  If ye failed to reach the goal—
If the glorious real came not
  At the strong prayer of each soul.
By the path ye've trod to duty,
  Blessings yet to man may flow,
Though the proud and stately beauty
  Of your structure lieth low.

Low as that which Salem mourneth,
  On Moriah's holy hill;
While the heathen proudly scorneth,
  Yet the wrecks are glorious still:
Like the seven columns frowning,
  On the desert city down,
Or the seven cedars crowning
  Lofty Lebanon.

Poet wanderer, hast thou bent thee
  O'er such ruins of the soul?
Pray to God that some Nepenthe
  May efface that hour of dole.
We may lift the shrine and column,
  From the dust which Time hath cast;
Choral chants may mingle solemn,
  Once again where silence passed;

But the stately radiant palace,
  We had built up in our dreams,
With Hope's rainbow-woven trellis,
  And Truth's glorious sunrise beams—
Our aims of towering stature,
  Our aspirations vain,
And our prostrate human nature—
  Who will raise *them* up again?

THE IRISH MINSTREL.

BY EVA. (MISS MARY EVA KELLY.)

I HEAR cold voices saying, that she my queen, is dead,
And those sad chords may never more their tones of music shed;
That I, who wildly loved her, must weep in mute despair—
Ah! they know not how true love will cling though blight and
    death be there!

I have no joy or triumph to swell my minstrel lay,
I have no hope to cheer me on the dark and lonely way;
But in this feeble soul there's still a might they dream not of,
While living springs are in my breast of deep unswerving Love!

Yes, pale one in thy sorrow—yes, wrong'd one in thy pain,
This heart has still a beat for thee—this trembling hand a strain;
They cannot steal the golden stores the *past* has left to me—
Or make me shrink with broken faith, asthore machree,* from thee

Oh! hear—my darling hear me!—'tis no cold pulse meets thine own,
Its burning throbs would warm to life, an' thou wert changed to
    stone:
I'll call the colour to thy cheek, the light into thine eye—
I know at least if *thou* art dead my love can *never* die!

'Twould make the air around thee warm with breath of living
    flame,
In life or death, or joy or woe, 'twill cling to thee the same—
No—never in the gladdest hour, when thou wert proud and strong,
Was deeper worship pour'd than now in this low mourning song.

     * *Asthore machree,*—Love of my heart.

I knelt before you long ago, when a crown was on your brow,
I lov'd you then with fervent love—I love you firmer now;
And that which makes the ivy green around the mould'ring tree—
Will make my voice all tuneful still, asthore machree for thee!

THE ANCIENT RACE.

BY T. D. M'GEE.

WHAT shall become of the ancient race—
The noble Celtic island race?
Like cloud on cloud o'er the azure sky,
When Winter storms are loud and high,
Their dark ships-shadow the ocean's face—
What shall become of the Celtic race?

What shall befall the ancient race—
The poor, unfriended, faithful race?
Where ploughman's song made the hamlet ring,
The village vulture flaps his wing;
The village homes, oh, who can trace?
God of our persecuted race!

What shall befall the ancient race?
Is treason's stigma on their face?
Be they cowards or traitors? Go
Ask the shade of England's foe;
See the gems her crown that grace;
They tell a tale of the ancient race.

They tell a tale of the ancient race—
Of matchless deeds in danger's face;
They speak of Britain's glory fed
On blood of Celt right bravely shed;
Of India's spoil and Frank's disgrace—
They tell a tale of the ancient race.

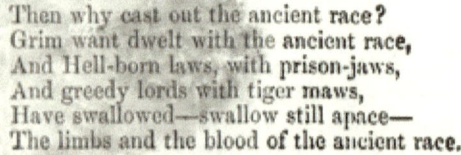

Then why cast out the ancient race?
Grim want dwelt with the ancient race,
And Hell-born laws, with prison-jaws,
And greedy lords with tiger maws,
Have swallowed—swallow still apace—
The limbs and the blood of the ancient race.

Will no one shield the ancient race?
They fly their father's burial place;
The proud lords with the heavy purse—
Their father's shame—their people's curse—
Demons in heart, nobles in face—
They dig a grave for the ancient race!

They dig a grave for the ancient race—
And grudge that grave to the ancient race!
On highway side full oft were seen,
The wild dogs and the vultures keen,
Tug for the limbs and gnaw the face,
Of some starv'd child of the ancient race!

What shall befall the ancient race?
Shall all forsake their dear birth-place,
Without one struggle strong to keep
The old soil where their fathers sleep!
The dearest land on earth's wide space—
Why leave it so, O ancient race?

What shall befall the ancient race?
Light up one hope for the ancient race;
Oh, Priest of God—*Soggarth aroon!*
Lead but the way—we'll go full soon;
Is there a danger we will not face,
To keep old homes for the Irish race?

They will not go, the ancient race!
They must not go, the ancient race!
Come, gallant Celts, and take your stand—
The League—the League—will save the land;
The land of faith, the land of grace,
The land of Erin's ancient race!

They will not go, the ancient race!
They *shall* not go, the ancient race!
The cry swells loud from shore to shore,
From em'rald vale to mountain hoar—
From altar high to market place—
They shall not go, the ancient race

THE YOUNG PATRIOT LEADER.

BY SPERANZA (MRS. W. R. WILDE).

Oh! he stands beneath the sun, that glorious *Fated One*,
  Like a martyr or conqueror, wearing
On his brow a mighty doom—be it glory, be it gloom,
  The shadow of a crown it is bearing.

At his Cyclopean stroke the proud heart of man awoke
  Like a king from his lordly down lying;
And whereso'er he trod, like the footstep of a god,
  Was a trail of light the gloom outvying.

In his beauty and his youth, the Apostle of the Truth,
  Goes he forth with the words of Salvation,
And a noble madness falls on each spirit he enthralls,
  As he chants his wild Pæans to the nation.

As a Tempest in its force, as a Torrent in its course,
  So his words fiercely sweep all before them,
And they smite like two-edged swords, those undaunted thunder
      words
  On all hearts, as tho' Angels did implore them.

See our pale cheeks how they flush, as the noble visions rush,
  On our soul's most dark desolation—
And the glorious lyric words—Right, Freedom, and our Swords!—
  Wake the strong chords of life to vibration.

Ay—right noble, in good sooth, seem'd he battling for the Truth
  When he poured the full tide of his scorn
Down upon the Tyrant's track, like an Alpine cataract—
  Ah!—such men wait an Æon to be born.

So he stood before us then, one of God's eternal men,
  Flashing eye, and hero mould of stature,
With a glory and a light circling round his brow of might,
  That revealed his right royal kingly nature.

Lo! he leadeth on our bands, Freedom's banner in his hands,
    Let us aid him, not with words, but *doing;*
With the marches of the brave, prayers of might that strike and
        save,
    Not a slavish spirit's abject suing.

Thus in glory is he seen, though his years are yet but green,
    The Anointed as Head of our Nation—
For High Heaven hath decreed that a soul like his must lead,
    Let us kneel then in deep adoration.

Oh! his mission is divine—dash down the Lotus wine—
    Too long is your trancèd sleep abiding,
And by Him who gave us life, we shall conquer in the strife
    So we follow but that Young Chief's guiding.

HIGHWAY FOR FREEDOM.

BY J. C. MANGAN.

"MY suffering country SHALL be freed,
    And shine with tenfold glory!"
So spake the gallant Winkelreid,
    Renowned in German story.
"No tyrant, even of kingly grade,
    Shall cross or darken *my* way!"
Out flashed his blade, and so he made
    For Freedom's course a highway !

We want a man like this, with power
    To rouse the world by *one* word ;
We want a chief to meet the hour,
    And march the masses onward.
But chief or none, through blood and fire,
    My Fatherland lies *thy* way!
The men must fight who dare desire
    For Freedom's course a highway !

Alas! I can but idly gaze
    Around in grief and wonder ;
The PEOPLE'S will alone can raise
    The People's shout of thunder.

Too long, my friends, you faint for fear,
  In secret crypt and by-way;
At last be Men!   Stand forth and clear
  For Freedom's course a highway !

You intersect wood, lea, and lawn,
  With roads for monster waggons,
Wherein you speed like lightning, drawn
  By fiery iron dragons.
So do!   Such work is good, no doubt :
  But why not seek some nigh way
For *Mind* as well?   Path also out
  For Freedom's course a highway !

Yes! up! and let your weapons be
  Sharp steel and self-reliance !
Why waste your burning energy
  In void and vain defiance,
And phrases fierce and fugitive ?
  'Tis deeds, not words, that *I* weigh—
Your swords and guns alone can give
  To Freedom's course a highway.

Emigrant Ballads.

SALUTATION TO THE CELTS.

BY T. D. M'GEE.

Hail to our Celtic brethren, wherever they may be,
In the far woods of Oregon, or o'er the Atlantic sea—
Whether they guard the banner of St. George in Indian vales,
Or spread beneath the nightless North experimental sails,
        One in name, and in fame
        Are the sea-divided Gaels.

Tho' fallen the state of Erin, and changed the Scottish land,
Tho' small the power of Mona, tho' unwaked Lewellyn's band—
Tho' Ambrose Merlin's prophecies degenerate to tales,
And the cloisters of Iona are bemoaned by northern gales,
        One in name, and in fame
        Are the sea-divided Gaels.

In Northern Spain and Brittainy, our brethren also dwell—
Oh! brave are the traditions of their fathers that they tell.
The eagle and the crescent in the dawn of history pales,
Before their fire, that seldom flags, and never wholly fails.
        One in name, and in fame
        Are the sea-divided Gaels.

A greeting and a promise, unto them all we send—
Their character our charter is, their glory is our end—
Their friend shall be our friend, our foe whoe'er assails
The past or future honours of the far dispersed Gaels.
        One in name, and in fame
        Are the sea-divided Gaels.

THE WOODS OF KYLINOE.

My heart is heavy in my breast—my eyes are full of tears,
My memory is wandering back to long departed years—
To those bright days long, long ago,
When nought I dreamed of sordid care, of worldly woe—
But roved, a gay, light-hearted boy, the woods of Kylinoe.

There, in the spring time of my life, and spring time of the year,
I've watched the snow-drop start from earth, the first young buds
    appear;
The sparkling stream o'er pebbles flow,
The modest violet, and the golden primrose blow,
Within thy deep and mossy dells, beloved Kylinoe!

'Twas there I wooed my Mary *Dhuv*, and won her for my bride,
Who bore me three fair daughters, and four sons, my age's pride;
Though cruel fortune was our foe,
And steeped us to the lips in bitter want and woe,
Yet cling our hearts to those sad days, we passed near Kylinoe!

At length by misery bowed to earth, we left our native strand—
And crossed the wide Atlantic to this free and happy land;
Though toils we had to undergo,
Yet soon content—and happy peace 'twas ours to know,
And plenty, such as never blessed our hearth near Kylinoe!

And heaven a blessing has bestowed, more precious far than wealth,
Has spared us to each other, full of years, yet strong in health:
Across the threshold when we go,
We see our children's children round us grow,
Like sapling oaks within thy woods, far distant Kylinoe.

Yet sadness clouds our hearts to think that when we are no more,
Our bones must find a resting place, far, far from Erin's shore,
For us—no funeral sad and slow—
Within the ancient abbey's burial ground shall go—
No, we must slumber far from home, far, far from Kylinoe!

Lament of the Irish Emigrant.—Vol. i., p. 299.

Yet, oh! if spirits e'er can leave the appointed place of rest,
Once more will I revisit thee, dear Isle that I love best,
O'er thy green vales will hover slow,
And many a tearful parting blessing will bestow
On all—but most of all on *thee*, my native Kylinoe!

LN. F,

LAMENT OF THE IRISH EMIGRANT.

BY LADY DUFFERIN.

I'M sittin' on the stile, Mary,
  Where we sat side by side
On a bright May mornin' long ago,
  When first you were my bride:
The corn was springin' fresh and green,
  And the lark sang loud and high—
And the red was on your lip, Mary,
  And the love-light in your eye.

The *place* is little changed, Mary,
  The day is bright as then,
The lark's loud song is in my ear,
  And the corn is green again;
But I miss the soft clasp of your hand,
  And your breath, warm on my cheek
And I still keep list'nin' for the words
  You never more will speak.

'Tis but a step down yonder lane,
  And the little church stands near,
The church where we were wed, Mary,
  I see the spire from here.
But the grave-yard lies between, Mary,
  And my step might break your rest—
For I've laid you, darling! down to sleep
  With your baby on your breast.

I'm very lonely now, Mary,
  For the poor make no new friends,
But, oh! they love the better still,
  The few our Father sends!

And you were all *I* had, Mary,
    My blessin' and my pride :
There's nothing left to care for now,
    Since my poor Mary died.

Your's was the good, brave heart, Mary,
    That still kept hoping on,
When the trust in God had left my soul,
    And my arm's young strength was gone;
There was comfort ever on *your* lip,
    And the kind look on your brow—
I bless you, Mary, for that same,
    Though you cannot hear me now.

I thank you for the patient smile
    When your heart was fit to break,
When the hunger pain was gnawin' there,
    And you hid it for *my* sake !
I bless you for the pleasant word,
    When your heart was sad and sore—
Oh! I'm thankful you are gone, Mary,
    Where grief can't reach you more !

I'm biddin' you a long farewell,
    My Mary—kind and true !
But I'll not forget *you*, darling !
    In the land I'm goin' to ;
They say there's bread and work for all,
    And the sun shines always there—
But I'll not forget old Ireland,
    Were it fifty times as fair !

And often in those grand old woods
    I'll sit, and shut my eyes,
And my heart will travel back again
    To the place where Mary lies ;
And I'll think I see the little stile
    Where we sat side by side :
And the springin' corn, and the bright May morn,
    When first you were my bride.

THE LAST REQUEST.

BY WILLIAM KENEALY.

You're going away, *Alanna*, over the stormy sea,
And never more I'll see you—Oh! never, *Asthore machree!*
Mavrone! I'm sick with sorrow—sorrow as black as night :
Mabouchal* goes to-morrow, by the blessed morning's light.

Oh! once I thought, *Alanna*, you'd bear me to the grave,
By the side of your angel sisters, before you'd cross the wave :
Down to the green old churchyard, where the tree's dark shadows
    fall—
But now, *Achorra!* you're going, you'll not be there at all.

The strangers' hands must lay me down to my silent sleep,
And *Shemus*, you'll not know it beyond the rolling deep.
Oh, *Dheeling! dheeling! Avourneen*,† why do you go away,
Till you'll see the poor old mother stretch'd in the churchyard clay?

My heart is breaking, *Alanna*, but I mustn't tell you so,
For I see by your dark, dark sorrow, that your own poor heart is
    low.
I thought I'd bear it better, to cheer you on your way ;
But, *Achorra! achorra!* you're going, and I'll soon be in the clay!

God's blessing be with you, *Shemus*—sure, you'll come back again,
When your curls of brown are snowy, to rest with your mother then ;
Down in the green old churchyard, where the trees' dark shadows
    fall—
Asthorach! in the strangers' land you couldn't sleep at all !

THE WANDERER.

"Whence come you, pallid wanderer, so destitute and lorn,
With step so weak and faltering, and face so wan and worn?
Our eyes are used to misery, that day by day endures,
Yet never have they looked upon so sad a form as yours."

---

* *Mabouchal,*—My Boy.
† *Dheeling, Avourneen,*—God be with us, my dear.

"In a glen of distant Munster, my infant breath I drew,
Where the summer sun falls brightly on the lovely Avondhu—
Oh! oftentimes beneath his beams I've watch'd the river shine,
And never thought such bitter woe and hardship would be mine.

I was born to strive with poverty, as all my people were,
But I never thought of better, and my heart was free from care;
We knew that ours must be a life of penury and toil,
For what were we but Irish—the children of the soil?
But the famine and the pestilence swept o'er us with their breath,
And gather'd many a one I lov'd into the arms of death;
While, crueller than famine—than pestilence more sure,
Came the landlord's hireling drivers—the wreckers of the poor.

Then woe unto the cabin homes within that little glen,
We never felt dependence in its bitterness till then;
The living and the dying lay unsheltered on the sod,
No earthly succour near them—no refuge save in God.
When our friends and our defenders rais'd the emerald flag on high,
And hope had whisper'd a return of long lost liberty,
Thus did our masters counsel those who to the standard pour'd,
'Be tranquil, and be loyal, or ye perish by the sword.'

But better had it been for them to lie among the slain—
Than to end a life of sorrow by a lingering death of pain;
And hardly would the sword have struck all that the famine slew,
In thy glens of rushing waters—my lovely Avondhu!
Now I, a lonely wanderer, come in my sorrow forth,
To seek for help and pity in the bosoms of the North.
An orphan and a stranger—in sickness and in woe,
May Heaven return the merciful the mercy they bestow!"

———

THE DAWN OF THE PARTING DAY.

"OH, mother, the dreary winter night is passing fast away—
The Eastern sky has a gleam of light 'neath its gloomy veil of grey,
And ever the light is growing more bright—I may no longer stay,
The lark is winging his morning flight, 'tis the dawn of our parting
    day.

I'm going away to the stranger's land in the season of manly toil,
To join with a strong and earnest band in tilling an alien soil;
There's a labour grand for the fearless hand, a noble prize to be
    won—
The ship is waiting beside the strand, now bless your first-born son."

" Oh, the blackest night I would sooner see, with never a hope of
    dawn,
Than the morning that takes you away from me, my darling, my
    Carroll *ban !*
'Tis lonely and dark my home will be when the light of your
    smile is gone—
When your clear voice ringing so true and free is heard by my
    heart alone !

And when I sit weeping my life long woe at evening beside my
    door,
And strangers their scornful pity throw on the widow so lone and
    poor,
I'll miss your soft eyes' kindling glow, as you vow with a true
    son's pride,
That you'd rather be mine in my grief-worn show than king of
    the world beside !

Alas! the children I loved the best, my noble, my fond and brave,
Are scattered afar from their mother's breast, or laid in the silent
    grave ;
And the *one* God left me, my hope, my stay, is going across the sea.
Oh, how can I bear the sad words to say that will send you away
    machree ! "

" Mother, I saw how my brethren went from your loving heart
    and home,
To gladden your life their strength was spent, now on me the
    proud task has come ;
And I saw my bright-eyed sisters mourn o'er the griefs that their
    brothers bore,
To finish the work my soul has sworn, your home shall be bright
    once more ! "

" Ah, well I knew how your noble heart is wrung by your mother's
    woe,
And strong in your choice of the toiler's part to strive for my
    weal you go ;

But the God that made you so pure and true will guard you and
　help you on—
To Him I pour forth my prayers for you, as mothers pray for an
　only son!"

THOMASINE.

MARY'S GRAVE.

BY THE REV. GEORGE HILL.

[In the ancient burying-ground of Buono-Margy, near Ballycastle, there is
the grave of a young woman who died when her parents and the other members of the family were about to emigrate to America. They were obliged, by
her illness, to postpone their departure for a time, and the gloom of approaching death was deepened and rendered more appalling to her, by the thought
that none of her kindred would be near to visit her grave.]

"O LIFE and Hope, ye faint, ye fail!
　How blithely once to me
On sweet Rathnona's heights, the gale
　Came o'er the summer sea!
But soon this heart shall cease to beat,
　These sleepless eyes shall close,
And in the grave's serene retreat,
　My weary head repose.

Sweet friends, and when ye lay me where
　Our fathers' ashes lie,
Say, will ye sometimes think of her
　Whose love can never die?
And when you leave our peaceful glen
　To cross the distant wave,
Oh, will ye ever come again,
　To see your Mary's grave?"

Full many a year has pass'd, and she,
　The best beloved of all,
Sleeps, from her cares and sorrows free,
　Beside the old church wall.—
The bee at noontide murmurs there
　The shamrock flowers among;
And in the evening's silent air,
　How sweet the redbreast's song!

THE CONNAUGHT CHIEF'S FAREWELL.

BY T. D. M'GEE.

[Scene.—Galway Bay after sunset. A Connaught Chief and his daughter on the deck of a departing ship. Time—1652. A few days after the surrender of Galway city to the Parliamentarians.]

" My Daughter! 'tis a deadly fate, that turns us out to sea,
Leaving our hearts behind us, where our hopes no more can be—
The fate that lifts our anchor, and swells our sail so wide,
Will have us far from sight of land ere morning's on the tide.

Why does the darkness lower so deep upon the Galway shore?
Will no kind beam of moon or star shine on the cliffs of Moher?
My child, you need not banish so the heart's dew from your eye,
We cannot catch an utmost glimpse of Arran sailing by.

Thus all that was worth fighting for, for ever passed away,
The true hearts all were given to death—the living turned to clay—
No wonder, then, the shamefaced shore should vail itself in night,
When slaves sleep thickly on the land, why should the sky be
    bright?

Yes, thus their light should vanish, as vanished first their cause.
Its hills should perish from our sight, as sunk its native laws,
Its valleys from our souls be shut like chalices defiled,
Nought have I now to love or serve, but God and you, my child."

" My father, dear—my father, what makes you talk so wild?
To God place next your country, and after her, your child ;
Though the land be dark behind us, and the sea all dim before,
A morrow and a glory yet shall dawn on Connaught's shore ;

What! though foul Fortune has her will, and stern Fate fills our
    sail,
The slaves that sleep must waken up, nor can the wrong prevail ;
What! though they broke our altars down, and rolled our Saints
    in dust,
They could not pluck them from that Heaven in which they had
    their trust."

U

" May God and his Saints protect you, my own girl wise as fair,
An angel wrestling with my will, indeed, you ever were,
Oh, sure, when young hearts hold such hope, and young heads
    bare such thought,
Defeat can ne'er be destiny, nor the crimson fight unfought!

Good land—green land—dear Ireland, though I cannot see you,
    still
May God's dew brighten all your vales, His sun kiss every hill;
And though henceforth our nights and days in strange lands must
    be past,
Our hearts and hopes for your uprise will keep watch till the last."

———

THE PARTING.

ANON. (MARY.)

WE are quitting our own land, darling, the ship will sail to-day,
Which bears us from our pleasant home, and kind old friends away;
We grew up children there, Mary, and never thought to go
From the cabin and the garden green, we loved and clung to so!

We saw our children, too, Mary, play o'er that smiling ground—.
But they in quiet graveyard now more lasting home have found;
Oh! don't we envy them, Mary? They sleep in their own land,
And none can lay their bones in death upon the foreign strand!

'Tis *that* I dread the most, Mary, when the dark death is nigh,
With strange—strange faces all around, I cannot bear to die!
I think that I could work and toil in other lands awhile,
If I might fill a grave at last in my own darling isle!

'Tis very cruel now, Mary, to talk in this wild way;
For well I know your loving heart is sore as mine to-day!
And I should comfort you, Mary, and speak of brighter years;
The heart *within* is breaking, and I cannot help my tears!

Oh! lift your face to mine, Mary, I'll kiss it o'er and o'er!
Oh! twine your arms around me, I'll never leave them more!
Oh! were it not for you—for you, I'd send one prayer on high,
And ask the blessed God of Heaven, to will that I might die!

Close—closer to your heart, Mary, my own will burst at last—
My brain is all on vivid fire with thinking of the past!
Oh! bid the ship sail on—sail on, and hold me fast to thee!
The waves around bathe Irish ground, they're sorely tempting me!

THE COUNTY OF MAYO.

(FROM THE IRISH.)

BY GEORGE FOX.

[This specimen of our ancient Irish Literature, is one of the most popular songs of the peasantry of the counties of Mayo and Galway, and is evidently a composition of the seventeenth century. The original Irish, which is the composition of one Thomas Lavelle, has been published without a translation, by Mr. Hardiman, in his Irish Minstrelsy; but a very able translation of it was published by Mr. Ferguson, in a review of that work in the *University Magazine* for June 1834. The original melody of the same name is of very great beauty and pathos, and one which it is desirable to preserve with English words of appropriate simplicity of character:—]

ON the deck of Patrick Lynch's boat I sat in woful plight,
Through my sighing all the weary day, and weeping all the night,
Were it not that full of sorrow from my people forth I go,
By the blessed sun, 'tis royally I'd sing thy praise, Mayo.

When I dwelt at home in plenty, and my gold did much abound,
In the company of fair young maids the Spanish ale went round—
'Tis a bitter change from those gay days that now I'm forced to go,
And must leave my bones in Santa Cruz, far from my own Mayo.

They are altered girls in Irrul now; 'tis proud they're grown and
  high,
With their hair-bags and their top-knots, for I pass their buckles
  by—
But it's little now I heed their airs, for God will have it so,
That I must depart for foreign lands, and leave my sweet Mayo.

'Tis my grief that Patrick Loughlin is not Earl in Irrul still,
And that Brian Duff no longer rules as Lord upon the hill;
And that Colonel Hugh Mac Grady should be lying dead and low,
And I sailing, sailing swiftly from the county of Mayo.

THE EMIGRANTS.

BY DIGBY PILOT STARKEY, M.R.I.A.

BEHOLD! a troop of travellers descending to the shore—
Strong, stalwart youths and maidens, mixed with those in years
    and hoar;
With stealth they glide towards the tide, like walkers in their sleep :
Where are ye going, lonely ones, that thus ye walk, and weep?

No answer : but the lip compressed argues a tale to tell—
A studied silence seems to hold them bound, as with a spell;
They pass me by abstractedly, their gaze where, near at hand,
Rolls through the shade the heavy wave upon the sullen strand.

Stop—whither go ye? See, behind, e'en yet the landscape smiles—
The broad sunset illumines yet these pleasant western isles,—
Why, why is it that none will turn and take one look behind,
But rather face the billows there, to light and counsel blind?

Peace! questioner—we know the sun upon our soil doth rest—
Though EMIGRANTS, we have not cast all feeling from our breast;
But still, *we go*—for through that shade hope gilds the distant
    plain,
While round the homes we've left we look'd for nourishment in vain !

Well, *thou* art strong; thy stubborn strength may make the de-
    sert do;
But, see! a weeping woman here—some shivering children too :
Deluded female, stop! for *thee* what hope beyond the tide?
For *me?*—and seest thou not I have my husband by my side?

And thou, too, parting! thou, my friend, that loved thy home
    and ease?
Ay—see my brothers— sisters here—what's country without *these?*
But then, thy hands for toil unfit—thy frame to labour new?
What then? I work beside my friends—come *thou* and join our
    crew.

Yes, come! exclaims a reverend man—glad will we be of thee—
We go in Christian fellowship our mission o'er the sea :—
I've left a large and happy flock, that loved me, too, full well;
Yet I take heart, as I depart where godless heathens dwell.

Alas! and is it needful then, that from this ancient soil,
Where wealth and honour crowned so long the hardy yeoman's
    toil,
The goodliest of its offspring thus should bid the canvass swell,
And to the parent earth in troops wave their last sad farewell?

I'm answered from the swarming ports, the everstreaming tide
That pours on board a thousand ships my country's hope and
    pride :—
I'm answered by the fruitless toil of many a neighbour's hand,
And the gladsome shouts of prosperous men in many a distant
    land.

Stay, countrymen!—e'en yet there's time—we'll settle all your
    score—
We cannot spare such honoured men—'twould grieve our hearts
    too sore ;—
Things will go smooth—why quit the scene a thousand things
    made dear,
That wealth may deck ye in the spoils torn from affection here?

Torn is the last embrace apart—the vessel quits the shore—
They're waving hands from off the deck—we hear their voice no
    more :—
God bless ye, friends! I honour ye, adventurous, noble band!
Farewell! I would not call ye *now* back to this wretched land!

Why not myself among ye, loved associates of my day?
Why not with you embarked to share the perils of your way?
Because, though hope may be *your* sun, remembrance is *my* star—
Farewell—I'll die a watcher where my FATHER's ashes are.

THE EXILE'S REQUEST.

BY T. D. M'GEE.

On, Pilgrim, if you bring me from the far-off lands a sign,
Let it be some token still of the green old land, once mine ;
A shell from the shores of Ireland would be dearer far to me,
Than all the wines of the Rhine land, or the art of Italie.

For I was born in Ireland—I glory in the name—
I weep for all her sorrows, I remember well her fame!
And still my heart must hope that I may yet repose at rest,
On the Holy Zion of my youth, in the Israel of the West.

Her beauteous face is furrowed with sorrow's streaming rains,
Her lovely limbs are mangled with slavery's ancient chains,
Yet, Pilgrim, pass not over with heedless heart or eye,
The Island of the gifted, and of men who knew to die.

Like the crater of a fire-mount, all without is bleak and bare,
But the vigour of its lips still show what fire and force was there,
Even now in the heaving craters, far from the gazer's ken,
The fiery heel is forging that will crush her foes again.

Then, Pilgrim, if you bring me from the far-off lands a sign,
Let it be some token still of the green old land, once mine;
A shell from the shores of Ireland would be dearer far to me,
Than all the wines of the Rhine land, or the art of Italie.

THE DEPARTURE.

BY B. SIMMONS.

The breeze already fills the sail, on yonder distant strand,
That bears me far an exile from my own inclement land,
Whose cloudy skies possess nor balm, nor brilliance, save what
    lies
In lips twin-sisters with the rose, and blue beloved eyes.

Dear misty hills! that soon to me shall o'er the ocean fade,
Your echoes ever in my ears exulting music made—
For with your torrents' rushing falls, and with your tempests'
    power,
Familiar voices blent their tones in many a festal hour.

How oft, in sunnier clime afar—in summer's glowing halls—
When on the lonely stranger's head the dew of welcome falls,
His pining spirit still shall hear, 'mid Beauty's thronging daughters,
The fairy steps that glance in light by wild Glen-seskin's waters.

And memory-prompted Hope shall dream, that where amid the
    West
The Harp's fair children lull the night with melody to rest,
Some simple strain may then recall remembrance faint of Him
Whose heart is with them in that hour across the billows dim.

HOME THOUGHTS.

BY T. D. M'GEE.

If Will had wings, how fast I'd flee,
To the home of my heart o'er the seething sea!
If Wishes were power—if Words were spells,
I'd be this hour where my own love dwells.

My own love dwells in the storied land,
Where the Holy Wells sleep in yellow sand;
And the emerald lustre of Paradise beams,
Over homes that cluster round singing streams.

I, sighing alas! exist alone—
My youth is as grass on an unsunned stone,
Bright to the eye, but unfelt below—
As sunbeams that lie over Arctic snow.

My heart is a lamp that love must relight,
Or the world's fire-damp will quench it quite.
In the breast of my dear, my life-tide springs—
Oh! I'd hurry home here, if Will had wings.

For she never was weary of blessing me,
When morn rose dreary on thatch and tree;
She evermore chanted her song of Faith,
When darkness daunted on hill and heath.

If Will had wings, how fast I'd flee
To the home of my heart o'er the seething sea!
If Wishes were power, if Words were spells,
I'd be this hour where my own love dwells.

THE IRISH EMIGRANT'S MOTHER.

BY D. F. M'CARTHY.

" Oh! come, my mother, come away, across the sea-green water;
Oh! come with me, and come with him, the husband of thy
    daughter;
Oh! come with us, and come with them, the sister and the brother,
Who, prattling, climb thine aged knees, and call thy daughter—
    mother.

" Oh! come, and leave this land of death—this isle of desolation—
This speck upon the sun-bright face of God's sublime creation,
Since now o'er all our fatal stars the most malign hath risen,
When Labour seeks the Poorhouse, and Innocence the Prison.

" 'Tis true o'er all the sun-brown fields the husky wheat is bending;
'Tis true God's blessed hand at last a better time is sending;
'Tis true the island's aged face looks happier and younger,
But in the best of days we've known the sickness and the hunger.

" When health breathed out in every breeze, too oft we've known
    the fever—
Too oft, my mother, have we felt the hand of the bereaver;
Too well remember many a time the mournful task that brought him,
When freshness fanned the Summer air, and cooled the glow of
    Autumn.

" But then the trial, though severe, still testified our patience,
We bowed with mingled hope and fear to God's wise dispensations;
We felt the gloomiest time was both a promise and a warning,
Just as the darkest hour of night is herald of the morning.

" But now through all the black expanse no hopeful morning
    breaketh—
No bird of promise in our hearts, the gladsome song awaketh;
No far-off gleams of good light up the hills of expectation—
Nought but the gloom that might precede the world's annihilation.

" So, mother, turn thine aged feet, and let our children lead 'em
Down to the ship that wafts us soon to plenty and to freedom;
Forgetting nought of all the past, yet all the past forgiving;
Come, let us leave the dying land, and fly unto the living.

"They tell us, they who read and think of Ireland's ancient story.
How once its Emerald Flag flung out a Sunburst's fleeting glory;
Oh! if that sun will pierce no more the dark clouds that efface it,
Fly where the rising Stars of Heaven commingle to replace it.

"So come, my mother, come away, across the sea-green water;
Oh! come with us, and come with him, the husband of thy
    daughter;
Oh! come with us, and come with them, the sister and the brother,
Who, prattling, climb thine aged knees, and call thy daughter—
    mother."

"Ah! go, my children, go away—obey this inspiration;
Go, with the mantling hopes of health and youthful expectation;
Go, clear the forests, climb the hills, and plough the expectant
    prairies;
Go, in the sacred name of God, and the Blessed Virgin Mary's.

"But though I feel how sharp the pang from thee and thine to
    sever,
To look upon these darling ones the last time and for ever;
Yet in this sad and dark old land, by desolation haunted,
My heart has struck its roots too deep ever to be transplanted.

"A thousand fibres still have life, although the trunk is dying—
They twine around the yet green grave where thy father's bones
    are lying;
Ah! from that sad and sweet embrace no soil on earth can loose
    'em,
Though golden harvests gleam on its breast, and golden sands in
    its bosom.

"Others are twined around the stone, where ivy blossoms smother
The crumbling lines that trace thy names, my father and my
    mother;
God's blessing be upon their souls—God grant, my old heart
    prayeth,
Their names be written in the Book whose writing ne'er decayeth.

"Alas! my prayers would never warm within those great cold
    buildings,
Those grand cathedral churches, with their marbles and their
    gildings;

Far fitter than the proudest dome that would hang in splendour
    o'er me,
Is the simple chapel's white-washed wall, where my people knelt
    before me.

" No doubt it is a glorious land to which you now are going,
Like that which God bestowed of old, with milk and honey flowing;
But where are the blessed saints of God, whose lives of his law
    remind me,
Like Patrick, Brigid, and Columbkille, in the land I'd leave be-
    hind me?

" So leave me here, my children, with my old ways and old notions;
Leave me here in peace, with my memories and devotions;
Leave me in sight of your father's grave, and as the heavens
    allied us,
Let not, since we were joined in life, even the grave divide us.

" There's not a week but I can hear how you prosper better and
    better,
For the mighty fireships o'er the sea will bring the expected letter;
And if I need aught for my simple wants, my food or my winter
    firing,
Thou'lt gladly spare from thy growing store a little for my
    requiring.

" Remember with a pitying love the hapless land that bore you;
At every festal season be its gentle form before you;
When the Christmas candle is lighted, and the holly and ivy
    glisten,
Let your eye look back for a vanished face—for a voice that is
    silent, listen!

" So go, my children, go away—obey this inspiration;
Go, with the mantling hopes of health and youthful expectation;
Go, clear the forests, climb the hills, and plough the expectant
    prairies;
Go, in the sacred name of God, and the Blessed Virgin Mary's."

MEMORIES.

BY T. D. M'GEE.

I LEFT two loves on a distant strand,
One young, and fond, and fair, and bland;
One fair, and old, and sadly grand,—
My wedded wife and my native land.

One tarrieth sad and seriously
Beneath the roof that mine should be·
One sitteth sibyl-like, by the sea,
Chaunting a grave song mournfully.

A little life I have not seen
Lies by the heart that mine hath been;
A cypress wreath darkles now, I ween,
Upon the brow of my love in green.

The mother and wife shall pass away,
Her hands be dust, her lips be clay;
But my other love on earth shall stay,
And live in the life of a better day.

Ere we were born my first love was,
My sires were heirs to her holy cause;
And she yet shall sit in the world's applause,
A mother of men and blessed laws.

I hope and strive the while I sigh,
For I know my first love cannot die:
From the chain of woes that loom so high
Her reign shall reach to eternity.

THE IRISH EXILES.

BY MARTIN MAC DERMOTT.

WHEN round the festive Christmas board, or by the Christmas
    hearth,
That glorious mingled draught is poured—wine, melody, and mirth!

When friends long absent tell, low-toned, their joys and sorrows
    o'er,
And hand grasps hand, and eyelids fill, and lips meet lips once
    more—
Oh! in that hour 'twere kindly done, some woman's voice would
    say—
" Forget not those who're sad to-night—poor exiles, far away!"

Alas, for them! this morning's sun saw many a moist eye pour
Its gushing love, with longings vain, the waste Atlantic o'er,
And when he turned his lion-eye this ev'ning from the West,
The Indian shores were lined with those who watched his couchèd
    crest ;
But not to share his glory, then, or gladden in his ray,
They bent their gaze upon his path—those exiles, far away!

It was—oh! how the heart will cheat! because they thought,
    beyond
His glowing couch lay that Green Isle of which their hearts were
    fond ;
And fancy brought old scenes of home into each welling eye,
And through each breast pour'd many a thought that filled it like
    a sigh!
'Twas then—'twas then, all warm with love, they knelt them
    down to pray
For Irish homes and kith and kin—poor exiles far away!

And then the mother blest her son, the lover blest the maid,
And then the soldier was a child, and wept the whilst he
    prayed,
And then the student's pallid cheek flushed red as summer rose,
And patriot souls forgot their grief to weep for Erin's woes ;
And, oh! but then warm vows were breathed, that come what
    might or may,
They'd right the suffering isle they loved—those exiles, far away!

And some there were around the board, like loving brothers met,
The few and fond and joyous hearts that never can forget ;
They pledged—" The girls we left at home, God bless them!"
    and they gave,
" The memory of our absent friends, the tender and the brave!"
Then up, erect, with nine times nine—hip, hip, hip—hurrah!
Drank—" Erin *slautha gal go brogh!*" those exiles far away.

Then, oh! to hear the sweet old strains of Irish music rise,
Like gushing memories of home, beneath far foreign skies,
Beneath the spreading calabash, beneath the trellised vine,
The bright Italian myrtle bower, or dark Canadian pine—
Oh! don't these old familiar tones—now sad, and now so gay—
Speak out your very, very hearts—poor exiles, far away!

But, Heavens! how many sleep afar, all heedless of these strains,
Tired wanderers! who sought repose through Europe's battle
    plains—
In strong, fierce, headlong fight they fell—as ships go down in
    storms—
They fell—and *human* whirlwinds swept across their shattered
    forms!
No shroud, but glory, wrapt them round; nor prayer nor tear
    had they—
Save the wandering winds and the heavy clouds—poor exiles far
    away!

And might the singer claim a sigh, he, too, could tell how tost
Upon the stranger's dreary shore, his heart's best hopes were lost;
How he, too, pined, to hear the tones of friendship greet his ear,
And pined, to walk the river side, to youthful musing dear,
And pined, with yearning silent love, amongst *his own* to stay—
Alas! it is so sad to be an exile far away!

Then, oh! when round the Christmas board, or by the Christmas
    hearth,
That glorious mingled draught is poured—wine, melody, and
    mirth!
When friends long absent tell, low-toned, their joys and sorrows
    o'er,
And hand grasps hand, and eyelids fill, and lips meet lips once
    more—
In that bright hour, perhaps—perhaps, some woman's voice would
    say—
"Think—think on those who weep to-night, poor exiles, far
    away!"

THE EXILE'S DEVOTION.

BY T. D. M'GEE.

IF I forswear the Art Divine
   Which deifies the dead—
What comfort then can I call mine,
   What solace seek instead?
For from my birth our country's fame
   Was life to me, and love,
And for each loyal Irish name,
   Some garland still I wove.

I'd rather be the bird that sings
   Above the martyr's grave,
Than fold in fortune's cage my wings
   And feel my soul a slave;
I'd rather turn one simple verse
   True to the Gaelic ear,
Than sapphic odes I might rehearse
   With Senates list'ning near.

Oh! Native Land dost ever mark
   When the world's din is drown'd,
Betwixt the daylight and the dark
   A wandering solemn sound,
That on the western wind is borne
   Across thy dewy breast?
It is the voice of those who mourn
   For thee, far in the West!

For them and theirs, I oft essay
   Your ancient art of song,
And often sadly turn away
   Deeming my rashness, wrong;
For well I ween, a loving will
   Is all the art I own,
Ah, me, could love suffice for skill,
   What triumphs I had known!

My native land, my native land,
　Live in my memory still!
Break on my brain, ye surges grand!
　Stand up, mist-covered hill!
Still in the mirror of the mind
　The land I love I see,
Would I could fly on the western wind.
　My native land to thee!

Pathetic Ballads.

LAMENT FOR CLARENCE MANGAN.

BY R. D. WILLIAMS.

"Oft, with tears, I've groan'd to God for pity—
     Oft gone wandering till my way grew dim—
Oft sang unto Him a prayerful ditty—
Oft, all lonely in this throngful city
          Raised my soul to Him!
And from path to path His mercy track'd me—
     From a many a peril snatched He me,
When false friends pursued, betrayed, attacked me,
When gloom overdarked, and sickness racked me,
          He was by to save and free!"
                              CLARENCE MANGAN.

YES! happy friend, the cross was thine; 'tis o'er a sea of tears
Predestined souls must ever sail, to reach their native spheres;
May Christ, the Crowned of Calvary, who died upon a tree,
Bequeath His tearful chalice, and the bitter cross to me!

The darken'd land is desolate—a wilderness of graves;
Our purest hearts are prison-bound, our exiles on the waves;
Gaunt Famine stalks the blasted plains—the pestilential air
O'erhangs the gasp of breaking hearts, or stillness of despair.

The ebbing blood of Ireland is shed by foreign streams,
Where our kinsmen wake lamenting when they see her in their
     dreams;
Oh! happy are the peaceful dead!—'tis not for thee we weep,
Whose troubled spirit rests at length in calmly laurelled sleep.

No chains are on thy folded hands, no tears bedim thine eyes,
But round thee bloom celestial flowers in ever tranquil skies;
While o'er our dreams thy mystic songs, faint, sad, and solemn
flow,
Like light that left the distant stars ten thousand years ago.

How sweet thy harp in every string!—wild, tender, mirthful,
grand—
Of fairy pranks, of war, or love, or bleeding Fatherland!
And long the mournful *caoina* of Tyrconnell and Tyrone,
Like midnight waves on cavern'd coasts, around their tombs shall
moan.

Still "Boating down the Bosphorus," with thee we gaily go;
And still the "Elfin Mariners" o'er tiny brooklets row:
The phantom "Lady Agnes" still roams in awful woe,
And Irish hearts o'er "Cahal Mor" and "Roisin Dubh" shall
glow.

Thou wert a voice of God on Earth—of those prophetic souls,
Who hear the fearful thunder in the Future's womb that rolls:
And the warnings of the Angels, as the midnight hurried past,
Rush'd in upon thy spirit, like a ghost-o'erladen blast.

Then the woes of coming judgment on thy tranced vision burst—
To call immortal vengeance on an age and land accurst—
For where is Faith, or Purity, or Heaven in us now?
In power alone the times believe—to gold alone they bow.

If any shade of earthliness bedimmed thy spirit's wings,
Well cleans'd thou art in sorrow's ever salutary springs;
And even bitter suffering, and still more bitter sin
Shall only make a soul like thine more beautiful within.

For every wound that humbles, if it do not all destroy,
Shall nerve the heart for nobler deeds, and fit for purer joy;
As the Demigod of Fableland, as olden legends say,
Rose up more strong and valorous each time he touched the clay.

And wisely was a weakness with thine ecstacies allied,
Thus Heaven would save a fav'rite child from God-dethroning
pride;
And teach the Starland dreamer that his vision'd milky-way
Is but the feeble reflex of his sire's transmitted ray.

X

As aforetime the Apostle wept to bear an earthly thorn,
While his raptured spirit floated through the portals of the morn;
For bards, like saints, have secret joys, none other mortals know,
And He who loves would chasten them in weakness and in woe.

Tears deck the soul with virtues, as soft rains the flow'ry sod,
And the inward eyes are purified for clearer dreams of God.
'Tis sorrow's hand the temple-gates of holiness unbars—
By day we only see the Earth, 'tis night reveals the Stars.

Alas! alas!—the Minstrel's fate!—his life is short and drear,
And if he win a wreath at last, 'tis but to shade a bier;
His harp is fed with wasted life—to tears its numbers flow—
And strung with chords of broken hearts, is Dreamland's splendid
      woe!

But now—a cloud transfigured, all luminous, auroral—
Thou joinest the Trisagion of choir'd immortals choral;
While all the little discords here but render more sublime
The joybells of the universe from starry chime to chime!

O Father of the harmonies eternally that roll
Life, light, and love, to trillion'd suns, receive the Poet's soul!
And bear him in Thy bosom from this vale of tears and storms,
To swell the sphere-hymns thundered from the rushing starry
      swarms.*

In sacred lustre rolling where the constellated throngs
Peal down through Heaven's chasmata † unutterable songs,
And the myriad-peopled systems, beneath, around, above,
Resound with adoration—reverberate with love!

Sleep, happy friend! The cross was thine—'tis o'er a sea of tears
Predestined souls must ever sail to reach their native spheres.
May Christ, the crown'd of Calvary, who died upon a tree,
Vouchsafe his tearful chalice and the bitter cross to me!

---

* See Humboldt's Cosmos.
† Idem.   Interstellar spaces in the nearer heavens, through which are beheld
innumerable nebulæ, and clusters of stars so distant that astronomers have
called them star-dust.

MY GRAVE.

BY THOMAS DAVIS.

SHALL they bury me in the deep,
Where wind-forgetting waters sleep?
Shall they dig a grave for me
Under the green-wood tree?
Or on the wild heath,
Where the wilder breath
Of the storm doth blow?
Oh, no! oh, no!

Shall they bury me in the Palace Tombs,
Or under the shade of Cathedral domes?
Sweet 'twere to lie on Italy's shore;
Yet not there—nor in Greece, though I love it more.
In the wolf or the vulture my grave shall I find?
Shall my ashes career on the world-seeing wind?
Shall they fling my corpse in the battle mound,
Where coffinless thousands lie under the ground?
Just as they fall they are buried so—
Oh, no! oh, no!

No! on an Irish green hill-side,
On an opening lawn—but not too wide!
For I love the drip of the wetted trees—
I love not the gales, but a gentle breeze,
To freshen the turf—put no tombstone there,
But green sods deck'd with daisies fair,
Nor sods too deep; but so that the dew,
The matted grass-roots may trickle through.
Be my epitaph writ on my country's mind,
"He served his country, and loved his kind"—

Oh! 'twere merry unto the grave to go,
If one were sure to be buried so.

A LAMENT FOR THOMAS DAVIS.

BY J. FRAZER.

Is he gone from our struggle—the pure of the purest—
The staff that upheld our green banner the surest—
    Is *he* gone from our struggle away?
Oh! Heaven, that the man who gave soul to our strife—
The heart with the lightnings of liberty rife,
    Should be suddenly stricken to clay;
But yesterday lending a people new life,
    Cold—mute—in the coffin to-day!
        Wo, wo;
Strong myriads stunned by the one fatal blow—
The loved is departed—the lofty laid low!

Though his form was to me as a far-dwelling stranger,
Did I need a defender from falsehood or danger,
    I would call on his voice—or his arm!
Romance and reality blended, in sooth,
The firmest of manhood, and freshest of youth,
    In honour's most beautiful form;
Not even to save the whole cargo of truth,
    Would he cast out a part in the storm!
        Gloom, gloom.
The firmness and freshness are nipped in the bloom!
Broad and dark is the shadow that falls from his tomb!

Go—mix with the crowds where his praises are spoken,
Go—watch the wet eyes that hang over each token
    His genius hath given of its birth:
Would millions in one common grief be combined,
If some spell-work embracing the heart and the mind
    Of man in its magical girth,
Were not left, like a scroll from his spirit, behind,
    To circle and gird up the earth?
        Grief, grief—
The minstrel-magician, the patriot chief,
To praise him is some—oh! how little—relief.

The water runs clear from the high, rocky fountain,
And rapid the river that bursts from the mountain:
    So rapid and clear was the stream

Of his song—for the bard was exalted above
The gross of the world, both by lore and by love,
   When country and kind were his theme,–
Oh! his soul was a seraph that ceaselessly strove
    To soar to its own native beam.
         Dear, dear—
Are the prunings of pinion that dropped from him here;
His own is the torch-light that flames round his bier.

From a spirit intensely to liberty cleaving—
From a heart that grew yet more enlarged by its heaving,
   He fired into energy all,
Whose nature looks up to the loftiest mind,
Since, like loftiest bough, it first catches the wind,
   And is last into stillness to fall;
He banded the glowing—he guided the blind,
   Who grappled and tugged with their thrall—
        Grave, grave—
Onward may still be the sweep of the brave;
But the bright crest of foam—it is gone from the wave.

To cowards and despots a hatred undying,
For freedom a passion intense and relying,
   A pride in the resolute hand;
A hope that could see not a danger to shun,
When bonds should be broken, and liberty won—
   A faith in the book and the brand,
The song and the standard—had made him the sun
   Of a fair, but a shadowy land—
        Blight, blight—
How sad are the banner and book in our sight,
Ah! the brow of the country grew grey in a night!

The gallant, good heart, that was fitted to clamber
The rockiest path, is now cold in the chamber
   Of death, as the basest can be—
No minstrel again to his greatness shall grow,
Though many shall spring from the one lying low.
   Like twigs from the felled forest tree;
But still, at his bidding, the fettered shall throw
   Their chains on the earth, and be free!
        Clay, clay—
Thou sooner shalt steal the broad sun from the day,
Than the luminous spirit of DAVIS away!

THE KEEN.*

(FROM THE IRISH.)

I NURSED you at this withered breast,
This hand baked your marriage cake;
The mother that sung to your childhood's rest
Now keens at your manhood's wake—
Ullagone!

I fed you with my heart's best blood,
And *your own* flows red before me—
By yours and your children's *cradle* I stood—
The plumes of your hearse must wave o'er me—
Ullagone!

Your children sit by your bloody bier,
To my side in terror clinging—
But thou, *my* child, *thou* art not here,
And my heart with grief is wringing—
Ullagone!

* *Keen,* properly *Caoine.*—the dirge sung over the dead in Ireland. The word is derived from the Hebrew, "*cina,*" pronounced "*keen,*" which signifies weeping, with clapping of hands. That the reader may have some notion of the *keen,* we give the following (which is a literal translation) from Croker's Keens of Ireland. It is the Lament of a mother for her son:—

"Cold and silent is thy bed. Damp is the blessed dew of night; but the sun will bring warmth and heat in the morning and dry up the dew. But thy heart cannot feel heat from the morning sun: no more will the print of your footsteps be seen in the morning dew, on the mountains of Ivera, where you have so often hunted the fox and the hare, ever foremost amongst young men. Cold and silent is now thy bed.

"My sunshine you were. I loved you better than the sun itself; and when I see the sun going down in the west, I think of my boy and of my black night of sorrow. Like the rising sun, he had a red glow on his cheek. He was as bright as the sun at midday; but a dark storm came on, and my sunshine was lost to me for ever. My sunshine will never again come back. No! my boy cannot return. Cold and silent is his bed.

"Life-blood of my heart—for the sake of my boy I cared only for this world. He was brave; he was generous; he was noble-minded; he was beloved by rich and poor; he was clean-skinned. But why should I tell what every one knows? Why should I now go back to what never can be more? He who was every thing to me is dead. He is gone for ever; he will return no more. Cold and silent is his repose."

I remember thee in thy manly youth,
  When thy face like the sun's was beaming—
And brightly it shone out in joy or in ruth
  Like a ray o'er my darkness gleaming—
                    Ullagone!

I saw your form bound through the dance—
  Your arm gather victory;
And I cast on those days a sorrowful glance,
  For my son was the world to me—
                    Ullagone!

And none was like him to his own Aileen—
  The wife to his bosom given—
In the glance of her blue-eyed babes is seen,
  The image of her in heaven.
                    Ullagone!

And many a suitor strove to wed
  Aileen with the yellow tresses,
But she left her wealth for thy lowly bed,
  And gave thee the love that blesses—
                    Ullagone!

Aileen was beautiful and good—
  One love in your souls was burning—
And my old heart laughed in a mother's mood,
  By her son's bright hearth sojourning—
                    Ullagone!

Pleasantly passed your youthful days,
  Till the dark destroyer's coming;
Then the light of joy left your gloomy gaze,
  And sorrow your youth was o'ercoming—
                    Ullagone!

I laughed no more—for the dismal cloud
  Of ruin above ye hovered—
It hung on your hearts till an early shroud,
  Your wife in her coffin covered—
                    Ullagone!

You see her again—your own Aileen—
  In the bright place where she's staying,

And tell her the words of the sorrowful *Keen*,
  Your desolate mother is saying—
                Ullagone !

Tell her your mother loves her well—
  Left alone to her bitter wailing ;
And her fatherless babes, if they could would tell,
  How their orphan hearts are ailing.
                Ullagone !

I nursed you at this withered breast,
  I kneaded your bridal bread,
And she that rocked you, a babe, to rest,
  Now sits by your corpse's head.
                Ullagone !

LAMENT OF THE IRISH MOTHER.

Oh ! why did you go when the flowers were springing,
  And winter's wild tempests had vanished away,
When the swallow was come, and the sweet lark was singing,
  From the morn to the eve of the beautiful day ?
Oh ! why did you go when the summer was coming,
  And the heaven was blue as your own sunny eye ;
When the bee on the blossom was drowsily humming—
  Mavourneen ! mavourneen ! oh, why did you die ?

My hot tears are falling in agony o'er you,
  My heart was bound up in the life that is gone ;
Oh ! why did you go from the mother that bore you,
  Achora, macushla ! why leave me alone ?
The primrose each hedgerow and dingle is studding ;
  The violet's breath is on each breeze's sigh,
And the woodbine you loved round your window is budding—
  Oh ! *Maura, mavourneen !* * why, why, did you die ?

The harebell is missing your step on the mountain,
  The sweetbrier droops for the hand that it loved,
And the hazel's pale tassels hang over the fountain
  That springs in the copse where so often you roved.

    All these Irish words are terms of endearment,—these two mean,—
" Mary, my dearest."

The hawthorn's pearls fall as though they were weeping,
  Upon the low grave where your cold form doth lie,
And the soft dews of evening there longest lie sleeping—
  Mavourneen! Mavourneen! oh, why did you die?

The meadows are white with the low daisy's flower,
  And the long grass bends glistening like waves in the sun;
And from his green nest, in the ivy-grown tower,
  The sweet robin sings till the long day is done.
On, on to the sea, the bright river is flowing,
  There is not a stain in the vault of the sky;
But the flow'rs on your grave in the radiance are glowing—
  Your eyes cannot see them.   Oh! why did you die?

Mavourneen, I was not alone in my sorrow,
  But he whom you loved has soon followed his bride;
His young heart *could* break with its grief, and to-morrow
  They'll lay him to rest in the grave by your side.
My darling, my darling, the judgment alighted
  Upon the young branches, the blooming and fair;
But the dry leafless stem which the lightning hath blighted
  Stands lonely and dark in the sweet summer air.

When the bright silent stars through my window are beaming
  I dream in my madness that you're at my side,
With your long golden curls on your white shoulders streaming,
  And the smile that came warm from your loving heart's tide;
I hear your sweet voice fitful melodies singing;
  I wake but to hear the low wind's whispered sigh,
And your vanishing tones through my silent home ringing,
  As I cry in my anguish—oh! why did you die?

Achora, machree, you are ever before me—
  I scarce see the heaven to which you are gone,
So dark are the clouds of despair which lie o'er me.
  Oh, pray for me! pray at the Almighty's throne!
Oh, pray that the chain of my bondage may sever,
  That to thee and our Father my freed soul may fly,
Or the cry of my spirit for ever and ever
  Shall be—"Oh, *mavourneen!* why, why did you die?"

                                        TINY.

THE PEASANT GIRLS.

THE Peasant Girl of merry France,
  Beneath her trellis'd vine,
Watches the signal for the dance—
  The broad, red sun's decline.
'Tis there—and forth she flies with glee
  To join the circling band,
Whilst mirthful sounds of minstrelsy
  Are heard throughout the land.

And fair Italia's Peasant Girl,
  The Arno's banks beside,
With myrtle flowers that shine like pearl,
  Will braid at eventide
Her raven locks; and to the sky,
  With eyes of liquid light,
Look up and bid her lyre outsigh—
  "Was ever land so bright?"

The Peasant Girl of England, see,
  With lip of rosy dye,
Beneath her sheltering cottage tree,
  Smile on each passer by.
She looks on fields of yellow grain,
  Inhales the bean-flower's scent,
And seems, amid the fertile plain,
  An image of content.

The Peasant Girl of Scotland goes
  Across her Highland hill,
With cheek that emulates the rose,
  And voice the skylark's thrill.
Her tartan plaid she folds around,
  A many-coloured vest—
Type of what varied joys have found
  A home in her kind breast.

The Peasant Girl of Ireland, she
  Has left her cabin home,
Bearing white wreaths—what can it be
  Invites her thus to roam?

Caoch the Piper.—Vol. i., p. 331.

Her eye has not the joyous ray
  Should to her years belong;
And as she wends her languid way,
  She carols no sweet song.

Oh! soon upon the step and glance
  Grief does the work of age;
And it has been her hapless chance
  To open that dark page.
The happy harvest home was o'er,
  The fierce tithe-gatherer came;
And her young lover, in his gore,
  Fell by a murderous aim.

Then, well may youth's bright glance be gone
  For ever from that eye,
And soon will sisters weep upon
  The grave that she kneels by;
And well may prouder hearts than those
  That there place garlands, say—
"Have Ireland's peasant girls such woes?—
  When will they pass away?"

UNA.

CAOCH THE PIPER.

BY J. KEEGAN.

ONE winter's day, long, long, ago,
  When I was a little fellow,
A piper wandered to our door,
  Grey-headed, blind, and yellow—
And, oh! how glad was my young heart,
  Though earth and sky look'd dreary—
To see the stranger and his dog—
  Poor "Pinch" and Caoch O'Leary.

And when he stowed away his "bag,"
  Cross-barr'd with green and yellow,
I thought and said, "in Ireland's ground,
  There's not so fine a fellow."

And Fineen Burke and Shane Magee,
  And Eily, Kate, and Mary,
Rushed in, with panting haste to "see,"
  And " welcome " Caoch O'Leary.

Oh! God be with those happy times,
  Oh! God be with my childhood,
When I, bare-headed, roamed all day
  Bird-nesting in the wild-wood—
I'll not forget those sunny hours,
  However years may vary;
I'll not forget my early friends,
  Nor honest Caoch Ó'Leary.

Poor Caoch and "Pinch" slept well that night,
  And in the morning early
He called me up to hear him play
  "The wind that shakes the barley."
And then he stroked my flaxen hair,
  And cried—" God mark my deary,"
And how I wept when he said "farewell,
  And think of Caoch O'Leary."

And seasons came and went, and still
  Old Caoch was not forgotten,
Although I thought him " dead and gone "
  And in the cold clay rotten.
And often when I walked and danced
  With Eily, Kate, and Mary,
We spoke of childhood's rosy hours,
  And prayed for Caoch O'Leary.

Well—twenty summers had gone past,
  And June's red sun was sinking,
When I, a man, sat by my door,
  Of twenty sad things thinking.
A little dog came up the way,
  His gait was slow and weary,
And at his tail a lame man limped—
  'Twas " Pinch " and Caoch O'Leary!

Old Caoch! but ah! how woe-begone!
  His form is bowed and bending,
His fleshless hands are stiff and wan,
  Ay—Time is even blending

The colours on his threadbare " bag "—
  And " Pinch " is twice as hairy
And " thin-spare " as when first I saw
  Himself and Caoch O'Leary.

" God's blessing here," the wanderer cried.
  " Far, far, be hell's black viper;
Does any body hereabouts
  Remember Caoch the Piper ?"
With swelling heart I grasped his hand;
  The old man murmured " deary !
Are you the silky-headed child,
  That lov'd poor Caoch O'Leary ?"

" Yes, yes," I said—the wanderer wept
  As if his heart was breaking—
" And where a vhic machree,"* he sobbed,
  " Is all the merry-making
I found here twenty years ago ?"—
  " My tale," I sighed, " might weary,
Enough to say—there's none but me
  To welcome Caoch O'Leary."

" Vo, Vo, Vo !" the old man cried,
  And wrung his hands in sorrow,
" Pray lead me in asthore machree,
  And I'll go home to-morrow.
My ' peace is made '—I'll calmly leave
  This world so cold and dreary,
And you shall keep my pipes and dog,
  And pray for Caoch O'Leary."

With " Pinch," I watched his bed that night
  Next day, his wish was granted ;
He died—and Father James was brought,
  And the Requiem Mass was chaunted—
The neighbours came ;—we dug his grave,
  Near Eily, Kate, and Mary,
And there he sleeps his last sweet sleep—
  God rest you ! Caoch O'Leary.

      * Son of my heart.

THE DYING GIRL.

BY R. D. WILLIAMS.

FROM a Munster vale they brought her,
   From the pure and balmy air,
An Ormond peasant's daughter,
   With blue eyes and golden hair.
They brought her to the city,
   And she faded slowly there,
Consumption has no pity
   For blue eyes and golden hair.

When I saw her first reclining
   Her lips were mov'd in pray'r,
And the setting sun was shining
   On her loosen'd golden hair.
When our kindly glances met her,
   Deadly brilliant was her eye,
And she said that she was better
   While we knew that she must die.

She speaks of Munster valleys,
   The patron, dance and fair,
And her thin hand feebly dallies
   With her scattered golden hair.
When silently we listen'd
   To her breath with quiet care,
Her eyes with wonder glisten'd—
   And she asked us, what was there?

The poor thing smiled to ask it,
   And her pretty mouth laid bare,
Like gems within a casket
   A string of pearlets rare.
We said that we were trying
   By the gushing of her blood,
And the time she took in sighing
   To know if she were good.

Well, she smil'd and chatted gaily,
  Tho' we saw in mute despair
The hectic brighter daily,
  And the death-dew on her hair.
And oft her wasted fingers
  Beating time upon the bed,
O'er some old tune she lingers,
  And she bows her golden head.

At length the harp is broken
  And the spirit in its strings,
As the last decree is spoken
  To its source exulting springs.
Descending swiftly from the skies,
  Her guardian angel came,
He struck God's lightning from her eyes,
  And bore him back the flame.

Before the sun had risen
  Thro' the lark-loved morning air,
Her young soul left its prison,
  Undefiled by sin or care.
I stood beside the couch in tears
  Where pale and calm she slept,
And tho' I've gaz'd on death for years,
  I blush not that I wept.
I check'd with effort pity's sighs
  And left the matron there,
To close the curtains of her eyes,
  And bind her golden hair.

SHE IS FAR FROM THE LAND.

BY THOMAS MOORE.

[This ballad was written to commemorate the feelings of Sarah Curran, daughter of the celebrated Irish barrister of that name, and of her lover Robert Emmet. It is of them that the following sketch has been written:—" Every one must recollect the tragical story of young Emmet, the Irish patriot; it was too touching to be soon forgotten. During the troubles in Ireland he was tried, condemned, and executed, on a charge of treason. His fate made a deep impression on public sympathy. He was so young—so intelligent—so generous—so brave—so every thing that we are apt to like in a young man. His conduct under trial, too, was so lofty and intrepid. The noble indignation with which

he repelled the charge of treason against his country—the eloquent vindicatio.
of his name—and his pathetic appeal to posterity, in the hopeless hour of co:
demnation—all these entered deeply into every generous bosom, and even h
enemies lamented the stern policy that dictated his execution. But there wa:
one heart, whose anguish it would be impossible to describe. In happier days
and fairer fortunes, he had won the affections of a beautiful and interesting
girl, the daughter of a late celebrated Irish barrister. She loved him with the
disinterested fervour of a woman's first and early love. When every worldly
maxim arrayed itself against him; when blasted in fortune, and disgrace and
danger darkened around his name, she loved him the more ardently for his
very sufferings. If, then, his fate could awaken the sympathy even of his foes,
what must have been the agony of her whose whole soul was occupied by his
image! Let those tell who have had the portals of the tomb suddenly closed
between them and the being they most loved on earth—who have sat at its
threshold, as one shut out in a cold and lonely world, from whence all that was
most lovely and loving had departed."—*Irvine's Sketch Book.*

SHE is far from the land where her young hero sleeps,
   And lovers are round her, sighing;
But coldly she turns from their gaze, and weeps,
   For her heart in his grave is lying!

She sings the wild song of her dear native plains,
   Every note which he lov'd awaking;—
Ah! little they think who delight in her strains,
   How the heart of the Minstrel is breaking!

He had liv'd for his love, for his country he died,
   They were all that to life had entwin'd him;
Nor soon shall the tears of his country be dried,
   Nor long will his love stay behind him.

Oh! make her a grave, where the sunbeams rest,
   When they promise a glorious morrow;
They'll shine o'er her sleep, like a smile from the West,
   From her own loved island of sorrow!

MARGREAD NI CHEALLEADH.

BY EDWARD WALSH.

[This ballad is founded on the story of Daniel O'Keeffe, an outlaw, famous
in the traditions of the County of Cork, where his name is still associated with
several localities. It is related that O'Keeffe's beautiful mistress, Margaret
Kelly (*Mairgread ni Chealleadh*,) tempted by a large reward undertook to de-

liver him into the hands of the English soldiers; but O'Keeffe having discovered in her possession a document revealing her perfidy, in a frenzy of indignation stabbed her to the heart with his *skian*. He lived in the time of William III. and is represented to have been a gentleman and a poet.]

At the dance in the village
Thy white foot was fleetest;
Thy voice mid the concert
Of maidens was sweetest;
The swell of thy white breast
Made rich lovers follow;
And thy raven hair bound them,
Young Mairgréad ni Chealleadh.

Thy neck was, lost maid!
Than the ceanaban * whiter;
And the glow of thy cheek
Than the monadan † brighter:
But Death's chain hath bound thee,
Thine eye's glazed and hollow
That shone like a Sun-burst,
Young Mairgréad ni Chealleadh.

No more shall mine ear drink
Thy melody swelling;
Nor thy beamy eye brighten
The outlaw's dark dwelling;
Or thy soft heaving bosom
My destiny hallow,
When thine arms twine around me,
Young Mairgréad ni Chealleadh.

The moss couch I brought thee
To-day from the mountain,
Has drank the last drop
Of thy young heart's red fountain,
For this good *skian* beside me
Struck deep and rung hollow
In thy bosom of treason,
Young Mairgréad ni Chealleadh.

* A plant found in bogs, the top of which bears a substance resembling cotton, and as white as snow. Pronounced Cânavân.

† The monadan is a red berry that is found on wild marshy mountains. It grows on an humble creeping plant.

Y

With strings of rich pearls
Thy white neck was laden,
And thy fingers with spoils
Of the Sassenach maiden:
Such rich silks enrob'd not
The proud dames of Mallow—
Such pure gold they wore not
As Mairgréad ni Cheallcadh.

Alas! that my loved one
Her outlaw would injure—
Alas! that he e'er proved
Her treason's avenger!
That this right hand should make thee
A bed cold and hollow,
When in Death's sleep it laid thee,
Young Mairgréad ni Chealleadh!

And while to this lone cave
My deep grief I'm venting,
The Saxon's keen bandog
My footsteps is scenting:
But true men await me
Afar in Duhallow,
Farewell, cave of slaughter,
And Mairgréad ni Chealleadh.

LAMENT OF MORIAN SHEHONE FOR MISS MARY BOURKE.

(FROM THE IRISH.)

" THERE's darkness in thy dwelling-place, and silence reigns above;
And Mary's voice is heard no more, like the soft voice of love.
Yes! thou art gone, my Mary dear; and Morian Shehone
Is left to sing his song of woe, and wail for thee alone.
Oh! snow white were thy virtues—the beautiful, the young—
The old with pleasure bent to hear the music of thy tongue:
The young with rapture gazed on thee, and their hearts in love
were bound,
For thou wast brighter than the sun that sheds its light around.

My soul is dark, oh! Mary dear! thy sun of beauty's set;
The sorrowful are dumb for thee—the grieved their tears forget;
And I am left to pour my woe above thy grave alone;
For dear wert thou to the fond heart of Morian Shehone.

Fast flowing tears above the grave of the rich man are shed,
But they are dried when the cold stone shuts in his narrow bed;
Not so with my heart's faithful love—the dark grave cannot hide
From Morian's eyes thy form of grace, of loveliness, and pride.
Thou didst not fall like the sere leaf, when Autumn's chill winds
    blow—
'Twas a tempest and a storm blast that has laid my Mary low.
Hadst thou not friends that loved thee well—hadst thou not
    garments rare?
Wast thou not happy, Mary—wast thou not young and fair?
Then, why should the dread spoiler come, my heart's peace to
    destroy,
Or the grim tyrant tear from me my all of earthly joy?
Oh! am I left to pour my woes above thy grave alone?
Thou idol of the faithful heart of Morian Shehone!

Sweet were thy looks and sweet thy smiles, and kind wast thou
    to all:
The withering scowl of envy on thy fortunes dared not fall;
For thee thy friends lament and mourn, and never cease to weep:
Oh! that their lamentations could awake thee from thy sleep!
Oh! that thy peerless form again could meet my loving clasp!
Oh! that the cold damp hand of Death could loose his iron grasp!
Yet, when the valley's daughters meet beneath the tall elm tree,
And talk of Mary as a dream that never more shall be;
Then may thy spirit float around, like music in the air,
And pour upon their virgin souls a blessing and a prayer.
Oh! am I left to pour my wail above thy grave alone?"
Thus sinks in silence the lament of Morian Shehone!

A CAOINE.

BY EVA. (MISS MARY EVA KELLY.)

GONE, gone from me and from the earth, and from the Summer
　　sky,
And all the bright, wild hope and love that swelled so proud and
　　high ;
And all this heart had stored for thee within its endless deep—
With me—with me, Oh ! never more thou'lt smile, or joy, or
　　weep !

There are gold nails on your coffin ; there are snowy plumes above;
They pour their pomp and honours there, but I this woe and love—
The hopeless woe, the longing love, that turn from earth away,
And pray for refuge and a home within the silent clay !

Come, wild deer of the mountain-side ! come, sweet bird of the
　　plain !
To cheer the cold and trembling heart that beats for you in vain!
Oh ! come, from woe, and cold, and gloom, to her that's warm and
　　true,
And has no hope or throb for aught within this world but you !

To the sad winds I have scattered the treasures of my soul—
The sorrow that no tongue could speak, or mortal power control—
And wept the weary night and day until my heart was sore,
And every germ of peace and joy was withered at its core.

In vain, in vain, this yearning cry—this dark and deep despair !
I droop alone and trembling here, and thou art lying *there*.
But though thy smile upon the earth I never more may see,
And thou wilt never come to me—yet, I may fly to thee !

I never stood within your home—I do not bear your name—
Life parted us for many a day, but Death now seals my claim;
In darkness, silence, and decay, and here at last alone,
You're but more truly bound to me—my darling, and my own !

THE MOTHER'S LAMENT.

BY GERALD GRIFFIN.

My darling, my darling, while silence is on the moor,
And lone in the sunshine, I sit by our cabin door;
When evening falls quiet and calm over land and sea,
My darling, my darling, I think of past times and thee!

Here, while on this cold shore, I wear out my lonely hours,
My child in the heavens is spreading my bed with flowers,
All weary my bosom is grown of this friendless clime,
But I long not to leave it; for that were a shame and crime.

They bear to the churchyard the youth in their health away,
I know where a fruit hangs more ripe for the grave than they,
But I wish not for death, for my spirit is all resigned,
And the hope that stays with me gives peace to my aged mind.

My darling, my darling, God gave to my feeble age,
A prop for my faint heart, a stay in my pilgrimage;
My darling, my darling, God takes back his gift again—
And my heart may be broken, but ne'er shall my will complain.

THE ORANGEMAN'S WIFE.

BY CARROLL MALONE.

I WANDER by the limpid shore,
  When fields and flowrets bloom;
But, oh! my heart is sad and sore—
  My soul is sunk in gloom—
All day I cry ochone! ochone!*
  I weep from night till morn—
I wish that I were dead and gone,
  Or never had been born.

* *Ochone!* an exclamation of deep sorrow, as, Oh, my grief!

My father dwelt beside Tyrone,
  And with him children five;
But I to Charlemont had gone,
  At service there to live.
O brothers fond! O sister dear!
  How ill I paid your love!
O father! father! how I fear
  To meet thy soul above!

My mother left us long ago,—
  A lovely corpse was she,—
But we had longer days of woe
  In this sad world to be.
My weary days will soon be done—
  I pine in grief forlorn;
I wish that I were dead and gone,
  Or never had been born.

It was the year of Ninety-Eight,
  The Wreckers came about;
They burned my father's stack of wheat,
  And drove my brothers out;
They forced my sister to their lust—
  God grant my father rest!
For the Captain of the Wreckers thrust
  A bayonet through his breast.

It was a dreadful, dreadful year;
  And I was blindly led,
In love, and loneliness, and fear,
  A *loyal* man to wed;
And still my heart is his alone,
  It breaks, but cannot turn:
I wish that I were dead and gone,
  Or never had been born.

Next year we lived in quiet love,
  And kissed our infant boy;
And peace had spread her wings above
  Our dwelling at the Moy.
And then my wayworn brothers came
  To share our peace and rest;
And poor lost Rose, to hide her shame
  And sorrow in my breast.

They came, but soon they turned and fled—
  Preserve my soul, O God!
It was my husband's hand, they said,
  That shed my father's blood.
All day I cry ochone! ochone!
  I weep from night till morn;
And oh, that I were dead and gone,
  Or never had been born!

TO THE MEMORY OF THOMAS DAVIS.

BY JOHN FISHER MURRAY.

WHEN on the field where freedom bled,
  I press the ashes of the brave,
Marvelling that man should ever dread
  Thus to wipe out the name of slave;
No deep-drawn sigh escapes my breast—
  No woman's drops my eyes distain,
I weep not gallant hearts at rest—
  I but deplore they died in vain.

When I the sacred spot behold,
  For aye remembered and renowned,
Where dauntless hearts and arms as bold,
  Strewed tyrants and their slaves around;
High hopes exulting fire my breast—
  High notes triumphant swell my strain,
Joy to the brave! in victory blest—
  Joy! joy! they perished not in vain.

But when thy ever mournful voice,
  My country calls me to deplore
The champion of thy youthful choice,
  Honoured, revered, but seen no more;
Heavy and quick my sorrows fall
  For him who strove, with might and main,
To leave a lesson for us all,
  How we might live—nor live in vain.

If, moulded of earth's common clay,
   Thou hadst to sordid arts stooped down,
Thy glorious talent flung away,
   Or sold for price thy great renown;
In some poor pettifogging place,
   Slothful, inglorious, thou hadst lain,
Herding amid the unhonoured race,
   Who doze, and dream, and die in vain.

A spark of HIS celestial fire,
   The GOD of freemen struck from thee;
Made thee to spurn each low desire,
   Nor bend the uncompromising knee;
Made thee to vow thy life, to rive
   With ceaseless tug, th' oppressor's chain
With lyre, with pen, with sword, to strive
   For thy dear land—nor strive in vain.

How hapless is our country's fate,—
   If Heaven in pity to us send
Like thee, one glorious, good and great—
   To guide, instruct us, and amend;
How soon thy honoured life is o'er—
   Soon Heaven demandeth thee again;
We grope on darkling as before,
   And fear lest thou hast died in vain.

In vain,—no, never! O'er thy grave,
   Thy spirit dwelleth in the air;
Thy passionate love, thy purpose brave,
   Thy hope assured, thy promise fair.
Generous and wise, farewell!—Forego
   Tears for the glorious dead and gone;
His tears, if tears are *his*, still flow
   For slaves and cowards living on.

THE RECONCILIATION.

BY JOHN BANIM.

[The facts of this ballad occurred in a little mountain-chapel, in the county of Clare, at the time efforts were made to put an end to faction-fighting among the peasantry.]

THE old man he knelt at the altar,
　His enemy's hand to take,
And at first his weak voice did falter,
　And his feeble limbs did shake ;
For his only brave boy, his glory,
　Had been stretched at the old man's feet,
A corpse, all so haggard and gory,
　By the hand which he now must greet.

And soon the old man stopt speaking,
　And rage, which had not gone by,
From under his brows came breaking
　Up into his enemy's eye—
And now his limbs were not shaking,
　But his clench'd hands his bosom cross'd,
And he looked a fierce wish to be taking
　Revenge for the boy he had lost !

But the old man he looked around him,
　And thought of the place he was in,
And thought of the promise which bound him,
　And thought that revenge was sin—
And then, crying tears, like a woman,
　"Your hand !" he said—"ay, *that* hand !
And I do forgive you, foeman,
　For the sake of our bleeding land !"

THE "HOLLY AND IVY" GIRL.

BY J. KEEGAN.

[John Keegan was born of humble parents in a village by the Nore, in the Queen's County, and died about forty years of age, in 1849. He was born and bred amongst the people,—he shared their occasional privations,—he thought and acted with them,—and was happy to die amongst them. He was plainly but well educated. At an early age he contributed tales and sketches to the Irish periodicals; and in course of time, became a well-known contributor of ballads to the *Nation*. Some of his best prose articles appeared in *Dolman's Magazine*,—to which he contributed also some poetry illustrative of the legends popular amongst the people, as well as upon the hard realities of their every day life. There were few men who surpassed him in knowledge of the legends and superstitions of the country; of these he was preparing a volume for publication, when he was hurriedly summoned to his eternal home. He was a poor man, who wrote for bread. His poems are thoroughly idiomatic, and as Irish in their gush of feeling and sentiment, as they are full of purity and tenderness.]

" COME, buy my nice, fresh Ivy, and my Holly sprigs so green;
I have the finest branches that ever yet were seen.
Come buy from me, good Christians, and let me home, I pray,
And I'll wish you ' Merry Christmas Times, and a Happy New
    Year's Day.'

Ah! won't you take my Ivy?— the loveliest ever seen!
Ah! won't you have my Holly boughs?—all you who love the
    Green!
Do!—take a little bunch of each, and on my knees I'll pray,
That God may bless your Christmas, and be with you New Year's
    Day.

This wind is black and bitter, and the hailstones do not spare
My shivering form, my bleeding feet, and stiff entangled hair;
Then, when the skies are pitiless, be merciful I say—
So Heaven will light your Christmas and the coming New Year's
    Day."

'Twas thus a dying maiden sung, whilst the cold hail rattled down,
And fierce winds whistled mournfully o'er Dublin's dreary town;—
One stiff hand clutched her Ivy sprigs and Holly boughs so fair,
With the other she kept brushing the hail-drops from her hair.

So grim and statue-like she seemed, 'twas evident that Death
Was lurking in her footsteps—whilst her hot, impeded breath
Too plainly told her early doom—though the burden of her lay
Was still of life, and Christmas joys, and a Happy New Year's
    Day.

'Twas in that broad, bleak Thomas-street, I heard the wanderer
    sing;
I stood a moment in the mire, beyond the ragged ring—

My heart felt cold and lonely, and my thoughts were far away,
Where I was, many a Christmas-tide, and Happy New Year's
    Day.

I dreamed of wanderings in the woods amongst the Holly Green;
I dreamed of my own native cot, and porch with Ivy screen;
I dreamed of lights for ever dimm'd—of Hopes that can't return—
And dropped a tear on Christmas fires, that never more can burn.

The ghostlike singer still sung on, but no one came to buy;
The hurrying crowd passed to and fro, but did not heed her cry:
She uttered one low, piercing moan—then cast her boughs away—
And smiling, cried—"I'll rest with God before the New Year's
    Day!"

*   *   *   *   *

On New Year's Day I said my prayers above a new-made grave,
Dug decently in sacred soil, by Liffey's murmuring wave;
The Minstrel maid from Earth to Heaven has winged her happy
    way,
And now enjoys, with sister-saints, an endless New Year's Day.

THE CONVICT OF CLONMELL.

(FROM THE IRISH.)

BY J. J. CALLANAN.

[Who the hero of this song is, I know not; but convicts, from obvious reasons, have been peculiar objects of sympathy in Ireland. Hurling, which is mentioned in one of the verses, is a thoroughly national diversion, and is played with intense zeal, by parish against parish, barony against barony, county against county, or even province against province. It is played, not only by the peasant, but by the students of the university, where it is an established pastime. Twiss, the most sweeping calumniator of Ireland, calls it, if I mistake not, the cricket of barbarians: but though fully prepared to pay a just tribute to the elegance of the English game, I own that I think the Irish sport fully as civilized, and much better calculated for the display of vigour and activity. Strutt, in his Sports and Pastimes, eulogises the activity of some Irishmen, who played the game about twenty-five years before the publication of his work, (1801,) at the back of the British Museum, and deduces it from the Roman harpastum. The description Strutt quotes from old Carew is quite graphic.]

How hard is my fortune,
  And vain my repining!
The strong rope of fate
  For this young neck is twining.
My strength is departed;
  My cheek sunk and sallow;
While I languish in chains,
  In the gaol of Clonmala.*

No boy in the village
  Was ever yet milder,
I'd play with a child,
  And my sport would be wilder.
I'd dance without tiring
  From morning till even,
And the goal-ball I'd strike
  To the lightning of heaven.

At my bed-foot decaying,
  My hurlbat is lying,
Thro' the boys of the village,
  My goal-ball is flying;
My horse 'mong the neighbours
  Neglected may fallow,—
While I pine in my chains,
  In the gaol of Clonmala.

Next Sunday the patron
  At home will be keeping,
And the young active hurlers
  The field will be sweeping.
With the dance of fair maidens
  The evening they'll hallow,
While this heart, once so gay,
  Shall be cold in Clonmala.

* Cuanmeala,—Recess or bed of honey.—Irish of Clonmell.

THE VOICE OF THE POOR.

BY SPERANZA (MRS. W. R. WILDE).

WAS sorrow ever like to our sorrow?
  Oh! God above!
Will our night never change into a morrow
  Of joy and love?
A deadly gloom is on us, waking, sleeping,
  Like the darkness at noontide
That fell upon the pallid mother, weeping
  By the Crucified.

Before us die our brothers of starvation;
  Around are cries of famine and despair!
Where is hope for us, or comfort, or salvation—
  Where—oh! where?
If the angels ever hearken, downward bending,
  They are weeping, we are sure,
At the litanies of human groans ascending
  From the crush'd hearts of the poor.

When the human rests in love upon the human,
  All grief is light;
But who bends one kind glance to illumine
  Our life-long night?
The air around is ringing with their laughter—
  God has only made the rich to smile;
But we—in our rags, and want, and woe—we follow after,
  Weeping the while.

And the laughter seems but uttered to deride us,
  When, oh! when
Will fall the frozen barriers that divide us
  From other men?
Will ignorance for ever thus enslave us,
  Will misery for ever lay us low?
All are eager with their insults; but to save us
  None, none, we know.

We never knew a childhood's mirth and gladness,
  Nor the proud heart of youth free and brave;

Oh, a deathlike dream of wretchedness and sadness
  Is life's weary journey to the grave.
Day by day we lower sink and lower,
  Till the godlike soul within
Falls crushéd beneath the fearful demon power
  Of poverty and sin.

So we toil on, on with fever burning
  In heart and brain,
So we toil on, on through bitter scorning,
  Want, woe, and pain.
We dare not raise our eyes to the blue Heaven
  Or the toil must cease—
We dare not breathe the fresh air God has given
  One hour in peace.

We must toil though the light of life is burning,
  Oh, how dim!
We must toil on our sick-bed feebly turning
  Our eyes to Him,
Who alone can hear the pale lip faintly saying,
  With scarce-moved breath,
While the paler hands uplifted and the praying.
  "Lord, grant us Death!"

THE COOLUN.*

BY MARTIN MAC DERMOTT.

THE scene is beside where the Avonmore† flows—
'Tis the spring of the year, and the day's near its close;
And an old woman sits with a boy on her knee—
She smiles like the evening, but *he* like the lea!
Her hair is as white as the flax ere it's spun—
His brown as yon tree that is hiding the sun!
      Beside the bright river—
      The calm, glassy river,
  That's sliding and gliding all peacefully on.

---

* This is the name of one of the most beautiful of our ancient melodies
† The Avonmore is the Munster Blackwater.

"Come, granny," the boy says, "you'll sing me, I know,
The beautiful Coolun, so sweet and so low;
For I love its soft tones more than blackbird or thrush,
Though often the tears in a shower will gush
From my eyes when I hear it.   Dear granny, say why,
When my heart's full of pleasure, I sob and I cry
            To hear the sweet Coolun—
            The beautiful Coolun—
    An angel first sang it above in the sky?"

And *she* sings and *he* listens; but many years pass,
And the old woman sleeps 'neath the chapel-yard grass;
And a couple are seated upon the same stone,
Where the boy sat and listened so oft to the crone—
'Tis the boy—'tis the man, and he says while he sighs,
To the girl at his side with the love-streaming eyes,
            "Oh! sing me sweet Oonagh,
            My beautiful Oonagh,
    Oh! sing me the Coolun," he says and he sighs.

That air, *mo stor*, brings back the days of my youth,
That flowed like a river there, sunny and smooth!
And it brings back the old woman, kindly and dear—
If her spirit, dear Oonagh, is hovering near,
'Twill glad her to hear the old melody rise
Warm, warm, on the wings of our love and our sighs—
            "Oh! sing me the Coolun,
            The beautiful Coolun!"
    Is't the dew or a tear-drop is moistening his eyes?

There's a change on the scene, far more grand far less fair—
By the broad rolling Hudson are seated the pair;
And the dark hemlock-fir waves its branches above,
As they sigh for their land, as they murmur their love:
Hush!—the heart hath been touched, and its musical strings
Vibrate into song—'tis the Coolun she sings—
            The home-sighing Coolun,
            The love-breathing Coolun—
    The well of all memory's deep-flowing springs.

They think of the bright stream they sat down beside,
When he was a bridegroom and she was his bride;
The pulses of youth seem to throb in the strain—
Old faces, long vanished look kindly again—

Kind voices float round them, and grand hills are near,
Their feet have not touched, ah, this many a year—
      And, as ceases the Coolun,
      The home-loving Coolun,
Not the air, but their native land faints on the ear.

Long in silence they weep, with hand clasped in hand—
Then to God send up prayers for the far-off Old land;
And while grateful to Him for the blessings He's sent—
They know 'tis His hand that withholdeth content—
For the Exile and Christian must evermore sigh
For the home upon earth and the home in the sky—
      So they sing the sweet Coolun,
      The sorrowful Coolun,
That murmurs of both homes—they sing and they sigh.

Heaven bless thee, Old Bard, in whose bosom were nurst
Emotions that into such melody burst!
Be thy grave ever green!—may the softest of showers
And brightest of beams nurse its grass and its flowers—
Oft, oft, be it moist with the tear-drop of love,
And may angels watch round thee, for ever above!
      Old bard of the Coolun,
      The beautiful Coolun,
That's sobbing, like Eirè, with *Sorrow* and *Love*.

A MUNSTER KEEN.

BY EDWARD WALSH.

[Edward Walsh was born in Londonderry in the year 1805, and died in Cork
on 6th August 1850, in the forty-fifth year of his age. Of the number of poets
which Ireland has produced during the last fifty years, there was none more
Irish than our author. It was his boast that he belonged to an old Sept which
was settled on the borders of Cork and Kerry ages before the English invasion;
and it would be rare to meet a man of purer heart or more sterling sentiment.
His father, who was a small farmer in the county of Cork, eloped with a young
lady much above his own position in life. Shortly after marriage his difficulties increased, and to avoid them, he enlisted in the militia, and was quartered
in Londonderry when his son was born. Our author having received a good
education, in early life became a private tutor. Some time after he taught
school in Millstreet, county Cork, from which he removed in 1837, and went to
teach in Toureen, where he first began to write for the Magazines. After some
time he went up to Dublin, where he soon became disappointed, and was at

last elected schoolmaster to the convict station at Spike Island. In a year or two he left this place and became teacher at the Workhouse in Cork, where he remained till his death. He married early, and has left a wife and family to mourn his loss. Two volumes of his poetical translations from the Irish have been published, with the *original* text on the opposite page. He was a great proficient in the fairy and legendary lore of the country; indeed, second only to Crofton Croker himself. His contributions to Irish literature have been both considerable and creditable; there is a singular beauty and fascinating melody in his verse which cheers and charms the ear and heart. His translations preserve all the peculiarities of the old tongue, which he knew and spoke with graceful fluency. His ballads are the most literal and characteristic which we possess. His 'Jacobite Relics of Ireland,' published by that persevering and spirited promoter of Irish literature, John O'Daly of Dublin, contains some of the best specimens of his muse.]

On Monday morning, the flowers were gaily springing,
The skylark's hymn in middle air was singing,
When, grief of griefs! my wedded husband left me,
And since that hour of hope and health bereft me.
        Ulla gulla, gulla g'one! &c., &c.*

Above the board, where thou art low reclining,
Have parish priests and horsemen high been dining,
And wine and usquebaugh, while they were able,
They quaffed with thee—the soul of all the table.
        Ulla gulla, gulla g'one! &c., &c.

Why didst thou die? Could wedded wife adore thee
With purer love than that my bosom bore thee?
Thy children's cheeks were peaches ripe and mellow,
And threads of gold, their tresses long and yellow.
        Ulla gulla, gulla g'one! &c., &c.

In vain for me are pregnant heifers lowing;
In vain for me are yellow harvests growing;
Or thy nine gifts of love in beauty blooming—
Tears blind my eyes, and grief my heart's consuming!
        Ulla gulla, gulla g'one! &c., &c.

Pity her plaints whose wailing voice is broken,
Whose finger holds our early wedding token,
The torrents of whose tears have drain'd their fountain,
Whose piled-up grief on grief is past recounting.
        Ulla gulla, gulla g'one! &c., &c.

* The keener alone sings the extempore death-song; the burden of the ulla-gone, or chorus, is taken up by all the females present.

I still might hope, did I not thus behold thee,
That high Knockferin's airy peak might hold thee,
Or Crohan's fairy halls, or Corrin's towers,
Or Lene's bright caves, or Cleana's magic bowers.*
Ulla gulla, gulla g'one! &c., &c.

But, O! my black despair! when thou wert dying
O'er thee no tear was wept, no heart was sighing—
No breath of prayer did waft thy soul to glory;
But lonely thou didst lie, all maim'd and gory!
Ulla gulla, gulla g'one! &c., &c.

O! may your dove-like soul, on whitest pinions,
Pursue her upward flight to God's dominions,
Where saints' and martyrs' hands shall gifts provide thee—
And, O, my grief! that I am not beside thee!
Ulla gulla, gulla g'one! &c., &c.

THE DYING MOTHER'S LAMENT.

BY J. KEEGAN.

"Oh God, it is a dreadful night,—how fierce the dark winds blow,
It howls like mourning *Banshee*,† its breathings speak of woe
'Twill rouse my slumbering orphans—blow gently, oh wild blast,
My wearied hungry darlings are hushed in peace at last.

"And how the cold rain tumbles down in torrents from the skies,
Down, down, upon our stiffened limbs, into my children's eyes :—
Oh God of Heaven, stop your hand until the dawn of day,
And out upon the weary world again we'll take our way.

"But, ah! my prayers are worthless—oh! louder roars the blast,
And darker frown the pitchy clouds, the rain falls still more fast;
Oh God, *if* you be merciful, have mercy *now*, I pray—
Oh God forgive my wicked words—I know not what I say.

* Places celebrated in fairy topography.
† *Banshee*—a spirit, or being of Irish superstition, which comes to mourn the approaching death of individuals destined for the grave.

"To see my ghastly babies—my babes so meek and fair—
To see them huddled in that ditch, like wild beasts in their lair:
Like wild beasts! No! the vixen cubs that sport on yonder hill,
Lie warm this hour, and, I'll engage, of food they've had their fill.

"Oh blessed Queen of Mercy, look down from that black sky—
You've felt a mother's misery, then hear a mother's cry;
I mourn not my own wretchedness, but let my children rest,
Oh watch and guard them this wild night, and then I shall be blest!"

Thus prayed the wanderer, but in vain!—in vain her mournful cry;
God did not hush that piercing wind, nor brighten that dark sky:
But when the ghastly winter's dawn its sickly radiance shed,
The mother and her wretched babes lay stiffened, grim, and dead!

LAMENT FOR THOMAS DAVIS.

BY EVA. (MISS MARY EVA KELLY.)

I MOURN thee, Thomas Davis—dark, dark, and wearily;
Oh! shut the light from out my eyes, I cannot bear to see;
I cannot look upon the world, and you no longer there—
'Tis now, and evermore will be, as my heart is, cold and bare.
Thomas Davis! Thomas Davis! *acushla sthore machree!*
My heart, my heart is pouring out black bitter tears for thee.

Oh! how can I believe it?—it can't be as they say,
That all the gifts so near to heav'n are quench'd within the clay :—
It cannot be, it cannot be, that all the noble dower
Of worth, and strength, and genius high, on this earth no more
    has power.
Thomas Davis! Thomas Davis!—is that a phantom name—
An empty, silent, churchyard word, so full of life and fame?

Oh! let me think upon him. And are all the thoughts of years,
So firm and bright around him twined, for ever steeped in tears;
And must we have but *memories* of all that he has been,
Like autumn's dry and wither'd leaves, we saw so fresh and green
Thomas Davis! Thomas Davis! sure, sure it is not true!
Oh, who, since first we heard your name, e'er thought of death
    with you?

Bright sparks of gold are dancing upon the river's breast,
And soft and calm the sky appears, it lies in gentle rest ;
The sun is slumb'ring warm and fair, on fields so still and green.
And stately look the mountains down, on the peaceful smiling
    scene ;
Nought is changing, nought is changing, the sound of life goes on—
There is no change, there is no change, and sure he can't be gone.

Ah ! woe is me, on this sad day—I know my tears are true—
Ah ! deep within the change that's come, 'twas well—too well, I knew ;
And you, oh ! you, *Mavourneen Oge,* our glory and our trust,
Oh ! who could ever think such might could crumble into dust.
Can we ever, can we ever, mind love or hope again,
When brightest hope and truest love, no more to us remain.

I see the hills of Ormond—the Shannon's pleasant shore—
I think how well you lov'd their sight, you'll look on them no more ;
You lov'd them well, *Mavourneen,* every stream and mountain
    blue—
You lov'd them in your bosom's core, oh! won't they mourn for you?
Won't they sorrow, won't they sorrow, this sad and woful day,
And, Thomas Davis lying low, within the darksome clay.

And will your voice, oh never, be heard where it hath pour'd,
Among the friends so fondly lov'd, the free and fearless word ;
And won't you see their banners wave, nor hear their triumph
    swell,
When they chase the foreign foe from the land you lov'd so well.
Oh ! the *caoine,* oh ! the *caoine,* will mingle with the tide
Of loud resounding triumph when we think of him who died

Oh ! why am I still able to pour my depth of woe,
Oh ! why am I not lying now where you are lying low ;
Embalm'd in all your lofty deeds, and thoughts so proud and high,
Above your grave in misery we're left this day to lie.
As the green moss—as the green moss, from off the stone is torn,
So you were taken from our hearts, and we are left forlorn.

END OF VOLUME I

PATTISON JOLLY, Steam-Press Printer, 21, Essex-street, West, Dublin.